KU-054-912

ONE STEAMY NIGHT

BRENDA JACKSON

TEMPTED BY THE BOLLYWOOD STAR

SOPHIA SINGH SASSON

MILLS & BOON

All rights reserved including the right of reproduction in whole or in part in any form. This edition is published by arrangement with Harlequin Enterprises ULC.

This is a work of fiction. Names, characters, places, locations and incidents are purely fictional and bear no relationship to any real life individuals, living or dead, or to any actual places, business establishments, locations, events or incidents. Any resemblance is entirely coincidental.

This book is sold subject to the condition that it shall not, by way of trade or otherwise, be lent, resold, hired out or otherwise circulated without the prior consent of the publisher in any form of binding or cover other than that in which it is published and without a similar condition including this condition being imposed on the subsequent purchaser.

® and ™ are trademarks owned and used by the trademark owner and/or its licensee. Trademarks marked with ® are registered with the United Kingdom Patent Office and/or the Office for Harmonisation in the Internal Market and in other countries.

First Published in Great Britain 2023
by Mills & Boon, an imprint of HarperCollins*Publishers* Ltd
1 London Bridge Street, London, SE1 9GF

www.harpercollins.co.uk

HarperCollins*Publishers*
Macken House, 39/40 Mayor Street Upper,
Dublin 1, D01 C9W8, Ireland

One Steamy Night © 2023 Brenda Streater Jackson
Tempted by the Bollywood Star © Sophia Singh Sasson

ISBN: 978-0-263-31769-5

1023

This book is produced from independently certified FSC™ paper
to ensure responsible forest management.

For more information visit: www.harpercollins.co.uk/green

Printed and Bound in the UK using 100% Renewable Electricity at
CPI Group (UK) Ltd, Croydon, CR0 4YY

ONE STEAMY NIGHT

BRENDA JACKSON

To the man who will always and forever be the wind
beneath my wings and the love of my life.
My everything: Gerald Jackson, Sr.

A man that hath friends must shew himself friendly: and
there is a friend that sticketh closer than a brother.

—*Proverbs* 18:24

In loving memory of my childhood friend and
Delta Sigma Theta Soror, Lynda Ravnell.
Losing you was hard, and I will forever appreciate the
memories. Rest in peace.

Prologue

Jaxon Ravnel threw out a card before glancing around the crowded room. Including himself, there were over fifty men in attendance at the first ever Westmoreland Poker Tournament. Some were men who were born a Westmoreland or who, like the Outlaws, were cousins of the Westmorelands. Then there were those who'd married into the family. All were accounted for and all but four players had been eliminated from the game. Those were the ones who were either sitting around observing or hanging out at the bar. An assortment of whiskeys were in decanters and everyone was helping themselves. There was also beer in a huge refrigerator.

The room was quiet for now. Storm Westmoreland was no longer cursing, which meant he was either holding a good hand or he wanted the three others seated at the table with him to assume he was. The room where the game was being played was the spacious poker room, located on the third floor of Westmoreland House.

Westmoreland House was the three-story building Dillon Westmoreland had built on his property, located in what the locals in Denver referred to as Westmoreland Country. Because the Westmorelands were big on family and enjoyed get-togethers, the building contained a humongous kitchen on the ground floor and a huge banquet room with the capacity to seat anywhere from two to five hundred people.

There was also a theater room for the ladies to watch movies, as well as a huge playroom for the younger children that resembled an indoor playground. Not to be overlooked, the teens had their own game room equipped with arcade consoles, mounted televisions, pinball machines, pool tables, board games and a refrigerator stocked with energy drinks.

The entire third floor belonged to the men. That's where the bar, pool tables, man cave and sleeping quarters for overnight poker games were located. Jaxon thought this was a nice setup. The beginning of the tournament required several games going on at once and this room was spacious enough to accommodate everyone. There was a men-only rule and food had been catered by a restaurant in town.

It was close to midnight now, and this was night two of the tournament. Over the past year he'd gotten to know all the Westmorelands, those based out of Atlanta, Montana, Texas, California and Denver. And he was building a bond with his newfound cousins, the Outlaws.

Since the Outlaws and their Westmoreland cousins were such a close-knit group, Jaxon had been included as an honorary member of the Westmoreland family. As an only child, he wasn't used to a huge family, but he was finding out just how such a family operated, thanks to the Westmorelands and the Outlaws. Getting to know all of them, which included the wives and husbands who'd married into the family, had been overwhelming at first. Now he felt comfortable and at ease around them.

More than anything, he appreciated their acceptance of him as one of them. That was the main reason he figured here at the tournament was just as good a place as any for the announcement he needed to make. He wasn't sure how the men would take what he had to say, but he wanted to be up front and honest with them, and then let the chips fall where they may.

Another hour passed before the intensity of the game lessened as King Jamal Yasir of Tehran, who was married to Delaney Westmoreland, told everyone about the new school that had been built in his country. When he'd finished talking, Jaxon decided to make his announcement in a voice loud enough to be heard by everyone.

"Just so all of you know, I plan to marry Nadia."

Like he figured it would, the room became quiet. More than fifty pairs of eyes stared at him. At first no one said anything, and then his cousin, Senator Jess Outlaw, the only one who'd been privy to Jaxon's plan, made sure everyone's mind was free of confusion by asking, "Nadia Novak?"

Jaxon fought back a grin. That was the only Nadia he knew and would guess that was the only one the others knew as well. "Yes, Nadia Novak."

"I didn't know you and Nadia were seeing each other," Zane Westmoreland said after taking a sip of his brandy.

"We aren't."

"Then how are you going to marry her? What's your plan of action?" Derringer Westmoreland asked.

A slow smile broke across Jaxon's lips. "A very serious courtship."

"Good luck with that," his cousin Maverick Outlaw said. "I think all of us have heard Nadia say more than once that she plans to stay single for a long time. Possibly forever."

"Hey, that's what Gemma claimed," Callum Austell said in his strong Australian accent. "It took me three years, but I eventually won her heart."

Jaxon had heard the story of how Ramsey Westmoreland's best friend from Australia had come to Denver to help Ramsey start his sheep farm. One day he had seen Ramsey's sister Gemma and what had been intended as a one-year trip to America for Callum had become three. It had taken the man that long to win Gemma over.

"I don't have three years," Jaxon said. "I want to marry Nadia before New Year's." He knew that was a big initiative given this was August.

"I hate to be the bearer of bad news, but Nadia doesn't like overconfident men," Canyon Westmoreland said, grinning.

Jaxon noticed several others nodding their heads in agreement. "I don't consider myself an overconfident man. Just a self-assured one."

"You're also a very disciplined one, but with Nadia it won't matter," Stern Westmoreland piped in to say. "I suggest you think things through, Jaxon. Trying to win Nadia over might be taking on a little too much. I love her to death but she's a renegade. She's headstrong, opinionated and sassy."

"Sounds like she hung around Bailey too long." Walker Rafferty grinned, commenting on his wife. "At least I've never heard Nadia use any curse words."

Jaxon raised a brow. "Bailey curses?" He couldn't imagine such a thing of the woman he'd gotten to know.

Laughter broke out around the room. Hilarious laughter. "Worse than a sailor," Ramsey Westmoreland said, taking a sip of his drink. Jaxon figured Ramsey should know since he was Bailey's oldest brother. "Bailey would use curse words not even in the English language," Ramsey kept on. "You wouldn't believe how many times Dillon and I had to wash her mouth out with soap. Now we let Walker deal with it."

Jaxon had heard how the parents, the aunts and uncles of the Denver Westmorelands had died in a plane crash over twenty years ago, leaving Dillon, the oldest cousin and Ramsey, who was next to the oldest, with a family of fifteen.

Several of the siblings and cousins had been under sixteen at the time. When the state of Colorado tried forcing Dillon to put the youngest in foster homes, he had refused.

Walker chuckled. "Now that we have kids of our own, Bailey's gotten a whole lot better and rarely says a curse word. Thank God."

"So, in other words," Sloan Outlaw said, "Nadia will be a challenge you might not want to take on, cuz. We've seen her give more than one guy the boot. We'd hate for you to be the next."

Jaxon didn't say anything for a minute as he glanced around the room and met each man's gaze. "I am very much aware that Nadia has a strong personality. However, I don't have any choice about taking Nadia on. I've fallen in love with her."

Words like "damn," "crap" and "shit" escaped several of the men's lips.

"Have you taken the time to get to know her?" Riley Westmoreland asked.

"No, but it doesn't matter. I fell in love with her the moment we were introduced. But then that's how things work in the Ravnel family."

"They work that way in the Austell family, too, so I know where you're coming from," Callum said, grinning. "Falling in love for some men might be a slow and reluctant process, but for me it was automatic. I fell in love with Gemma the moment Ramsey introduced us."

"It was that way for me, as well," Dylan Emanuel said. He'd become the most recent addition to the Westmoreland family when he'd married Charm Outlaw ten months ago. "I'm a firm believer in love at first sight."

"That's all well and good, but I'm not sure five months will give you enough time to grow on Nadia. She can be stubborn," Reggie Westmoreland, the other senator in the family, said.

Jaxon leaned back in his chair. "I believe it can be done... without any interference from any of you."

"As long as you don't plan to do anything illegal or break her heart."

It was the first time Dillon had spoken. Any input from Dillon meant a lot since Nadia was his wife Pam's youngest sister. Jaxon knew Nadia was not just Dillon's sister-in-law, but that he also considered her the baby sister he never had since his parents had had six boys.

"I won't do anything illegal, and I won't break her heart. I just need all of you to know my intentions. And like I said, I prefer no interference."

"That means we can't tell our wives," Thorn Westmoreland said. "That shouldn't be a problem. We abide by the rule that whatever we say in this room stays in this room."

All the men agreed. However, Dillon said, "I'm telling Pam. Nadia is her youngest sister and I feel she has a right to know. Don't worry about her interfering because she won't. She knew about Aidan and Jill and didn't interfere with them."

Jill was another of Pam's younger sisters. Jaxon had been told of Aidan and Jill's secret love affair during medical school. Little had they known that Pam and Dillon had been fully aware of what was going on between them.

"You and Pam were too perceptive," Aidan said, grinning over at Dillon.

"Some things just can't be hidden," Dillon responded. He glanced back at Jaxon. "I'm trusting you to do the right thing by Nadia."

"And I will, I promise you. Like I said, I want her to be my wife and will do my best to win her over."

"Well, just be prepared that with Nadia, your best might

not be good enough," Durango Westmoreland said, shaking his head. "To be honest, Nadia isn't the one I'm worried about."

"Same with me," Stone Westmoreland said, laughing. "In other words, Jaxon, we'll be here to help tend to your bruises when Nadia gives you the boot."

Jaxon actually saw a look of pity in a number of the men's eyes. Even Dillon's.

"You guys aren't scaring me any," Jaxon said, laughing and tossing out another card.

"Don't say we didn't warn you," Jared Westmoreland said, smiling.

At that time, King Jamal Yasir, who'd acted as dealer, went around the table to ask each player if they wanted to bet or call. No one raised the bet, and they began showing their hands.

Everybody groaned loudly when Jamal proclaimed Storm Westmoreland the winner of the tournament.

One

"Did you hear us, Nadia?"

Nadia Novak rubbed her temples and wished she hadn't heard what her sisters Jillian and Paige had said. Jaxon Ravnel was in Gamble scouting out land to expand his business. Why? Hadn't he bought enough land last year in Forbes, Texas, for the same reason? Besides, it wasn't like Gamble was a major city in Wyoming, even if it had grown in population over the past few years.

When her oldest sister, Pam, had married Dillon Westmoreland fifteen years ago and packed up a thirteen-year-old Nadia, a fifteen-year-old Paige and a seventeen-year-old Jillian to live with them on his huge spread in Denver called Westmoreland Country, Gamble had been a town with a population of barely five thousand. There had been only one hotel, few fast food places and a theater that showed movies months after they were released.

Now thanks to a progressive mayor, Gamble's population had quadrupled. There were several hotels and theaters and a slew of fast food places. Sprawling housing developments had sprouted up as well as a megamall. With rumors circulating about a possible ski resort coming in about five years, Nadia figured one day Gamble would be as popular as Jackson Hole.

Years ago, her great-grandfather Jay Novak Sr. had purchased the two-hundred-acre spread that he named the Novak Homestead. More than anything, she appreciated her sister Pam for not selling it when they'd moved to Denver. She'd retained it as part of their family legacy.

Nadia didn't regret moving back to Gamble. She would admit it got lonely here at times, living in this huge house by herself. There had never been a boring moment in Westmoreland Country with so many Westmorelands living close by each other. It helped, too, that since Denver was only an hour's flight away, she often returned to Westmoreland Country for visits.

Her sister Jillian, who was fondly called Jill, was a neurosurgeon and was happily living in Florida with her cardiologist husband, Aidan Westmoreland. Nadia thought it was awesome that her sisters—Pam and Jill—had married Westmoreland men who were cousins.

Her sister Paige had followed in Pam's footsteps to become an actress in Hollywood. She'd made a name for herself and had starred in several movies. Paige hadn't hesitated to give up the glitz and glamor to marry Senator Jess Outlaw. Jess was a cousin to the Westmorelands, and he and Paige made their home in the nation's capital.

Nadia had attended the University of Wyoming for four years, before graduating from Harvard with an MBA. She had returned to Gamble three years ago. The timing had been perfect since the acting school her sister Pam owned, the Dream Makers Acting Academy, had been in need of someone to manage it. Nadia loved her job and found it rewarding as well as challenging.

Over the past year the student count at the academy had increased substantially, mainly because of Pam's contacts back in Hollywood. Oftentimes an actor friend would teach a class for a semester or two, or would do a once-in-a-lifetime symposium or workshop. Last year they'd added classes for aspiring stuntmen taught by folks from Hollywood. The academy was now in demand and already there was a waiting list for the next school year.

Although Nadia and her sisters now lived thousands of miles apart, they would carve out time to share a conversation or two at least once a week. Because of Pam's hectic schedule, she would jump on the call whenever she could. Although Pam was twelve years older than Jill, fourteen years older than Paige and sixteen years older than Nadia, the four of them were extremely close.

"Nadia, are you listening to us?"

"No," she said honestly. They'd lost her after mentioning Jaxon's name and that he was in Gamble to scope out land. The idea of them being in the same town was troubling. There was no way she would tell her sisters the impact the man had had on her from their initial meeting. For some reason, she couldn't shake off her intense attraction to him. What was pathetic was that whenever their paths crossed, he barely seemed to notice she existed.

Except for that one time at Charm's wedding last year. They'd held a pretty long conversation. Nadia figured the reason had been he'd been too kind to walk away when the others in the group had dispersed, leaving them alone.

"Well, get your mind off the acting school for a minute," Jill said.

Nadia had news for them. Her mind had not been on the acting school, although maybe it should have been since she was in a dilemma. The new school year had begun two weeks ago and yesterday the sponsor for this year's holiday play, the Dunnings Financial Group, had filed for bankruptcy. That meant she needed to find another sponsor and fast. The students had returned energized and ready to start work on the play. Auditions were already being held.

"Okay, what did I miss?" Nadia asked, turning her attention to the conversation with her sisters.

"You didn't make a comment when we told you how to treat Jaxon."

She frowned. "And just how am I supposed to treat him?"

"We want you to be hospitable to him, Nadia," Paige said.

Hospitable? "Why wouldn't I be? I don't recall being any other way around him."

"When you're not trying to avoid him. And what's up with that?" Jill asked.

Nadia rolled her eyes. Leave it to Jill to notice. "I just don't see the need to fawn over him like the rest of you do."

If only they knew that, in private, she did more than fawn over him. She had naughty thoughts that actually made her panties wet. Not to mention those dreams she had of him, the contents of which would probably give her sisters a stroke.

"We don't fawn over him, Nadia," Paige defended. "We just think highly of him for what he did. Can you imagine what would have happened if he had not come forward with that information on Phire's father?"

Phire was married to Maverick Outlaw, the youngest brother of Paige's husband. Nadia had never met Phire's father, but she'd heard about all the money he'd swindled from the Outlaws for close to twenty-five years. "And?" Nadia braced herself knowing her sisters were about to sing Jaxon Ravnel's praises.

"And," Paige continued, "Jaxon is the Outlaws' newfound

cousin, and the Westmoreland family has embraced him as one of theirs, so you know what that means."

Yes, she knew. The Westmorelands and Outlaws were now one big happy family. Heck, her three sisters were married to Westmorelands and an Outlaw, which made them official members of the clan. "Like I said, I'm always pleasant to Jaxon, but I refuse to fawn over him." But she had no problem drooling in private.

"Well, please don't cause problems, Nadia. You can be rather hard on men and for no reason," Jill said.

A deep frown settled on Nadia's face as she leaned back in her chair. "I have plenty of reasons whenever I'm hard on a man. Should I remind you about Kemp, Paige?"

Kemp had been Paige's actor boyfriend who'd made news when he'd betrayed her with another actress while filming a movie. The news had caused a scandal that had taken social media by storm.

"And the three of us can't ever forget Fletcher Mallard and what he tried to do," she added.

Fletcher had been engaged to marry Pam with devious intentions. Luckily Dillon had arrived on the scene and put an end to that foolishness. He'd stopped Pam and Fletcher's wedding ceremony just in the nick of time.

"Those are just two men, Nadia. You can't judge the entire male population by them," Jill said.

In all honesty, there were three. One she'd never told her sisters about. Namely Benson Cummings. He was a guy she'd met during her first year at the University of Wyoming. He'd been a senior and she'd thought she was in love until she'd discovered her name was on a Freshmen Girls to Do list. A list circulated by senior guys, and Benson had been assigned to do her. She was grateful she'd found out about the list before sleeping with him.

"Just think of all the Westmoreland and Outlaw men and how wonderful they are," Paige tacked on for good measure.

"Okay, I will admit they're one of a kind," Nadia said. "But then I'm partial where they are concerned. I don't know Jaxon Ravnel that well."

In truth, she didn't know him at all. She only knew how he made her feel whenever he was around her. Just being in the same room with him reminded her that she was a woman. A woman whose body sizzled every time she saw him. That was a reaction she'd rather do without and that was the primary reason she avoided him.

"Well, now is your chance to get to know him since he'll be in Gamble for a while."

Nadia's frown deepened. "How long is 'a while'?"

"He told Jess he planned to be there for at least three months," Paige said. "Possibly four."

"Why don't you invite him to dinner?" Jill suggested. "You love to cook and always complain about wanting to prepare all those dishes but having no one there to eat them."

They had to be kidding. There was no way she would invite Jaxon to dinner. What if he picked up on just how attracted she was to him? That's the last thing she wanted to happen. However, if she didn't invite him, her astute sisters would figure out why. "Fine, I'll call him in a few days to see if he's available. Give me his number." Paige wasted no time in rattling it off.

"And Nadia?"

"Yes, Jill?"

"Please remember Jaxon is a nice guy. Don't do or say anything that will make us regret suggesting you invite him to dinner."

"Well, if he's as nice as the two of you claim, then you won't have anything to worry about. Now, can we change the subject and talk about something else?" she asked.

The conversation about Jaxon stirred up sensations inside of her that she didn't need to be stirred. She was convinced it was merely a phase she was going through. It had to be. At twenty-eight her body was trying to convince her it was past time to end her virginal state. But she refused to do so merely to quench a case of lust. For her sex had to be more meaningful than that. But what if nothing meaningful ever came along? Should she continue to deny herself the experience of making love to man? Especially if it was anything like Jill and Paige claimed it was? Nadia couldn't help but be curious as to whether the real thing was anything compared to her dreams.

"I got a call from Taylor today," Paige said, intruding into Nadia's thoughts.

Taylor Steele Saxon was the sister to Cheyenne, who was married to Quade Westmoreland. "How is she doing?"

"She's doing fine. Quade is giving Cheyenne a surprise birthday party next month and Taylor is helping him with the invitations."

Nadia smiled, thinking about Quade and Cheyenne's triplets. While in high school she had kept the three for a week while their parents had celebrated their fifth wedding anniversary in India. Now the triplets were in their early teens.

"Give me the date so I can mark it on my calendar. Now if you guys don't mind, I need to finish this report before I can go home."

After ending the call with her sisters, Nadia glanced at her watch and then looked at the stack of papers on her desk. Standing, she moved to the window. The Dream Makers Acting Academy had once been a spacious house on two hundred acres of land that had been owned by Pam's high school acting instructor, Louise Shelton. Ms. Shelton, a former actress herself, had been instrumental in getting Pam a scholarship to attend college in California.

When Ms. Shelton died, she willed the house and all the land it sat on to Pam with stipulations. Pam could never sell it and it had to be used as an acting/drama academy. Pam had managed the school until she'd married Dillon, but then had left her friend Cindy in charge. When Cindy's husband, Todd, who'd been mayor of Gamble for several years, decided to run for state senator, and had won, Todd moved his family to Cheyenne, the state's capital. That's when Pam had offered the job to Nadia.

Pam had since opened a second school in Denver. Like this one, it operated at full capacity. A couple of years ago, Pam purchased land for a third drama academy in the DC area. Currently Paige was managing that one.

Returning to her chair, Nadia sat back down. The school had closed an hour ago, but she was still here. Some of the students were rehearsing downstairs, all excited about this year's holiday production. She refused to think it wouldn't be happening unless she found a replacement sponsor and fast. The Dunnings Financial Group pulling out was a hiccup of the worst kind.

Starting tomorrow she would begin making calls to several businesses in town. She wasn't sure how that would work out since most of them had already donated to the school and were contributing to other local charities.

Leaning back in her chair, she wondered where on earth would she get the extra money needed for the school's holiday play.

Jaxon Ravnel stood at the window in his hotel room and gazed out at downtown Gamble, Wyoming. If anyone had told him two years ago that the decision to expand his family's technology business would bring him here, he would not have believed them.

The home office for Ravnel Technologies was in Virginia,

and so far he'd purchased land to expand into Forbes, Texas. Now he was considering, of all places, Gamble. He would admit it was mainly because of a particular woman. At least that had been the case a few days ago when he'd first arrived in town. However, it didn't take him long to discover Gamble was Wyoming's best-kept secret.

Although the town's growth began a few years ago, there were a number of national corporations unaware of the city's potential and attractiveness. That lack of awareness was in his favor. He could purchase all the land he needed at a fair market price before there was a business boom. He was also satisfied knowing there would be adequate housing for his employees who relocated here. There was no doubt in his mind that Gamble would be an ideal place to live, work and raise a family.

As for him personally...it was the perfect place to pursue a certain woman he wanted. Nadia Novak.

Jaxon was a man who could appreciate a beautiful woman whenever he saw one, and Nadia had taken hold of his senses the first time he'd laid eyes on her. That had been a little over a year ago at his cousin Maverick Outlaw's wedding reception. The minute she'd entered the banquet room of the Blazing Frontier Dude Ranch there had been something about her that demanded a second look and then a third. Never in his life had he been so captivated by a woman. He'd asked his cousin Jess about her and when Jess had said Nadia Novak had a rather feisty personality, that had made Jaxon even more interested.

Unlike some men, he preferred a woman with a strong personality mainly because over the years most of those he'd dated had had anything but. They'd assumed in order to capture the interest of the Ravnel heir, they had to be mild, meek, the epitome of social decorum, grace and sophistication. That's where they'd been wrong since he found that type of woman boring as hell.

Jaxon wanted a woman who was tough, independent and spirited—like his mother. His father, Arnett Ravnel, said the first thing that had attracted him to Ingrid Parkinson was her energy, sassiness and spunk. Those were traits Jaxon's mother still possessed and his father still admired.

His father had also said that a Ravnel man would know the woman he was destined to share his life with the moment he saw her. Jaxon had always assumed it would be someone from his home state of Virginia. He hadn't been prepared to be taken with the likes of a Wyoming-born beauty named Nadia Novak.

Getting Nadia to be as taken with him as much as he was with her would be a challenge, but like he'd told the males in her family, it was one he was up to. Whenever he'd seen her she'd been friendly and pleasant, but she never had much to say. At least not to him. And there were times when he thought she was avoiding him. Jaxon figured the main reason for that was because she hadn't gotten to know him. That assumption was what had led him here.

Never in his thirty-three years had he ever pursued a woman. Because of the Ravnel name and wealth, it had always been the other way around. He'd been warned by the Westmorelands and Outlaws that he had his work cut out for him. There were some who even jokingly referred to her as the "Renegade Novak."

He had to be patient and not overplay his hand. For her to get to know him, they needed to spend time together. He'd been in Gamble a little more than a week and as part of his plan, he had deliberately not looked her up. Tomorrow he would drop by the drama academy and invite her to lunch or suggest dinner. It would come across as nothing more than a friendly gesture on his part since they were connected to the same families. He smiled, liking that approach.

He turned away from the window at the sound of his phone. Moving across the room he picked it up off the nightstand, not recognizing the caller's ID. "Yes?"

"Jaxon, this is Nadia Novak."

He pulled in a surprised breath. What were the odds that the very woman he'd been thinking about would call him? "Nadia, how are you? This is a surprise."

He felt sensations in his lower extremities just from hearing the sound of her voice. "What can I do for you?" He asked the question while his mind was filled with several scenarios of all the things they could do for each other.

"I was talking to my sisters earlier this week and they mentioned you were in Gamble."

"Yes, I'm here on business."

"That's what they said, and I'd like to invite you to dinner."

"Dinner?"

"Yes. Tomorrow. In my home at the Novak Homestead. It's the least I can do since we have close ties to the same families."

A smile spread across his lips. That had been the same angle he'd planned to use. "I wouldn't want you to go to any trouble."

"I won't. I enjoy cooking and look forward to doing so for someone other than myself for a change."

"All right, if you're sure?"

"I'm positive."

"In that case, I accept. What's your address?" he asked, reaching for the pen and notepad off the nightstand.

She rattled it off to him and he jotted it down. "Thanks for the invitation. What time do you want me to come?"

"How about five o'clock? Will that work for you?"

Little did she know he would make any time work when it came to her. "Yes, five o'clock is fine."

"Good. I'll see you tomorrow. Goodbye, Jaxon."

"Goodbye, Nadia."

Jaxon's smile widened as he disconnected the call. Of all the luck. Getting that call from Nadia had certainly made his day. He couldn't wait to see her tomorrow.

Two

What a man, what a mighty good-looking man…

Nadia stood at the kitchen window and watched Jaxon get out of his car. She definitely appreciated what she saw and from where she was standing, she was seeing a lot. This particular window was designed in a way that gave anyone looking through it a good view of approaching visitors without being seen. In other words, you could watch them without them knowing they were being observed. It was a clever idea and she appreciated her great-grandfather Jay Novak for having thought of it.

Jaxon was carrying a huge bouquet of flowers and she figured they were for her. How thoughtful. The women in the Westmoreland and Outlaw families who'd gotten to know him thought he was considerate and kind, a true Southern gentlemen who had a strong sense of doing what was right. He'd certainly proved the latter when he'd exposed the wrongdoings of Simon Bordella to the Outlaws.

Nadia placed a hand over her heart when it began beating fast. The closer he got, the more he worked on all of her female senses. There was something about Jaxon Ravnel that did things to her each and every time she saw him. What was there about him that made her feel vulnerable? Make her want to toss caution to the wind and...

And do what? Risk giving her heart to another man? Have another man place her on his *agenda*? Trample both her heart and her pride? Refusing to think about what Benson had done to her, she concentrated on studying Jaxon instead. Why did he have to look so good?

He had coffee-colored skin, dark brown eyes and a solid, bearded jaw. She also knew he had black hair under that Stetson he was wearing. He had handsome features on a definitely sensual face, features any woman would drool over. He was also tall with muscular shoulders, a tight abdomen and a broad and powerful-looking chest. Definitely a body that was well-built.

The business jacket he wore over a white, collared shirt fit him perfectly, and she figured his taut thighs were why those slacks looked so darn good on him. Altogether—his looks, clothes and walk—made up a very alluring package. Now for the umpteenth time she was wondering if she should have her head examined for following Jill's and Paige's advice and inviting him to dinner.

She nearly jumped at the sound of the knock at the door. Drawing in a deep breath, she moved away from the window and left the kitchen. She glanced around the living room and wondered what he would think of her home. Although the Novak Homestead encompassed a lot of acres of land, the two-story, five-bedroom, four-bath house wasn't all that big. At least not in comparison to the monstrosity of a ranch house she'd heard Jaxon owned in Virginia. Paige had visited there a few times with Jess. Dumfries, Virginia, was less than thirty miles from the nation's capital. Paige had told her all about Jaxon's horse ranch and the beautiful thoroughbreds he owned.

Not wanting Jaxon to know she'd been spying on him from the moment his car had pulled into her yard, she asked, "Who is it?"

"Jaxon."

She opened the door. Although she'd seen his approach, every single step of it, she still blinked. Up close he was even more handsome, and when he smiled, making dimples appear, she was a goner. She forced her attention from his face to the two top buttons on his shirt that were undone, exposing a dark, hairy chest. Her heart rate increased. She couldn't help but appreciate his total maleness although she resented her reaction to it.

"Hello, Nadia."

His greeting made her look back into his face. "Jaxon. Welcome to my home," she said, easing back for him to enter while pulling herself together. He smelled good. She thought that same thing each and every time she was around him.

"These are for you," he said, handing her the flowers and then removing his Stetson and placing it on the hat rack by the door.

"Thank you. They are beautiful. You didn't have to," she said, lowering her head to draw in the scent of the flowers. They were a beautiful mixture of pink daisies, white peonies, orchids, bluebells and roses. But what had really gotten her was the feel of his hand when he'd given her the flowers. She had felt the touch all the way to her toes.

She glanced back up at him, smiled. "But I'm glad you did. I love flowers and these are some of my favorites."

"I'm glad."

"Excuse me while I put them in a vase of water. Make yourself at home. The table is set and dinner is ready."

"It smells good."

"Thanks." She'd asked his Outlaw cousins about his favorite foods. Not surprisingly most were Southern dishes. One year while in high school she'd spent the entire summer with the Atlanta-based Westmorelands. That summer she had worked in Chase Westmoreland's restaurant and learned how to cook most of the foods Jaxon liked.

It didn't take her long to find a vase while recalling her reaction when their hands had touched. Just remembering it made her feel light-headed. Why now? She'd been around him before, although for short periods of time. That one time the two of them had engaged in a longer conversation was at Charm's wedding. She had felt somewhat light-headed then, and had to fight back from drooling.

Now that they were completely alone in her home, more than anything, she needed all the self-discipline she could muster to handle her attraction. The last thing she wanted or needed was for her body to look for some excuse to be drawn closer to him, to desire him any more than she already did. That had been her mistake with Benson. She had been taken with him from the first.

After putting the flowers in water, she headed back to the living room.

Jaxon turned from studying the huge portrait when he heard the sound of Nadia returning. He watched, appreciating her shapely backside as she crossed the room to place the vase of flowers on a table in front of a window. She then turned to him with a huge smile on her face.

"I think they look perfect here, don't you?" she asked.

He honestly thought she looked pretty damn perfect in her blue maxi-dress. It had a drawstring that emphasized her small waistline, and she'd complemented it with a short suede vest and a pair of black leather boots.

He'd seen her a few times in a shorter dress and knew

she had a gorgeous pair of legs. He especially liked the out-fit she was wearing because it showcased all her shapely curves. "Yes, they look nice there," he said. He then turned back to the huge portrait he'd been looking at earlier. Last thing Nadia needed to see was how aroused he'd gotten from looking at her.

"This is a nice family picture," he said, trying to concentrate on the huge, framed portrait that hung over her fireplace. It was a picture of an older couple surrounded by four beautiful younger girls. "You look so young."

He knew the moment she'd come to stand beside him and glanced over at her. For a second, maybe two, their gazes held. That's when he felt it. A sexual connection she was trying to fight the same way he was. Had he misread her all these times? Had this been the reason she'd avoided him?

She quickly broke eye contact with him to glance up at the picture. "I was six. This picture was taken a few months before Pam left for college in California. Although we were all smiling, my, Jill and Paige's hearts were breaking. We didn't want Pam to leave us and go so far away."

He nodded. "The four of you are close?" Although he asked the question, he already knew the answer. Anyone observing the four whenever they were together could see that.

"Yes. Pam is the best oldest sister anyone could have. We have different mothers. Her mother died when Pam was three and Dad married my mother, Alma, on Pam's tenth birthday. Pam says my mom was the best birthday present she'd ever gotten. Mom filled the void she'd had in her life after losing her mother."

He glanced back at the picture. Alma Novak had been a beautiful woman and he could see her catching the eye of the widowed rancher Jay Winston Novak Jr. It was probably the same way her youngest daughter had caught his. "Your mother was a beautiful woman and your father, quite a handsome man. They had a beautiful family," he said, glancing over at her.

"Thank you. If you want to take off your jacket, there's a closet near the door next to the hat rack, Jaxon."

"All right." He removed his jacket and then walked over to the closet to put it in before returning to the living room. He saw that she was staring at him. "Is anything wrong?" he asked.

"No. Nothing is wrong. In fact, dinner is ready," she answered. "I left work early to come home to prepare it."

"You didn't have to go to all that trouble." He said the words, although he was glad she had since this gave him the opportunity to not only see her again but to spend time with her.

She waved off his words. "No trouble since I love to cook. Unfortunately, there isn't anyone here to cook for."

It was on the tip of his tongue to say that she could cook for him anytime but he decided to keep that to himself. "Is there a place where I can wash my hands?"

"Yes, just follow me."

She led the way and he couldn't help how his heart missed a couple of beats while admiring the sexiness of her walk. "Here's the powder room. The kitchen and dining room are through that door."

"Okay."

Moments later when he walked through the door that led to the kitchen and dining area, he paused. She was leaning down to take a tray of bread out the oven. He couldn't help appreciating the shape of her backside while she did so.

He cleared his throat to let her know he was there. She glanced over at him while placing the tray on a cooling rack on the counter. "Please have a seat at the dining room table. What would you like to drink?"

"What do you have?"

"A little bit of everything. Thanks to Spencer, I never run out of wine and I make sure I have beer, wine coolers and coffee on hand for whenever those Westmorelands or Outlaws decide to visit." Spencer Westmoreland and his wife, Chardonnay, owned Russell Vineyards which was located in Napa Valley.

Jaxon tilted his head to look at her. "They do that a lot? Come visiting?"

She grinned as she placed several rolls of bread on a tray. "They do it enough, just to check up on me. Not as much now as they did when I first moved back here. I guess they're now convinced that I can take care of myself."

He was glad to hear that. When he had arrived on her property and had seen how massive it was and how far away the location was from town, he became concerned with her living here alone. The good thing was all the security cameras installed around her land. "Wine will be fine," he said.

It was only when she finally sat down at the table that he did so as well. After she'd said grace, she glanced over at him. "I hope you like everything." She then took the lids off the platters.

He couldn't stop the smile that spread across his lips. All the things she'd uncovered were foods he loved to eat. There was no way this was a coincidence. He was not a person who believed you had to wait for Thanksgiving to feast on turkey and dressing. Then there was a medley of garlic roasted mixed vegetables, potato salad and hot yeast rolls.

"Dig in and make sure you leave room for dessert. I baked a chocolate cake."

His eyes lifted. "You did?" Chocolate cake was his favorite.

"Yes."

He looked at the platters again before gazing back at her. "You did all this for me?"

He watched her shrug a pair of feminine shoulders. "Like I said, I enjoy cooking and finding out about the foods you liked was easy." She chuckled and said, "Chase told me whenever you're in Atlanta and patronize his restaurant you always get the turkey and dressing off the menu. Jason told me that you do the same thing whenever you're in Denver and go to McKays restaurant."

"True. I'd eat turkey and dressing every day of the week if I could."

"Well, just so you know, I learned how to make the turkey and dressing from Chase, so it ought to be good."

"I'm sure it will be." After taking his first bite, he saw that it was. "Nadia, this is delicious."

He watched her lips ease into a smile. "Thanks."

Now they were getting somewhere. He could still feel sexual chemistry flowing between them, and he had a feeling she was trying hard to suppress it. He didn't want it quelled one iota. In fact, knowing she wasn't immune to him as he'd thought, gave him hope. However, he wanted her to feel relaxed around him, at ease and to lower that guard he felt she'd put up for whatever reason.

They began eating. When he glanced up to look at her, he saw her looking at him. Like they'd done earlier in front of the fireplace, their gazes held for an intense few seconds before she looked back down at her food. Whatever he'd been about to say had been wiped from his mind, so he resumed eating while thinking just how strikingly beautiful she was. So much so that she'd nearly taken his breath away just now.

But then that's the same reaction he'd gotten the first time he'd seen her at Maverick and Phire's wedding reception. Even from a distance, the first thing he'd noticed were her eyes. They were chocolate brown and almond shaped. Then there had been her hair, a thick mass of dark brown sister locks that flowed around her shoulders and complemented her honey-brown skin tone.

Jaxon figured the silence between them would continue unless he said something, so he did. "I understand you moved from Gamble when Dillon married Pam."

She looked over at him. "Yes, that's right."

"What made you move back?"

She smiled again and he felt a deep fluttering in the pit of his stomach from that smile. "For the longest I had no intention of returning here. There was even a time when Paige, Jill and I tried convincing Pam to sell, but she wouldn't. She wanted to hold on to it for our legacy. I'm glad she did. I hadn't known how much I'd missed the place until we came back one weekend to attend a play at Pam's acting school. That's when I realized something."

"What?"

"That saying 'there's no place like home' was true."

She took a sip of her wine then added, "Don't get me wrong, I love Westmoreland Country, too. But I was born here. In this very house, and coming back that time made me realize it means a lot to me." She paused for a moment. "What about your home in Virginia, Jaxon? I heard it's beautiful."

There was no need to ask where she'd heard that from since her sister Paige and his cousin Jess were frequent visitors whenever Jaxon was home. He liked that DC was less than an hour away from his ranch. "Thanks. Like you, I was born on the Circle R Ranch. My parents signed it over to me when they retired and decided to move closer to the city."

"They were involved with your family's company, right?"

After taking a sip of his wine, he said, "Yes. My father was CEO of Ravnel Technologies, and Mom was CEO of the Ravnel Institute of Technology. Now I'm CEO of both. Luckily, I have good people working for me."

He paused a moment and said, "The Circle R Ranch will

always be home for me, although because of all my travels I'm not there as often as I'd like."

She nodded. "I understand you raise horses, Jaxon. And that you own several prized thoroughbreds. Some of which have competed in the derbies."

It seemed that she was trying to keep the conversation on him and not her. He intended to remedy that. "Yes, the Circle R started out as a horse ranch with my great-grand-father. It still is and I have a devoted staff whose job is to handle the horses."

He leaned back in his chair. "Now, enough about me. Tell me about you, Nadia."

Three

Nadia glanced over at Jaxon again, wishing he hadn't said her name like that and wishing even more that her body didn't react whenever he did. He pronounced it with a Southern drawl that seemed to roll off his lips. Those same lips she enjoyed watching every time his mouth moved. Was there anything about him that she didn't find a total turn-on?

"There's not much to tell," she finally said after forcing herself to stay focused on their conversation. "You already know that I'm Pam, Jillian and Paige's youngest sister. And I'm sure you've heard the story of how we tried to ruin Pam's engagement to this guy name Fletcher."

He chuckled. "Yes, I heard about that."

"Pam thought going through with a loveless marriage was something she had to do to save us from losing this house. It was a blessing that Dillon stopped by when he did. I don't want to think where we'd be if he hadn't."

Jaxon nodded and then took a sip of his wine. She couldn't help looking at his lips again. "There's a lot about this house that reminds me of Dillon's home," he said, after placing his wineglass down. "They are similar in design."

She smiled. "Yes, and there's a reason for it. My great-grandfather Jay Winston Novak Sr. and Dillon's great-grandfather Raphel Westmoreland were once business partners. I'm told that Raphel liked the design of this house so much that years later when he settled in Denver and built his own home, he used this same architectural design."

"Dillon mentioned that the two great-grandfathers had been business partners here in Gamble. What sort of business was it?"

Nadia thought he was doing a good job of keeping the conversation flowing between them. She was glad since it eliminated any awkward moments, and she was beginning to feel comfortable around him. However, that comfort level didn't decrease her attraction to him.

"It was a dairy business. However, from the journals Pam and Dillon discovered in a trunk in the attic, Raphel took care of the horses. I understand he was very good with them. Those Westmoreland cousins in the horse-training business probably inherited their love of horses from him."

"Your great-grandfather raised horses?"

"Yes, and he passed his love of them to his son and my father. I'm sure Dad wanted at least one son instead of four daughters but that didn't stop him from making sure we loved horses, too. He also made sure we knew how to take care of them, and he taught us how to ride."

She took a sip of her own wine and then added, "I've been riding since I was two. Dad was a wonderful trainer and over the years all his girls had received awards for their riding skills."

"All four of you?"

"Yes. Pam was a pro since she'd been riding longer. Jill wanted to be as good as Pam, and since Dad thought she had potential he sent her to horse-riding school. She competed nationally until Dad got sick. That's when money was needed to pay for his medicine and care."

"Did you enjoy living in Denver?"

Evidently, he saw the sadness in her eyes from remembering that time when her father was sick and he had quickly changed the subject. She appreciated him doing so. That hadn't been easy time for the Novak sisters. Pam, who'd had a bubbling career in Hollywood as an actress, had come home to help take care of their father as well as her three younger sisters.

In a way Nadia knew that's what made Dillon and Pam the perfect couple. Just like Pam had put her sisters' needs before her own, Dillon had done the same by raising his siblings and cousins after his parents, uncle and aunt had died in a plane crash.

"Yes, I enjoyed living in Denver. When Dillon married Pam the entire Westmoreland family claimed us as theirs. Pretty much like they're doing to you now. That's the Westmoreland way. They are big into family."

She watched the smile that spread across his lips and fought hard for her body not to respond. "I can see that," he said. "I had a younger sister who died before her first birthday of a heart defect. I grew up without any cousins and admit the Westmorelands and Outlaws were a bit overwhelming at first. There are so many of them."

"I'm sorry to hear about your sister." She touched his arm. "But you seemed to have fit right in with our families."

"They didn't give me much of a choice," he replied, grinning.

She couldn't help but grin back, knowing exactly what he meant. It had been that way for her and her sisters as well. In no time it was as if they'd known the Westmorelands all their lives. She'd observed Jaxon with them over the past year and like she'd told him, he seemed to fit right in. They included him in just about everything. She'd heard he'd flown to Denver, Montana and Atlanta a number of times to take part in those infamous Westmoreland poker games.

"I understand you attended Harvard," he said in a voice that felt like warm honey being poured over her skin.

"Yes, I did. However, first I attended the University of Wyoming for my bachelor's degree. Then I went to Harvard for my MBA."

He nodded. "An MBA is impressive, especially one from Harvard. I was in a long line of Ravnel men who'd attended MIT and decided not to break tradition. I did, however, go to Harvard Law School."

"Did you practice law?"

"I did for a couple of years as one of the firm's attorneys. However, when my father let it be known he would be retiring in a few years I figured that was my cue to get ready to take over the reins as CEO."

Nadia had googled him and knew all about his family and how they'd acquired their wealth. She'd read how Jaxon's paternal grandfather founded the Ravnel Institute of Technology and how it was revered the likes of MIT in providing technological advances in higher learning. There was a waiting list to get master's degrees in technology management from the institute and the majority of the students were all but guaranteed six-figure jobs upon graduating. A good number went to work for Ravnel Technologies Incorporated, which was reputed to be one of the most successful technology firms in the nation. At some point, the firm had decided to expand in several parts of the country.

"I understand you're VP of the acting school here," Jaxon said, intruding into her thoughts.

"Yes. My original plan was to move back to Denver after college and go to work at Blue Ridge Land Management," she said, mentioning the billion-dollar corporation owned by the Westmorelands. "However, Pam knew I was interested in moving back to Gamble and when this position came up, she thought I'd be good for it and she offered it to me."

After taking another sip of her wine, she added, "The school depends on donations to award scholarships to deserving students as well as to put on special programs and projects each year. One of my jobs is to make sure we continue to receive funds for all those things."

"Sounds like you're kept pretty busy."

"Not too busy. Once in a while it requires some travel, but I like what I do." That was true. Even now when she needed more funds for the upcoming play and had no idea where they would come from.

They continued conversing through dinner and it was easy to tell that Jaxon was confident with himself but not overly so and definitely not cocky. He had the type of voice that whenever he spoke, she couldn't help but listen. It was just that captivating. She was glad she was taking this time to get to know him and a part of her wished she would have done so sooner.

The reason she hadn't done so was her fear of him realizing just how attracted she was to him. Even now she hoped he hadn't figured it out. The thought that he might have sent panic skidding up her spine. More than once he'd caught her staring at him. Each time, he'd just given her a friendly smile before striking up another conversation.

"I understand you're looking for land to expand here in Gamble," she said when they had finished their meal and had pushed their plates aside.

"Yes, that's right."

"Why Gamble? What made you turn your sights here, Jaxon?"

Jaxon fought back telling her that *she* was the reason he had set his sights on Gamble. However, if truth be told, once he had visited the town, he'd discovered it was truly a hidden treasure.

Something similar had happened last year. His actual reason for arriving in Forbes, Texas, was to expose Simon Bordella and his betrayal of the Outlaws. His claim about wanting land to expand had been a ruse. But, in the end, just like in Gamble, he'd seen the potential of actually expanding his business in the area.

"The suggestion to expand here actually came from Dillon," he said. That much was the truth. It had happened the night of the poker tournament, when he'd announced his intentions toward Nadia. "He mentioned he'd thought about expanding Blue Ridge Land Management to Gamble because land was plentiful here and at a reasonable price."

She nodded. "I recall Dillon changed his mind after deciding Wyoming was too close to Colorado and if he was going to expand it would be best to do so in another part of the country."

"Yes, and he suggested that I come and check out Gamble. I've only been here a little more than a week and so far I'm impressed with what I see. Wyoming is the least populated state in this country. There's a lot of untouched land here and a lot of ranches. I can see why Wyoming is considered the Cowboy State."

"Yes, we are known to have our cowboys, which equates to plenty of rodeos," she said.

That made him wonder. Nadia was a beautiful woman and with so many cowboys around, he could see her catching their attention. Had none caught her eye? A lot of women went for the rugged, bronco, chaps-wearing type. Jess and Maverick claimed they'd never known her to be involved in a serious relationship. The Westmorelands had claimed the same. He couldn't help wondering why. Had some man broken her heart at some point in time?

Then there was that sexual attraction flowing between them. Sensations seeped through his veins every time he looked at her and every time she looked at him. She had to be feeling it. He now knew for certain that she wasn't as immune to him as he'd originally assumed. It had taken them being alone for him to hone on to it.

"Are you ready for dessert, Jaxon?"

He recalled she'd made a chocolate cake. Dessert was the end of the meal and the thought of that dampened his spirits. He had enjoyed the time he'd spent here with her talking and getting to know her. Listening to the sound of her voice stirred all sorts of longing within him.

It had taken all his willpower to contain himself as he watched her eat. Damn, he actually envied her fork each time she'd stuck it in her mouth. He could just imagine her tongue twirling around it. Another thing he thought was that he had yet to see the renegade side of Nadia. Was she putting on her best behavior for his benefit? Why? More than anything he wanted her to be herself.

Knowing she was waiting for a response, he said, "I'm ready for dessert. Everything was delicious, Nadia. You're a wonderful cook. I find it hard to believe there aren't any hungry cowboys around these parts who would appreciate a home-cooked meal."

He hoped his comment would open the discussion as to why, at twenty-eight, she wasn't seriously involved with anyone. He saw the expression on her face change from a smile to a frown and wondered why. Had what he'd said hit a nerve? She stood and tossed him a haughty look. He had a feeling he was finally about to see the very sassy, outspoken Nadia.

"You're right, there are quite a few hungry cowboys around here, but trust me when I say that I have no interest in feeding them."

Whoa... Well, she'd certainly told him. However, he felt

there was a deeper meaning in her answer, and he had no problem digging. He leaned back in his chair. "Care to share the reason why?"

Her frown turned to a glare that sharpened on him. "Let's just say I'm picky when it comes to men."

"Picky in what way?"

"That's none of your business."

He couldn't help but smile because everything about her was his business. This was the Nadia Novak he'd heard about and the one he'd been waiting to see. "Remind me to never ask you a question."

"Oh, you can ask all you want, just as long you know that I reserve the right not to answer."

"Touché. And just for the record, I understand your position because I'm picky as well when it comes to the opposite sex."

She lifted a brow denoting her curiosity. "Are you?"

"Yes. So, I guess you can say we have something in common."

He could tell by the stiffening of her shoulders that she didn't agree with that assessment. "If you'll excuse me, I'll go get those slices of cake." She then walked out of the dining room toward the kitchen and said over her shoulder, "I'm not sure if we have anything in common or not, Jaxon Ravnel."

He couldn't help the way his lips twitched into a smile and was glad she hadn't turned around to see it.

Four

Nadia leaned against the kitchen cabinet, determined to get her anger in check and her desires under control. Dining with Jaxon had been nice, especially with them getting to know each other. But then his question about inviting cowboys to dinner had rubbed her the wrong way because it had reminded her of that incident with Hoyle Adams.

When she'd moved back to Gamble there had been men—namely cowboys—practically coming out of the woodwork, asking her out. It was a full year before she'd decided to go out with Hoyle. She'd played it safe and accepted his invitation to the movies a few times before inviting him to dinner. That had been a mistake. He had assumed she would be the after-dinner delight. After the meal she'd prepared, while she'd been in the kitchen to get the banana pudding she'd baked, he'd slipped out to his truck for his duffel bag. He'd actually assumed he would be staying the night and couldn't believe it when she'd asked him to leave.

That's when he'd acted like a total ass. He even had the nerve to tell her that all the single women in Gamble, and a few married ones as well, wanted him, and that she should be grateful she was the object of his attention. She'd told him just what he could do with all that attention.

He'd left with a bruised ego, but not before accusing her of being frigid just because she'd refused to sleep with him. Newsflash! She didn't do anything just for the hell of it, especially when it concerned her body. As far as Nadia was concerned it was no big deal that at twenty-eight she hadn't yet met a guy she felt was worthy of sleeping with. In fact, she'd never thought of making out with any man…

Until she'd met Jaxon.

Her sisters didn't know that since meeting him, she dreamed about him most nights. In secret he'd become her fantasy man. There was just something about him that pushed all her buttons in ways she hadn't thought was possible. During dinner when he'd licked a dab of gravy from around his mouth with his tongue, she could imagine him using that tongue to lick all over her the same way. She'd never had such thoughts before, but she had imagined them with Jaxon.

Nadia let out a frustrated sigh. She had to pull herself together. Sitting there talking with him, eating and sipping wine while getting to know him, had made her lower her guard and get too comfortable. But then why did she think she had to be uncomfortable around him? He'd been a perfect gentleman since he'd arrived. It wasn't his fault that bringing up the issue of her feeding a cowboy had pressed the wrong button and set her off. She could just imagine what he thought of her now. Probably Dr. Jekyll and Ms. Hyde.

Knowing she had hung out in the kitchen long enough, she drew in another deep breath and grabbed both plates of cake to walk back to the dining room. He looked up when she entered and stood. "Need help with those?" he asked.

"No, I got this," she said, setting plates with slices of cake on the table and then sliding one across to him.

He didn't sit back down until she did and she couldn't help but admire his manners. The Westmorelands and Outlaws behaved the same way. They might get rowdy at times but they respected women. She knew that some men didn't bother with all that chivalry stuff anymore because they assumed most women preferred they didn't. She wasn't one of them. Her father had raised his daughters to expect men to treat them like ladies.

"You think I can eat this huge slice?" he asked, picking up his fork while eyeing the cake she'd placed in front of him.

It didn't seem like her earlier flippant remarks had bothered him and she was glad they hadn't. "Yes, I think you can handle it," she said, wishing her gaze wasn't drawn to the hand that had picked up his fork. Why on earth would she think he had sexy fingers?

When he smiled over at her, flutters invaded her stomach. "Maybe, but I'll be hitting the hotel's fitness room in the morning," he teased.

She watched as he sliced into the cake with his fork and then slid a bite into his mouth. Seeing the way his lips parted sent an intense throbbing between her legs. Nothing like that had ever happened to her before. Not with Benson or Hoyle and she'd seen both men eat. In fact, the way Hoyle had chomped on his food had been annoying.

"This is delicious, Nadia." He took another bite before glancing over at her with bunched brows. "Aren't you going to eat any?" He was probably wondering why she was sitting there staring at him. Specifically, his mouth. Instead of answering, she nodded and reached out to pick up her fork.

"Don't bother. I got this," he said, leaning across the table to bring his fork with a bite of cake on it to her mouth.

She met his gaze. Did he not know how intimate such a thing was? It was his fork, the same one he'd used. He continued to hold the cake close to her mouth while she studied the look in his eyes, thinking there was something in the dark depths staring back at her. She didn't want to consider the possibility of that being true. Her attraction to him was one thing. The thought the attraction might be reciprocated was something she wasn't sure she could handle.

She could tell him thanks but no thanks, that she could very well slice into her cake and use her own fork. But there was something about the way he was staring at her and the patient way that cake was being held close to her lips. Sensations rushed through her at the thought of them sharing the same fork.

Without saying a word, she parted her lips and he fed her the cake.

The moment Nadia parted her lips Jaxon knew he'd made a mistake.

Or, maybe not if her soft moan was anything to go by. He had a feeling the sound wasn't because her taste buds were exploding from the sensational flavor of the cake. Instead, he chose to believe it had everything to do with another type of sensation entirely. One he could feel himself. All the way down to his gut. And when her tongue darted out to grab a crumb left on the fork, he nearly lost it.

"You like it?" he asked her in a voice that sounded way too throaty for his own ears.

Still holding his gaze, she nodded and said, "Of course I like it. I baked it, didn't I?"

He couldn't help but smile at the bit of defiance in her voice. "Yes, you baked it."

She then asked him in a somewhat mellow tone, "You liked it?"

He was trying like hell to concentrate on what she was saying and not how turned on he was getting each and every time her lips moved. "Yes. I told you it was delicious. Didn't I?"

Then, as if she accepted his comeback as her due, she nodded and said, "Yes, you did. Thanks for letting me sample yours, but I can eat my own. I can also feed myself."

"I know you can, but I enjoyed feeding you."

"Why?"

She would have to ask. "I like the thought of us sharing the same fork."

The surprised look on her face was priceless. It started at her eyes and then spread to her cheeks. Although his response had been honest, maybe he should not have been so bold. His only excuse was that at that moment...or any moment he was around her... Nadia had an impact not only on his male senses, but on his mind.

"Why?"

She was certainly asking a lot of questions. As far as he was concerned, he had no problem telling her whatever she wanted to know. He didn't like playing games anyway. "For me, doing so was a form of intimacy. I wanted to know how you tasted and I wanted you to know the same about me."

Before her mouth could form the word *why*, he quickly added, "I'm sure by now you've figured out that I'm interested in you." He wouldn't go so far as to admit to falling in love with her. She wouldn't believe him. However, he had no problem to at least admitting to being attracted to her. He had a strong feeling the attraction was mutual.

He saw a defiant look appear in the depths of her eyes before she placed her fork down. The gaze staring at him was sharp, like it might rip him to shreds at any moment. "You're interested in me for what reason, Jaxon?"

He figured any other man would clam up under her piercing gaze. Instead, he was trying like hell to ignore a multitude of sensations escalating through him. Did she not feel the heat flowing between them? It was heat he welcomed, but he had a feeling she was fighting hard to control her reaction.

"For the reason any man would be interested in a woman, Nadia," he said, then took a sip of wine.

Something flashed in her eyes. Was he mistaken or was it disappointment? If so, why? Granted, a number of people were never prepared for his outright honesty. He would have thought, however, that she would be. She didn't come across as a woman who preferred a man spouting bullshit.

She sat up straight in her chair and her gaze sharpened even more. "If that's your way of letting me know your interest in me is nothing more than sex, then let me set you straight. That's not how I roll, and I'm disappointed you think that I do." And then as if that ended the conversation, she picked up her fork and began eating her cake.

"Sex?" he asked, surprised. "What makes you think that's my only interest in you?"

"What other interest would there be? You did mention the word *intimate* earlier. And what's more intimate than sex?" she asked. "Just so you know, the last man I invited to dinner who assumed it was all about sex was asked to leave. Should I show you to the door as well?"

She had it all wrong. Damn did she have it all wrong. He wouldn't say he didn't think about making love to her, because he did. A lot. Every night. But to him making love to her was synonymous with the love he felt for her. "You misunderstood me, Nadia. And you definitely misunderstood my intentions."

"Did I?"

"Yes," he said, placing down his wineglass.

"Then what did I misunderstand? What are your intentions?"

Jaxon hadn't wanted to tell her so soon. At least not before spending more time with her, before courting her properly. However, she left him no choice. It was either tell her what she needed to know or let her group him in the same class as the other assholes who hadn't left a positive impression on her.

To make sure she fully understood what he was about to say, he leaned slightly toward her. Holding tight to her gaze, he said, "My intention, Nadia Novak, is to marry you."

Five

Nadia tilted her head and stared at Jaxon. He didn't look as if he was teasing. That could only mean… Sliding back her chair, she walked around the table and placed the back of her hand to his forehead.

"What are you doing?" he asked.

"I figure you must have a high temperature for you to be so delusional."

"I'm in my right mind, Nadia."

Removing her hand, she returned to her chair. "There's no way you can be to say something as asinine as that, Jaxon. Think about it. There's no way you can want to marry me. You don't even know me."

"I would like to get to know you."

She didn't say anything for a moment. "Who put you up to this? Sloan or Maverick?"

She watched as a dumbfounded look appeared on his face. "What makes you think they put me up to anything?"

"Mainly because the three of us are known to play tricks

on each other. I figured they owed me for that time I set them up with blind dates from hell a couple of years back."

"Trust me, Sloan nor Maverick have nothing to do with my decision to marry you."

His decision to marry her? Honestly, she didn't believe for one minute he was serious. And even if he was delusional to think such a thing, what man told a woman they barely knew of his plans to marry her? As if it was a done deal and she didn't have anything to say about it?

She wasn't born yesterday and knew she wasn't his type. It wasn't just the fact he was wealthy, since the Westmorelands and Outlaws had plenty of money as well. She would think a man like Jaxon preferred a sophisticated type, a cultured and graceful woman. A woman totally opposite from her. That one time she'd looked him up on the Internet she'd seen images of him from the society pages of several newspapers. In all of them, his date looked the part of a high-class, refined goddess.

"First of all, Jaxon, you won't be marrying me so stop saying such nonsense. And if Sloan nor Maverick put you up to this foolishness then who did?"

"No one put me up to anything. I'm speaking the truth."

She rolled her eyes. "Get serious."

"I am serious, trust me."

She leaned back in her chair and crossed her arms over her chest. "No, you aren't if you think for one minute that one day you'll be my husband."

"Don't you plan to marry?"

She shrugged her shoulders. "Possibly."

"Then what's the problem?"

She couldn't help but glare across the table at him. "The problem is you. How dare you say something like that, like you have the ability to speak such a thing into existence regardless of how I might feel about it happening. Marriage isn't and never will be at the top of my to-do list. Unlike some women, I don't worry about a biological clock ticking."

There was no way he didn't hear the irritation and strong conviction in her voice because she meant every word. "So, just in case you fell and hit your head on the way over here and are serious about thinking of marrying me, let me go on record to say that it won't be happening." She frowned when he had the audacity to smile.

"We shall see, Nadia."

We shall see? Had he actually said that? In that case, now was the time to show him the door. Easing from her chair, Nadia said, "I think you should leave now, Jaxon."

He glanced down at his cake. "I haven't finished eating."

"Then I suggest you take it with you."

He stared at her for a minute and then said, "I'm sorry if what I said upset you. However, it's my belief that honesty is the best policy."

Nadia stared at him and then she eased back down in her chair, totally confused. Although she hadn't gotten to know Jaxon as well as the others in her family had, at no time had she assumed he wasn't operating with a full deck. Until now. Therefore, she decided to use another approach.

"When did you decide you wanted to marry me?"

"The moment we were introduced."

Now she'd heard everything. "You honestly want me to believe that?" she asked, chuckling, finding what he'd said totally absurd.

"I don't see why not when it's the truth, Nadia."

Nadia would admit to feeling something when they'd first been introduced as well. However, she would call it what it was. Lust of the worst kind. She then thought about what he'd said. If he'd been taken with her from the first, why hadn't he approached her before now? The only reason he was here was because she had called and invited him to dinner. He'd even admitted he'd been in town a while, yet he hadn't looked her up. So how was she supposed to believe he was interested in her to the point of intending to marry her? That made this entire thing even more outrageous.

"That was truly delicious."

She blinked and glanced down at his plate. It was clean. He had eaten all of his cake. "I'm glad you enjoyed it."

"I've enjoyed everything about this evening with you, Nadia."

She drew in a deep breath, refusing to get baited. Standing, she said, "I had a rather interesting and enjoyable evening with you. Now it's time to call it a night."

"When can I see you again?"

She shrugged. "Not sure that's a good idea."

"Why? Because I told you of my future plans for us?"

He was frustrating her to the point where she wanted to stomp her feet. "There are no future plans for us, Jaxon. I am absolutely sure of that."

"If you're so certain of it then there should be no reason for me not to see you again, right? Dinner will be on me the next time. You pick the place." He then he stood as well. "I know it's a workday tomorrow for the both of us. I'll be seeing more land."

"So you are in town for that purpose?"

He smiled over at her. "That's one of them, yes."

"Meaning?"

"Meaning, while I'm here I hope to get to know you better." Then he changed the subject by saying, "I'll help you clear off the table."

"That's not necessary."

"It is for me. I'll even roll up my sleeves and wash the dishes if you need help."

"I don't. And you don't have to help clear off the table."

"You sure?"

"I'm positive." What she needed was for him to leave. Now. She couldn't think straight with him around. And she desperately needed to think. Do an instant replay and a total reevaluation of everything he'd said, especially the part about his future plans for them.

"Okay, if you're certain, Nadia."

"I am."

"Then please come walk me to the door."

She should have declined his request. After all, he knew the way there without her assistance. But then she decided to extend the same courtesy to him she would have expected of him had she been his guest for dinner. Besides, she didn't want him to think he'd rattled her with his nonsense, even if he had.

"You didn't say if you'll have dinner with me," he said.

They had walked side by side from the dining room and had reached the front door. He opened the closet to get his jacket. She was so focused on him sliding the jacket over his broad shoulders that she almost missed what he'd said. "I'll think about it." Although she'd said she would, she honestly knew she wouldn't. Right now, she needed him gone.

"All right. And like I said, I want you to pick the place."

Although she hadn't agreed to anything, she asked, "When?"

"Doesn't matter. I'm free whenever you are." He was standing there in front of her. She was about to take a step back when he reached out and placed both hands at her waist. The moment he touched her, heat spread to all parts of her body.

He was going to kiss her. She didn't say anything as she absorbed that fact into her brain. Regardless of the craziness he'd said about marrying her, what he'd said earlier was something she couldn't deny. She *had* wanted to know how he'd tasted and licking that fork hadn't been enough. Even with the sweetness of the chocolate cake, a part of her wanted to believe she had also gotten a taste of him. And it was a taste she wanted to experience again.

"Nadia?"

"Yes?"

"I hope you don't lose much sleep over what I said tonight."

She lifted her chin. "I don't plan on losing any sleep when I know it won't be happening."

"We'll see."

"No, you'll see," she said in an annoyed tone.

They stood there, staring at each other, squaring off. She wished all those sensations she'd felt all through dinner weren't still there. Jaxon was taking her breath away without even trying. If that wasn't bad enough, the nipples pressed against the material of her dress suddenly seemed achy. That was a first for her as well.

"It's getting late," she said, trying to dismiss the desire for him that was hitting her full force. It couldn't be helped, with the way his dark eyes were latched on to hers as if daring her to look away. For some reason, she couldn't. She felt herself falling victim to everything about him. Never had she been so mesmerized with any man, and she couldn't understand why she was this way with him. And then there was his mouth. The shape of it from corner to corner and that little dip in the middle fascinated her. She didn't have to be a rocket scientist to know that she was out of her element with Jaxon. The man was definitely out of her league. Yet...

"Then I guess I need to say good night."

His words cut into her trance. Before she could offer a response of *Yes, you do*, he leaned forward, drew her closer and captured her mouth in his.

Her lips immediately parted under his. The moment their mouths touched, thoughts fled from her mind. She'd needed this to happen. Was glad it was happening. For the past year, she'd wondered about his mouth. Fantasized about it. Dreamed about it. Not only how it would taste but also how well he could use it for kissing.

Now she was finding out and had no complaints. He'd stuck his tongue inside her mouth at the exact moment she released a sigh of pleasure. There was something about the way he was kissing her that sent jolts of heat through her. Never had she been kissed this way, with such mastery and finesse. So vibrantly and with so much passion. It was both mind-blowing and torturous.

He was devouring her mouth with one stoke of his tongue while slowly mating with it with another stroke. It was as if he was methodically and intentionally creating an avalanche of need and pleasure within her. Unable to help herself, she wrapped her arms around his neck to hold, certain if he stopped kissing her, she would melt in a puddle at his feet. Needs she didn't know she had, and a degree of pleasure she hadn't known could be derived from a kiss, were taking over her senses.

Without warning, he deepened the kiss and drew her even closer. That's when she felt him. His aroused body hard against the junction of her thighs. Knowing he wanted her as much as she wanted him had temptation running rampant through her. Temptation to try some of those things with him that she'd dreamed about. Fantasized about doing.

Suddenly he broke off the kiss, but she soon discovered that he wasn't through with her yet when he traced the tip of his tongue across her lips, corner to corner. Then he stopped and slowly eased back, although he hadn't removed his hands from around her waist.

"I have to fly out tomorrow to Forbes to check on a few things but will return in a day or so. I will be thinking of you, Nadia and I hope you'll be thinking about me."

Before she could respond, mainly to tell him that she wouldn't be thinking about him, he grabbed his Stetson off the hat rack, opened the door and left.

Jaxon had driven a mile from the Novak Homestead when he pulled his car to the shoulder of the road to inhale and exhale. Never had kissing a woman left him so weak. He'd only stopped kissing her when breathing had become a necessity. Then it had taken all his strength to finally release her and walk out the door.

He rubbed his hand down his face. It had not been his intent to tell her he planned to marry her, and, as expected, he'd put her on the defensive. She would probably avoid going out with him for that reason. He could see her putting roadblocks in his paths.

But Jaxon could never forget the look on her face when he'd broken off the kiss. She hadn't been happy about how she was feeling, if the look on her face was anything to go by. And yet, she had enjoyed it as much as he had. He was certain of it. He'd also felt the way the hardened nipples of her breasts poked into his chest. That was a sure sign of arousal.

His plan was to tear down any wall she tried erecting between them, one brick at a time. Although more than anything he would love to be married to her by New Year's, he knew that some things just couldn't be rushed. He loved her and he had to be patient for her to fall in love with him. He had to believe that eventually she would.

He would give her a few days to think about tonight, just like he would. Then he would call and follow up on his invitation to dinner. No matter what she might be thinking now, there would definitely be a next time for them.

He would see to it.

Six

"You can close your mouth now, Rissa," Nadia said the next morning to the woman sitting across from her desk. Marissa Phelps had been Nadia's best friend since second grade. When Pam had moved her sisters with her to Denver, Nadia and Rissa had stayed in touch by engaging in summer visits, occasional sleepovers and then attending the same university after high school. It was at the University of Wyoming where Rissa had met Shayne, the man she married. The couple had three beautiful children under the age of ten.

Rissa closed her mouth but leaned forward in her chair with her eyes still widened. "Jaxon Ravnel actually told you that he intends to marry you?"

"Yes, that's what he said. Can you imagine anything so downright ridiculous?"

"I guess you can," Rissa said, eyeing her speculatively.

"Of course I can. What man tells a woman something like that?"

Rissa shrugged her shoulders as she sat back in her chair. "A man who knows the woman he wants and intends to get her. A man who wants more than a bed partner. He wants a future with the woman he loves. A man who—"

"Love has nothing to do with it," Nadia interrupted, frowning. "Jaxon doesn't even know me." Rissa's words had put her on the defensive. "You can't love someone you don't know."

Rissa scoffed at that. "I heard it happens that way at times. Otherwise, there would not be any of those love-at-first-sight situations."

Nadia shook her head. She didn't believe in that kind of phenomenon either. "Get real, Rissa. Jaxon Ravnel doesn't love me. Besides, I'm definitely not his type. He's a man who'd prefer a woman with a high degree of sophistication. One who possesses style, grace and pedigree. Not someone who for years was a tomboy. Even now I only act prim and proper when there's a need. I have no problem being outspoken and opinionated. Being known as a rebel and renegade doesn't bother me one bit."

"Maybe he likes you the way you are."

"Let me say this again, Rissa. Jaxon doesn't know the way I am because he doesn't know me. Besides, I'm not sure I even like him."

Rissa smiled. "If you recall, I didn't like Shayne at first either. However, he eventually grew on me. But then, maybe not liking Jaxon right off the bat is a good thing. You were smitten with Benson the minute he got in your face at that football game, and you see what happened with that."

She wished Rissa didn't make her remember that day or the guy. Yes, she might have been smitten with Benson the first time he'd turned those dreamy hazel eyes on her, but it was only after he'd taken her on a couple of movie dates that she had convinced herself he was a supernice guy. That's when she had fallen in love with him. Supernice her ass. He had proven just what a scum he was.

"Well, I don't want Jaxon, or any man for that matter, to

grow on me nor do I want to grow on him. I'm not in the mood."

"Obviously you were in the mood for that whopper of a kiss he laid on you last night," Rissa said, grinning.

There were days Nadia regretted that Rissa kept her in check. Unlike her sisters, who hadn't a clue about her attraction to Jaxon, Rissa knew everything. She'd even told Rissa about the kiss that still had her swooning. When Paige and Jill had called that morning to see how dinner with Jaxon had gone, Nadia had told them everything had gone well. What she hadn't told them was what he'd said about marrying her. Nor had she told her sisters about their heated kiss.

"That kiss took me by surprise. I hadn't been kissed in a long time, so my mouth was more than ready for some action."

Rissa chuckled. "I guess it helped that the action was delivered by the same man you've been dreaming about for over a year. Don't you want to compare the dream with the real thing? You can't even say it's been a long time since you've slept with a man because you've never slept with one. I've told you more than once what you're missing."

Yes, Rissa had. Too many times. To the point where Nadia had gotten curious, too curious for her own good. It didn't help when Jill and Paige would go on and on about how much they enjoyed their husbands in the bedroom. That was one of the reasons Hoyle had been such a disappointment. She had figured although she hadn't been looking for anything long-term with him, that maybe after they'd gotten to know each other better, a little roll between the sheets wouldn't be so bad. It would have rid her of her virginity and appeased her curiosity. Like with Benson, she was glad she'd discovered just what an ass he was before sharing her body with him.

"Are you going to tell your family what Jaxon said about his plans to marry you?" Rissa asked, interrupting her thoughts.

"Heck no. They like Jaxon. If anything, they would pity him for even contemplating such a thing and warn him off." She paused and then said, "Benson taught me a hard lesson. When I do marry…if that day ever comes… I will marry for love. I will know beyond a shadow of doubt that the man I marry loves me. Truly loves me. I won't take a chance with my heart again."

"Does that mean you won't sleep with a guy until you marry him?"

"No, I didn't say I had to love whatever guy who will become my first. To be quite honest, he doesn't even have to love me. However, I need to feel that I truly do know him and there won't be any surprises later on that I couldn't handle."

"So, what are you planning to do, Nadia? You might want to come up with a plan because I have a feeling Jaxon Ravnel has one of his own. Sounds like he intends to wear down your resistance like Shayne did to me. And if that kiss is anything to go by, he's already begun his attack."

The last thing Nadia wanted to think about was that the kiss had been part of a planned attack by Jaxon. In fact, she didn't want to talk about him at all anymore. That meant it was time to send Rissa on her way; otherwise he would remain the topic of their conversation.

Looking at her watch, she said, "Shouldn't you be leaving for work?"

Rissa was the assistant manager of a bank that was a half a mile up the road. Since the bank didn't open until ten, it was Rissa's normal routine after dropping her kids off at school to stop by Dream Makers Acting Academy every weekday morning to share a cup of coffee and girl-talk with Nadia.

Rissa gave Nadia a knowing eye, fully aware of why she'd asked. "Not yet." After taking another sip of her coffee, Rissa inquired, "Has anyone signed on as a sponsor of this year's Christmas play yet?"

Nadia released a frustrated breath. She honestly didn't want to talk about that either. "No. Although I can go to the Westmoreland Foundation as a last resort, I prefer not doing so since they bailed this place out a couple of times before I began working here. The reason Pam hired me is because she believed I could keep sponsorships intact. I can't disappoint her."

"It's not your fault that the Dunnings Financial Group went bankrupt."

"I know, but I should have had a Plan B in place."

"I disagree. Dunnings has always been one of the most prominent employers in the city. A company that could be depended on to fund community projects. It's unfortunate they had to close their doors when they did. Just think of the number of people who lost their jobs. People who were making good salaries." Rissa took a sip of her coffee then added, "At least I can admire them for giving everyone a nice severance package with enough funds to last them for the next six months. Everyone is hoping that by then another huge employer will come to town."

Nadia hoped so, too. Rissa was right. Dunnings was one of the few corporations in Gamble to pay top salaries and who readily funded community projects. They had been sponsoring the Christmas play for years. No one had asked who the new sponsor would be. She figured most people thought she had one.

"Just so you know, Nadia, the mayor and Gamble's Better Business Bureau had a meeting yesterday. Jaxon Ravnel's name came up. They know he's in town looking for land to expand his business. They're hoping he likes the area. Ravnel Technologies is three times the size of what Dunnings was."

"Although Jaxon is looking for land here, there's no guarantee he'll buy any," Nadia interjected.

"I know, but we can all hope," Rissa said standing. "It will certainly solve the unemployment crisis Gamble will be facing within a few months." She glanced at her watch. "It's time for me to skedaddle. I'll see you again this time tomorrow."

After Rissa left, Nadia leaned back in her chair and for the umpteenth time replayed in her mind everything that had transpired last night between her and Jaxon. He'd been the perfect gentleman the entire time. She'd been so busy fighting her attraction to him that she hadn't noticed he'd been attracted to her.

Until he'd fed her that cake.

She had noticed him staring at her a number of times but assumed he'd done so because he had caught her staring at him. It now appeared they had been staring at each other. She figured the reason she hadn't picked up on an attraction on his end was because he hadn't been giving her any predatory, I-want-to-take-you-to-bed looks.

What had rocked her world more than anything had been that kiss. What she'd told Rissa was true. She hadn't been prepared for it. She doubted any woman would have been. What man kissed like that? The way he had taken her mouth, locked his tongue around hers while he greedily mated with it had sent sparks escalating through every part of her body.

And talking about a body... While he'd held her tight in his arms, with her body pressed hard against his, she had felt him. Namely his arousal. Just knowing the intensity of his desire had matched hers sent a wave passion rushing through her. She was convinced if he hadn't stopped kissing her when he had, she would have gotten her first orgasm ever, right there in his arms. His kiss had been hotter than any she'd ever shared with a man before. Just thinking about it sent sensuous chills through her. That was the last thing she wanted or needed.

A couple of hours later Nadia was working through the stack of papers her administrative assistant, China Evans, had placed on her desk earlier. She glanced up at the knock on her door. "Come in."

China walked in carrying a huge vase of flowers. Nadia grimaced and sat up in her chair, having an idea who'd sent them. But that didn't make sense when Jaxon had brought her flowers yesterday when he'd arrived for dinner. Why would he be giving her more flowers today? But if they weren't from him, then who else would have sent them?

"These are for you, Ms. Novak." The younger woman of nineteen, who was attending the local community college, smiled from ear to ear as she placed the a dozen red roses on the desk.

"Thank you, China," Nadia said, not bothering to pull off the card that was attached.

"You're not eager to see who they're from?" China asked. "I've never known you to get flowers when it wasn't your birthday or Valentine's Day."

That was true. She always got flowers from various people on her birthday, and Dillon had always sent his Denver Westmoreland female cousins—Megan, Gemma and Bailey—flowers on Valentine's Day. After marrying Pam he'd added Nadia, Paige and Jill to his list. He was such a thoughtful brother-in-law. The best.

"I'll read the card later," Nadia said, turning her attention back to the stack of papers on her desk.

"I guess that means you know who sent them."

"Maybe," Nadia said and that was all she would say on the matter. China was at that impressionable age where she believed in love. The forever kind. Nadia remembered when she had been that way as well. Her parents, as well as Dillon and Pam, had been great role models. Then Benson had broken her heart and from that day forward she'd shied away from falling in love.

Seeing she was not getting any information out of Nadia, China said, "Well, I guess I'll get back to my desk."

As soon as China closed the door behind her, Nadia pulled the card off the arrangement and read it.

Thinking about you,
Jaxon

Nadia placed the card back in the envelope and slid it into her desk drawer. If Rissa was right and Jaxon was trying to wear down her resistance, first by feeding her cake, then the kiss and now with more beautiful flowers, she had her work cut out for her. She had to make sure he knew a marriage between them wouldn't be happening.

She sighed deeply as she stared at the beautiful red roses. Of course she would thank him for the flowers. However, she would text him instead of calling him, not sure she could handle hearing his voice. And as far as his dinner invitation, she might as well decline that, too, while she was at it. Hopefully, in due time he would discover she would not participate in whatever games he wanted to play.

Jaxon drove to the airport, glad to finally be leaving Forbes. The trip had taken a day longer than planned due to a glitch in the data system of one of the firm's top clients. He was glad the malfunction had been corrected and now he was on his way back to Gamble.

He wished he could say he'd been too busy to think about Nadia, but that had not been the case. He had thought about her a lot. Each time her face entered his thoughts, he felt emotions so profound that more than once he had to pause to pull himself together and refocus.

If there had been any doubt in his mind that Nadia was the One, it had been dispelled on the night they'd shared dinner together. Specifically, the moment she'd opened the door. Never before had a woman caused his entire body to burn.

Up close she'd been even more beautiful and by the end of the evening she'd had him tied in knots in the most sensual way. Any other man would think such an intense attraction to a woman wasn't normal. However, to him it was. He'd figured it would be that way when he'd found his soulmate, the woman destined to have a special place in his life.

Jaxon was well aware she had issues with accepting that place. Quite frankly, she didn't believe that place existed. The text messages he'd received from her before leaving Forbes pretty much confirmed it. One had thanked him for the roses and the other had turned down his invitation to dinner. She had then proceeded to tell him that she hoped he enjoyed the rest of his stay in Gamble.

If Nadia thought that was the end of them, she was mistaken. There was nothing stopping him from figuring out a different approach.

His thoughts shifted to the call he'd gotten from his administrative assistant advising him of Gamble's mayor's request to meet with him. A meeting had been scheduled for next week but he would have preferred scheduling time with Nadia instead.

He'd dismissed their sexual chemistry as one-sided until she had stood beside him while they'd discussed the huge family picture over her fireplace. That's when he'd felt it, not only the vibes coming from him but from her as well. And the chemistry had been there each and every time their gazes met during dinner. He'd known every time she'd looked over at him because it had resulted in him looking at her.

It didn't take him long for him to realize the reason she hadn't picked up on all those sexual vibes coming from him was because she'd been too busy trying to ignore those coming from her. That's when he'd decided to feed her the cake. Doing so had certainly turned up the heat, which was the very thing he'd wanted to happen. It had been the very thing that had prompted her to remove her blinders.

What he'd thought about most over the last three days had been the kiss they'd shared. It had been everything he'd thought it would be and more. Although it had been intense and invigorating, it hadn't been enough.

A few hours later he was back in his hotel room in Gamble. It was close to seven and he hadn't responded to the two text messages Nadia had sent him. Now he would.

Instead of texting her back he decided to call her. Picking up his cell phone he punched in her number. The phone rang several times and for a minute he thought perhaps she would not answer once she saw the call was from him. He was about to disconnect when she clicked on.

"Hello."

He pulled in a deep breath the moment he heard her voice. "Nadia, I got your messages. I'm glad you liked the roses."

She paused before saying, "They are beautiful. Thank you again."

"You are welcome. As for my dinner invitation, I'm sorry you've decided not to go out with me. I regret that what I said the other night scared you off."

She hesitated and then said, "Nothing about what you said scared me."

He couldn't help but smile at her strong denial. "Didn't it?"

"No. There was no reason it should when it's apparent you're living in a delusional world."

Undaunted by her words, he said, "That's your opinion. We could meet and discuss it further if you weren't so afraid to face the truth."

"Truth? There's no truth in what you're thinking, Jaxon. I don't like overconfident men."

That's what he'd been told. "You're getting a self-assured man confused with an overconfident one. I know what I want, and I want you. I've been up front with you. I don't like playing games with a woman any more than I like a woman playing games with me."

He could just imagine her glaring him down through her phone. "Anyway, you've made your decision. Have a nice night, Nadia."

"Wait!"

He took his time answering. "Yes?"

"I'll have dinner with you, and you'll see how unafraid I am of you. And you can decide on the place."

"Fine. I will do that and call you in a few days with the details. Goodbye, Nadia."

"Goodbye."

He couldn't help but smile when she ended the call.

Seven

Nadia stood in the same spot she had last week when she'd watched Jaxon arrive. Unlike then, when she hadn't known what to expect, she knew now. He was a nice guy although a delusional one. There was no other way for her to describe a man who'd told her, without as much as blinking an eye, that he intended to marry her. Regardless of the fact that other than the surface stuff, they knew nothing about each other. Then there was the reality that they weren't in love. In fact, the verdict was still out as to whether she would even consider them friends.

She'd heard from Rissa that he had met with the mayor yesterday. No one knew how that meeting went, although she had more than a hunch what was discussed. Nadia had no idea how much of an expansion Jaxon was contemplating and wondered would it be enough to help the job employment crisis the city would soon be facing. More than likely, Ravnel Technologies would be relocating a lot of their present employees and might not need additional staff. At least not to the magnitude the city was hoping for.

Thinking it was best to move away from the window, she did so. There was no need for her adrenaline to get revved up when he got out of the car. She would have more time to fully check him out later and hoped she could contain herself when she did so.

She quickly left the kitchen and moved to the living room with no intention of giving him the chance to knock. Grabbing her purse and shawl, she opened the door and stepped out on the porch, locking the door behind her. He had called a few days ago saying dinner plans had been finalized. When she'd asked where and suggested she just meet him there, seeing no reason for him to drive to her house to pick her up, he refused to do that, saying his definition of a date was the guy picking up the woman from her home and returning her there. He never did say where they were going.

She studied him as he got out of the car. He was talking on his cell phone and hadn't looked up to see her. Since he'd told her to dress casually, she'd opted for a skirt and blouse. It was her first time wearing the ensemble that she'd purchased earlier that year while shopping with her sisters in New York. Her sisters thought she looked good in them.

From the expression that appeared on Jaxon's face when he put his phone in his jacket pocket and glanced up and saw her, he agreed with her sisters. She thought he looked good, too, dressed in a pair of dark slacks, a tweed jacket and that black Stetson on his head.

He had stopped walking and stood there in a masculine stance that caused her heart rate to increase. The sun was going down behind him and the backdrop—orange and gold over the mountains—was a breathtaking sight that complemented a breathtaking-looking man. Seeing it before her eyes stirred something deep within her and she just couldn't understand it. She'd been raised around eye candy, ultrahandsome men, mainly the Westmorelands, and then there were the Outlaws. She would even say she'd met a few cowboys in town she thought were good on the eyes. But at that moment, the memory of any other man faded to black. Jaxon Ravnel was in a class all by himself. His lips curved into that killer smile that showed all his dimples as he began walking again.

Nadia drew in slow, steadying breaths and wished Jaxon's smile didn't affect her the way it did. Having a handsome man stare at you with male appreciation in his eyes was one thing. Throw a sexy smile in the mix and it was lethal. "Hello, Jaxon."

"Nadia. You look nice."

"Thanks. I hope what I'm wearing is appropriate for where we're going."

"It is. Are you ready to go?"

"Yes."

She wished he hadn't reached for her hand, leaving her no choice but to give it to him. The moment he touched it, goose bumps appeared on her skin. Suddenly, images floated through her mind, namely that of his arms wrapped tight around her as she'd kissed him as deeply and thoroughly as he'd kissed her.

He walked her to his car and opened the door. Releasing his hand, she slid onto the leather seat. She hadn't missed how his gaze had lowered to her legs when the hem of her skirt had inched up a little. "Is anything wrong, Jaxon?" she asked, after making sure her seat belt was securely fastened.

He moved his gaze to her face and his lips curved into a smile. One that sent flutters through her stomach. "No, nothing is wrong."

A short while later they had driven past downtown, where most of the popular restaurants were located. She glanced over at him, and evidently anticipating her question, he said, "Where we're going is a surprise."

"And what if I don't like surprises?"

"Then I'll make doubly certain you like this one."

When the interior of the car got too quiet to suit her, she said, "I understand you had a meeting with the mayor the other day."

He grinned and gave her a sideways glance. "Yes, that's right."

Was he going to tell her anything? When moments passed and he didn't, she figured he wouldn't. Then he said, "That was awful what happened to the Dunnings Financial Group. I understand a lot of people lost their jobs. However, I'm glad they got a good severance package."

"I'm glad, too, but unfortunately it doesn't extend to our school."

He looked at her when he brought the car to a stop. "What do you mean?"

She wished she hadn't said anything, but since she had, she might as well give him an answer. "Every year the school puts on this huge holiday play. This year a well-known movie director from Hollywood, who is a good friend of Pam's, is volunteering his time here. It will be the biggest production the school has put on so far and also the most expensive. Unfortunately, Dunnings was our major sponsor. Their bankruptcy pretty much left us in a bind."

"I'm sorry to hear that. Will you have to cancel the event?"

"I hope not. I'm working hard to find a replacement sponsor." She stopped talking when she looked out the car's window. "Why are we at the airport?"

He brought the car to a stop and smiled over at her. "Because we'll be dining on my jet."

Jaxon thought the look of surprise on Nadia's face was not only priceless, but it was also one of the most sensuous expressions he'd ever seen. The way her lips parted in an "oh" followed by her eyes lighting up and ending with a smile that spread wide across her lips. That smile went straight to his heart. Not that there had been any doubts about his feelings for her before, but if there had been, they had dissolved at that moment.

"You're kidding, right?" she asked him, her smile widening ever more.

"No, I'm not kidding."

When she realized he was serious, she rocked her body in her seat in a happy dance.

He threw his head back and laughed, loving her excitement. He hadn't been sure what to expect when he'd thought of the idea. "I guess that means you have no problem with flying."

"Heck no. I think the Denver Westmorelands shied away from owning a corporate jet because of what happened to their parents, but those Atlanta-based Westmorelands have no reservations about it. And flying is a way of life for those Outlaws in Alaska."

Jaxon knew that to be true. The Westmoreland triplets, Clint, Cole and Casey, were licensed pilots. And because of Alaska's road system, people living there owned more planes than cars. All six of the Outlaws owned planes. In fact, Garth, the oldest Outlaw son, was married to Regan, their company's pilot.

It seemed Nadia was in a good mood and he intended to take full advantage of her joviality. "Ready to go aboard?"

"Yes."

Now he was glad for all the special arrangements he had made. He had gone out of his way to impress her tonight. Getting out of the car, he came around on her side to open the door. This time he tried not to be so obvious when he glanced down at her legs. Taking her hand, he walked over to the plane, where his pilot and flight host were waiting. Introductions were made before he escorted her up the steps.

"My parents always had the company jet, and I had a Cessna since I rarely did international travel. But now that I'm in charge, I decided to get a jet that fit my needs. I've only had this one for six months," he told her when he saw her glancing around curiously.

"This is nice," Nadia said. "The only other time I've been on a corporate jet was during one of Charm's bridal showers. It was given to her in flight by Regan. We had so much fun during the three-hour flight. We never did land. The entire shower was held while we were in the sky."

"Who was the pilot that night?" he asked as he escorted her over to the seats. He would give her a tour of the jet later.

"A girlfriend of Regan's. Garth had volunteered but he was told no husbands or significant others were allowed on that trip. I'm glad. Things got pretty wild."

"Were there half-naked men on board?"

She threw up her head and laugh. "I'll never tell. Don't you know what goes on at the bridal shower stays at the bridal shower? I'm sure men have the same rule for the bachelor party."

"I guess they do." He was tempted to say not only was that the rule for a bachelor party but that had been the case for that poker tournament a couple of months ago as well.

Nadia sat in the seat facing him and they both followed instructions when the pilot told them to buckle up. She was deliberately looking everywhere else but at him. That was fine since he had no intentions of looking anywhere else other than at her.

"You have big plans for the weekend?" he asked, not just for conversational purposes but as a way to get her to glance over at him. She did so and when their gazes met, he felt it. He had a feeling she did, too. The attraction was stronger than ever. He was beginning to think that the more they were alone the more the sexual chemistry increased between them.

She looked over at him at the exact moment the plane began moving down the runway. "Not big plans. Normal chores that need to be done. What about you?"

"I'm flying home tomorrow. My parents like to see their only child every once and a while."

She nodded. "You're close to them?"

"Very."

"I heard they were nice."

He could tell by her expression that she regretted saying that because it meant his name had come up in a discussion she'd had with someone. Before he could ask who had told her that, she cleaned up her comment by adding, "I believe Paige mentioned she met them at one of Jess's fundraising dinners."

"She did. My parents are big on making financial contributions to their favorite political candidates. Now that they consider Jess, as well as Reggie Westmoreland, as family, they wanted to attend and do their part."

"That was kind of them."

"I have kind parents." He truly meant that. As long as he could remember they'd always been there for him, encouraging him to be his own man. The only thing they'd demanded of him was to always have respect for others, especially women. Now was not the time to tell her that he'd told his parents about her, and they were looking forward to meeting her.

When the plane had leveled off in the sky and the pilot indicated it was okay to move around, he unbuckled his seat belt and stood. By the time he had walked over to her, she had unbuckled her own and was standing as well. "You're ready to show me around?" she asked excitedly.

In all honesty, he wanted to do a lot more than that. Taking her hand, he said, "Yes, I am ready to show you around before dinner is served."

Eight

Nadia was impressed by everything she saw on Jaxon's private jet. From the thick rich carpeting to the smooth leather seats in his sitting room. However, what touched her most was the table set for dinner. It was just as impressive as any table in a five-star restaurant.

He introduced her to the chef, who was also on the flight. The food had tasted wonderful and she'd wasted no time letting the chef know. Dessert was banana pudding cake. Evidently Jaxon had inquired about her favorite dessert the way she'd done for him.

"I can't eat a thing more," she said, pushing back from the table. "Your cook outdid himself with dinner and so did you."

He chuckled. "I didn't cook."

"No, but you arranged all of this," she said, using her hand to encompass the dining table. "A beautifully set table, great food, champagne and a delicious dessert, all the time while flying high in the sky. Things can't get any better than this."

In all honestly, that's what bothered her. She hadn't wanted to be impressed by anything he'd done tonight. She had decided tonight would be her chance to use any means possible to make him think twice about pursing any type of relationship with her. But whenever he gave her a warm smile, like he was doing now, she couldn't stop the desire flowing through her. Desire she knew he not only felt but reciprocated.

Why was the sexual chemistry stronger between them tonight than it had been at dinner last week? She figured that kiss had a lot to do with it. The same kiss she couldn't get off her mind. The kiss that had her licking her lips every morning and night, and a few times in between, to see if his taste was still there.

"Do you want to go in the sitting room to look out at the stars?"

She hesitated a minute before she said, "Yes, I'd love to."

"I think you'll love the view," he said, grabbing the bottle of wine off the table.

"I'm sure I will."

The sitting room had a beautiful leather sofa that faced a huge window. It was a beautiful night and the sky was clear and the stars appeared to be everywhere. They'd been in the air a couple of hours now and every so often the pilot would announce what state they were flying over. They were now in Idaho and would do a zig-zag across Montana before returning to Wyoming.

"Too bad Dylan is away on a concert tour and Charm is with him. Otherwise we could have dropped in to say hello," he said.

"That would have been nice," she said, easing down on the sofa. Charm owned her own Cessna and Dylan's ranch in Idaho had an airstrip. The flight distance between their ranch and Gamble was less than an hour. Charm would often fly into the Gamble airport, pick up Nadia and two of them would fly to Westmoreland Country.

Charm's husband, Dylan, was an award-winning singer

and guitarist. He'd won another award earlier that year and had called Charm on stage while making his acceptance speech to introduce her to all his fans.

Nadia settled down on the sofa and was surprised when Jaxon came to sit beside her. She thought he would take the single chair across from her and quickly scooted over to make room.

"It's a beautiful night, isn't it?" he said, refilling their wine-glasses.

"Yes, and you were right, I love the view."

"So do I."

She noticed he wasn't looking out the window but his gaze was on her. Was he flirting with her? The last thing she wanted was to send out an erroneous message that she was in any way entertaining the thought of what he claimed the other night. Namely, that he intended to marry her. Rissa thought she should at least be flattered, but she wasn't.

"So what do you see when you glance out the window?" she asked him.

He looked out the window and then back at her. "I see an array of beautiful stars dotting a dark sky and a quarter moon peeking out at them. Now ask me what I see when I look at you."

She wasn't sure she wanted to know as she felt the heat flowing between them. However, drawing in a deep breath, she asked, "So, what do you see?"

"A woman I want to dance with."

She lifted a brow. "Dance?"

"Yes. So will you dance with me?"

"Without music?"

"What makes you think that?"

She was about to say because no music was playing when he reached for the remote on the table. With a press of his finger, music came through speakers. Of course it would be a slow tune.

Standing, he reached out his hand to her. "Please dance with me, Nadia. I need to hold you in my arms."

She could make a comeback that she didn't need to hold him in hers, but the thought of having her body pressed to his while his arms were wrapped around her was too tempting to deny.

Placing her hand in his, he eased her to her feet and when he gently pulled her into his arms, she didn't hesitate. The moment her body pressed against his, it seemed everything woman inside of her went into overdrive. Instinctively she rested her head on his chest and inhaled his manly fragrance.

This was not supposed to be happening. She had done her research, had looked up the top twenty ways to scare a man away. Yet she hadn't tried any of the suggestions tonight. She had been too impressed with sharing dinner with him thirty thousand feet off the ground to concentrate on anything other than him.

She needed to take a big pause and catch her breath. But not now. Not even tonight. Jaxon was in control, and she didn't want to fight against this. His looks, his aroma, his personality and the way he made her feel…

No matter what, she had to get a grip on reality. The last thing she wanted to do was encourage him in his nonsense that he would marry her one day.

"I love dancing with you, Nadia."

His low, husky and sexy voice sent her heart pounding. "Do you?"

"Can't you tell?"

If he was hinting at the fact that dancing with her had aroused him, then yes, she could tell. She wondered if he could tell she was just as aroused. Her breasts, as they pressed against his chest, felt sensitive. Could he tell her nipples had hardened? Were poking into him?

"Are you okay, sweetheart?"

She wondered why he used that term of endearment. She wasn't his sweetheart. And why had he even asked her that? Had she moaned and hadn't realized she had done so? Was he feeling the intense heat leaving her body and going to his? She lifted her head off his chest to look at him and wished she hadn't. The dark eyes staring down at her caused flutters in her stomach. "I'm fine, Jaxon, why do you ask?"

"No reason."

There had to have been a reason, but she knew better than to push the issue. She was smart enough to know when and how to operate on the side of caution. Tonight, she would ignore any endearments or sexual innuendos. Deliberate or otherwise.

The music stopped and then another tune began playing. She was going to suggest they sit this one out, cool things off a minute, but when he pulled her closer Nadia decided not to say anything at all. She liked the feel of the warm hard body pressed close to hers, the even breathing near her ear and the way he gently rubbed strong hands up and down her back. Point blank, more than anything, she wanted to savor the moment.

As if he had the ability to read her thoughts, he whispered, "I love holding you in my arms and will find any excuse to do so."

"Even by dancing?" She lifted her face from his chest to ask him while looking into his dark eyes.

"Yes, even by dancing. But it's just the beginning."

"The beginning of what?"

"Our courtship that will end in marriage."

Jaxon saw the flare of defiance that leaped into Nadia's eyes and wondered if she knew how beautiful she looked when she was filled with fire. His gaze then shifted to her mouth. A mouth he was tempted to kiss and devour.

"Why can't you get it through that thick skull that a marriage between us won't be happening, Jaxon?"

He shifted his gaze back to her eyes. "Mainly because I believe it will, Nadia."

She let out a frustrated sigh. "Why are you being so difficult?"

"Why are you?" he countered.

"I am not being difficult ,just realistic. I don't know how things operate in your world. Maybe the wealthy Ravnels of Virginia are used to doing things this way."

"What way?"

"Saying what they want and then getting it regardless of people's feelings, thoughts or pride?"

"That's not how my family operates, Nadia."

"Isn't it?"

"No."

"Well, that's how it seems to me." She pushed out of his arms and placed her hands on her hips. "What would make you think I'd want to marry a man who doesn't love me or one who I don't love? Did it ever occur to you that I might want a marriage where I know my husband loved me, and I wouldn't have to worry about…"

He frowned. "About what?"

"It doesn't matter."

Jaxon thought it did. The Westmorelands claimed that as far as they knew, Nadia had dated on occasion but had never been in a serious or exclusive relationship. Now he wondered if there had been someone they hadn't known about. Some man who had broken her heart?

"I think it does matter," he said.

"No, it doesn't."

He decided not to push the issue. "All right then. Let's talk about the issue of love. You don't think two people can fall in love with each other?" he asked, deciding not to admit he was already there. No need to bring that into the conversation when she wouldn't believe him.

"Yes, but they fall in love first and then talk about marriage and not the other way around, Jaxon."

"The reason I talked about marriage was because I wanted to be honest with you up front, to let you know my intentions toward you were honorable, Nadia. I am not a womanizer or a man on the prowl. I want you as part of my future."

"But you don't know me."

"I know you are a very beautiful and desirable woman. A woman who is deserving of a man who will love you, cherish you and make you happy."

"And you believe you are that man?"

"I know I am. All I need is a chance for you to get to know me and for me to get to know you better."

She shook her head. "What if once you get to know me you don't like me after all? But I discover I like you? All I can see is another heartbreak, Jaxon, and I won't go through something like that again."

Another heartbreak? He'd guessed right. At that moment the pilot asked them to take their seats for the landing. They had returned to Gamble. He inwardly cursed the timing. It was just as he'd suspected. Some man had broken her heart. Was it someone she'd met during the six years she'd been in college? Had it been someone she'd met after moving back to Gamble? One of those cowboys she'd gotten so uptight about?

He needed to convince her that they should spend more time together. It would only be then that she would believe he'd never break her heart. Instead of saying anything else to him, she left the sitting room to return to her seat in the cabin.

By the time he got there she was already buckled in and staring out the window. She didn't even look over at him.

After sitting down and snapping his seat belt in place, he glanced over at her. "Nadia?"

She turned from the window to look at him. "Yes?"

"I want to see you again. Spend time with you."

"I don't think that's a good idea."

He disagreed—he wanted to get to know her—but one thing he knew how to be was flexible. Normally, he wasn't one who liked changing the rules of any game, but for her he would. Apparently telling her up front that he wanted to marry her hadn't been a good idea. Yet he couldn't backtrack on it now or else she would think he really didn't know his own heart and mind.

"I'm not interested in anything other than an acquaintance type of relationship while you're in Gamble," she continued. "Of course when we're around the Westmorelands and Outlaws it can extend to one of friendship. There's no way we can avoid it being any other way when we're there."

He didn't like what he was hearing. "And if I don't want that kind of relationship?"

She frowned at him. "You don't have a choice."

She was wrong—he did have a choice—but he would let her assume she was calling the shots. "I will give you what you want."

"Thank you."

"However, I am open to you changing your mind at any time."

"I won't change my mind, Jaxon. Unlike some women, I don't need a man in my life."

He nodded. More than anything he was determined to make sure she did, and that man would be him.

Nine

"I would help you out if I could, Nadia, you know that. However, I just donated to the community's college scholarship drive."

Nadia released a disappointed sigh. "I understand, Marv. Tell Harriett and the boys hello for me."

"Will do. Goodbye."

"Goodbye."

Nadia disconnected the call and marked Marvin Booster's name off the list of possible sponsors for the holiday play. She, Marvin and his wife, Harriett, had gone to the same church as kids when their parents were alive. He owned one of the largest ranches in Gamble and was a big supporter of community projects.

She frowned when she saw the next name, Fletcher Mallard. Shaking her head, she marked through his name as well, refusing to call and ask him for anything. Fletcher had been Pam's fiancé years ago and swore Nadia and her sisters were the reason Pam hadn't married him. He would conveniently forget the lie he'd told to get Pam to agree to marry him in the first place. It was the lie Dillon exposed at the wedding in the nick of time.

Nevertheless, the man still wanted to blame Nadia and her sisters anyway. Unfortunately, he was wealthier now than before. His chain of grocery stores had grown and was in almost every state in the Midwest and still expanding. She'd also heard he was on his fourth wife.

She was about to pick up the phone to call the next person when the buzzer on her desk sounded. Pressing the button, she asked, "Yes, China?"

"Someone is here to see you. A Mr. Jaxon Ravnel."

A frown settled on Nadia's face. Why was Jaxon here? She hadn't seen or talked to him since that night he'd taken her to dinner on board his jet. That had been over a week ago. She would be lying if she said she hadn't thought about him because she had. More times than she wanted to.

Telling him there would only be an acquaintanceship between them had meant no kisses and no holding hands. When he had taken her home, he had walked her to the door, told her how much he had enjoyed her company and made sure she had gotten inside the house safely before leaving.

"Ms. Novak?"

Releasing a deep sigh, she said, "Please show Mr. Ravnel in."

"Trust me when I say it will be my pleasure, Miss Novak."

Nadia rolled her eyes as she moved from behind her desk. She recognized that voice. It was the same one China used whenever one of the Westmoreland or Outlaw men arrived in town and would take her to lunch. She could understand a young girl of China's age getting all hot and bothered seeing such eye candy, and Jaxon was definitely that.

The door opened and seeing Jaxon again took her breath away. Literally. Why did he have to look so ultraenticing and mouthwateringly appealing in his business suit? Looking like the billion dollars he probably was. And why couldn't she control her gaze from roaming over him, appreciating how his muscles filled out that jacket?

"Jaxon," she said, moving toward him to shake the hand he'd extended. She had to fight back the reaction she felt the moment their hands touched. "It's good seeing you again."

Too late, she watched China's brow inch up in curiosity. Her administrative assistant had latched on to the word *again*, which meant Nadia and Jaxon had seen each other before.

"It's good seeing you again, as well, Nadia," he said with a smile that complemented everything about him. His masculine power and that virile strength were definitely radiating from him today.

Nadia glanced to China. "Thanks for escorting Mr. Ravnel to my office. That will be all."

Once China had left and closed the door behind her, Nadia turned back to Jaxon. "And the reason for your visit?" she asked, offering him a seat in the chair in front of her desk.

"The reason I'm here, Nadia, is strictly business."

"Is it?" she asked, going back around her desk to sit down.

"Yes."

"And what kind of business is there that would bring you here?"

It was only after she'd taken her seat that he took the one she'd offered him. As usual he was displaying impeccable manners. She wished the way his slacks stretched across a pair of masculine thighs when he sat down didn't send her heart racing.

"An article will be appearing in the *Gamble Daily Tribune* tomorrow that Ravnel Technologies has acquired over fifteen hundred acres of land to expand our business here."

She couldn't help the smile that spread across her lips. For both him and the city. "Congratulations. That's a lot of land."

"Yes, it is. The city was instrumental in helping me acquire what I needed."

Nadia could just imagine. They probably saw it as a boom to Gamble's economy.

"Thanks for letting me know, but you didn't have to come all the way over here to tell me." In a way she wished he hadn't. When it came to Jaxon, out of sight, out of mind worked best. She'd managed to get by on her dreams of him at bedtime and memories of their one and only kiss.

"That's not why I'm here."

"Oh? Then what is the purpose of your visit?"

"To offer you a proposal. I decided to do so here first before moving on to some other entity."

Now he had her curious. "And what is this proposal?"

He leaned forward in his chair as if to make sure he had her absolute attention. There was no need for him to do that since he'd had it the moment he'd walked into her office. "Ravnel Technologies wants to replace the Dunnings Financial Group as the sponsor for this year's holiday play."

She didn't say anything for a minute because she was too stunned to speak. His company partnering with the school for the play would be wonderful. A prayer that was answered. A...

A thought suddenly popped into her head, and she looked at Jaxon. He was staring at her. For some reason she couldn't turn away and the thought that had taken root in her head began growing. She broke eye contact and looked down at the notepad on her desk and then back at him. He was still staring at her.

"Why, Jaxon?"

He lifted a brow. "Why what?"

"Why do you want to partner with Dream Makers Acting Academy? What do you think you're going to get out of doing so?"

* * *

Jaxon figured there were several answers he could give her. The main one being her idea of being acquaintances wasn't working for him and he was determined to make sure it didn't work for her either. The moment he had walked into her office, everything faded to black except her. Desire, to a degree he had never felt before for any woman, had rushed through him while he had taken in every single thing about her. Her dark slacks and pink blouse made her look feminine as hell, and her hair, a mass of locks around her face, highlighted her features and emphasized what a totally beautiful woman she was.

Now he was here and she was there, right within his radar, and he had come up with a plan that would keep her there. But he wouldn't admit that. Her question meant she suspected he had an ulterior motive for choosing this school to partner with. She was right, yet he would not only downplay her suspicions, but he also intended to eliminate them completely. He was a businessman and she'd never seen the business side of him before. Now she would.

"What exactly are you asking me, Nadia?"

She leaned forward and placed her elbows on her desk to rest her chin on her hands. Her eyes pierced into his, but he had no problem with it because his gaze was just as penetrating. "Does your decision have anything to do with me?"

He had to fight back telling her that everything had something to do with her. Instead, he said, "To be quite honest, it only pertains to you because you mentioned last week that you needed a sponsor for the play. My reason for deciding to replace Dunnings Financial Group has everything to do with my relationship to the Westmorelands and Outlaws. As you indicated the other night, you and I don't have a relationship, we have an acquaintanceship. I made it clear then, and I'm making it clear now, that I will abide by your wishes."

He paused before continuing, "Ravnel Technologies likes to bond with the towns they become a part of. When we purchased that land in Forbes last year we partnered with the Boys and Girls Clubs there. Therefore, it would make perfect sense to align my company with an institution connected to a group I now consider as family."

He allowed a lull in the conversation to let what he'd said to sink in before adding, "If you have a problem with it, please say so."

"I don't have a problem with it."

He nodded. "The sponsorship I'm offering is strictly business. You will be required to periodically keep my company abreast of how things are going with the play. Will you agree to that?"

She stared at him and a part of him knew Nadia was stubborn enough to say no, she didn't agree. She had just that much nerve and was just that defiant. Seconds had almost ticked into a full minute before she said, "Yes, I'll agree."

"Good. My administrative assistant, Langley Easton, will be contacting you later today to complete the necessary paperwork and ask questions for the newspaper article."

"The newspaper article?"

"Yes. Sometime this week your local newspaper will announce my company's plans to build here. Whenever such an announcement is made, Ravnel Technologies uses that opportunity to assure the citizens of our commitment to the community by making it known what nonprofit organization we plan to partner with the first year. Typically, we rotate annually. Since this is almost the end of the year, it was decided that sponsoring the holiday play would work in our favor. In January, we will open it up so other local nonprofits can apply."

"I see."

He stood. "Do you have any other questions for me?"

"No. I don't have any questions."

"Like I said, Langley will be contacting you later today. However, at any time you can reach me at this number," he said, extending his business card to her.

"I have your number already."

"You have my personal number. This is my business number."

She took the card. "Thank you."

"Have a good day, Nadia." Then, without saying anything else, he walked out of her office.

An hour later Jaxon walked into his hotel room. He hoped what he'd told Nadia had squashed her suspicions about his company's motives for the sponsorship. He had finished ordering room service when his cell phone rang. He couldn't help but smile as he clicked on. "Dad. Are you and Mom back?" His parents had flown to Barcelona. No special occasion, just a two-week getaway. They did that a lot now that they'd both retired.

"Yes, we're back but not for long. Your mom wants to spend a couple of weeks in Toronto before the cold weather sets in."

Jaxon nodded. It was no secret that Ingrid Ravnel didn't like cold weather. She barely tolerated it. "I take it Barcelona was nice."

"Yes, it was. And I understand we've acquired more land."

"Yes, we have. It was a good deal. Like Forbes, they presented an economic development plan that will benefit the town and our company."

"That's good to hear." Although Jaxon kept his father in the loop, he appreciated that Arnett Ravnel never questioned his judgment about any business decisions. "And just so you know, Ravnel Technologies is sponsoring a holiday play being produced by the acting school here."

"What's the title of the play?"

"It's a Wonderful Life."

"That's one of your mother's holiday favorites. We can't wait to see it."

So, in other words, they would be visiting Gamble. Jaxon knew his parents. Ever since that day he'd shared with them that Nadia Novak was the woman he intended to marry, they'd been anxious to meet her.

He talked to his father for a few minutes more before they ended the call. He had time to shower before room service arrived with dinner. Getting into bed before nine was first on his list. If Nadia thought she had seen the last of him for a while, then she was mistaken.

Ten

"Did he really say that, Nadia?" Rissa asked, after taking a sip of her coffee and leaning forward in her chair. It was early morning and the two of them were sitting in Nadia's office, sharing coffee and chitchatting like they usually did. Nadia had just told Rissa what had happened yesterday with Jaxon.

"He didn't have to. Giving me his business card said it all as far as I'm concerned."

Rissa rolled her eyes over her cup of coffee. "Well, you did want him to leave you alone. Not that I thought he was bothering you. Telling a woman of his intentions to marry her is not a bad thing. In fact, I think it's romantic."

Now it was Nadia who rolled her eyes. "I don't agree and you're missing the point."

"Okay, what is the point?" Rissa asked, leaning back in her chair.

"First of all, the more I think about it, the more I get upset that Jaxon had the nerve, the very gall, to tell me of his plans to marry me. He probably only did it because some men have an entitlement complex. Benson thought he was entitled to me and so did Hoyle."

"And?" Rissa asked, as if she expected more.

"And once I put Jaxon in his place by letting him know I wouldn't tolerate his foolishness, he stopped."

Confusion lined Rissa's features. "But that's what you wanted him to do, right?"

"But he didn't put up a fight, which proves he wasn't serious about anything to begin with."

"You don't know that, Nadia."

"Yes, I do. Nobody can turn their feelings off like that. Granted, he hadn't said he felt anything for me, but still. It's obvious he no longer wants to marry me."

"And that bothers you, doesn't it?" Rissa asked, giving her an odd look. A look Nadia had gotten used to over the years. It was one of Rissa's analytical looks. There were times she thought her friend was wasting her time in the financial industry and should own a psychiatry office.

Nadia knew it was imperative that she made her best friend understand. "What I don't like is the thought of him being overconfident in thinking he could marry me and telling me such when he had no intentions of doing it."

Rissa chuckled. "Now you're being dramatic. You either want Jaxon to show interest in you or you don't. You told him not to and he is following your request. Now you're upset about it. That makes no sense, Nadia, unless..."

"Unless what?"

"Unless...deep down you did like the thought of him wanting to marry you one day."

"That's ridiculous."

Rissa tilted her head. "Is it? You act offended that he took you at your word and is leaving you alone. Had he continued to pursue you, then you could have complained that you were being harassed. So, being the gentleman you say that he is, he is abiding by your wishes. Now the acquaintanceship has moved to a strictly business relationship and for some reason that is bothering you. I'd think you would appreciate him stepping in as a sponsor for the play. That's wonderful and takes a load off your mind."

"Yes, and I do appreciate it."

"So, what's the problem? What's the real reason your panties are in a twist?"

Nadia didn't say anything for a minute and then she said in a soft voice, "Whether or not I wanted him to pursue me or not, the moment I pushed back he moved on. That meant he wasn't serious about a future with me anyway."

Rissa smiled. "You like him, don't you?"

Nadia shrugged. "He was moving too fast. He was talking marriage and didn't even know me."

"Then you should have told him to slow down. Instead, you sent him away. Do you know what I think?"

Nadia didn't want to ask but figured her best friend would tell her anyway. "No, what?"

"That you like Jaxon more than you want to admit, and that you'll give anything for another kiss, another taste of his mouth, his tongue, the opportunity to be your first rumple between the sheets and—"

"Rissa!"

"Just keeping it real, my friend."

"I refuse to involve myself with a man who only wanted to connect himself with me because…"

Rissa lifted a brow. "Because of what?"

Nadia ran a hand down her face. "I honestly don't know."

Rissa stood after checking her watch. "Then maybe it's time you stop assuming and find out the answers. The real answers, Nadia. And how about taking a look in the mirror.

You're beautiful. That's why he wanted to connect with you. You're not a bad catch and Jaxon Ravnel isn't either. Just so you know, the word is out and he's already at the top of every single woman's hit list in town."

After draining the last of her coffee and tossing the cup in a nearby trash can, Rissa smiled over at her and said, "See you tomorrow. Same place. Same time. However, I certainly hope you have a different attitude."

By the end of the day, Nadia was clearing off her desk and getting ready to leave when her cell phone rang. She smiled upon recognizing the caller. "Hello, Pammie." Calling her oldest sister by her nickname whenever they spoke was something Nadia hadn't outgrown.

"Nadia, I just heard the good news. I understand Jaxon will replace the Dunnings Financial Group as the sponsor of this year's holiday play. That's wonderful!"

Pam was the second person to sing Jaxon's praises. Rissa had been the first. Nadia figured there would be others tomorrow when news of his company expansion to Gamble, as well as his being sponsor of the play, appeared in tomorrow's newspaper. His personal assistant, Langley Easton, had called and introduced herself. The woman sounded very professional and young.

That had prompted Nadia, out of curiosity, to check out Ravnel Technologies' website. Now she wished she hadn't. Not only was Miss Easton professional and young. She was also attractive and single. It said she had been Jaxon's personal assistant for a few years. Had the two ever dated? Been romantically involved? Why on earth did Nadia care if they had?

"Nadia?"

"Yes?"

"You are glad about it, too, aren't you? I'm sure you had

everything under control as far as getting a replacement, but Jaxon has made your job easier."

"Yes, and I appreciate him doing so. But…"

"But what?"

Pam was the last person Nadia needed to tell about her complex relationship with Jaxon. But then, to be honest, she and Jaxon didn't have a relationship. That thought made her ask her sister something she had wondered about for years. "Pammie, at the time you met Dillon you were engaged to marry Fletcher. What made you fall in love with Dillon when you were promised to another man?"

Pam didn't say anything for a moment, and then said, "I didn't love Fletcher. Our marriage was to be one of convenience. However, I'd agreed to a sexual relationship since we both wanted kids. But I looked at my engagement to Fletcher as a business deal, which is why I wouldn't sleep with him before the wedding."

Pam paused and Nadia figured she was remembering that time fifteen years ago. "That day when you, Jill and Paige called me outside to let me know a man was there to see me, and I saw Dillon for myself, engaged or not engaged, the moment I gazed into his eyes I was not only attracted to him, but knew, if given the chance, I could feel more."

If given the chance she could feel more…

Nadia wondered if it could it be that way for her with Jaxon. "Why didn't you fight it? After all, you were engaged."

"Trust me, I tried. But there are some things you aren't equipped to fight. An attraction that could lead to falling in love is one of them."

"Did it scare you? Your inability to resist your attraction?" Nadia asked.

Pam chuckled. "It petrified me because I didn't know Dillon. I had just met him and he certainly didn't know me. Yet

I felt things for him that I hadn't felt for Fletcher. I wasn't even physically attracted to Fletcher. With Dillon it was another story altogether. The sexual chemistry between us was strong."

Nadia would admit the same thing between her and Jaxon. There was something about him that stirred sensations deep within her each and every time they were near each other. Just dancing with him the other night had jarred her senses in a way they'd never been jarred before.

"The sexual chemistry between us was even stronger whenever we were alone," Pam cut into Nadia's thoughts to say. "I knew I was in deep trouble that day he returned to go through that trunk in the attic. We were at the house alone."

"Oh." Just like the night Nadia and Jaxon had been alone when she'd invited him to dinner. The same house.

"Is there a reason you're asking me these questions, Nadia?"

"No. There's no particular reason, Pammie. I just think you and Dillon make the best couple ever."

"Thanks. There was a connection between us that we were both trying hard to ignore, given the fact I was an engaged woman."

"What if Dillon had told you he wanted to marry you after you guys had only known each other a few days? Would you have broken things off with Fletcher to marry him?"

"No. Although I was attracted to Dillon, I didn't feel I knew him and he didn't know me. But then I'd agreed to marry Fletcher because I had thought I knew him when in essence, I didn't know him at all. I've discovered people can fall in love without fully knowing each other or knowing everything about each other. It has to start with something. I'm glad that once I discovered a connection between me and Dillon that I didn't fight it. And that connection between us, combined with a hefty dose of sexual chemistry, got stronger every time we saw each other."

Nadia took in everything Pam had said. Had Rissa been right? Had she overreacted to Jaxon's claim that he intended to marry her? She would admit she'd felt a connection to him that got stronger each time they saw each other. Did that mean anything?

"Well, I'll let you go, Nadia. It's time for you to leave for today, right?" Pam said.

"Yes. I was just wrapping things up."

"Have a safe drive home. And Nadia?"

"Yes, Pammie?"

There was a pause and then, "Nothing. Goodbye."

Jaxon opened the paper and saw that news of Ravnel Technologies' expansion into Gamble was all over the front page. His company's PR department had also arranged a slate of local interviews, and Langley had a list of other nonprofit projects his company intended to be a part of during the coming year.

Once he'd made the decision to expand his company beyond Virginia, he knew what that would entail, from strategy to execution. One of the first things to do was strengthen the company's presence in the chosen community. In Forbes, his company had hosted a fundraising event to raise money for a new building for the Boys and Girls Club. It was to be built on land that Ravnel Technologies had donated. Not only had they donated the land, but also would match all contributions made.

In Gamble, he would start with sponsoring the holiday play. He'd seen the budget but wanted Nadia to think bigger. No reason to host the event in the school's auditorium when there was a theater in town. He'd had Langley check it out already.

He had finished drinking his coffee and was about to go into the bedroom of his hotel suite to get dressed when his phone rang. It was his business line. Heat flowed through his body at the possibility it was Nadia. He picked up the phone, and saw the call was from his administrative assistant. "Yes, Langley?"

"Mr. Ravnel, I got a call from Sue Ellen Donovan, talk show host of *Good Morning Wyoming*. A show produced at a television station that's located in the valley between Gamble and Jackson Hole. The show not only broadcasts in those two areas but several other towns scattered about. She wanted to know if you're available one day this week to appear on her show. She's interested in why you selected Gamble for expansion."

The real reason, he thought, was a well-guarded secret. He'd done television interviews in the past but usually Paul Maloney, the person in charge of PR for the company, handled that sort of thing. "Is there a reason Paul can't do the interview?"

"Ms. Donovan specifically asked for you."

Jaxon rubbed his chin, feeling somewhat annoyed. "Did she?"

"Yes. She said it would have a greater impact if you did it. She thinks it would give the interview more community appeal. I told her in that case she should also invite Nadia Novak of the Dream Makers Acting Academy. That way the two of you could inform the viewers how Ravnel Technologies' move into the community will benefit Gamble and surrounding areas. Already your company has partnered with the academy to sponsor their holiday play. Personally, I think publicity for the school might boost interest in nearby towns, which will result in more ticket sales."

Jaxon smiled, liking the way Langley thought. It would

also be a way for him and Nadia to share space, even if it was only on a stage at a television studio. "Since it's a community piece I agree that both Ms. Novak and I should be interviewed together."

"Does that mean you will do the interview?"

"Yes."

"I'll suggest that Ms. Donovan call Ms. Novak to invite her to join you on the show. I've checked your schedule and this Friday morning will work for you. It airs at ten."

"Make sure that date and time works for Ms. Novak as well. If not, I expect the station to be flexible with both of us."

"Yes, sir."

Jaxon hung up the phone thinking his day was off to a good start. Things could not have worked out more perfectly if he'd arranged it himself. He knew Nadia was still trying to figure him out. To fight what she'd felt, and, for whatever reason, she refused to lower her guard not even an inch. He knew before he could gain a place in her heart, he would have to gain her trust. That also meant she had to deal with whatever pain still lingered from a love that had gone bad. A love he had to somehow convince her hadn't been meant to be anyway.

His father had told him that it had taken his mother almost a year to see the light. Jaxon wasn't sure he would last a year. He wanted Nadia just that much. He wanted her physically, sexually and all those ways in between. But he also wanted her for more than that. He wanted her to be a part of his life, the mother of his children, his partner in love until death do them part.

He had told Dillon he wouldn't break Nadia's heart, and he intended to keep that promise. However, the one thing Dillon and the others failed to realize was that if something went wrong, he might be the one who ended up with the broken heart.

* * *

Nadia returned to her office from lunch thinking that everyone in town must have read the paper's headlines. Rissa had brought her a copy with a huge smile on her face. No doubt she was hoping the bank she managed would get the Ravnel business account.

Settling in the chair behind her desk, Nadia was pleased that the newspaper had also mentioned that Ravnel Technologies would be the sponsor of this year's holiday play. She had just taken a file off her desk when her buzzer went off. "Yes, China?"

"Sue Ellen Donovan, of *Good Morning Wyoming*, Station WKJP, is on the line."

Nadia lifted a brow, wondering why Ms. Donovan would be calling. Earlier that year Nadia had reached out to the woman for an interview on one of their shows to promote the school's spring pageant. The woman had turned down the request saying the event wasn't important enough. Over the years, what had started out as a community awareness show was now only interviewing the rich and famous vacationing in the area. Specifically, on the ski slopes in Jackson Hole.

"Please put the call through, China."

"Okay."

Upon hearing the connection, Nadia said, "This is Nadia Novak. May I help you?"

"Ms. Novak, this is Sue Ellen Donovan of *Good Morning Wyoming*. We are excited that Ravnel Technologies will be expanding into Gamble and we understand your school will benefit. On Friday morning we will be interviewing Mr. Ravnel. Since we want this as a community piece, and it was announced that his company will be the major sponsor of your school's holiday play this year, it would be great if you could be a part of the show as well."

So now the show wanted to highlight something other than celebrities vacationing in the area? What a switch. "That sounds wonderful, and I would love to be on your show."

"Great. I'll see you Friday at ten."

After disconnecting the call, Nadia leaned back in her chair. She would take free publicity for the school any way she could get it. The students were excited about the news and that made her appreciative of Jaxon's company helping out. Specifically, bailing her out.

And he *had* bailed her out. He'd even admitted he'd selected the school not only because of the family connection, but also because she'd mentioned she didn't have a sponsor for the play. She would admit that was thoughtful of him. She would also admit something else. She did like him…a little. Her conversation with Pam yesterday had helped somewhat. Then there were the memories of the words Jaxon had spoken to her weeks ago.

My intention, Nadia Novak, is to marry you.

She quivered each and every time she remembered them. His words had been precise and he'd said them in a deep, husky voice that had flowed from those sexy lips of his. The tone had been so smooth it had taken her a minute to respond. Although at first she'd taken what he'd said as a tease, it didn't take long for her to realize he was serious. Even when he shouldn't have been.

During their coffee and chitchat time this morning, Rissa had come down on Nadia pretty hard. Rissa had accused Nadia of always whining about what the men in the past had done to her and how much of a disappointment they'd been, of letting her past hurts and heartbreaks be the cause of her not having a relationship with a man. She'd gone on to say that Nadia would never find out if Jaxon was or was not the man for her without giving him a chance.

Well, it was a moot point now since all there was between them was business. Besides, one heartbreak had been enough for her. She wasn't ready to risk her heart on another. But what she *was* ready for was to be intimate with a man.

At twenty-eight it was probably past time and she probably would have eventually gone all the way with Hoyle if he hadn't acted like an ass about it. Like he thought not only was he entitled, but also that he was the best thing in her lifetime, as if she would be a fool to pass up the chance to roll between the sheets with him. He was a typical male who thought his balls were made of gold. That was the type of man she wanted no part of.

So far Jaxon hadn't come across that way. Other than thinking that one day they would marry, he was an okay guy. Even when she'd told him they could not have any type of relationship, he had respected her wishes. However, she couldn't get their kiss out of her mind. Just the memory of it made her heart pump wildly in her chest and her mouth hunger for more.

For years she'd heard Rissa, Jillian and, more recently, Paige whisper about how wonderful it was to share a bed with a man. She'd even come home from college unexpectedly one weekend and walked into Dillon's house to the sound of Pam screaming all over the place. It didn't take long to comprehend they'd been screams of pleasure and not pain.

Her curiosity about the kind of pleasure that could make you scream was what had sparked her interest in Hoyle. Now, after sharing that kiss with Jaxon, her curiosity was not just sparked; it had been ignited. Maybe it was time for her to finally do something about it.

How would he handle her change in attitude of them going from acquaintances to just business to personal and intimate? Would he think she was fickle as hell? Probably. More importantly, would it bother him that she was still a virgin at twenty-eight?

Years ago, she'd overheard a conversation between the two Westmoreland cousins, Derringer and Riley, where they said the last kind of woman any man wanted to have in his bed was a virgin. Mainly because no man wanted to be a woman's first, and most men wanted an experienced woman in their bed. Because of Derringer's and Riley's reputations at the time, she'd had no reason to think they hadn't known what they were talking about. If that was true, then how would she handle what she definitely saw as a problem?

And another problem—Rissa had said the gold diggers around these parts would be honing their predatory skills on Jaxon. For some reason Nadia didn't like the thought. But then if Jaxon wanted to marry her like he claimed, wouldn't that give her an advantage over the other women?

How many times had Rissa said that Jaxon came across as the type of man who went after what he wanted? News flash! Nadia was that type of woman, and right now she wanted Jaxon. Not for anything long-term but rather for the short-term. She needed her curiosity appeased about sex once and for all to see what the hoopla was about.

Her approach to Jaxon had to be subtle. No man wanted to think he'd been targeted. That was another thing she'd heard the Westmoreland cousins say. A man didn't like being seduced. They preferred being the seducer. So how would that work for her?

Picking up the phone, she called Rissa. Her best friend should be on her way home from work now. Rissa picked up on the first ring and from the sound of it, she was in her car and the phone call was coming through by Bluetooth on her car's speakers.

"You're alone?" Nadia asked, wanting to make sure her kids weren't in the car with her.

"Yes, I'm alone. Why?"

"I have a question for you and I want it for your ears only. Just give me an answer, no inquiries, please. Will you do that?"

Rissa hesitated a minute, then said, "Yes."

Satisfied her friend would do what she said, Nadia asked, "How do you get a man to make love to you without seducing him?"

Eleven

Jaxon got out of his car and strolled up the walkway to Nadia's front door. She had left a message on his business phone last night while he'd been in the shower. She'd taken her car to the shop yesterday and it wouldn't be ready for today's trip to the valley. Nadia wanted to know if she could catch a ride with him. He had called her back and in the most professional voice he could deliver, he'd told her that yes, she could, and he would arrive to pick her up around eight.

To be quite honest, he'd been surprised by her call. Especially when her request meant they would be sharing the same vehicle to get to their destination. But then he figured since she was getting free publicity for the school and the holiday play she would tolerate anything or anyone. Including him.

The door opened and she stood there. She held his gaze and he held hers. Had it been just a few days ago when he'd seen her last? He should have been prepared but he wasn't. Now he couldn't help but zero in on everything about her. She was dressed in a two-piece business suit that made her look both professional and gorgeous to a degree that left him speechless. Her hair was pinned up on her head and twisted in a ball. Her makeup wasn't heavy; it was just enough not to overtake her natural beauty.

It seemed each and every time their paths crossed the sexual chemistry between them increased. Even now it flowed between them, and they both knew it and there wasn't a damn thing either of them could do about it. It was a raw physical force made up of her hormones and his testosterone that had taken over not only their minds but also their bodies.

The sound of his phone alarm going off broke the spell. He glanced away momentarily to pull it out of his pocket and turn it off. When he glanced back at her he saw the same sexual awareness in her features that he figured she saw in his. Only thing they could do was try and ignore it.

"Good morning, Nadia. Are you ready to go?"

"Yes. Just let me grab my coffee. Would you like a cup?"

If he said yes, that meant she would have to invite him in. That would definitely be a change from the last time he'd been here, when she'd been waiting outside on the steps with no need for him to come inside.

"Yes, if you don't mind. I wasn't sure how traffic would be getting here this morning, so I didn't stop for coffee."

"No problem," she said, moving aside for him to come in.

He turned back to her when he heard the door close behind him. "You look nice."

"Thanks. So do you. And how do you like your coffee?"

"Black."

"Okay. I'll be back. I'm sure you want us to get on the road as soon as possible."

When she left and headed for the kitchen, he was drawn to that huge photo over the fireplace just like the last time he'd been here. That photo of her parents and sisters. This time he really studied it. She was the perfect combination of both parents. That's what he wanted for them. Him and her. Kids who would look like the both of them. He could envision a daughter with her eyes and smile; and a son who would have his height and mouth. It was a mouth his mom often referred to as the Ravnel mouth. She said that was one of the first things that drew her to his father. The shape of his mouth and the darkness of his eyes.

"Here you are."

He turned around and she was there, handing him coffee in a to-go cup with a lid. "Thanks. Cup's convenient," he said, accepting the coffee she offered. Their hands touched in the process and he felt a flutter in the pit of his gut.

"I keep a ton of them here. I have two cups of coffee every morning. One before I leave here while getting dressed and another when I get to school, from Rissa."

"Rissa?"

"Yes, Marissa Phelps, my best friend."

He lifted a brow. "Your best friend is living in Gamble?"

"She's lived here all her life. We separated when I moved to Denver but we stayed in touch and went to the same college in Wyoming." She glanced at her watch and then at him. "I'm ready to leave if you are."

Yes, he was ready. The sooner they got out of this house the better. "I'm ready."

"Are you attending Cheyenne's surprise birthday party?"

Nadia glanced over at Jaxon. They were out of Gamble's city limits and were in the part of Wyoming the locals called the valley. It was the area between Gamble and Jackson Hole. Sparse towns were scattered about and most of the people were ranchers.

She nodded resolutely and said, "Yes, I plan to go. What about you?"

"Yes, I'm going. I wouldn't think of missing it."

She turned to look out the window again, at the objects

they passed. Now they were on a two-lane road with very little traffic. The television station was in Valley Bluff, a small town between here and Jackson Hole.

Nadia thought about her conversation with Rissa yesterday. Needless to say, her best friend had given her an earful. According to Rissa, if a woman wanted a man and the man wanted her, then no seduction was needed. Just roll with the flow. She suggested that when Jaxon returned Nadia home, she should invite him in. When he kissed her goodbye, she should let him know she enjoyed it. That sort of thing fired up a man's libido. A deeply aroused man could make you just as aroused as he was.

Nadia recalled how aroused Jaxon had been when dancing with her, and how aroused she'd gotten knowing he wanted her. Even now, while sharing car space with him, she was getting aroused. What on earth was happening to her? It was as if since she'd decided not to hold back where he was concerned, her body was yearning for what was to come. But what if he didn't want to make the switch from business to pleasure? What if he'd decided she wasn't worth the trouble and just wanted a platonic relationship between them?

What gave her hope was the strong sexual chemistry still flowing between them. So far they'd managed to keep up a steady stream of conversation, and she was glad of that. She'd taken the time to tell him of the excitement buzzing around town about his company's plans to expand in Gamble. A lot of people were wondering what type of positions would be available. He'd told her about the job fair his company planned to hold in the spring.

Jaxon also shared that they anticipated it taking a year and a half for the Ravnel Technologies' state-of-the-art complex to be built. In the meantime, they would be leasing space— namely six floors—in the Lesswick Building in town. She appreciated him sharing that much information with her.

He asked her about the play and mentioned it was his mother's favorite for the holidays, and his parents looked forward to attending. She was glad to hear that and intended to make sure they got special seats in the front of the auditorium.

"I like Langley," she said truthfully. They had talked a few times and the woman seemed efficient at her job. But still, Nadia couldn't help wondering if Jaxon and the woman had ever been involved.

The car had come to a traffic light and he glanced over at her. "She keeps me pretty much on point."

"Has she been your administrative assistant long?"

"Around four years now. I hired her right out of college."

"She seems like a nice person and efficient in what she does."

"She is. That's the reason I hate losing her."

Nadia raised her brow. *Losing her?* "She's leaving?"

"Yes. Langley is getting married in June to Rick, her college sweetheart. He took a government job in Amsterdam, and she'll be moving there after the wedding."

Nadia didn't say anything for a minute as she inwardly admitted that she'd been jealous of the beautiful young woman, which honestly didn't make any sense. There was never a time she'd gotten jealous of any woman over a man. Such a thing just wasn't in her makeup. At least, it never had been before.

"I take it you've been interviewed by Ms. Donovan before," Jaxon said, cutting into her thoughts.

Nadia rolled her eyes. "Not hardly." At the strange look he gave her she decided to explain. "Although *Good Morning Wyoming* started off as a one-hour show to keep the viewers abreast of the things going on in the four communities it serves, a couple of years ago the producers switched gears."

"Switched gears how?"

"They switched their focus to celebrities who visited the

area to ski and hang out in and around Jackson Hole. Would you believe Ms. Donovan turned me down each and every time I called to ask for time on her show?"

"That's a missed opportunity for her," Jaxon said, shaking his head as he moved the car forward when the traffic light changed. "I hear you're doing great things at the academy."

She figured Pam told him that but decided to ask him anyway. "You heard that from who?"

"The mayor and some others."

That made her feel good. "I'm convinced the only reason I got an invite to the show was because of you."

"Me?"

"Yes. It would make more sense to show what your company is doing to help the community by hearing from the first recipient of your company's kindness."

He didn't say anything, and she figured he'd agreed with what she'd stated. "We're here," he said. When Jaxon brought the car to a stop he glanced at his watch. "We're almost an hour early."

She nodded. "It's better to be early than late." Then after a moment she said, "I want to thank you, Jaxon."

"No problem since I was coming this way."

"No, I want to thank you for everything. For replacing the Dunnings Financial Group as the play's sponsor. Although the students had faith in me to find a replacement. Unfortunately, they were wrong."

Nadia watched as he eased the car seat back to give himself more room to stretch out his legs. "No, they weren't wrong. You got a replacement."

She shook her head. "No, I didn't. Miraculously, you came to me."

He shrugged. "Does it matter?"

Yes, it mattered to her that this tall, ultrahandsome, broad-shouldered, sexy-as all-outdoors man helped her save face with not only the students but everyone involved in the play, including the community, which looked forward to seeing the performance every year. It was a time when the residents came together to support a good cause.

"It does to me."

He nodded. "Then I'm glad my company could help."

She didn't say anything. He hadn't said he was glad that he could help but that *his company* could help. Was that his way of reminding her that she'd made it pretty clear she didn't want any type of relationship between them? She'd made a shambles of things with Jaxon, and she knew it was up to her to undo the mess she'd made.

Sue Ellen Donovan was smiling into the camera. "Today our guests on the show are Jaxon Ravnel, CEO of Ravnel Technologies, along with Miss Nadia Novak, the VP of Development and Community Civic Engagement for the Dream Makers Acting Academy in Gamble."

Jaxon watched the camera switch from Ms. Donovan to zero in on him before shifting to Nadia. He saw how strikingly beautiful she was on camera. As far as he was concerned Sue Ellen Donovan's introduction of him took way too long. By the time it was finished everyone knew more about his family and their wealth than they needed to. She also harped on the fact he was single and a prime catch. He thought the statement was inappropriate and was tempted to say he was officially off the market because the woman he wanted to marry was sitting on stage beside him.

"Thank you two for coming and sharing information with our viewing audience," Sue Ellen Donovan said, reclaiming his attention. "First, I want to begin with you, Mr. Ravnel. I'm aware of your company's decision to expand in Texas as well as Wyoming. What made you choose Gamble?"

Of course he'd been expecting that question and provided

the same answer he'd given others who'd asked. After instituting a plan for growth, it became a business decision to expand in other states. Mainly as a way to improve and further develop products and services.

Sue Ellen Donovan continued to ask questions so that his responses could fully explain the benefits in communities when big businesses made such a move.

She then turned her attention to Nadia. However, she only asked one question before moving her attention back to him. Then the woman's questions began centering on his private life, which annoyed the hell out of Jaxon. It became obvious that she was turning this into some sort of celebrity interview.

He saw the disappointment in Nadia's eyes. After he finished answering the last question Sue Ellen had asked, and she was about to ask him another, a rebellious Nadia spoke up and said, "I think it would be wonderful to tell the audience about the play the academy is producing."

Before the woman could say whether it would be wonderful or not, Jaxon agreed. "I think that is a great idea, Ms. Novak. After all, the purpose of this interview was to highlight what my company will be doing in the community and not focus on my personal life." He then turned to Sue Ellen Donovan. "Isn't that right?"

A chagrined expression appeared on the woman's face. "Yes, of course."

Nadia began speaking and Jaxon took in the richness of her voice as she explained things in a way that would get viewers excited about the event. She went into detail about how an acclaimed director from Hollywood had volunteered to direct the show. From Sue Ellen Donovan's expression it was obvious she hadn't known that.

He chimed in on occasion and told everyone how excited his company was to partner with the school as sponsor, and

he shared the names of other charities his company was looking into sponsoring in the near future. At the end he mentioned his company would be setting up a job fair because
he wanted to hire as many qualified individuals in the area
as possible, in addition to relocating some of his own people.

Sue Ellen opened the network call lines and some of the
viewers had questions about Jaxon's company, as well as the
school's play. Some callers even made comments that it was
great hearing about something else other than movie stars
and they hoped the television station did more such shows.
Jaxon hoped the producers took that under consideration.

At the end of the show the production assistant rushed on
stage to remove the mics off their clothes. That's when Sue
Ellen invited Jaxon to lunch. It didn't go past him that she
didn't extend the invitation to Nadia.

"Thanks, but Ms. Novak and I have made plans for lunch
before returning to Gamble."

"Oh."

"I want to thank you for finally having me on your show,"
Nadia said, giving Sue Ellen a smile that even Jaxon could
tell didn't quite reach her eyes.

Sue Ellen nodded, pulling a business card out of her jacket.
Handing it to Jaxon, she said, "I would love for you to call
me sometime. I'll be glad to tell you more about the area and
even show you around."

He took the card more out of courtesy than anything else.
"Thanks, I'll keep that in mind," he said, although he had
no plans to do so. He then turned to Nadia. "Are you ready
to go, Ms. Novak?"

She nodded. "Yes, Mr. Ravnel. I'm ready."

When they were buckled inside the car, he glanced over
at Nadia before starting the engine. "Where do you want to
go for lunch? You're more familiar with the area than I am."

She gave him a smile that had his stomach churning with

sexual need. "There's a great bar and grill in the next town. It's owned by friends of mine and the food is great."

"That sounds good," he said, putting on his aviator-style sunglasses. Although it was chilly outside, the bright sun was shining over the mountains.

He glanced over at her. "Are you in a hurry to return to Gamble?"

"No, why do you ask?"

"There are several stops I need to make before we head back." The truth of the matter was that he was in no hurry to get her back home.

"No problem. I'll call and let China know I'm taking the rest of the day off. I need time off anyway. It's been a while since I've taken any."

Now that he knew that bit of information, he was going to make sure she enjoyed today with him.

Twelve

After leaving the television station they had lunch at Gravel, a bar and grill owned by a college friend of Nadia's named Lilli. For years Lilli's parents had run the place and had recently turned it over to Lilli when they retired.

Jaxon placed his hand in the center of her back while they walked into the restaurant. His touch had an effect on her. All sorts of feelings rippled through her, and she was totally conscious of him as a man. And from the feminine looks they got when they entered, quite a few other women were aware of him as well.

She could tell Jaxon liked Lilli when they were introduced. Most people did. She had that kind of personality. He also liked Aaron, Lilli's husband. Since Aaron was originally from Norfolk, Virginia, the two had a lot to talk about, being from the same state.

Lilli had been Nadia's friend long enough to detect something between her and Jaxon, although she'd introduced him as a business associate. Had Nadia's interest in him been obvious? She discovered her answer when, after placing her

order, she excused herself to go to the bathroom and deliberately cornered Lilli. "What gives, Lil?"

Lilli threw her head back and laughed. "You tell me, girlfriend. I can't wait until I talk to Rissa. Business associate,
my ass. The sexual chemistry between you and Jaxon Ravnel is so thick I can feel it."

"It's not," Nadia scoffed.

"It is, too. I'm sure even Aaron felt it and he has a tendency to let stuff go over his head. Another thing I noticed
is that Jaxon can't keep his eyes off you, so the desire isn't
just coming from you, kiddo."

She hoped not. Otherwise, she'd been reading the vibes
all wrong. But then she didn't have that much experience
with men to read the signs Rissa had told her to look out for.
She was well aware of the fire raging inside her whenever
he glanced her way, gave her a smile or when he'd placed
his hand at the center of her back. Returning to her table,
she tried to stay composed but it was hard. Never had she
been this taken with a man. Jaxon had the ability to short-
circuit her senses.

She'd ordered a hamburger, fries and a strawberry milk-
shake. He had a brisket sandwich with sweet potato fries and
a vanilla shake. Over lunch he told her how he'd recently gone
into partnership with the Westmorelands' horse-training business. She had heard that from Paige but enjoyed listening to
him tell her about it. She sat there trying to convince herself
her enjoyment had nothing to do with the deep, husky sound
of his voice. Nor did it have anything to do with how sensuous his mouth looked whenever it moved.

"How did your parents meet?" she asked, curious about the
two people who'd raised him. She'd heard from Paige, who'd
met them, that his mother was gorgeous and the epitome of a
defined and elegant woman. She probably had more sophistication in her pinkie finger than Nadia had in her entire body.

He smiled at her question, and she immediately felt a quivering in the pit of her stomach. "Mom and Dad were the two most unlikely people to get together. He needed more land to expand the institute and she was president of this group whose sole purpose was to protect lands and natural resources from excessive development. Needless to say, they butted heads."

"I can imagine."

"I don't think you can. I still find it hard to believe at times. I understand back in the day Dad was a rather stern businessman who was used to having things his way. Mom was a tough cookie. At the time Dad was the most eligible bachelor in town and was known to dazzle most women."

Probably like his son, she thought. "So how did they come to a compromise?"

"I don't think they did. At the time she was a college professor at a community college in Dumfries. He thought she was the most temperamental, unmanageable, outspoken and sassy woman he'd ever met."

Nadia laughed. "She sounds like a woman I can truly admire."

"She was one he could admire, too. Dad says he fell in love with Mom the moment he walked into her office to give her hell. He was immediately taken with her because she was the first woman who didn't treat him like he was a prize catch. Instead, she treated him like he was a nuisance she was forced to deal with." He took a sip of his iced tea and then said, "Needless to say, less than a year after they met they got married."

Nadia nodded. "What was the outcome of the land your father wanted but she didn't want him to have?"

"Since the primary concern of her organization was the trees on the property that had been there for over one hundred years, Dad promised to build around them. Although that meant having the architectural plans redone, which was costly."

A short while later, after they'd eaten, Jaxon told her how much he'd enjoyed his meal. To her surprise, when they were leaving, he told Lilli and Aaron he would be coming back.

When they left Gravel, he reminded Nadia of the errands he had to make in Jackson Hole. They went to several men's shops looking for shirts and ties. He also purchased another Stetson. Last was a pair of boots. At first it felt odd going shopping with him but after a while it seemed like a natural act. He asked her opinion about several ties and bought the ones she told him she liked the best.

By the time they'd finished with all his shopping it was close to five o'clock and he suggested they grab dinner. They dined at a very elegant restaurant in Jackson Hole. The moment she walked into the Jagged Edge she recalled hearing about it from Cash Outlaw's wife, Brianna. This was where Cash had brought her for their wedding dinner. It was just as beautiful as Brianna had said. The restaurant was massive as well as impressive with a set of triple stairs that led to other dining areas, high cathedral ceilings and beautiful chandeliers.

Dinner had been delicious and instead of discussing anything personal, she'd asked him about what he'd said during Sue Ellen Donovan's interview. Specifically, those community projects he was adding to his agenda for next year. One conversation led to another and he shared with her his plans for his company. With the acquired land in Wyoming, he was finished expanding for now. His concentration would be on hiring the most qualified people to manage both the Forbes and Gamble expansions.

"I hadn't meant to keep you away so long," he said when they were headed back to Gamble. They had enjoyed conversing so much that neither of them had realized how late it had gotten. It was close to eight o'clock.

"That's fine. I enjoyed taking a day off work." And she truly meant it. What she hadn't added was that she had enjoyed spending the time with him.

"What in the world!"

She heard the startled astonishment in his voice, and then he pulled the car over to the shoulder of the road. She followed his gaze as he stared out the window and into the sky. She saw what had him so captivated. The Milky Way could occasionally be seen in this part of Wyoming.

It was known that the state of Wyoming was one of the only states in the country where an individual could enjoy the beauty of the universe. Over the years she'd seen planets, nebulae, a multitude of stars and galaxies. It was the best place for stargazing and most people around these parts owned telescopes. Tonight, you didn't need one. The sight before them was a spectacular view with clarity.

"I've never seen anything so beautiful."

She nodded, understanding completely. That was usually a person's reaction upon seeing the Milky Way for the first time. "On those nights when the skies were really dark, Dad and Mom used to gather us up in our pjs and drive us to Peake Row. It's the best place around here to see the Milky Way."

"Peake Row? I'd love to go there. And I'd love for you to go with me. You can even wear your pj's."

She turned to look at him and could see the seriousness in his gaze. He wasn't teasing. Clearing her throat, she said, "Thanks for the invite, but I'll pass."

She glanced back into the sky when suddenly a mass of red seemed to circle around the stars in the shape of an arrow. "My goodness!" Now she was the one with startled astonishment in her voice.

"What is it?" he asked, staring up into the sky and seeing the same thing that she did.

"That rarely appears, what looks like a huge ball of fire encircling a cluster of stars. It's beautiful."

"It is. Have you ever seen it before?"

"No." There was no need to tell him that around these parts there were some who believed if a couple saw it together, it was a sure sign of everlasting love. She was glad she wasn't one of those believers.

When the sky began getting dark again, he said, "I guess the show is over."

"Yes, I guess it is. It was beautiful while it lasted though."

An hour later they were pulling up in her yard. The floodlights from the house shone into the car and highlighted his features. "It's late but at least I got you back safe and sound."

"And I appreciate it," she said, flashing him a smile.

"I enjoyed your company," he said, opening his door to get out.

She watched him come around to her side of the car to open the door and wondered if he'd felt the sexual chemistry between them that she'd been feeling all day. She'd spent the entire day with him and had enjoyed it. When they reached her front door, she thanked him for the ride into Valley Bluff.

"Don't mention it. Are you sure you have a way to pick up your car tomorrow?"

"Yes. Rissa will be taking me. Like I told you, Steve's Auto Repair Shop is open all day on Saturdays."

"Okay. Flick the blinds when you get inside to let me know you're safe."

Nadia nodded, a little disappointed he hadn't asked to come inside. Would he kiss her goodbye? He was standing close but not too close. "I will. Thanks. Good night."

"Good night, Nadia."

Her key was in her hand and she turned to her front door. She heard his footsteps moving down the stairs and when she opened the door to go inside, she turned to look over her shoulder, certain he'd made it to his car by now. He hadn't. Instead, he stood on the last step. Their gazes met and held.

She was going to ask if anything was wrong, but couldn't. It was as if she was in a trance where her vocal cords weren't working. Nadia swallowed as she slowly turned back around to face him. She felt the pull, the connection, and all that chemistry Lilli had teased her about earlier that day. She also felt something else she couldn't explain.

Time appeared to drone on endlessly before he spoke in a low, deep voice. "You're killing me, Nadia."

She was killing him? Did he not know what he was doing to her?

"How?" she heard herself asking.

"Do you not feel it? All that chemistry? Have you not felt it all day?"

No need for her to play dumb. They were both adults after all. "Yes, I feel it and yes, I've felt it all day."

From his expression it was obvious her response had surprised him. He slowly began walking back to her. When he came to a stop in front of her, he asked, "Do you want to go inside and talk about it?"

Nadia nibbled nervously on her bottom lip. Was that what she wanted? Or did she want something more? Although she didn't believe seeing that sign in the sky had anything to do with love, maybe it was the universe's way of letting her know it was time to make one important move in her life. And if that was true, then why not make that move with him?

Wasn't that the advice Rissa had given her? To invite him in? The chemistry between them was hot and there was no doubt in her mind he had the ability to rock her world. But more than anything, she believed that unlike Benson, he wasn't the type of man who would break a woman's heart without caring that it might cause her pain.

"Nadia?"

Making her decision, she said, "No. I don't want to go inside and talk about it, Jaxon. I want to go inside and do something about it."

Jaxon followed Nadia inside and closed the door behind them. After she strolled to the living room, she kicked off her shoes. The heels weren't high enough to be considered stilettos, but had looked sexy on her legs nonetheless. His gaze focused entirely on her as she removed her jacket and began unbuttoning her blouse. "Don't you think we need to talk first?" he asked.

"No." She slanted him a cool yet decisive look. Determined. "But we do need to get the status of our relationship squared."

He watched as she finished unbuttoning her blouse. It hung open, revealing a sexy black lace bra. "Squared in what way, Nadia?"

"You said if I wanted to change the status of our relationship you'd grant me the courtesy of doing so."

He lifted a brow. "And are you doing so?"

"Yes. I want more than an acquaintanceship or a business relationship between us. At least for tonight anyway."

"Do you?"

"Yes."

If she thought this would be a single sexual encounter, a once-in-a-lifetime-thing for them, she was wrong. He'd engaged in casual sex before but he wouldn't do so with her. Never with her. Regardless of whether she accepted it or not, she was the woman who would be his future wife. Once they made love there was no turning back.

He slowly crossed the floor to stand in front of her. "So what do you want from me, Nadia?"

In her bare feet, she took a step closer and he immediately breathed in her scent. The same scent that had captivated him during the drive all day. The same scent that could send desire rippling through him whenever it flowed through his nostrils.

Jaxon took a sharp breath when she deliberately pressed her body against his. There was no way she couldn't tell he was aroused. Every cell in his body throbbed due to over-loaded testosterone. Maybe he should warn her just how long it had been since he'd been with a woman. Not since meeting her more than a year ago and wanting her to be the only woman he made love to for the rest of his life. That meant his entire body was in a sexually deprived state.

She then leaned toward him, where their mouths were almost touching, and whispered, "I want one steamy night, Jaxon. I've never had one before, and I want you to give me one."

She'd never had one before? Questions flared in his mind. Was she saying no man had ever given her a night to re-member? The Big O? Satisfied her to the degree she had ex-pected? Or was she stating something else altogether? That she'd never…

The thought that suddenly entered his mind was way too much to imagine as a possibility. After all, she was twenty-eight. Then he stopped thinking at all when she leaned in closer and used the tip of her tongue to swipe across his lips.

He wrapped his arms around her waist and pulled her to-ward him and kissed her long, hard and deep. She wanted a steamy night and he intended to give her one.

Nadia sighed deep in her throat. Jaxon was giving her a kiss that topped any kiss she'd ever shared. It was a kiss that even made the first one they'd shared weeks ago seem tame in comparison.

He released her mouth to give her a moment to draw in a much needed breath before capturing her mouth again. The feel of his tongue dueling with hers stimulated her in a way she'd never been stimulated before. Tonight his mouth was greedier, more demanding.

Suddenly she pulled back, breaking off the kiss, parting her lips to draw in another deep breath, her gaze focused solely on him. She kept her gaze on Jaxon while licking her lips. Never had a man tasted so delicious. He stood there with his arms wrapped around her, giving her time to…do what? Slow down the rapid beating of her heart? The urgent throb between her legs? His gaze was as intently focused on her as hers was on him.

"You have beautiful lips, Nadia."

His words made her swipe her tongue across them, and she saw how his gaze followed the movement. "I think you have beautiful lips, too." She wasn't good at small talk. But then she wasn't good at flirting either.

In a surprise move, he slid his hands beneath her blouse to caress her back. It was the same spot he'd placed his hand several times today but now he was touching her skin. The moment he did so, something flared in his eyes and heat filled her completely.

Then, in an unexpected move, he swept her off her feet and into his arms. "Which way?"

"Upstairs. First bedroom on your right."

How he managed to maneuver the stairs while holding her firmly in his arms, she wasn't sure. But he did. After placing her on the bed, he leaned in and kissed her again. A jolt of sexual energy rushed through her body when their tongues began devouring each other.

When he finally released her mouth, he straightened and stared down at her. More heat than she could ever have imagined suffused her. She could only lie there, propped against her pillow, and stare back. No man had ever made her feel this way from a kiss. Desire was actually clawing at her and each breath she took caught on a surge of yearning so sharp it felt painful.

"I don't think you have any idea how much I want you, Nadia."

She had news for him. She doubted he knew how much she wanted him, too. Arousal coiled in the very core of her. She'd never considered herself an overly sexual being. Until him. Not in a million years would she have asked any man to give her one steamy night. However, she had done so with him.

"What's going on in that pretty little head of yours, Nadia? You aren't changing your mind about tonight, are you?"

She was surprised he'd asked. Most men would not have. They would have taken the ball she'd placed in their court and played it without caring that she might be having doubts. "No, I'm not changing my mind."

He nodded and the serious expression on his face eased into a smile. "In that case, whose clothes come off first? Yours or mine?"

Knowing her answer would seal her fate, a fate she was looking forward to, she said, "Yours. More than anything I want to undress you, Jaxon."

Thirteen

Nadia's words did something to him. They fired up his libido even more. Undressing him was just one of the things he wanted her to do to him. "Then come undress me."

His heart kicked up a notch and his erection pressed hard against the zipper of his pants when she eased off the bed and slowly walked over to him. He couldn't help noticing just how uneven her breath was with every step she took. From the first, he'd thought her to be sexy as hell. That hadn't changed. Although after tonight her place in his life still might be unclear to her, at least it would be a start.

And speaking of a start…she looked unsure about where and how to begin. Those earlier thoughts he'd had regarding her experience level returned. But then it honestly didn't matter. He would gladly introduce her to everything any other man had fallen short in doing.

He stared down at her and she stared up at him. Her beautiful chocolate-brown eyes held a level of innocence he hadn't expected. Then, as if the look in his eyes motivated her, she pushed the jacket from his shoulders and began unbuttoning his shirt. His heart rate increased with every button she touched. Moments later, when she eased his shirt from his trousers and it hung open, she seemed transfixed with his chest.

"I love a man with a hairy chest, Jaxon."

He was glad to hear that. "What else do you love about a man?"

She switched her eyes from his chest to his face. "I love a man who cares enough about his health to stay in shape. You have nice abs as well."

He chuckled at that. "Thanks. I think you have nice abs, too."

She lifted a brow. "You've never seen my abs."

"Yes, I have."

"When?"

That wasn't hard for him to recall. "The weekend I was in Westmoreland Country for Bane's second set of triplets' first birthday. You were getting out of their swimming pool." The image of her in that two-piece bikini had permanently fried his brain. She had looked just that hot. "You looked sexy as hell."

"You liked what you saw, did you?" she asked, tracing a slow path up and down his chest.

He couldn't stop the sharp breath that escaped his lips. "I most certainly did. I liked it a lot."

She tilted her head and looked at him questioningly. "Yet you never showed any sign of interest."

Since he'd promised not to mention marriage again, he wouldn't tell her that he'd decided the day they'd been introduced that she would be his wife. "The interest was there, Nadia. I'm just not a man who likes rushing into anything. That's not my style."

Nadia didn't say anything to that. Instead, she lifted her hands to push his shirt off his shoulders. Then she lowered her hands to his belt, but not before again tracing a path through the hair on his chest. She'd obviously been serious when she said she liked a hairy chest.

Jaxon was trying hard to keep his control in check when she unbuckled his belt and eased it from the loops. He almost stopped breathing when her hands went to his zipper to slide it down. Because of his erection, her doing so wasn't an easy task. He glanced down and watched her, saw the determined look on her face and hoped like hell she didn't ask him to suck it in. There was no way he could.

When she'd finally slid the zipper all the way down, she looked up at him and met his gaze with a huge smile of accomplishment on her face.

"Now what?" he asked, thinking just how much he loved her.

"Your shoes and socks have to go before I can tackle your pants and briefs."

"Okay," he said, thinking he definitely didn't have a problem with her tackling anything when it came to him.

Easing down on the bed, he removed his shoes and socks as she watched him intently. When he stood back up, she was there, reaching out her hand for the waistband of his slacks. "Maybe I shouldn't tell you this," she said softly, "but I like how you dress. With your suits. Makes you stand out as the businessman that you are."

He chuckled. "You mean you don't prefer seeing me in jeans and a Western shirt?"

She glanced up at him. "I've seen you dressed that way in Westmoreland Country, and I liked it, too. But there is something about you in a suit and Stetson. Especially when you don't wear a tie. I like the open-shirt look."

She would say that after he'd purchased three new ties that day. "Because of the hairy chest?"

She smiled. "Precisely."

He wondered if Nadia realized she was giving him too much information. However, he had no intention of telling her that, but he would file it in the back of his mind for future use.

Jaxon ceased thinking when she eased his slacks down his hips and legs and stooped to assist while he stepped out of them. When she stood back up, she stared at his middle. He was in a pair of black briefs and the size of his erection couldn't be helped. He wanted her just that much.

"Now for that last piece," she said in a somewhat nervous tone. The last thing he wanted was for her to get cold feet now.

"I'm all yours, Nadia." He meant that more than she would ever know.

She glanced up at his face from staring at his groin and then took a step toward him. He watched with bated breath as she eased down the last piece of his clothing.

For the longest time she stared down at his aroused shaft. It was as if she was seeing a man—up close and personal—for the first time. That niggling thought he'd forced to the back of his mind earlier tried to make its way to the forefront yet again. He pushed it back.

Then as if she pulled herself out of a trance, she shifted her gaze to other parts of him. With a huge smile on her face, she met his gaze and said, "Well, I guess I'm finished."

He smiled back and said, "Not quite."

Not quite? Nadia figured a dumbfounded look had to be on her face. Finding her voice, she decided to ask. "What else is there?"

Instead of answering, he leaned down and picked up his slacks to pull something out of one of the pockets. He opened his hand to show her what he had. Condom packets. Several of them. "Oh."

"You want to do the honors, Nadia?"

She arched a brow. He had to be kidding. Although she was sure some women might not have a problem doing such a thing, she did. She wouldn't know where to start. And the thought of holding him in her hand while figuring out a condom was too much to think about. Even now his erection jutted proudly from a dark thatch of hair. Why did the sight of it make her want to reach out and run her fingers through those curls?

"Nadia?"

She raised her gaze to him. He was waiting for her response. "Thanks, but I'll let you do it."

"You're sure?"

"Positive."

He nodded and she stood there and watched him. When he finished, he glanced back at her. "Now it's my turn."

Nadia swallowed. She had gotten so caught up in watching him sheath himself that she couldn't comprehend his words. "Your turn?"

"Yes. It's my turn to undress you."

Not wasting any time, he pushed her blouse from her shoulders. Then he unhooked the front clasp of her bra, which made her breasts spill out. "Your breasts are beautiful. So damn shapely," he said, staring at them.

It was on the tip of her tongue to say they were also real. "Glad you like them."

"I'm going to prove just how much I like them in a moment. There aren't any limitations tonight, right?"

She blinked at his question. "Limitations?"

"Yes. You want steamy and I want to make tonight as steamy for you as it can get."

His words had heat gathering in the area between her legs. "There are no limitations, Jaxon."

"Good."

He finished undressing her by removing her skirt. Crouching down in front of her, he lowered her black lace panties down her legs and then remained there to stare at her feminine mound. It was as if he was fascinated by it, and she knew why. Although she wasn't sexually active, she wanted to look pretty down there regardless. That was why she routinely got a French bikini wax with a little artwork thrown in. The curls left down there were in the shape of a heart.

"That design is beautiful," he said, standing back on his feet.

"Thanks."

"And just so you know, Nadia, tonight will be a night of pleasure for the both of us. Especially for you."

She tilted her head to look up at him. Did he know about her virginity? "Why especially for me?"

"Because you deserve a man cherishing your body while making love to it."

His words touched Nadia. Her first time with a man was playing out how she'd hoped, how she'd fantasized it could be. She'd always wanted her first to be someone who wouldn't rush things. Someone who'd want to pleasure her, and Jaxon just said he would.

Her breath took on a different pattern when Jaxon's gaze moved from her eyes down her naked body—head to toe— before returning to the juncture of her thighs.

Feeling emboldened, she took a couple of steps to him and wrapped her arms around his neck. Doing so made them skin-to-skin, hard to soft.

She whispered, "I'm ready for the Jaxon Ravnel experience."

Fourteen

The Jaxon Ravnel experience?

No woman had ever termed making love with him that way, Jaxon thought. Coming from Nadia, he would take it. Not only would he take it, but he would try like hell to make it an experience she would never forget. It took more than great sex to bind a woman to a man and vice versa, but at least it was an explosive connection.

Sweeping her into his arms he carried her over to the bed. By the end of the night, she would be his physically. He would continue to work on her mentally by having them get to know each other more, showing her how good they could be together and making sure she fully understood the impact she had on his heart and the place he had designed for her in his life.

After placing her on the bed, he joined her there. Pulling her into his arms, he zeroed in on her mouth for a kiss. More than anything, he wanted to not only give Nadia intense pleasure, but he also wanted them to savor the night so she'd want plenty of steamy nights with him. The kiss was long, deep and passionate. It fired up everything inside of him and, from the sound of her moans, it fired her up as well.

Simultaneously, his hands were all over her. His fingers touched areas on her body he intended to give his full concentration to later. Right now, his focus was on her mouth and her taste. From their first kiss he'd found her flavor addictive and mind-blowingly delicious. He could kiss her all day or every chance he got. Holding back and not kissing her good-night when he'd brought her home after dinner on his jet had been the hardest thing he'd ever had to do.

Finally, he broke off the kiss and stared down at her. Her lips glistened, and he lowered his head to lick the wetness from them with the tip of his tongue. After licking and nibbling around her mouth a while, he licked toward her neck. From there he licked his way to her breasts and took a swollen peak into his mouth. He heard a whimper escape her lips as he sucked harder. Like he'd told her, she had beautiful breasts. They were the perfect size and shape. When he'd removed her bra to reveal them, sensations ripped through him. It had taken everything he had to hold himself in check. He'd never considered himself a breast man. Of course he liked looking at them and sampling them on occasion. But he'd never wanted to gobble up a pair like he was doing to Nadia.

Then he eased his finger between her legs. He began to shamelessly stroke her there while he devoured her breasts. Her feminine scent got to him, arousing him in a way he hadn't thought possible. It was then that he knew it was time to go further south. Shifting his body, he pulled away from her breasts and moved down to her stomach, licking and nibbling. Her skin was soft, delicate beneath his tongue, and the taste was incredible. He figured if her skin tasted this awesome, he could just imagine how tasty the area between her legs would be.

"Jaxon…"

Although her thighs opened when he'd placed his head between them, the way she'd said his name made him think no other man had gone down on her before. He glanced up and saw how she was looking at him with a mixture of want, need and curiosity. He knew then he would take his time, feast on her properly, to ensure this part of lovemaking was something she enjoyed.

He lowered his head and went to work. Grabbing hold of her hips, he eased his tongue inside of her. He loved the moan she made; he'd made one as well. She was so damn delicious. Her delectable flavor seemed to send his tongue into a licking frenzy. Locking his mouth to her feminine mound while holding her hips tight, he began devouring her. She grabbed his head to hold him to her. Such a thing wasn't needed since he had no intention of going anywhere. Never had his tongue been so eager to satisfy a woman.

He knew from the sudden jerking of her body that she was climaxing, but he refused to pull his mouth away. He kept it there while his tongue enjoyed the taste of her feminine juices. They invigorated him, filled him with a craving the extent of which he'd never felt for a woman. After lapping up as much of her as he could, he pulled his mouth away and looked up at her.

The satisfaction on her face touched him, sent sensuous shivers all through his body. She had enjoyed it as much as he had, and he was glad. Now it was time for the union of not only their bodies, but also their minds and souls.

Taking a deep breath, which included a whiff of her scent, he moved to ease his body over hers. While holding her gaze firmly with his, he slowly entered her. He knew the moment his earlier suspicions were confirmed. He was going where no man had gone before.

He was humbled and honored to be Nadia's first. Although she might not know it or accept it, she belonged to him in every way a woman could belong to a man. At twenty-eight he wasn't sure why she'd waited but she had and he would be the lucky guy. The only guy.

Their gazes held and as he stared into her eyes, he felt the same degree of desire he'd felt when he'd first met her, the same desire he felt whenever he was close to her. Now they were as close as two people could possibly be. All he could do was stare down into her beautiful face. With her hair spread out across the pillows, her features were even more striking. If it was possible to fall in love with her even more, at that moment he did.

He moved again and she widened her legs as if to welcome him in. When he had pushed his way inside her to the hilt, he asked, "You're okay?"

Reaching up, she wrapped her arms around his neck. She smiled and said, "Yes, I'm okay."

"Good, because I'm about to give you the ride of your life, sweetheart."

And he meant it.

Something inside of Nadia flared to life when Jaxon began thrusting. And when he growled low in his throat, every hormone inside of her sizzled as if she was burning alive from the inside out. She felt it in every pore, nerve and pulse. And then there was the sound of flesh slapping against flesh and the way his gaze held hers as if daring her to look away. She couldn't.

He managed to go deeper and deeper and she wondered how her body was keeping up with his urgent demands. She'd begun moving her body as well; she couldn't help but respond. Her body throbbed in areas it never had before.

Then there was the feel of his pubic hair rubbing against hers. It seemed everything surrounding them was on overload. His manly scent seemed to envelop her and when he leaned in to nibble on her earlobe, the feel of his hot breath near her neck made her heart skip a beat.

Each time he made a downward thrust, her feminine muscles tightened and tried holding him in while her hands glided up and down his naked back. Was this what made her sisters wear such satisfied smiles whenever they talked about their husbands' abilities in the bedroom? Now she fully understood what she'd been missing by not doing this with a man. But a part of her knew that it might not have been this good, this overwhelming, this hot with any other man but Jaxon. For reasons she didn't understand, they connected on every level.

Suddenly, he moved his mouth from her ear to her lips at the same time he used his hands to lift her hips to a more secure fit while moving inside of her. This kiss was hotter than any they'd ever shared. It was a full contact, wet-tongue kiss that made her head reel and her senses spin. And when his tongue captured hers, she clamped his face with her hands while returning the kiss with the same hunger and need he was plowing into it.

Then she felt it. It was as if every roll of his hips, every hard thrust into her body and the mind-blowing kiss had prepared her for this. It felt like a sexual explosion tearing her body apart with pleasure. She pulled her mouth from his and let out a scream as she felt her body splinter into a thousand pieces. Each piece filled with frissons of fire and passion.

Then she heard him holler out her name at the same time his body jerked hard while he continued to pound inside her, hard and deep. That pushed her into another orgasm. She welcomed it, needed it and desperately wanted it. She clenched her inner muscles around him tighter and knew he was giving her all he had. Yet she wanted more. Arching her back, her inner muscles clamped down on him, trying to draw everything out of him. She was determined to receive it all.

And just like she wanted, it happened for the third time. And she screamed yet again.

"Nadia?"

She forced open her eyes, feeling drained and depleted of all strength. Meeting Jaxon's gaze she forced a single word from her lungs. "Yes?"

"I need to go into the bathroom and come back to take care of you."

"Take care of me, how?"

"Last night was your first time and if I don't put you in a tub of warm water, you're going to be sore tomorrow."

She was glad that once he'd discovered she was a virgin he hadn't stopped making love to her. "I'm not ready to move just yet. Besides, I won't be too sore. I ride a lot."

He chuckled and tenderly kissed her lips. "Yes, sweetheart, but tonight you weren't the one doing the riding."

That was true but as far as she was concerned, it didn't matter. She wasn't ready for their bodies to separate, which was why her legs had a firm grip across his back. He couldn't go anywhere until she released him. "I liked it and want to do it again."

Seeing those lips she loved ease into a smile made her pulse rate increase. "I don't suggest we do that."

"Why?"

"It might make you even sorer."

"I'll chance a little discomfort for another few rounds."

He lifted a brow. "Another few rounds?"

"Yes. Now that I have you where I want you, I'm not ready to let you go." Too late she realized what she'd said and knew how her words could be misconstrued. She quickly added, "What I meant is that this is all new to me and I wondered how it would be. Now that I know and I like it, I'm wondering what took me so long to try it."

"Not that I'm complaining, but what did take you so long?" he asked, nuzzling his lips near her earlobes again.

Since he'd been her first, a position most men didn't want, and he hadn't made a fuss about it, she did owe him some sort of explanation. "I'll tell you, but not tonight. I want you again, Jaxon."

He stared down at her and she could feel him expanding inside of her. "I need to change condoms."

She knew he probably should, especially after hearing how Maverick had gotten Phire pregnant. But still. "Maybe the next go-round. I'm not ready for you to come out of me yet. Just so you know I am on the pill and I'm safe."

He stared at her and then said, "I'm safe as well."

A smile touched her lips. "Then there's no reason for us to worry about a condom, is there?"

He pushed back a lock of hair that had fallen in her face. "You sure?"

"I'm positive." Tonight in his arms, while he was here in her bed, she felt feminine and safe. She also felt desired. His aroused body attested to that. Then there was that hum of lust that had infiltrated her brain, making her want more of him. She wanted to know how it felt for him to release his semen inside of her. Tonight, he had introduced her to something her body had never done before and she had enjoyed it immensely. Maybe a little too much. She would have to worry about that later.

She had asked for one steamy night and she was definitely getting it.

Fifteen

Jaxon came awake to the brightness of the sun coming in through the window and the sound of Nadia's even breathing. She was still sleeping while cuddled in his arms. He could definitely get used to waking up each morning this way. He couldn't imagine anything better than being in bed with the woman he loved, holding her close after a night of lovemaking.

He hoped like hell she'd be able to walk today but she'd gotten just what she'd asked for. He'd given her fair warning. However, she'd refused to take heed. He had removed the condom after their first lovemaking session but hadn't put another one on. The feel of being skin to skin with her had driven his own need to have her over and over again. Each and every time their bodies joined, he'd loved her that much more. It had been before dawn this morning when they'd finally drifted off to sleep wrapped in each other's arms.

As he lay there staring up at the ceiling he wondered what today would bring. Would she regret what happened last night? Ask him to leave? Assume last night was one and done? Had last night been only about lust for her? That meant it was up to him to show her the difference between lust and love. She might not love him now, but there was no reason for her not to love him eventually. He would have enough love for the two of them until she did. In time she would see that their lives were entwined, and he would never hurt her.

There was a knock at her front door. He glanced at the clock on her wall and wondered who would be paying her a visit before nine in the morning? Hell, it would be just his luck for one of those Westmorelands or Outlaws to be here. She'd said they were known to drop in unannounced.

When the knock sounded again, she stirred in his arms and then slowly opened her eyes. He knew the exact moment she brought him into focus. He tried to prepare himself for what was to come. She hadn't asked him to spend the night; it just happened that way. He wondered if she'd remember how many times her legs had held his body hostage.

She continued to stare at him as if trying to recall why he was there. Then it seemed as if she remembered and the recollection made her smile. He released a relieved breath. "Good morning, Nadia."

"Good morning to you, Jaxon."

She sounded like she was in a good mood and then she proved she was by leaning over and brushing her lips across his. Before she could move back, he took over the kiss, deciding to show her what a real good-morning kiss looked like. He captured her mouth and exploited it for all it was worth and for him, it was worth everything.

The knock at the door sounded again. Louder this time. Jaxon reluctantly pulled his mouth away from hers. However, out of necessity, he licked around her lips and asked, "Do you normally get visitors this early?"

She licked around his mouth as well. "It's probably Rissa. She was supposed to take me to pick up my car this morning. I should have called her. Since you're here you can take me. At least if you don't mind."

"No, I don't mind."

"She's probably seen your car and figures you're still here since I'd told her I would be catching a ride with you to the television station yesterday."

He nodded. "Do you have a problem with her knowing I spent the night?"

"Heck no." She eased out of bed. "I would call and tell her to go away but my cell phone is downstairs." It didn't seem to bother her that she was standing there naked. "I'll grab my robe and let her know you'll give me a ride to the repair shop. And you might as well put on some clothes, too. She'll want to meet you."

"Then I can't disappoint her," he said, getting out of bed and not missing how her gaze traveled the full length of his body. There was no need to ask if she liked what she saw. All during their lovemaking last night she'd kept saying she did.

"I'll go downstairs before she calls the police to report you've done harm to me and gotten rid of my body. Rissa's husband, Shayne, is a US Marshal and her mind gets carried away at times."

Jaxon could certainly arrest Rissa's fears about him getting rid of Nadia's body. And speaking of that body, he decided to ask, "How do you feel this morning? Are you sore?"

His question made her blush. "I'm fine, Jaxon. Of course I'm sore, but the best way to work out soreness is to keep the muscles moving."

He nodded. "May I use your bathroom to freshen up?"

"Sure and there's a toiletry bag beneath the vanity you can use."

"Thanks."

As Jaxon headed for the bathroom, he was glad Nadia had

no problem letting her best friend know he'd spent the night. As far as he was concerned, that was a good start.

"Please wipe that silly-looking grin off your face, Rissa," Nadia said, stepping aside to let her friend enter her home.

"Well, it took you long enough to open the door and with your robe on and probably wearing nothing underneath, what am I to assume?" Rissa replied with a smirk on her face.

"I don't know, you tell me," Nadia said, closing the door.

"Well, the one thing I can assume is that you're no longer a twenty-eight-year-old virgin."

Rissa didn't know just how right she was about that. "I won't say."

"You don't have to say with all those passion marks on your neck. I'm surprised you can still walk this morning."

In a way Nadia was surprised, too. Her body was sore but she felt wonderful. "You're a smart woman, Rissa. You saw Jaxon's car out front. After the second knock, you should have kept moving, knowing I would call you later."

"Are you kidding me? You wanted me to miss seeing a huge smile on your face so I can gladly say I told you so?"

Nadia shook her head. For years Rissa had tried telling Nadia what she'd been missing by not engaging in an intimate relationship with a man. Rissa had accused Nadia of letting Benson win by not getting over what he'd done while they'd been in college.

"Well?"

Nadia glanced over at Rissa. "Well what?"

"I want to see that morning-after smile. The glow is there but I want to see the smile. No way will I believe Jaxon Ravnel didn't put a smile on your face." Rissa then glanced around. "Where is he, by the way?"

"Upstairs, and if it will get you to leave, here's my smile."

Unashamedly, Nadia gave her friend a huge, wide smile. The widest she could make.

Rissa laughed. "I knew it!" She gave Nadia a big hug. "I knew the two of you were meant to be together and—"

"Whoa. Hold up." Nadia shook her head. "Now you're talking nonsense," she said, lowering her voice to a hushed tone. "Jaxon and I are not meant to be together. Last night was one and done. Nothing has changed. It's back to the way things were before."

Rissa rolled her eyes and responded in a hushed tone as well. "I hate to tell you but that's not possible."

"And why not?"

"Your body knows him. It will want him. It will need him."

"That's rubbish. I don't want nor will I need any man, Rissa," Nadia said.

"You'll see and when you do, don't say I didn't warn you."

Nadia waved off her words. "Whatever."

"Well, since I've seen your smile I'll leave now and—"

"I hope you're not leaving on my account," a male voice said behind them.

Nadia and Rissa glanced around to see Jaxon walking down the stairs. At least he was dressed in his slacks and shirt. Why did he have to look so darn sexy this morning?

Seeing Rissa staring at him as if in a daze, Nadia leaned over and whispered, "Remember, you're a married woman."

Rissa snatched her gaze from Jaxon to look at Nadia with a sheepish grin and whispered back, "I'm trying hard to re-member."

Shayne was a good-looking man. But Nadia had to admit, there was good-looking and then there was goody-looking. This morning, Jaxon was not only goody-looking; he was sexy, sensual and salacious.

They watched him come down the stairs. Nadia didn't know Rissa's thoughts but she definitely knew hers. *What a man, what a man…* This morning he was jaw-droppingly handsome. Just the thought that last night she had gotten as much of him as he'd gotten of her made goose bumps appear on her body. Even now her gaze was glued to the zipper on his pants as she remembered everything. Every lusty, hungry moment of last night.

When he came to a stop in front of them, Nadia made introductions. Then Jaxon said, "Rissa, I'm happy to meet you. Nadia has told me a lot about you."

Nadia lifted a brow. Had she? She mentioned that she and Rissa were best friends and had been since they were kids, but that was all. She figured he was just being kind…as usual.

"Thanks and welcome to Gamble. I understand your company is expanding here."

"That's right," he replied with that killer smile. "Will you be joining us for breakfast?"

Breakfast? Nadia wondered what made Jaxon assume he was staying for breakfast. "Rissa has a lot to do today and was just about to leave," she said, taking her best friend's arm and leading her toward the door.

"Yes, that's right. I was about to leave. It was nice meeting you, Jaxon."

"Same here, Rissa."

When Nadia closed the door behind Rissa, she turned to Jaxon, ready to light into him about his assumptions about breakfast or that he might be hanging around, period. Maybe she needed to make it clear to him that last night was one and done. She was about to open her mouth when he lowered his lips to hers.

She knew what was about to happen but didn't want to stop it. Jaxon was seducing her and she was letting him. He began torturing her mouth the way he'd done several times last night. After ending the kiss, he nibbled her lips from corner to corner and then used the tip of his tongue to lick around the lines of her mouth. When she made a breathless sigh, his tongue eased inside her mouth once again, took hold of her tongue and began an intimate, sensual duel.

If that wasn't enough, she could feel his erection pressed hard against her middle and the more they kissed, the bigger he got. Then suddenly, she was swept into his strong arms as he moved in the direction of the stairs.

Jaxon had a good idea just what Nadia had expected when he'd swept her into his arms to take her back upstairs. When he entered her bedroom, he hadn't placed her on the bed but kept moving to the bathroom. Once there he removed her robe before placing her in the warm sudsy water he had prepared for her.

"A good soak will help those sore muscles," he said, crouching down beside the tub.

"And what will you be doing while I'm soaking?"

He smiled and pushed a wayward lock from her face. "I'm going to the hotel to shower and change. Then I'll be back to take you to get your car. By then it will be lunchtime. Will you have lunch with me?" He knew to ask rather than to assume. The last thing he wanted was for Nadia to think he was calling the shots. He was beginning to know her well and the one thing she disliked was a man assuming he had any rights as far as she was concerned. So far everything she'd gotten was what she had asked for.

"Thanks for the invitation, but I have things to do today and I'm sure you do, too."

If she thought that was her way to get rid of him, she was sorely mistaken. He would give her space but he had no intention of leaving her alone completely. Last night was a game changer for them. He'd never known any woman who was more sensual, more uninhibited, more open to trying new things. He'd never forget the moment he realized she was still a virgin. His chest had expanded along with his shaft, knowing he was the first man to go inside her.

Once they'd established that she was on a reliable form of birth control and they both were safe health-wise, he had dispensed with the use of the condom. Each and every time he'd come inside her he'd experienced an earth-shattering orgasm. Hell, he'd lost count of how many times they'd come. They'd even hit multiples a few times. There was no doubt in his mind that he had placed his stamp all over her. Evidently, she hadn't yet seen those passion marks on her neck, not to mention other parts of her body. She now belonged to him as much as he belonged to her.

"Is there anything you need me to do before I leave?"

She lifted her chin. "Of course not. In fact you didn't have to do this. I could have filled my own tub with water."

"I know, but I liked doing it." And before she could say anything, he leaned in and brushed a kiss across her lips. "I'll be back in an hour."

"I can call Rissa to come back and take me to get my car."

Standing, he said, "I want to take you. Besides, earlier you said Rissa had a lot to do today. Whereas, I have plenty of time."

She frowned. "Well, I hope you don't plan to get underfoot by thinking last night meant anything."

Jaxon had news for her. Last night had meant everything. "Are you normally this grouchy in the mornings, Nadia?"

Her frown deepened. "I'm not grouchy."

"Yes, you are. While soaking, you should not only work out the soreness but also the grouchiness. I'll see you later."

He heard what she said when he walked out of the bathroom. Walker Rafferty had said he'd never heard Nadia curse. Jaxon just had, and his ears were still blistered.

He chuckled as he went down the stairs. Before it was all over, she would probably be inclined to say even more curse words. Nadia was headstrong, opinionated and had no problem stating how she felt about any given topic. She'd done so last night. She liked being in control and for a while he'd let her. He wouldn't change a thing about her. But he would straighten her out on a few things. He was a permanent part of her life and the sooner she accepted that fact the easier things would be for the both of them.

Sixteen

Nadia didn't lean back to relax in the water until she heard the sound of the front door closing and locking behind Jaxon. She couldn't help licking her lips. The man had more sensuality in his lips than some men had in their entire body.

And speaking of his body...

Granted she'd never been in the presence of a naked man, but she couldn't imagine one with a more trim and fit body than Jaxon. She had studied his physique like an architect would study a blueprint. Taking in the solid muscles that seemed to be everywhere. Even his coffee-colored skin tone had seemed to glow beneath her bedroom light.

And he was so well endowed. The thought of that particular body part being inside her most of the night, giving her pleasure, made her shiver at the memories. And when he'd placed his body above hers and stared down into her eyes, every inch of him had been compelling. She drew in a deep breath at the delicious and tantalizing memories. There was no reason to worry about her bathwater turning cold since the heat from her body was definitely keeping it warm. Jaxon

Ravnel had touched her in the right places and had made a lasting impression on her while doing so.

And that was the crux of her problem. She didn't want any man to make a lasting impression on her. But she couldn't refute the fact that he had. Jaxon had made her first time special. Way too special. Both mentally and physically. He had made it worth the wait. And for some reason that was a sore spot even when it shouldn't be.

She should be elated he had given her such tender, loving care. He'd even run bathwater for her in deference to her well-being. How many men would do such a thing? Some would not have hung around until morning. There were some who wouldn't even invite a woman to their home for the night, preferring to always go to hers. She would eye-roll any woman who allowed such a thing.

A short while later she eased out of the tub to get dressed. Jaxon said he would be back in an hour and there was no reason not to believe him. There was a lot about him she was trying to figure out. Did he see their relationship changing or did she just assume he did?

Earlier, when he'd invited her to lunch and she'd declined, he hadn't given any pushback. It was as if it hadn't mattered to him one iota if she accepted his lunch invitation or not. And last night, she'd been the one to tell him she wanted to change their relationship just for that night. Did his nonchalance mean anything?

As she slid into her jeans she wondered if she was overthinking the situation. All they'd had was last night. But what if he wanted more? Was he pretending he didn't want more to throw her off kilter? She pushed such a thought from her mind. Jaxon said he was a man who didn't play games with a woman and there was no reason to assume he was doing so now.

Exactly on the hour there was a knock on her door. Giving

herself one last look in the mirror, she quickly moved down the stairs to open it. Nadia was glad the weather was cool so it wouldn't look odd for her to be wearing a scarf. The last thing she needed was for anyone to see all those passion marks on her neck. It was bad enough Rissa had seen them.

She glanced through the peephole. It was Jaxon all right and like her, he was wearing jeans and a Western shirt with the top three buttons undone.

Was that on purpose since she'd told him she had a fetish for chest hair? If so, it was working. She could recall last night when she had dragged her fingers through it, buried her face in it. Her thighs quivered at the memories. And as if he knew she was watching him, he smiled. Dang. That smile would be the death of her.

Drawing in a deep breath, she opened the door without asking who it was. No point since he'd known she'd been watching him. "Jaxon, I'm ready and you look nice," she said, grabbing her purse and jacket without inviting him inside.

"So do you and I like your scarf," he replied as he waited for her to lock the door behind her.

"Thanks." Although she thanked him there was no doubt in her mind that he knew why she was wearing one.

They walked side by side down the steps to his parked car. Forever being a gentleman, he opened the door for her. "Thank you, Jaxon."

He smiled down at her. "You're welcome, Nadia."

She frowned when he closed the door to walk around to his side of the car. Why were they acting so formal with each other? This was the same man who had undressed her last night. The same man she had undressed. The man she'd given her virginity to, and who in the span of fourteen hours had taught her more positions for lovemaking than she'd thought were possible. He had packed a lot into those hours and she had no complaints.

When he got in the car, before starting the engine, he glanced over at her with concern on his features. "Still sore?"

She was about to tell him he was asking her something too personal but then pulled back. Hadn't she just thought they were acting formal with each other? For that reason, she decided to answer. "I'm fine, Jaxon. What about you? Are you sore?" She figured that question would shut him up. They were now discussing her inexperience versus his experience.

"Yes, in fact. I tried some positions with you I've never done with other women."

Yeah, right. "You could have fooled me. You seemed good at everything you were doing."

"Only because it was you."

She rolled her eyes. Did he honestly expect her to believe that? Deciding to change the subject, she said, "If the invitation is still open, I'll have lunch with you."

"Okay," he said, starting the car and driving it out of the yard.

Nadia didn't think he sounded all that enthused about it. "If you'd rather I didn't, then..."

"The invitation is still open, Nadia, and I would love for you to join me for lunch. However, I've made after-lunch plans."

"Oh."

"I'm going horseback riding."

"Horseback riding?"

"Yes. I understand the Ellerey Ranch arranges activities like that."

"They do, and they have some beautiful horses," she said.

"That's what I heard and you're welcome to join me if you like. You did say you can ride a horse, right?"

Did he not believe her? "Yes, and I recall saying I was pretty good at it."

"If you say so."

"And that's what I meant," was her retort.

Nadia wished he hadn't mentioned he was going to the Ellerey's ranch. Immediately, thoughts of Clementine Ellerey, the granddaughter of old man Ellerey, flashed in her mind. Twice divorced at thirty, the woman was known to be a man-eater. It didn't help matters that a lot of men around these parts thought she was absolutely gorgeous. Well, maybe she was. But that was no reason to deliberately sleep with some-one's boyfriend or husband just because she could, if rumors could be believed. Clementine had a reputation around town and not a good one. More than likely, she would be at the ranch, especially if she got wind that Jaxon was coming. Well, Nadia had news for Clementine. Not on her watch.

Nadia turned around in her seat to face Jaxon as he came to the gate that led off the Novak Homestead. "I'd love to join you, and I can't wait to show you how well I can ride."

After picking up Nadia's car, Jaxon followed her back home. Then they had lunch at a restaurant on the outskirts of town that, in his opinion, served the best BBQ ribs he'd eaten in a long time. When they reached the Ellerey Ranch two horses were saddled and ready for them to ride.

For some reason the man's granddaughter, a woman who looked to be in her late twenties, had saddled the second horse for herself. She'd assumed Jaxon would want company and had invited herself to go riding with him. Why she'd thought such a thing when he didn't even know her, he couldn't say.

It didn't take long to figure out what she was about and he wasn't having it. He let her know that Nadia would be his riding partner. From the way she'd glared at Nadia it was ob-vious the woman hadn't liked that too much. Not that he'd given a royal damn.

As soon as Nadia was seated in her saddle, she had taken off and he'd chased after her. It didn't take long for her to prove she was the expert horsewoman she'd claimed to be. Not that he'd doubted it for a second. He liked ruffling her feathers. He had enjoyed racing across the valley with her and then trotting along several paths.

"Oh, look," she called out and slowed her horse.

His gaze followed to where she was pointing. A fawn was caught between the fencing. They brought their horses to a stop and Nadia was off before Jaxon could help her down. She rushed over to where the baby deer was crying for its mother.

"Poor thing," Nadia said, glancing around.

"We need to untangle it and set it free," he said. "It's my guess the mother is around here somewhere, probably watching and hoping we don't do her baby any harm. I need to grab a pair of gloves from the saddle bag."

When he returned, he saw Nadia smoothing the animal with calming words and it was no longer crying. It took them working together to untangle the fawn only because the animal was skittish and frightened. Once they had set it free, the fawn took off. Up in the distance they saw it was joined by the mother and then both animals skedaddled into the woods.

"Well, that was our excitement for today," Nadia said, smiling.

"There's a lake over there. We might as well rest the horses and let them take a drink," he said.

Going back to the horses, they grabbed the reins and walked toward the lake. "When Dad was alive there were a lot of horses on the Novak Homestead," Nadia said, leaning against a tree. "We had to sell them all when he got sick since money was needed. That's when I lost my horse. He was one of the ones we had to sell."

Jaxon nodded. This wasn't the first time she'd told him how she and her sisters had made sacrifices when their father had taken ill. Sacrifices they had been glad to make so their father could get the best medical care. The first night

Jaxon had shared dinner at her place she'd told him how Pam had returned home after giving up acting. Jill had to stop her riding lessons. Yesterday, on the drive to Valley Bluff, they'd passed a dance studio and she told him Paige had been taking dance classes there until their father had gotten too sick for her to continue. Now, Nadia had told him she'd given away a horse that had meant a lot to her.

"What was your horse's name?" he asked, leaning against a tree opposite her. The fading sun highlighted her features. They were the same beautiful features he'd stared down into last night while making love to her.

"Cocoa. I named him when he was born because he was the color of rich, dark cocoa. He was the best horse a girl could ever have, and he was beautiful."

"I bet he was."

"I have a picture of me at eleven sitting on his back. It was the last one Cocoa and I took together."

Jaxon recalled seeing the framed picture on a wall in her bedroom. He could hear the sadness in her voice. It was sadness he wished he could take away. Deciding to change the subject, he said, "I wonder where this lake leads to."

Nadia told him the history of the Ellerey Ranch and how Jamie Ellerey was the descendant of one of the town's founders. She then told him more of the town's history and how her great-great grandfather had been one of the first to settle in the area as well. While she was talking, he wondered if she would consider living somewhere else. Or was she pretty rooted here since returning after living in Denver all those years? Gamble was the type of town that could grow on you. Everyone he'd met had been hardworking and friendly. That's why he knew if Nadia preferred living here permanently, then he would, too. His home would always be with her.

"What's the deal with Ellerey's granddaughter? I take it the two of you know each other."

Nadia nodded. "I've known Clementine all my life. Her father was old man Ellerey's only child and I understand he was a real decent man. When Clementine's parents were killed in an avalanche during a ski trip, old man Ellerey raised her alone. She was only three and needless to say he spoiled her rotten. She's always been a pain in everyone's side. Even as a kid. I'd hoped her attitude had improved when I moved back years later but it hasn't. She has this entitlement complex. She believes she's entitled to anything or anyone she wants."

Jaxon had gotten that same impression.

"I'm sure you noticed how beautiful she is," Nadia added.

Yes, he'd noticed. "I'm a man who believes inner beauty is just as important as outer beauty. Even more so." There was no need to add that he'd dated a number of women who'd had the looks of a goddess but possessed hearts of stone.

"It's time to get back, Jaxon."

He glanced at his watch. It had gotten late and he hadn't been aware so much time had passed. "I enjoyed today with you, Nadia." No need to tell her again how much he'd enjoyed his night with her, too. He had pretty much proved it last night.

She didn't say anything for a minute and then stated, "And I enjoyed being with you today, too, Jaxon. But nothing has changed."

"You're wrong about that. Everything between us has changed after last night." He wouldn't waste his time saying that as far as he was concerned last night sealed the deal. "I was your first," he added.

"But that doesn't mean you'll be my last."

"That's how I intend for it to be."

A frown appeared on her face. "Don't tell me you're the male version of Clementine with an entitlement complex."

"I won't tell you that, but I will tell you this," he said, crossing the distance separating them. "I don't make it a habit to have sex with virgins. In fact, I never have before. I could have stopped things before I finished the deed, but you know why I didn't?"

"Of course I know. The same degree of lust that consumed me also consumed you."

"Lust had nothing to do with it for me. It was love."

Her eyes widened. "Love?" She threw her head back and laughed. "Oh, that's rich. Weeks ago, you said you wanted to marry me when you didn't even know me. Now today you want me to believe you've fallen in love with me? Really?"

He glared at her. "Yes, really. I fell in love with you the moment we were introduced."

She frowned and glared back. "That's not possible. Besides, I don't want any man to love me or want to marry me."

"That's tough because I do and I will." Before she could say anything else, Jaxon leaned down and planted his mouth on hers.

She didn't pull away. Instead, she wrapped her tongue around his the same way she'd done last night. Somehow their mouths always mated in perfect unity. An intense flare of heat consumed his entire body while he held her in his arms and continued to kiss her like he never wanted to stop. She might be mad at him but it was obvious she wanted this kiss as much as he did.

What was she afraid of and why?

When he finally released her lips, he stared into her eyes, which had a look that all but said she couldn't believe she had let him kiss her and that she had kissed him back. Her next words proved it. "We should not have done that."

He tilted the Stetson back from his eyes to gaze down at her. "Everything we've done or are doing was meant to be, Nadia."

The glare was back in her eyes. "I disagree. I'm ready to go, Jaxon."

"Okay, but there's something I want to ask you first."

"What?"

"Who hurt you?"

She broke eye contact with him to look away and then she looked back at him. "I don't know what you mean."

"I think you do. There's a reason you hold yourself back."

She threw her head back and laughed again. "Hold myself back? What about last night? If anything, I let myself go."

"Yes, and it took you twenty-eight years to do so. I want to know what man broke your heart to make you not want to fall in love again. Twenty-eight-year-old virgins are rare these days."

"That's none of your business, Jaxon."

"That's where you're wrong. Every single thing about you is my business, Nadia."

Jaxon watched an angry Nadia walk over to her horse. After mounting it, she glanced over at him. "No, it's not. I don't want or need a man in my life."

"Well, I want and need you in mine, Nadia."

She glared at him before nudging her horse and taking off racing across the field.

Nadia was quiet on the drive back to the Novak Homestead. Jaxon thought about engaging her in conversation but decided against it. He'd said his piece so he let her stew. But anger or no anger, he could still feel the sexual chemistry surrounding them in the confines of the car. In a way, he really shouldn't have been surprised. If nothing else, last night proved just how combustible they were. How well connected. For her, it might only have been lust, but for him it was love.

When he brought the car to a stop in front of the house, she got out without waiting for him to come around to open the car door for her. "Don't bother. I can see myself inside."

Ignoring what she said, he got out anyway and walked a

few paces behind her. He shouldn't be noticing, but he liked the way her jeans shaped her backside and loved the sashay of her hips when she walked. The woman couldn't help being sexy no matter what she put on her body or took off of it.

When she reached the door and unlocked it, she did glance over her shoulder to say, "Thank you."

"You're welcome and flick the curtains or open the blinds to let me know you're safe inside. And Nadia?"

She slowly turned to him. He hadn't even come up the steps to the porch. Instead, he stood back. He knew if he got too close, he would want to pull her into his arms and kiss her. "I meant everything I said about my feelings for you. I love you and have from the moment we were introduced. If you change your mind about me, about us, then you know how to reach me."

He watched her go inside and closed the door. He didn't move off the steps to return to his car until she had flicked the curtain.

Seventeen

Nadia jumped when Rissa snapped her fingers in front of Nadia's face. She hadn't known her best friend had even moved out of the chair. Nadia frowned. "What did you do that for?"

Rissa returned to her chair in front of Nadia's desk. "To get your attention. You've been zoning out on me since I got here. Do you want to talk about it?"

She was about to tell Rissa that no, she didn't want to talk about it. Rissa had been trying to get information out of Nadia since the moment she'd arrived. However, the teasing glint in Rissa's eyes had been replaced with concern. She heard it in her friend's voice and saw it in her face.

Other than her sisters, Rissa knew Nadia better than anyone. If she could feel Nadia was out of sorts, then her worry was justified. Nadia was not one to let a man get under her skin. Yet Jaxon had done so.

"Jaxon and I argued."

Rissa nodded her head as if not surprised. "The two of you have been at odds since he told you he wanted to marry you. I thought you guys had declared a truce or something since you slept with him Friday night."

"It's gotten worse."

Rissa lifted a brow. "How?"

"Now he thinks he's in love with me."

Rissa stared at her for a moment and then asked, "He actually told you that?"

"Yes. It was when we'd gone riding at the Ellerey Ranch on Saturday. We were at the lake letting our horses rest and he said he loved me. He also said he felt entitled to me because he was the first guy I slept with."

Rissa frowned. "Did he really say that?"

"No, but that's the way he acted."

"Or is that the way you took it, Nadia? I know you. And the one thing I do know is you have a tendency to make a mountain out of a molehill."

When Nadia didn't say anything, Rissa leaned back in her chair and studied her. "Why do I have the feeling you aren't telling me everything?"

Probably because she wasn't, Nadia thought. She hadn't told Rissa of her unusual feeling of jealousy when she'd seen a picture of Jaxon's administrative assistant on his website and how relieved she was when he'd said the beautiful woman was getting married. Nor had she told her how she'd deliberately gone horseback riding with him just so Clementine Ellerey wouldn't get her clutches in him.

"I'm getting jealous where Jaxon is concerned."

Rissa raised a brow. "Jealous in what way?"

She then told Rissa of the two situations and when a smile spread across Rissa's lips, she asked, "Why are you smiling?"

"Because you're not a woman who makes a habit of getting jealous over a man. That could only mean one thing."

"What?"

"You care for Jaxon Ravnel more than you're admitting to me and, more importantly, to yourself."

"I don't want a man in my life. Especially not him."

"Why not him?" Rissa asked with a sheen of curiosity in her eyes.

Nadia inhaled deeply as she struggled to say the words to make Rissa understand. "Because Jaxon is too good to be true. Everybody likes him. I told you how he exposed that man who was deceiving the Outlaws. He didn't have to do that, but he did. Now the Westmorelands and Outlaws think he's a swell guy. Even all the women in the family like him."

"All the women but you." Rissa hadn't stated it as a question.

"I don't dislike him."

Rissa chuckled. "Heck, I hope not after all that bumping and grinding the two of you did Friday night and early Saturday morning."

Nadia shrugged. "Women have been known to sleep with men they don't like."

"Not most women and definitely not you." Rissa finished the last of her coffee and tossed the cup in the trash can at the side of Nadia's desk. "But I still don't understand. Why are you afraid of getting involved with Jaxon? Do you think he will play you like Benson did?"

"Of course not."

"Then what is it, Nadia?"

"I'm not his type. He should be interested in a woman with grace and refinement. One full of sophistication."

"That's utter nonsense. If Jaxon says he loves you and wants to marry you then that means you are the woman he wants. Besides, worrying about if you're Jaxon's type might be the least of your problems, Nadia."

"What do you mean?"

"You know Jaxon. Your mouth knows him. Your tongue

knows him. In other words, your entire being knows him. I bet you spent this weekend remembering how good things were with him. How the real thing was better compared to your dreams. How he knocked all your fantasies right out of the ballpark."

Nadia rolled her eyes, refusing to admit everything Rissa said was true. "You act as if Jaxon will become an addiction."

"It's a good chance he might. Maybe he already is. I think you've fallen for Jaxon, but you're fighting it like hell."

Nadia sat straight up in her chair. "I don't love Jaxon."

Rissa waved off her words. "You can deny it all you want but the signs are there. Anytime you mention his name your eyes light up. Your breathing changes. Personally, I think it's wonderful that he loves you and wants to marry you and has told you so. How many men are that up front with a woman?" Rissa then glanced at her watch and stood. "I gotta leave now to get to work on time. Remember I'll be out of town the rest of the week on that business trip to San Diego. However, if you need to talk, I'll just be a phone call away."

Nadia nodded, knowing this issue with Jaxon was something she had to figure out for herself.

It was past six on Thursday when Nadia finally left the academy for home. Usually, she didn't work so late but Langley had called with the budget for Ravnel Technologies' sponsorship. It was more than she and her staff had anticipated. Definitely a lot more than the Dunnings Financial Group had agreed to give them. Langley even mentioned that Jaxon had suggested using the local theater instead of the high school's auditorium. Additional funds would be allotted if she chose to do so.

She had immediately liked the idea and had called an impromptu meeting with her staff to see what they thought. Everyone got all excited. They couldn't wait to share the news with the students tomorrow.

Jill and Paige had called before Nadia had closed up her office. Both were excited about the surprise party for Quade Westmoreland's wife, Cheyenne, this weekend and wanted to know when she'd be arriving. When she'd told them she had just purchased her ticket that morning, Paige asked why she hadn't caught a ride with Jaxon on his plane. Saying he probably would not have minded since he would be attending the party, too.

She'd told Paige there was no way she could have imposed like that. What if he was bringing a date? Jill agreed with Nadia and said although Jaxon had never brought a woman to any of the family's functions before, that didn't mean he would never bring one. After all Jaxon was single and good-looking. Paige still thought it shouldn't be an issue. All Jaxon had to do was to tell his date that Nadia was nothing more than a family friend.

Nothing more than a family friend…

She hadn't yet told her sisters how her relationship with Jaxon had taken a turn since that time she'd invited him to dinner. In a way, she was glad she hadn't shared the news since she and Jaxon were back to not having a relationship at all, although according to Jaxon, he loved her and wanted to marry her.

She would admit she wasn't as shocked now by what he'd said as she had been on Saturday. That had been five days ago. Since then she'd done a lot of thinking. Rissa had been right. Nadia was falling for Jaxon.

It had taken her five days and sleepless nights to finally accept that. She had thought a lot about him since Saturday and now it was Thursday. She missed him and constantly re-played in her mind the time they'd spent together. She also replayed in her mind the dinners they'd shared, both at her home and on his jet.

However, more than anything she thought about that day last year when they'd been introduced. She had been attracted to him from the start and, according to him, he'd been more than attracted. He claimed he'd fallen in love with her. Could she believe that? Hadn't he said at lunch that day that his father had fallen in love with his mother the same way?

She'd also heard about such things happening to a couple of the Westmoreland men, like Bane. He swore he'd fallen for Crystal when he'd come upon her walking home from school. He hadn't hesitated to turn his motorcycle around and introduce himself. And Dillon claimed he'd fallen in love with Pam even though she'd been engaged to Fletcher. Could she believe such a thing happened to Jaxon?

Getting into her car, she started the engine. As she drove out of the parking lot, she thought about what she'd seen that night when they'd viewed the Milky Way. She hadn't mentioned it to Rissa because her friend was one of those believers and would have sworn that was the sign Nadia needed that she and Jaxon were destined to share everlasting love. Were they?

I meant everything I said about my feelings for you. I love you and have from the moment we were introduced. If you change your mind about me, about us, then you know how to reach me.

Why was she remembering Jaxon's words now? Why had she thought of them a lot this week? Why was her heart beating so fast? And why was she getting off the exit that would take her to Jaxon's hotel? It was one of the newest hotels in the city and she'd heard it was one of the fanciest. When it was first built it had seemed out of place in a ranch town. However, now it fit. More importantly, it fit a man like Jaxon.

She pulled into his hotel and parked her car. Why was she

here? Would he be upset that she showed up unannounced? She couldn't worry about that now. The one thing she did know was that she missed him and more than anything she wanted to see him.

Jaxon was about to order room service when he heard the knock at his hotel room door. He frowned, hoping like hell it wasn't Clementine Ellerey. The woman had had the audacity to come to his hotel room a few days ago. He'd opened the door, but of course he hadn't let her in.

He'd tried telling her in the nicest way that he wasn't interested. When it seemed his words were falling on deaf ears, he'd had to be frank. She wasn't his type and he would appreciate if she left him alone and moved on and not invite herself to his hotel room again. Ms. Ellerey hadn't liked that one iota and threatened to ruin his name in town by saying he'd sexually harassed him. There had been no doubt in her mind the townspeople would believe her over him. After all, she was a hometown girl and that meant something in Gamble.

He was glad he'd anticipated she would make such a move, after that stunt she'd tried on Saturday and after hearing Nadia's opinion of her. Saturday night he'd called Martin Lockley, the man who handled all his security, to run a check on her. He'd gotten Lockley's report first thing Monday morning and it was rather colorful and informative.

There were four men in Gamble she was currently sleeping with behind their wives' backs. When he'd told Ms. Ellerey everything he knew about her and assured her he wouldn't hesitate to share the report with the good people of Gamble if she carried out her threats, she quickly left.

He glanced out his door's peephole. It wasn't Clementine Ellerey but was the woman who'd been on his mind constantly since parting ways with her on Saturday evening. That had been five days ago and although he'd missed her like hell, he'd wanted to give her space to think about all he'd said. Things he had no intention of backing down on.

Had she come to give him another piece of her mind or was she here because she believed what he'd said? As if she knew he was staring at her, she stared back and sensations ripped through him. He had to breathe slowly for air to flow through his lungs.

Opening the door to his suite, he didn't bother to ask what she was doing there. It didn't matter because he was glad to see her. "Hello, Nadia."

"Hello, Jaxon. May I come in?"

As far as he was concerned, she could come in and stay and never leave. "Yes," he said and stepped aside for her to enter.

She was certainly getting a different reception than the one he'd given Clementine Ellerey. But then this was the woman he was deeply in love with. The one he wanted more than anything to share his life with. She looked good in her plaid pencil skirt, earth-tone suede knee-high boots and matching suede jacket.

He shoved his hands into the pockets of his pants. Otherwise, he would be tempted to reach out and pull her into his arms. Desire between them was always intense, heated and charged. Tonight, it seemed even more so. Sexual chemistry dominated the air they shared, like usual. They stood staring at each other, feeling it shimmering around them.

The moonlight filtering through the curtains seemed to fill the room with an ethereal light that bathed her in a radiant glow. Maybe it was his eyes, but she appeared even more beautiful tonight than ever before. The room seemed electrified. He was convinced all it would take was a touch to send sparks flying.

"I want to thank you for that suggestion you made for the academy to hold the play at the theater in town," she finally broke the silence to say.

He nodded. "You didn't have to come all the way over here to thank me, Nadia."

"I know. That's not the only reason I'm here."

"It's not?"

"No. I felt the need to talk to you about something, Jaxon."

He wondered what she wanted to talk about. Just her being here in his hotel suite was causing heat to stir in his groin. More than anything, he needed to keep his control in check. "Okay, come into the sitting area. We can talk there," he said, leading the way. His suite was spacious, but at the moment it seemed way too cozy.

"Please have a seat," he said, offering her the sofa. When she moved around him, her hips accidentally brushed against his. Suddenly, like a magnet, their bodies connected, and he drew her to him and lowered his head to hers.

Eighteen

The moment Jaxon's lips touched hers, Nadia felt energized, mesmerized and totally captivated. Automatically, her arms went around his neck and her body pressed hard against his. She felt him; there were just some things a man couldn't hide and a full-blown erection was one of them.

And now he was kissing her the way she wanted. The way she needed. It always amazed her how his tongue could work its way around her mouth, eliciting hers to participate and duel in the most sensuous way. Every bone in her body felt completely enthralled. Whenever he kissed her, she was incapable of holding back. He made her feel things she'd never felt before, and all from a kiss. But she knew tonight they would share more than a kiss. The reason she'd come was to talk, but she had no problem getting this first. Like him, she needed it now. Talking would come later.

When he swept her into his arms without breaking the kiss, she tightened her hold around his neck. He wanted her and she wanted him. Something else she knew now with all certainty was that she *did* love him. The moment he had opened the door and she'd looked into his face, she'd known. The face she had dreamed about for over a year, the face that belonged to her fantasy man. She could not fight emotions she'd been too afraid to face any longer.

Jaxon broke off the kiss when he placed her on the bed. Then he stepped back, held her gaze and began removing his clothes. Likewise, she began dispensing with hers. No words were spoken. None were needed. Their kiss had told them everything.

"I've missed you," he said in a deep, throaty voice.

She was about to tell him that he'd known where to find her, but didn't. She had needed the space, the distance and the longing. She was even glad Rissa had been out of town on that business trip. Nadia's feelings for Jaxon were something she'd needed to figure out for herself, and she had.

Staring deep into his gaze, she said, "And I missed you, too. I'm here now and so are you."

He nodded. "And that's all that matters."

Moving closer to the bed, he pulled her into his arms and she went willingly. Together they fell back onto the mattress with their lips joined. She doubted she would ever tire of being kissed by him. His kisses were always mind-blowingly hot.

Moments later, he broke off the kiss, and in a surprise move, he shifted his body so she was on top of him. At the questioning look he must have seen in her eyes, he said, "Tonight, I want you to ride me. After seeing you on a horse I know how good you are at it."

She smiled down at him. "I plan to do my best."

Jaxon quickly concluded that if Nadia got any better she would kill him. She was riding him right into another orgasm. The third for the both of them. She would come and he would follow like clockwork. It was like she hadn't gotten enough of him any more than he'd gotten enough of her. How long would they keep this up? Probably until neither had strength to do anything else.

With each and every upward thrust from him, she would grind her hips against his in a way that had an abundance of liquid heat coiling in his erection. He gazed up into her eyes and what he saw took his breath away. He didn't see lust-filled eyes but ones full of something else. But then, maybe he was seeing what he wanted to see and not what was really there.

All thoughts fled his mind when the sounds of Nadia's moans reached a high peak. Just the thought that she was riding him with the expertise she'd ridden that horse on Saturday made his breath rush from his lungs. She continued to take him inch by incredibly sweet inch.

Now her hips were coming down faster and harder. Every cell in his body was set and ready to explode the moment she did. She was still tight and he could feel her body tighten even more and pulse around him. And each time she came down on him their gazes caught and locked. He cupped a hand across her bottom, loving the feel of the movement she made every time their bodies connected.

"Jaxon!"

Then it happened. An explosion that plunged them into sweet oblivion. When she came downward on him again, he dragged his tongue over her face, licking the moisture that had accumulated there. Another shudder of pleasure tore through them and this time it was him who yelled out her name.

"Nadia!"

Waves of pleasure shot through every part of him and then detonated on glorious impact. He knew that for as long as he lived every time they came together would be burned into his memory as well as his heart. When her body collapsed on his, he wrapped his arms around her and held her tight. Unable to hold it back, he whispered. "I love you, Nadia."

She went still and then lifted her head off his chest and looked into his eyes. "And I love you, too."

Then she closed her eyes and slept.

Nadia came awake to the feel of someone's tongue licking across her face. Slowly opening her eyes, she met Jaxon's gaze. He was no longer in the bed with her but was sitting on the side of the mattress next to her. When she reached out to him, he pulled her into his lap and gave her a kiss that she felt all the way to her toes.

When he released her mouth, he said, "Did you mean what you said?"

She knew what he was asking and nodded. "Yes." She drew in a deep breath and with it came the scent of their lovemaking that was still very potent in the room. "There is so much I need to tell you, Jaxon."

"Okay, but we need to eat first."

"Eat?"

"Yes, I ordered room service. I don't know about you, but I'm famished."

She was hungry, too, since she hadn't eaten since lunch. She glanced over at the clock on his nightstand. "It's after ten?"

"Yes. We've been busy."

She couldn't help but smile. That was an understatement. He stood with her in his arms and placed her on her feet. "Do I need to run warm bathwater for you or are you okay?"

"I'm okay." Nodding, he went to the closet and grabbed one of the hotel's complimentary robes. It was a match to the one he was wearing. "I don't have a problem if you want to walk around naked, but I figure we need to give our bodies a rest while we eat."

She totally agreed. As soon as she slid into her robe, which he helped her do, he swept her back into his arms and carried her out of the bedroom to the dining area, where a table for two was set up. Complete with candles and wineglasses. Several bottles of champagne sat chilling in an ice-bucket.

"The table setting is beautiful. But what's with the champagne? You do know I have to go to work tomorrow, right?" she said, when he placed her in her chair.

"You sure you don't want to play hooky?"

"I want to but I'd better not. Besides, I'm getting off early tomorrow to pack and fly to DC tomorrow evening for Cheyenne's surprise birthday party."

"Cancel your flight. You can fly with me on my jet. I'm leaving tomorrow as well."

"What time?"

"Whenever you're ready to go. My time is your time."

"Thanks." She uncovered her dishes and smiled. "This looks delicious," she said of the steak and potatoes on her plate.

"It is. I've had it before and the chef here is pretty good. I believe you will enjoy it."

She did. Over dinner she told him how excited her staff was about his sponsorship and how a special assembly was scheduled tomorrow morning where it would be announced that the venue for the play would be the theater instead of the high school's auditorium.

"I can't wait to see the student's faces." She reached across the table and squeezed his hand. "Thank you."

He smiled at her. "I was happy to do it." He glanced at both their empty plates. "Are you ready for our talk now?"

She nodded. "Yes, I'm ready."

Not wanting Nadia too far away from him, Jaxon gathered her into his arms, carried her over to the sofa and sat down with her in his lap. "Now tell me what we need to talk about, sweetheart."

It took her a minute to speak, and he figured she was collecting her thoughts. That had to be the reason she was looking down while fidgeting with the buttons on her robe. Finally, she said, "His name was Benson Cummings. I met him at the University of Wyoming the second week of class. I immediately liked him since he seemed like a nice guy. It only took me five months to find out what a total ass he was when it was discovered he was keeping a journal of all the freshmen girls he'd slept with or planned to sleep with. I was on his to-do list. Not only that, he had the date by my name and his friends were going to video us doing it." She paused. "I was hurt since I honestly thought he liked me as much as I'd liked him. I had fallen hard for him, Jaxon."

"So what did you do about it?" he asked her when she got silent, looking back down at the buttons on her robe. He was fighting back the anger he felt for what the guy had done and had planned to do.

She lifted her head to gaze into his eyes. "What do you mean what did I do about it?"

Jaxon fought back a smile. Those innocent-looking eyes staring into his weren't fooling him any. She was a renegade, a rebel and a hellion. She would not have let that Cummings guy get away with anything. "Just what I asked, Nadia. What did you do about it?"

She went back to fidgeting with the buttons again. Clearing her throat she said, "Well, there was that time we emptied twenty-five bottles of chocolate syrup into his car and then dumped several bags of live ants in there as well."

Jaxon's eyes widened. "Who were 'we' and where did you get bags of live ants?"

She looked back up at him and smiled. "We, meaning me, Rissa and Lilli. And as for the live ants, it just so happens that one of the agricultural labs on campus was working on several ant farms. We got them from there." Nadia paused and said, "Then there was that other incident."

"What other incident?"

"The one that got him expelled from school."

Jaxon was almost too afraid to ask what Nadia had done to make that happen. "Tell me about it."

"We found out he was sneaking girls from another campus into his dorm room for pot parties. The kind that ended up being orgies. The security guy on campus got an anonymous tip about it and Benson, his roommates and several others were caught red-handed. All naked as the day they were born."

"I guess you were the one who provided the anonymous tip."

"Of course." She laughed and he couldn't help but laugh as well.

"Cummings never traced his misfortunes back to you?"

"Nope. I played the innocent. Besides, he had over twenty girls' names on that list. It could have been any of us out for revenge."

But it was you, he thought. Good for her. "And because of him you were cautious about getting serious about any guy again?"

"Yes. But years passed and when I moved back to Gamble, I decided to have an open mind. Especially with so many good-looking cowboys around here. The first one I met was Hoyle Adams. Like Benson, he seemed nice enough. He asked me out to the movies, and I enjoyed myself. He seemed to be a perfect gentleman. So I invited him to dinner one evening."

"And?"

She frowned. "And he thought the dinner invitation was really a sleepover. Imagine my shock when he went out to his truck for his overnight bag while I was in the kitchen getting dessert. He honestly thought he was spending the night. I tossed him and his overnight bag out the door."

He fought back a grin. "No wonder you went off on me that night I asked about inviting a cowboy to dinner."

"Yes, that was the reason." She got quiet and then said, "Just so you know, Jaxon, I was attracted to you from the first. But I thought it was one sided since you weren't paying me any attention. I didn't want to make a fool of myself so I deliberately avoided you."

"Like I told you, I was trying to play it safe by not showing my interest in you immediately. The last thing I wanted was one of my Outlaw cousins or the Westmorelands to challenge me to a fistfight for getting out of line with you."

She chuckled. "They would not have done that. If anything, they would have warned you away from me. They know how I can be at times."

"I take it you never told them about Cummings."

"There was no need. I handled it."

She most certainly had. "Is there anything else I need to know?"

She turned around to face him and wrapped her arms around his neck. "Nothing other than I meant what I said in bed. I love you. I fought it. I kept telling myself I couldn't love you because we didn't know each other. I even convinced myself it was just lust, but I was wrong."

"And when did you realize you were wrong and it was more than lust?"

"Tonight. The minute you opened the door. Seeing you again put a lot of things in perspective. I had missed you so much and it had only been five days. I wondered how I would handle it if it had been five weeks, five months or five years. That's when I knew I loved you, Jaxon."

"And I love you, sweetheart. And I meant what I told you that night. I intend to marry you one day. Granted, I hadn't planned to tell you about my plans that soon, but I felt I had to be honest with you. I didn't want you to think all I was interested in was sex."

She smiled. "It was hard to believe you were serious since most men run away from marriage."

"Not me. My parents set good examples for me to follow."

"Are you sure about me? I'm not a sophisticated or refined kind of woman."

"Trust me, you're the kind of woman I need, want and desire."

"And speaking of desire…" she whispered against his lips. "What will it take for you to give me one more steamy night?"

"All you have to do is ask."

"Well, I'm asking, Jaxon."

He stood with her in his arms and headed for the bedroom.

Nineteen

Nadia knew the moment her sisters Jill and Paige arrived at Cheyenne Steele Westmoreland's birthday party, which was being held in the nation's capital at the Saxon Hotel. The huge ballroom of the luxurious hotel was beautifully decorated with balloons and birthday streamers. Nadia had seen her sister Pam when she first arrived a short while ago.

To say Cheyenne had been surprised about the party was an understatement. Quade had told her they would be attending another joint fundraiser for his two senator cousins, Reggie Westmoreland and Jess Outlaw. She hadn't suspected a thing and the look on her face when she'd entered the ballroom to discover the party was in her honor was priceless.

Nadia thought it was good seeing so many Westmorelands and Outlaws together. If anyone found it odd that Jaxon was always by her side, they didn't mention it. However, several women in the family did give her curious looks. The men did not, and she thought that was rather strange.

She braced herself when she saw Jill and Paige make a beeline straight to her. None of her sisters had a clue about her and Jaxon. She hadn't had a chance to pull them aside to tell them anything yet.

After greeting everyone in the group standing around Nadia, Paige and Jill gave their sister a hug. "When did you arrive in town?" Paige asked.

"I got in early today." No need to tell her that her plans to arrive yesterday had been waylaid when instead of helping her pack like he claimed he would do, Jaxon had kept her on her back in bed. But then she'd kept him on his back a few times as well.

"That's why we couldn't reach you. You were probably in the air," Jill surmised.

"Probably. I caught a ride with Jaxon on his jet."

Both women shifted their gazes to Jaxon and smiled. "Thanks for getting her here. Does that mean you didn't bring a date?" Jill asked.

Jaxon lifted a brow. "A date?"

"Yes. We had suggested early in the week that Nadia catch a ride here with you, but she was worried you might be bringing a date and didn't want to impose," Paige said.

Jaxon smiled back. "Oh, I see. And to answer your question, yes, I brought a date. In fact, I brought the woman I intend to marry as soon as she's ready to tell me yes."

Nadia noticed several people around them had their eyes and ears on Jaxon and she knew why. He'd never mentioned being in a serious relationship with anyone. "Really?" Paige said, smiling brightly.

Jill's and Paige's gazes searched the group surrounding them before glancing around the room. They then turned their gazes back to Jaxon. "Where is she? We can't wait to meet her," Jill said.

A huge smile spread across Jaxon's lips. "She's standing right in front of you." He wrapped his arm around Nadia's waist before leaning in to brush a kiss on her lips.

"What! When! How!" Her sisters' squeals of excitement caused others to look their way. Then others came over to join them to hear the details.

"Don't tell me you and Jaxon pulled a secret affair like me and Aidan," Jill said, grinning from ear to ear.

Nadia chuckled as she leaned back against Jaxon. "There was nothing secret about us, trust me. None of you were in Gamble to get into our business."

Paige was about to make a comment when suddenly Clint Westmoreland, who was standing in the group, exclaimed, "Who the hell is that guy that just walked in?"

Everyone turned toward the entrance of the ballroom. It was Chance Steele, one of Cheyenne's cousins, who answered, "That's Dominic's best friend, Matt Caulder. They were raised together as brothers. Do you know him?"

Before Clint could answer, his brother Cole and his sister Casey, along with their spouses, walked up. Nadia noticed that the same shocked look that was on Clint's face was on his siblings'. His sister Casey asked Clint in a deep, emotional voice. "Do you see that guy's face, Clint?"

"Yes, I see it."

Now everyone was curious as to what was going on. Nadia studied the guy who seemed to be in his midforties and who she thought was very handsome and distinguished looking.

"Hey, while you're all interested in the guy, I want to know about the young woman with him," Alisdare Westmoreland said. "Is that his wife, girlfriend, sister or daughter?" Nadia could only assume Alisdare, who at twenty-nine was single and worked as a FBI agent, was hoping it was one of the latter two.

"The young lady with Matt is his daughter," Sebastian Steele, another one of Cheyenne's cousins, said. He turned to Clint. "Why the interest in Matt? What's wrong with his face?"

Clint glanced over at him and said, "Nothing, other than it's the spitting image of our Uncle Sid, and we want to know why."

It was after midnight when Jaxon opened his hotel room door and stepped aside to let Nadia enter. Thanks to Dominic everyone attending Cheyenne's birthday party was given complimentary accommodations. Jaxon had upgraded to one of the larger suites on the other side of the hotel for privacy.

A lot of celebrating had been going on, not just for Cheyenne's birthday but once news got around that the Westmoreland triplets—Clint, Cole and Casey—had found their long-lost cousin, the son of Sid Roberts, the legendary rodeo star and renowned horse trainer. Matt Caulder had never known the identity of his biological father, but that night he learned that Sid had hired someone to find him, and they'd looked for him for years, but they never found him. Everyone was excited when the triplets' father, Corey Westmoreland, had welcomed Matt to the Westmoreland family as an honorary member. In a shocking move, Bart Outlaw had done the same.

Jaxon was glad that since accepting his relationship to the Westmorelands, Bart was doing a better job of connecting. Jaxon's Outlaw cousins thought Bart's marriage to Claudia had a lot to do with it and Jaxon would agree. Bart could still be his ornery self at times but these days he was more hospitable and sociable. Jaxon's parents had even invited Bart and Claudia to Virginia over the summer, so his mother could visit with her cousin Bart. The two couples got along wonderfully.

"It was a great party, wasn't it?"

Nadia's words cut into Jaxon's thoughts as he leaned against the closed hotel room door and watched as she kicked off her stilettos. She had worn a short and sexy dress that showed what a great pair of legs she had. "Yes, it was. There were quite a number of revelations tonight. The one that really took me by surprise was Quade and Cheyenne's announcement that they're having another baby," Nadia said. "Their triplets are in their early teens. But they'd always said they wanted other kids. It will be funny if they have another set of triplets like Bane and Crystal."

"Well, according to Quade they aren't worried about it. If it happens, it happens," Jaxon said, moving away from the door. "And what do you think of Quade's father James's announcement that he's located more Westmorelands?"

Nadia chuckled. "From the cheers that went up around the ballroom, I think everyone was happy and excited about it. James is considered the genealogist in the family. I understand he's been on the trail of those particular Westmorelands for a while. Ever since it was reported in a national newspaper some years back that the wife of some man with the last name Westmoreland had given birth to quadruplets."

Jaxon smiled as he came to stand in front of her. "I'm sure that was the first clue there might be a connection."

"What?"

"Multiple births. It seems such a thing runs rampant with the Westmorelands and Outlaws."

Nadia threw her head back and laughed. "You noticed?"

"Can't help but notice. I think Adrian and Aidan get a kick out of fooling me every time. I still can't tell them apart."

She reached up and wrapped her arms around his neck. "Maybe one day I'll let you in on the secret as to how to do that."

He leaned in and nibbled around her lips. "Promise?"

"Um, yes. A number of people were surprised to discover we're together. Mostly the ladies. The men, however, didn't seem surprised. Would you care to explain that?"

He leaned back and stared down at her. "They weren't surprised because they knew I intended to marry you."

She lifted a brow. "And just how did they know that?"

"I told them when we were together at the poker tournament in Westmoreland Country."

"That was in August. Three months ago."

"I know," he said, smiling. "I knew from the first that you were the woman for me. Am I the man for you, Nadia?"

She lifted up on tiptoes to brush her lips across his and whispered, "Yes, Jaxon, you are definitely the man for me."

"Good." He then swept her into his arms and carried her to the bedroom. He placed her on her feet beside the bed. Stepping back, he reached for the duffel bag he'd placed there earlier and retrieved a small white box. Kneeling on one knee in front of her, he said, "If you believe that then will you marry me? Will you share my life, my name and my babies as my wife?"

Tears filled her eyes as she nodded and said, "Yes!"

Jaxon slid his ring on her finger, stood and pulled her into his arms. "You have made me a happy man, and just so you know, my parents knew about my intentions as well. I talked to them earlier and they want you to know they are excited to welcome you to the family."

"Oh, Jaxon," she said, wiping away the tears that had appeared in her eyes as she gazed down at her ring. "It's beautiful. I'm so happy."

"So am I, sweetheart. So am I."

He then leaned in and captured her mouth in his.

Epilogue

Nadia's heart nearly stopped when saw Jaxon standing beneath the beautifully decorated gazebo that overlooked Gemma Lake. It was a beautiful day in June and it was her wedding day. Jaxon had wanted a Christmas wedding, but she had talked him out of that. So much was already on her plate with the holiday play, and she wouldn't have time to plan the type of wedding she'd always wanted. Besides, she'd always wanted a June wedding.

For the time being, he had moved into the house on the Novak Homestead with her. He'd been kept busy with getting everything set up for the expansion of Ravnel Technologies into Gamble. The weekend following Cheyenne's birthday party, he had flown Nadia to his home in Virginia. She had fallen in love with his ranch immediately and couldn't wait to move there after they married. His parents had been awesome and were happy for them. She knew she was blessed to be getting such wonderful in-laws.

She glanced around at all the people in attendance—family, friends and some of Jaxon's business associates. Alpha,

Riley's wife, was the event planner in the Westmoreland family. Everything was beautifully decorated in colors of pink and black. Her sisters and the women in the family thought Nadia had gone loco when she told them of her decision to break from tradition and wear a black wedding dress instead of a white one.

The one person who thought it was a great idea was Jaxon's mother. She had worn black on her wedding day and offered Nadia her wedding dress to wear. It was beautiful and the moment Nadia had tried it on she thought it embodied elegance. Made of intricate floral lace appliqués and embellished with over five thousand beads and sequins. She especially loved the illusion plunge bodice and lace-trimmed keyhole back. The soft, sweeping skirt had a double slit that would swish with her every step.

Once she'd explained to them a black wedding dress symbolized the bride's undying love and commitment to her husband until death do them part, they understood. And when they saw her in it for the first time, they cried. Now seeing how Jaxon was staring at her let her know she'd made the right decision because he knew what wearing the black wedding dress meant.

"You're ready, Nadia?"

She glanced over at the man who would be walking her down the aisle and smiled. "Yes, Dillon. I'm ready." And she was. She loved Jaxon and was looking forward to sharing the rest of her life with him. She smiled as she strolled closer to him then looked over at her twenty bridesmaids, who were pretty in their beautiful pink gowns. Pam was her matron of honor and Jaxon's father was his best man. The groomsmen wore black tuxes with pink shirts and black bow ties.

Anyone who hadn't known of Nadia's plans to wear a black wedding dress were first sending choruses of "What?" around the room. And then those choruses were replaced with oohs and ahhs… She glanced at her mother-in-law, who winked at her, and she winked back. Her mother-in-law was silently telling her she looked beautiful. Nadia felt beautiful.

When they reached Jaxon and the minister asked who was giving her away, Dillon spoke up and then placed her hand in Jaxon's. Nadia leaned over to kiss Dillon's cheek and said, "Thanks for everything and thanks for marrying Pammie and making us a part of your family."

She then turned to Jaxon and smiled. Just like her wedding dress signified, he was the man she would love for the rest of her life.

"And where are you taking me, Jaxon?" Nadia asked as he held her hand.

"To my barn."

He glanced down at his wife of less than twenty-four hours. After the wedding and reception, instead of flying straight to the Maldives, where they would spend a two-week honeymoon, he had flown her to his ranch, where he wanted to present her with her wedding gift.

They had changed out of their wedding attire and were both wearing jeans. He doubted she would ever know how he felt the moment he'd seen her on Dillon's arm. Just knowing he was married to the beautiful woman by his side filled his heart with joy.

"Did I tell you how beautiful you looked in your wedding dress, Nadia?"

She smiled up at him. "Yes, but I'll never get tired of your compliments, so keep them coming."

He threw his head back and laughed. Both the wedding and reception, which had been attended by over three hundred people, had gone off beautifully. "What's up with Sloan's best friend Redford St. James and Leslie's best friend, Carmen Golan?" Jaxon asked.

Nadia chuckled. "So you noticed? Well, Carmen let it be known at Sloan and Leslie's wedding a few years ago that she's going to be the woman who ends Redford's womanizing ways. Redford doesn't intend for that to happen since he loves his life just the way it is. Usually, he tries to avoid Carmen, but it seems there was no such luck at our wedding."

"He might be avoiding her, but I denote some interest on his part," Jaxon said.

"Yes, but it's I-want-to-bed-you interest and not I-want-to-wed-you interest. The latter is what Carmen wants."

They stepped into his huge barn and when Nadia saw what he intended for her to see, she released a loud squeal. "Cocoa!"

She then raced over toward the horse. By the time Jaxon joined her she looked at him with tears in her eyes. "How did you find him? Cocoa was sold sixteen years ago," she said, hugging the huge stallion. It was obvious the horse remembered her as well.

"It wasn't easy. Luckily Pam knew the people he was sold to. Zane was able to track him down for me. Over the past sixteen years he's had four owners and each one used him as a stud horse. Zane was able to locate his present owner, a rancher in North Dakota. He didn't want to part with him until he saw how much I was willing to pay. And seeing the look on your face just now made buying him back worth it."

"Thanks so much. I want to go riding."

"You will but not with him, with me."

He knew the moment she'd figured out what he meant. Releasing the horse, she turned and wrapped her arms around his neck. "That can be arranged. When do we leave for the Maldives?"

"Anytime after breakfast in the morning."

Nadia's smile widened. "In that case, I want a wedding

night we will always remember. And I have no problem doing the riding."

Jaxon grinned. "Tonight, we will both ride. I plan to make our wedding night as steamy as hell."

When he swept her into his arms, she said, "Another steamy night is just what I need."

He then carried her out of the barn toward their home.

* * * * *

TEMPTED BY THE BOLLYWOOD STAR

SOPHIA SINGH SASSON

This book is dedicated to all those who feel that love will never happen for them. It will. Keep your heart open.

Thank you to the awesome Mills & Boon Desire Editorial team, in particular Stephanie Doig.

It's lonely being an author but the amazing community of South Asian romance writers always keeps me going.

Last and most important, I wouldn't be an author without the love and support of my family.

One

"If you tell me there are more script changes from the Bollywood prima donna, I'm going to scream."

Gail dropped a bulging manila folder on Mia's pristine desk and sank into a chair. She was wearing her standard outfit of dark cargo pants, a black tank top and silver hoop earrings that were too large for her delicate face. Her jet-black hair was scraped into a ponytail.

"She couldn't even send them electronically?" Mia picked up the envelope, weighing its heft.

"Saira worked on them during the eighteen-hour flight from Mumbai. Using a laptop on the plane gives her a headache."

"How are you able to say that with a straight face?" Mia rolled her eyes at Gail and tore open the envelope. She fanned the pages, the sight of the familiar, perfectly formed, handwritten letters making her stomach flutter. *I had this tutor in India who made me practice my cur-*

sive for hours until I got it right. It had been ten years since she and Saira had spent that month in Fiji. Ten years in which she'd finally moved on with her life. Mia almost hadn't taken this dream job because of Saira, but then she'd reminded herself that she had a reputation for being able to work with the angriest producers and the most narcissistic actors and actresses. Surely, she could handle Saira Sethi.

Mia threw the packet of papers on the desk, rattling the keyboard and mouse. "Shooting for *Life with Meera* begins in two days. The entire writers' room is ready to go on strike if I give them any more changes."

"We're not required to take her suggestions. Her contract gives her very limited powers, which she's grossly overstepping," Gail said carefully.

That's Saira. You give her an inch and she takes a mile.

"Want me to take the hit this round?"

Mia smiled gratefully at Gail. They'd met at the studio on the first day of their internship and compared notes on how many decaf soy lattes and no foam cappuccinos they'd fetched. In a city where relationships only lasted until the next job, they'd somehow managed to be friends for fifteen years. But even Gail didn't know about her history with Saira.

She stood and paced in her ten-by-ten office. The walls were covered with pictures and awards belonging to the previous director, Peter Denton. The carpet reeked of the cigarettes that he wasn't supposed to smoke inside. Mia stared at a picture of Peter holding an armful of Emmy awards. He held the record for the most Emmy nominations for outstanding producer and the most wins. In film school, Mia thought the key ingredient to success was talent, but she was wrong. It was opportunity. Shows succeeded when they had the budget to hire the best writers, stars and staff. Once a studio invested in producing the show, they spent money on marketing. Show popularity attracted better talent, and the cycle repeated. *Life with Meera* was Mia's opportunity.

Peter Denton had had to leave the show suddenly after his wife got sick. Mia had met Peter's wife at a party once; she was a kind woman and Mia sincerely hoped she recovered. But it was Peter's departure that had created this opportunity for Mia. The studio execs had finally noticed her and had given her a chance. It was her first big-budget show, and if the first ten episodes were a success, it would launch Mia's career.

Mia turned to face Gail. "I have to deal with Saira. When is she due in studio?" Mia had put it off as long as she could, but it was time to face her past, present and possibly her future. *Life with Meera* centered on a South Asian female lead, and the success of the show hinged on Saira's performance. She was the star. That gave Saira a lot of power, but Mia wasn't going to let Saira ruin her big chance.

"She's been here all morning—met with the studio execs, did the rounds."

Saira hadn't come to see Mia. At least she wasn't the only one avoiding their meeting.

Gail tapped on her phone. "Speak of the devil. She's in wardrobe, and Jessica says there's a problem."

Mia took a breath. Peter had let Saira run roughshod

over him. They were already behind schedule and over budget because of all the changes she'd requested. It was time to show her former lover that the new boss wasn't going to tolerate her diva behavior.

"There's really no reason to call the producer." Saira's stomach flipped at the thought of seeing Mia. She'd been mentally preparing all day, but she wasn't ready yet.

The costume designer, Jasmine, was frantically tapping on her iPad.

"Listen, it's not a big deal. We can choose a neutral color like black." Saira began to unravel the fuchsia pink saree she'd been trying on but was intercepted by a wispy man with a pincushion in his mouth.

"I need to mark the hemlines," he muttered.

Jasmine shook her head. She was tall, broad shouldered with salt-and-pepper hair and lips that disappeared when she scrunched her face, as she was doing now. "Mia said no changes without her approval. The set designer planned around these wardrobe colors."

Saira stared at the full-length mirror. The costume room was much smaller than she was used to and felt claustrophobic, with racks of clothes and bolts of fabric cluttering the space. She had no idea what pincushion man was doing, marking hemlines on a saree. Didn't he know that she could just tuck the excess fabric and adjust it any way they needed?

"I'm not asking to change the whole saree, just the blouse." She pointed to the crop top, hating the sudden high pitch in her voice. She didn't want to sound difficult on her first day, but everything had to be right. A lot was riding on this project, her one shot at transferring her Mumbai stardom to LA. It had taken her five years to find the right show; she'd been patient, waited for the project that would give her the wide visibility she needed. But she'd made a mistake. Once she saw the final script, she realized that the network was making the same tired, clichéd show American networks had made countless times before. The script had the same stereotypical non-sense that previous shows proliferated, the kind of stuff that had ruined her sister's life. Saira wasn't going to let that happen. Even if it meant going to war with everyone on the show, including Mia.

The mere thought of Mia sent a jumble of emotions twisting and churning inside her chest. Could she handle working with Mia? Being in such close proximity to the one person who had once meant everything to her? They hadn't spoken in ten long years. Did Mia remember any of the passion that had consumed them both, or was Saira a distant memory for her?

It doesn't matter how Mia feels. Saira steeled herself. She couldn't afford to be distracted by thoughts of Mia. All of her focus and energy had to be on making the show a success. The past was just that, and she needed to bury it once and for all if she had any hope of unlocking the future she wanted. It didn't matter that her heart had been racing all day at the thought of seeing Mia. Saira had to keep things professional and not let her feelings for Mia affect the show. Could she hide her feelings from Mia? She lifted her chin in the mirror. Saira had been acting all her life. Her first memory from childhood was hiding under the couch from her parents. It hadn't been until a few years ago that she realized the memory was from one of her movies. Putting on an act for Mia shouldn't be too difficult.

Mia's image filled the mirror and Saira froze. Their eyes met in the reflection. Saira followed all of Mia's social media accounts using an alias. She'd seen pictures of Mia, had been prepared for the sight of her. Or at least she'd thought so.

"How is it possible that you haven't aged in all this time?" Saira turned, keeping her voice light. Mia was wearing skinny jeans and an untucked T-shirt with the name of the studio emblazoned across her chest. Her blondish brown hair was loosely tied into a messy bun. She'd never worn much makeup, but Saira didn't miss the fresh touch of pale pink gloss on her lips and the swipe of brown mascara that brought out the green tones of her hazel eyes.

Mia turned to the costume designer. "Jessica, are you finished with Saira?"

Saira's back was turned to Jessica but she was pretty sure that the woman was making faces. There was a slight twitch in the very corner of Mia's lips; she was trying to keep a straight face. Saira could almost feel the softness of that corner beneath her own lips.

"We need to discuss Saira's request on this outfit. It's for the first day of shooting, I don't have time to make these changes." Jessica stepped toward Mia, iPad in hand, her fingers dancing on the screen.

Mia cut her eyes to Saira. "What's the problem with the saree?"

Mia's tone was cold and all business. Saira's heart

shrank. What did she expect after all this time? For Mia to throw everyone out of the room, embrace her and tell her how much she missed her? This wasn't a scene out of some romantic movie, and they weren't exactly long-lost lovers reuniting.

She took a steadying breath. "The blouse is the same fabric as the saree. It's too matchy-matchy. My character, Meera, is a stylish, young, Indian woman. No one like that would be caught dead in this old-fashioned style. You can replace it with a plain black blouse that won't take much time to make." If her tailor from India was here, he could do it in less than an hour.

Mia's mouth set into a straight line. "It's a fair point, but Jessica is on a tight schedule. We need to let it go for this episode, but she can go over the rest of the costume designs with you and we'll try to incorporate your suggestions in any of the outfits that haven't been completed yet." Without waiting for a response, Mia turned toward Jessica, issuing her directions.

Just like that, Saira had been dismissed. She gathered the silky material of the saree into her fists. *Deep breaths.* Arguing with Mia in front of her staff would just make her more confrontational. She needed to get Mia alone.

As Mia huddled with Jessica, pincushion man turned toward her. "Could you take this off now? I need to finish ironing it before I go for the day."

She gave him a tight smile. *This sure isn't Mumbai.* She was used to an army of assistants itching to please her. If anything, she longed for an empty dressing room, a break from the enthusiastic smiles and eager offers of assistance. One of the first things Mia had done as producer was cut her budget to bring staff from India. Saira hadn't argued because she wanted a break from the constant army that hovered over her. But now, as she watched pincushion man try to unwrap the five yards of saree fabric, she regretted her decision.

Saira was used to being scantily dressed in front of people. It was a necessity on set, but she suddenly felt conscious of Mia in the room. After taking off the petticoat, the long skirt worn underneath a saree, and the crop top blouse, she was left in a lacy black bra and matching panties. Pincushion man yelled for a robe. Feeling awkward, she pretended to study her forehead. Her agent had been encouraging her to get Botox before the wrinkles deepened but Saira had resisted. She'd seen too many of her fellow actresses get seduced by the promise of procedures and injections only to end up looking like puffedup versions of their former selves. Five more years, that's all she needed her body and skin to give her; less if those years were in Hollywood and she earned in US dollars. Then she could finally be free to live the life she wanted.

She caught Mia's eyes in the mirror and held her gaze. Her pulse kicked at the unmistakable appreciation that was written all over Mia's face. Black lace used to be Mia's favorite. Mia walked to one of the racks, grabbed a blue silk robe and threw it at Saira.

Saira shrugged on the robe, watching with satisfaction as Mia's eyes darkened before she looked away. Turning around slowly, Saira smiled. "Is this a good time for us to talk? In private?" She looked pointedly at Jessica. Pincushion man was already walking out, nearly tripping over the trailing length of saree he hadn't managed to fold.

Mia shook her head, but Jessica was already making her way to the door with ill-disguised relief.

"Please close the door," Saira yelled, her eyes never leaving Mia.

She stepped toward Mia. "Listen, while we are alone, I want to clear the air." She swallowed. "About us…"

Mia stepped back, her eyes flashing. "There is nothing to clear. What happened between us was a long time ago. I've moved on with my life, and I know you have too."

Moved on? Saira had scoured Mia's social media accounts. There were plenty of pictures with friends, but none that looked like a girlfriend.

"I tried to call, email, text, even tried to reach you on social media after Fiji."

"You made your feelings very clear when you said goodbye."

Mia turned away, clearly bolting for the door. Saira's chest tightened. She was used to a laughing, carefree Mia, who could warm her heart just by looking at her. Had ten years changed her so much, or was it that Mia hated Saira? "I want to explain what happened that day in Fiji…"

Mia whirled, facing Saira. Her eyes blazed an emerald green. "You don't need to explain. Either you were lying to me when we were together, or you were lying when you broke up with me. The distinction doesn't matter to me."

The ice in Mia's voice made Saira go cold. They had to make peace, the tension between them wasn't good for the show. Saira had to make it right.

"It does matter." She stepped close to Mia and placed a hand on her arm. The warmth of Mia's soft skin, the shine in her eyes made Saira's heart flutter uncontrollably. She'd waited ten years to say these words. "I hate the way I left things between us in Fiji. The things I said…"

Mia moved Saira's hand away with such gentleness that her chest tightened.

"I don't care about the past. There's only one thing that matters, and that's making this show a success. Other than that, we don't have anything to discuss."

The words stung. But what really hurt was the pity in Mia's voice. Saira hadn't really expected Mia to welcome her with open arms. She'd been ready for anger, even hatred—but not the look of sympathy that was in Mia's eyes.

Saira stepped back, her throat so tight she wasn't sure she'd be able to speak. "I am sorry, Mia," she managed to choke out.

Mia took a deep breath. "If you're sorry, then forget what happened ten years ago and work with me on making this show a success." Mia gave her a steely look. "I received the script edits that you sent. I know there's some leeway in your contract to provide input, but the read-through is tomorrow and shooting starts the day after. It's simply too late to…"

Saira interrupted her, her voice cracking with emotion. "Mia, please, this show is important to me and—"

Mia cut her off, her tone icy. "Great. Then stop sabotaging it. Every time you want to change something, the script, the costume, the set, it costs us time and money."

Saira crossed her arms. She didn't know what was

harder to take, the accusation that she was somehow purposely making things difficult, or the fact that Mia believed Saira would behave this way. Mia might be angry with her, but surely she had reviewed Saira's changes and could see what she was trying to accomplish.

"Have you looked at the changes I'm requesting? I've studied every South Asian show Hollywood has produced and they're mediocre at best. This show has to be different, and the way we do that is to…"

"Oh, of course you know better than all of us what's best for the show."

Saira's nails dug into her clenched fists as she struggled to keep her emotions in check. She could handle anger, even pain; what she couldn't quite reconcile was that the once warm and supportive woman she knew was now acting like every other know-it-all producer she'd ever worked with.

"I've been in the film industry for thirty years. I've done nine TV shows, thirty-seven movies, and I don't know how many guest appearances. Show me someone on your team who has more experience than I do."

"No one disputes that you're a great actress. That's why you're here. But acting is not the same as…."

Saira put her hand, palm out, toward Mia. If Mia was going to treat her like any other actress, then Saira was going to treat her like just another producer. "There's no reason to debate here. I believe my contract allows for final approval on all dialogue and mannerisms that relate to Indian culture."

Mia crossed her arms. "It's too late to make the changes."

"Then I suggest you consult your lawyer. I don't believe the contract specifies a timeline. You know as well as I do that scripts, costumes, sets…everything can be changed." She gave Mia a thin-lipped smile. Her bitch smile. If Mia wanted their relationship to be professional, then that's what she would get.

Mia narrowed her eyes "You're right. Everything can be changed. Including the heroine." She turned and opened the door. Just as she stepped out, Mia turned. "By the way, your husband called. He said he'll be here to support you on the first day of shooting."

Two

Mia slammed her door and stood against it, breathing deeply. Her heart thundered in her chest and she wiped her damp hands on her pants. Damn Saira! Mia thought she'd been prepared to see her, to deal with her, to stand up to her, but one look at that woman and Mia's stomach had turned to Jell-O. All she'd been able to think about was the feel of Saira's silky skin against hers, the way her mouth felt on her lips, the warmth of her breath on her core.

She slid to the floor, hugged her knees to her chest and buried her face in her arms. *What is wrong with me?* It's not as if Mia had been alone all this time. She'd been with several partners. Beautiful women, available women, women who were comfortable being openly lesbian. She had no problem meeting people. The TV and film industry was a constant churn of writers, artists, interns, set workers and on and on. There wasn't a day that went by where she didn't have the opportunity to ask someone out, or get asked out. There was no reason to want Saira.

Twelve weeks. She just had to get through the filming. Peter would be back before the next season, and if the show was a success, Mia could have her pick of producer jobs. She'd make sure she never had to work with Saira again.

A sudden knock on the door made her jump up. Before she could even take a step, the knob turned and the door began to open. Mia quickly sidestepped to avoid being hit.

"What is it?" she snapped, still a bit rattled by the unexpected interruption.

"Sorry!" Gail stuck her head around the door. "You're supposed to be meeting with Chris to go over the budget. You can't be late—you only have fifteen minutes with him."

Mia looked at her wristwatch and cursed. She hurried to the desk and picked up her laptop. Chris was an insufferable network executive who controlled the purse strings on the TV series. He kept sending Mia red envelope emails regarding show expenses, then ignored her reply questions. It had taken Gail begging, coercing, then finally bribing his assistant to get this meeting.

Mia nearly ran to the elevators, stabbing the buttons in frustration. There were eight elevators in the bank, and the electronic dashboard showed that none of them was close to her floor. Chris's office was thirty stories up. Even if Mia raced up, she'd never get there in time. At last a door dinged open and she exited onto the sixty-sixth floor. Mia had never been to this floor before, but she wasn't surprised to see that, unlike the commercial white square tile and gray carpet on her floor, the executive floor had hardwood floors with marble inlays, modern area rugs and polished leather couches and chairs in the waiting areas. The receptionist checked her ID and then pointedly looked at her watch. "You're two minutes late. You will have twelve minutes with him."

"Thirteen." Mia said through gritted teeth.

"It'll take you a minute to get to his office."

Mia tightened her grip on the laptop. "Can you let me in so I don't lose any more time?"

The receptionist took her time buzzing Mia into the inner chamber, which was separated from the outer waiting room by a glass wall. Another assistant greeted her with thin lips and pointed her to a slightly ajar door.

Mia hurried to the door, then froze. She'd recognize Saira's fake laugh anywhere. The first time Mia had heard it was when a fan had recognized Saira in Fiji. Saira had pretended that she was *oh so happy* that the fan wanted an autograph and not at all concerned when she asked to take a selfie with Saira and Mia. *This is my childhood friend. She's just like a sister to me.* That was the first time alarm bells had gone off in Mia's head. *And those alarm bells are still clanking.*

"You must be Mia."

Chris O'Toole was the stereotypical network executive. Average height, expensive suit that couldn't hide the middle-age bulge in his waistline, male pattern baldness that he clearly thought he had covered with a state of the art hair plug transplant. His voice was slightly nasal and immediately grated on Mia.

She stuck out her hand and mustered a friendly smile. "It's nice to finally meet you in person."

"Do you need a few more minutes before our budget meeting?" Mia looked pointedly at Saira and immediately wished she hadn't. Saira had changed out of the robe that she'd seen her in less than an hour ago. She was wearing a silky pearl white blouse with several top buttons open. Mia could practically see the drool from Chris's chin in the tantalizing dip of her cleavage.

Chris waved his hand dismissively. "The budget crisis is solved." He gestured for Mia to sit on the couch across from Saira. Chris's office was a spacious and stylishly designed room, big enough to fit most of Mia's apartment without much trouble. An L-shaped desk dominated one corner, with two sleek white monitors sitting atop it. The wall opposite the desk was made entirely of floor-to-ceiling windows, offering a breathtaking view of the distant mountain landscape. In another area of the room, a large conference table was surrounded by leather chairs that were far more comfortable than Mia's own desk chair. Currently, they were all seated in the living room portion of the office, a carafe of coffee and mugs bearing the network logo resting on the table between them. The air was filled with the invigorating scent of coffee and the warm aroma of whiskey.

"Saira has saved the day."

What has she done now?

Mia didn't dare look at Saira. She knew her gaze would wander down her blouse and she needed to keep her focus on the meeting. Instead, she locked eyes with Chris and asked, "What did I miss?" Her tone was friendly and composed, but inside, she seethed. How dare Saira go behind her back?

"Saira has agreed to reduce her fee by 32 percent."

Yeah, right. How many arms and legs did she ask for in return?

"That's quite generous." She looked at Saira, who gave her one of her dazzling fake smiles. It was the one she gave the cameras, the adoring fans—a toothy grin that left people basking in her glow.

"I'm just as invested in the success of this show as the network is," Saira said, setting the coffee mug on the table. "This way, there is room in the budget to make the changes that'll make the show better."

And there it is.

"Exactly what changes are we talking?" Mia shot Chris a look but his gaze was plastered on Saira. Or more accurately, the curve of Saira's breast that peeked through the V opening of her blouse every time she moved.

"Little things here and there." Saira's voice was sugar sweet. She met Mia's gaze. "Like the color of the saree blouse and the dialogue changes I requested."

"All those little things add up to personnel time and production delays." Mia couldn't keep the irritation out of her voice.

Saira narrowed her eyes. "Those little things can make the difference between the show trending in the top ten in online streaming or barely hitting six figures in viewership."

"Right you are," Chris said. "It is the little things that determine whether a show is good, or if it's great."

Mia bit the inside of her cheek to keep from reminding Chris that he was a financial weenie who probably couldn't tell the difference between a producer and a director.

"Well, thank you, Saira. I'm sure you have a lot still to do, so we won't keep you here any longer."

Chris shook his head. "Oh, no rush, I can cancel my next meeting, and I don't think there's anything more I need to discuss with Mia that we can't take care of over email."

Mia clenched her jaw to keep from saying something she'd regret.

Saira stood. "Actually, I am still a little jet-lagged. I should get some rest before the big read-through tomorrow. I'll let you get on with your meeting." She shot Mia a smile, one of her genuine ones. *Is it my imagination or is there an apology in her eyes?*

Chris made a show of walking Saira to the door. When he leaned in for a hug or a kiss, Mia wasn't sure which, Saira deftly sidestepped and held out her hand for a shake. Not to be deterred, Chris took her hand and kissed it, holding it to his lips longer than comfortable for anyone. Mia nearly laughed when Saira wiped her hand on her skintight jeans.

Chris walked to his desk, completely ignoring Mia. Not to be discouraged, she took a seat in the guest chair and placed her laptop loudly on the desk. As Chris swiveled in his chair, tapping on his keyboard to wake up his computer, he asked in a distracted tone, "Do we have anything else to talk about?"

Mia took a deep breath before responding, "Are you changing Saira's contract?"

Chris nodded, a determined look on his face. "Of course. I want to lock down her fee reduction before she changes her mind."

Mia pressed further. "Did she request any other changes?"

"Just some minor wording changes," Chris replied nonchalantly.

Mia sighed. "Her changes are not that minor. We can't give her more control over the show."

Chris turned toward her, his expression hardening. "The show is already 21 percent over budget, and we both know unexpected expenses will come up during filming. Whatever Saira needs, find a way to make it work."

Mia opened her mouth to lay out all the ways in which Saira's salary discount would end up costing them in the long run, but the door opened and his assistant walked in.

"Good work, Mia, keep it up," Chris said dismissively.

"Can I at least review the contract changes?"

"Ms. Strome, you're already five minutes over your meeting time and his next meeting is waiting," the assistant said, her tone brusque. Mia felt a hand on her arm, but she shrugged it off and walked out. She didn't see the point in causing a scene. As a producer with little clout and even less experience handling people like Chris, she had to pick her battles. What she needed was to get a handle on Saira—that was a problem she knew how to solve.

She was looking up Saira's cell number on the call sheet to see if it was the same number she had stored in her phone—the number she hadn't quite brought herself to delete—but she needn't have bothered. Saira was in the waiting room chatting with Jason Brossart, one of the senior vice presidents. *Dammit.* That was the guy in charge of entertainment content. *What is Saira up to now?*

She stepped up to them.

"Speak of the devil," Saira said as Mia approached, and she braced herself. Had Saira complained to Jason? Unlike Chris, Jason had the power to remove her as producer. *Hell, he has the power to cancel the show and send us all home.*

Jason turned and put out his hand. "I don't think we've actually met, Mia. Saira was just telling me how wonderful you are to work with. Thank you for pinch-hitting for Peter." Mia shook his hand and she found herself liking him. His grip was firm but not hard. Unlike Chris, who exuded a smarmy quality, Jason had warmth.

"It was a pleasure meeting you both. I wish I could stay and chat, but I'm late for a meeting."

As he walked away, Mia turned to Saira. "Thanks for putting in a good word." She meant it. Jason had the power to make her career, and even if Saira considered it a throwaway comment, he'd remember her name when it came across his desk in the future.

Saira gave her a small smile. "Whatever differences we have regarding the show, I want the very best for you, and if I can do anything to make it happen, I will."

Mia's breath caught. Saira's eyes shone and a lump formed in Mia's throat. This was the side of Saira that Mia had fallen in love with—the Saira who instinctively understood her wants and needs, who took genuine pleasure in doing something for someone else. It was easy to forget that Saira was like a kaleidoscope with constantly changing facets and reflections, depending on which way Mia was looking. The overwhelming, disconcerting feeling of being in Saira's orbit came rushing back to her.

"I was wondering…"

"Do you think we could…"

They both spoke at once, but Saira gestured for Mia to continue. "We should talk," Mia said.

Saira nodded. "How about dinner tonight?"

Mia agreed. "That sounds great. Do you want to go to the hotel and freshen up first?"

Saira glanced at her wristwatch. "If I go back to my room, I'll flop onto the bed and fall asleep for the rest of the night. How about we order room service and catch up over dinner?"

Mia's cheeks flushed as the image of room service dinners in Fiji flooded her mind. At the time, Mia had thought all the room service orders were because they couldn't stop having sex long enough to go out. She later realized Saira didn't want to be seen in public with her. Still, the memory of those dinners had tormented her for years. Especially the way they had chosen to eat dessert.

Tempting, oh so tempting.

Three

Despite it only being five o clock, the Thai restaurant was full, and they ended up at a bar table, which was noisy and packed with people. Not a great ambience for a heart-to-heart but it would have to do. If this were Mumbai, Saira would've gotten the best table in the house. *There will come a time when a crowd of fans will greet me in LA too. As long as I keep my focus on this show.*

Saira had thought she was ready to face Mia, but the day had been far more excruciating than she'd anticipated. The last few hours had been a roller coaster of emotions, memories and regrets flooding her mind with a dizzying intensity. The anger in Mia's eyes was palpable, and it cut through Saira's heart like a knife. It was clear that Mia was so focused on maintaining a wall between them that she wasn't being reasonable about the script and costume changes. Saira had to make it right; she couldn't let the weight of her past mistakes ruin her future. She had to make Mia understand why she'd left the way she had.

They ordered drinks—a Diet Coke for Mia and a mojito for Saira. Mia was staring at the menu as if it was a legal contract she was about to sign.

"Don't even pretend you're not getting the pad-see-ew."

Mia looked up at her defiantly. "Actually, I was thinking of the shrimp pad thai."

"Since when do you eat seafood?"

"A lot of things have changed in the last ten years, including my tastes."

You haven't changed in the slightest bit. You just want me to think you have. "So tell me what's new with you. What have you been up to since we last saw each other."

Mia took a long sip from her supersized Diet Coke, the sound of the straw sucking up ice and soda amplifying the silent tension between them. "Ten years is a long time. There have been a lot of milestones in my life:—my first show as producer, one Emmy nomination for assistant producer...many, many, girlfriends."

Saira bit her tongue to keep from asking exactly how many.

"Anyone serious?"

"You know how it is, Saira—it's so easy to think you're in love in the moment but it's really not much more than relationship excitement."

Her chest tightened as Mia flung her own words back at her. Words she had carelessly chucked at Mia in Fiji. They were the words of a young woman who hadn't yet understood what love was.

"I didn't mean what I said back then," she said quietly.

"You meant it when you said it."

Saira shifted under Mia's unrelenting stare. *She's still so angry at me. How do I make her understand?*

"I was scared and confused. You were my first girl-friend...my parents didn't know I'm a lesbian. *I* didn't fully understand my sexuality...."

"And you're just as confused now as you were back then. You're married to a man, for goodness' sake. You married him, what, two days after you broke up with me?"

"It's not a real marriage!" As she caught a few people turning around to look at her, Saira lowered her voice. "Rahul and I are good friends. He did me a favor—after the pictures of you and me in Fiji, there was an uproar in India. There were death threats against me, against my family. People aren't very tolerant in India, and it was even worse ten years ago. *Six months* after I returned from Fiji, I needed to do something drastic to save my career, to protect my family. Marrying Rahul was the only way to calm the public outcry against me."

"Do you think it was easy for me to come out as a teen-ager? Do you think things weren't difficult here? I know it's not quite the same, but there is plenty of stigma and hate crimes here as well. I'm not saying it's easy, but it is a choice—no one is forcing you to live a lie."

Mia would never understand. She'd grown up in America, where the streets were safe and girls whose parents disowned them had choices other than prostitution or begging. If Mia was the one getting death threats, the police would protect her, not help the perpetrators. She would never understand what it was like to be in Saira's shoes. To live in a country where she could go from being a loved icon to a symbol of hate-filled protests.

Just one social media post with a picture from Fiji and a question as to whether she was "unnatural," and she'd spent weeks dealing with spray-painted doors and windows, being shunned by her friends and family and losing two lucrative movie contracts. She'd been physically attacked twice, only surviving thanks to some very expensive bodyguards. Had it not been for Rahul and their wedding announcement, she would've been killed for sure. There was no point in telling Mia all this. Saira had sent her countless emails explaining, pleading, begging for understanding. All unanswered.

Saira took a sip of her mojito, then pushed the glass away. It was too sweet and not minty enough. She locked eyes with Mia. "It was so easy for you to ask me to give up my life. But what if I'd asked you to do the same? What if I'd asked you to leave your Hollywood life and come to Bollywood with me?"

"It's not the same." Mia's expression was inscrutable. "You can have a career, a life here. I don't speak any of the Indian languages. I wouldn't be able to get a job and I'd stick out like a sore thumb being a white woman."

"None of that affects me because America is so welcoming of brown people," Saira said, bitterness creeping into her voice. No matter how much she romanticized their past, there was a reason it hadn't worked out. Saira had to deal with obstacles and expectations that Mia couldn't even begin to understand, yet Mia had expected her to give up everything without being willing to do the same in return.

Mia was back to studying the menu and Saira did the same. *What was I thinking?* Until this morning, she'd thought she could handle seeing Mia. She'd almost convinced herself that she'd idealized their month in Fiji, and that the years had dampened the intensity of her emotions. But now, sitting with Mia, Saira's heart pounded uncontrollably. Ten years ago they'd both been young and carefree, unencumbered by the grind of daily life and lost in the magic of their romance. Sometimes she pretended it had all been a beautiful dream. But now, in Mia's presence, it felt all too real.

Saira hoped that apologizing to Mia, explaining why she'd broken up with her in such a heartless way would ease the restlessness in her heart. That closure on their relationship would finally let her move on, focus on what was really important, securing her future. But Mia still got under her skin. Mia with her irritating habit of sucking down ice-cold drinks, Mia with her half smiles and hazel eyes that looked green in the light and brown in the dark. It wasn't closure that she needed. It was Mia.

The waitress finally made her way to their table, placing a fresh glass of Diet Coke in front of Mia.

"I'll have the pork pad-see-ew," Mia said, then gave her a small smile. "I still order that every time."

Saira's heart fluttered. The waitress looked at her expectantly, and she couldn't remember what she wanted to order. "I'll have the same, thank you." She handed the menu to the waitress.

Mia took a long draw from her drink. "Look, I know working together is going to be complicated, but I want to bury the hatchet. I don't want to talk about Fiji. I've worked very hard to forget about it. What do you need me to say so we can move on from that?"

I want you to tell me that you haven't stopped thinking about me in the last ten years, just as I haven't stopped

thinking about you. I want you to tell me that seeing me again is messing with your head, just as it is mine. I want you to tell me that you forgive me.

"You're right. We should put the past behind us and focus on the show." If Mia wanted to leave the past behind, Saira would do her best to follow suit. *It's for the best.* She couldn't spend the next twelve weeks pining for what could have been. She needed to focus on what should be—her work, her future.

Maybe, just maybe, if she threw herself into her work, she could forget about Mia and move on with her life.

Four

Mia hated table reads. The one for *Life with Meera* promised to be an extra level of torture. Normally a read through this late in the production stage was designed to sharpen or fine-tune the dialogue. Peter had said they'd had one several weeks ago with Saira on Zoom. She hadn't been able to fly over because of her filming schedule in India. This read through was just to get Saira comfortable with the rest of the actors—a formality.

They were set up in a conference room, eight tables organized in a hollow square. There were sixteen actors for the show, with only five that had major roles. Mia began rearranging the tent cards that Gail had placed just moments earlier.

"Now I'm going to have to move the scripts," Gail moaned.

"Saira needs to be in the middle of the crowd, not at the head of the table."

"You do know she's the star?" Gail said. "And that this is a hollow square. There isn't really a head of table."

Mia picked up Saira's tent card and put her in an off-center seat near the corner. "Trust me—no one will need reminding that she's the star."

It was the first time everyone on the show would get to see Mia in action. How she dealt with Saira would determine their on-set dynamic for the next twelve weeks.

"What is your history with her?"

Mia avoided Gail's gaze. Her friend had a way of being able to tell when Mia was lying. "It's not important. We ran into each other ten years ago, and let's just say that she didn't leave the best impression on me."

Mia felt a twinge of guilt not telling Gail the full story. It wasn't as if they didn't talk about their love lives.

"Is working with her going to be a problem?"

Mia lifted her eyes and met Gail's look of worry. "There will be no problem. I know how to handle Saira."

"What if she knows how to handle you?"

Mia turned away. How well did Saira know her? *About as well as you know her.* She finished moving the name cards and stepped back to survey the table. Saira knew the old Mia. The one whose heart was open, the one who used to believe in peace and love and happily ever after. That Mia was long gone.

"Did you hear about George Valencia?" Gail chatted as they rearranged the scripts.

Mia shook her head. There was too much la-la land gossip to keep up with. She could count on Gail to keep her posted with whatever was relevant.

Gail stopped what she was doing and faced Mia dramatically. "His wife outed him last night at the Netflix party."

"Excuse me?"

"Yeah, they've been married for like ten years, and Tracey said they're getting a divorce because he's gay."

Mia shook her head. Relationships were messy but she'd worked with George. He was a nice guy. He didn't deserve to be publicly humiliated.

"That's not really nice of her to out him."

"It's not an amicable divorce, and she says he's been a hypocrite. He outwardly supports LGBTQ rights but won't come out because he's afraid it'll affect his career."

"There's always an excuse. There are plenty of LGBTQ actors and actresses in LA. It's not even news when someone comes out anymore. Why do people want to live a lie? Sneaking around, not able to openly be in a relationship, hiding who you are. It's no way to live." Mia stopped before she said anything more. She wasn't just talking about George Valencia.

Mia had opened up to her parents about being lesbian in her last year of high school. She came from a religiously conservative Southern family and it hadn't gone well. Her father had raged, her mother cried. They tried to talk, cajole and threaten her into changing her mind about being gay. Finally, they kicked her out of the house. A friend's family took her in so she could finish high school, and as soon as she'd turned eighteen, she'd headed to LA and film school on financial aid.

"Well, this time George being outed is big news. It's all over social media. People are saying he's a hypocrite. He should have come out."

Mia slapped the last script on the table. "Why did he

have to *come out*? Being sexually fluid is normal. What if we made everyone who is cis hetero come out and announce their sexuality?"

Gail stepped to her and put a hand on Mia's shoulder. "I didn't know you felt this strongly about it. I was just sharing news."

Mia softened. Who was she to judge anyway? She was a check writer where gay rights were concerned. She donated to organizations who worked on the ground level, but she didn't march, parade or attend protests.

"George Valencia being gay shouldn't have been a story. His wife shouldn't have been able to hold that over him and embarrass him by making an announcement."

Gail shrugged. "It's not a story because he's gay. It's a story because his show is on season ten, and his role is a seventies era mansplaining playboy. It's hard enough to renew a show once it gets to the double digits, but he's going to have a hard time convincing an audience that he's a lady killer."

Mia shook her head. "He's a talented actor who has convinced audiences for ten years that he can seduce women. The fact that his sexuality will affect his career is wrong. If the network doesn't renew, I hope he sues their asses."

"Have you ever been with a partner who was in the closet?"

Mia stiffened. Was Gail purposely asking about Saira? She shook the thought away. No one knew about her and Saira. It was too painful to talk about, so she didn't discuss it with anyone.

"Just once. That's why I don't date people who don't live their lives openly. The lying, the hiding, it all makes you feel like you're doing something wrong. The way we live our lives is not wrong. It shouldn't even be considered different."

"You know, you should join this group that the network...."

Mia held up a hand. "Please don't tell me to join a committee, working group or organization. That's another thing I disagree with. We shouldn't have separate committees to promote our rights. When we don't like the options from food services, we form a committee to tell them what they should serve. The more separate committees we have, the more we get othered. We should be part of every committee there is, we should be part of that stupid food services committee, telling them to serve rainbow sherbet. Instead, we're set aside in a committee of our own, made to feel like we should be grateful for any concession we get."

Gail held up her hands. "Rainbow sherbet?"

Mia smiled. "Bad example. But you know what I mean."

"Sorry I brought it up. I didn't know you felt so angry about this. Actually, I don't even know what you're angry about, exactly."

Neither did Mia. This was Saira's fault. It was Saira who was reminding her of all the reasons why she didn't date women who were in the closet. It was Saira whose ability to set her body on fire with just a look was making her do bizarre things like rearrange seating so she didn't have to look directly at her. She wasn't angry with LGBTQ committees, and she didn't even care about George Valencia and his life. She was angry with Saira, the woman she had loved, the woman she had wanted to spend her life with, who had chosen to live a fake life with a real husband.

They heard noise outside the room; others were starting to arrive. Gail leaned over and spoke softly. "If it makes you feel any better, you know who won by the announcement? Ned Hawkins. Apparently he and George have been lovers for years.

Mia shook her head. "I'll bet you money that Ned didn't win anything. He's spent years being alone, unable to take his lover to parties or dinner openly. Now that George is finally out, there'll be such a spotlight on them that they won't even be able to enjoy it. Everyone loses."

Mia walked away to greet the first actors that started to file in. Some gave her a hug, others an elbow bump, and a few air kisses. They had a catering table set with fruit, bagels, avocado toast and little flutes filled with muesli. Some people grabbed coffee, a few nibbled at the table. Saira hadn't shown up and Mia was definitely not watching the door for her.

After their dinner the night before, Mia had spent the night thinking about whether she'd been too harsh on Saira about her fake marriage. She didn't know what it was like to be a celebrity, or to live in India, but Mia had sacrificed a lot to live her life openly. To this day, she was estranged from her parents.

Where was Saira anyway? Mia scanned the room and startled when she landed on Saira, in her assigned seat and studying the sheets in front of her. She was wearing a see-through white shirt with a flaming red bra-like undershirt that showed off her figure in that casually sexy way that sent heat waves coursing through Mia. *Damn that woman.*

Saira looked up suddenly and Mia instinctively looked away, realizing a second too late how childish the gesture was.

"Mia!"

She turned toward Gail. "Sorry, what were you saying?"

"Do you want to start?"

Mia nodded distractedly. The faster they were done with the read through, the sooner Saira with her red bra and see-through top would be out of her line of sight.

Gail called the meeting to order and explained the process. Mia began with a welcome speech, talking about how she was honored to have the job, big shoes to fill and the most talented staff on network television. It was the speech every producer gave, and everyone nodded politely. Then the director, David, had to say his piece. Finally, they began.

The read through started off well. Everyone was perfectly timed, effortlessly dialoguing like a team of champion synchronized swimmers. Saira was brilliant, her tone and accent pitch-perfect.

They got through the opening scene and took a break. Mia began to relax and walked over to the catering table to grab a muffin.

"I see lemon poppyseed is still your go-to."

Mia closed her eyes for a second before turning to face Saira. "Nice job in the read through. You've got the accent down."

"About that. I don't think Meera should have an American accent."

I knew things were going too well.

"Why not?"

"She was born in Mumbai and moved here as a teen-ager. She's going to have an Indian accent."

"The TV show is airing here. Strong accents don't do well with audiences. They want to understand the char-acters, see themselves in them."

"Then what differentiates this show from all the oth-ers? Why not cast some American actress?"

Mia blew out a breath. "There are plenty of American actresses that we can cast if you'd rather not play the role."

Saira narrowed her eyes. "You need me for this role. The network is banking on selling the show in foreign markets, and I am an international star. I want this show to be authentic, not the same bullshit this network usu-ally puts out."

Mia crossed her arms, hugging herself to keep her temper in check.

"If you hate the network so much, why did you sign with us?"

"Because I was promised a different show, and I in-tend to make it happen."

She walked away, and Mia nearly shouted at her but stopped just in time. The other actors and crew were clearly pretending not to listen while straining for every word. Gossip on a set was like happy meals at McDon-ald's. Everyone wanted the special toy.

Mia pasted a smile on her face and made small talk with the other people milling around the coffeepot.

As soon as the second scene began, Mia knew it was going to be bad. Saira was saying her lines in her nor-mal accent. Mia loved the sound of Saira's usual inflec-tions. She had that upper-crust Indian accent that clearly enunciated each word. If Saira's co-actors were thrown off by the sudden accent change, they recovered quickly.

Mia waited until the end of the scene before speaking up. "That was good, but I don't think the accent is working, Saira. Let's go back to the one you used for scene 1." Mia congratulated herself on how calm and matter-of-fact her voice sounded. No trace of rage, frustration, or annoyance.

"I'd like to hear what the others think about the two accents," Saira said just as matter-of-factly. She gave Mia a thin smile and a hard look.

Gail spoke up first. "I think the American accent is more relatable."

"I like the Indian one—it fits better with the character." The actress playing Meera's boss spoke up. Mia dug her nails into her hands to keep from saying something she'd regret.

"Not saying that you don't do the American accent well, but it sounds fake, y'know, I think the Indian one sounds better too," the actor playing Meera's best friend chimed in.

"I think we should consider it," David, the director, said.

Et tu, David? If there was one person Mia could count on to veto last-minute changes, it was David. He was a meticulous planner. If he thought this was a good idea, was Mia shooting it down just because it came from Saira? Mia mentally shook her head. She had considered the accent issue days ago, and after researching it and talking with the marketing people, she had agreed with Peter's original decision.

"Thanks for the input, everyone. Let's take an early

lunch break while I listen to the recording." Mia dismissed the group. The lunch catering hadn't been set up so most of the group dispersed. Mia caught Saira just as she was about to leave.

"Can I have a word in my office, please."

They rode the elevators in silence. Once in her office, Mia shut the door.

"What's your plan, exactly?" Mia stood with her hands on her hips. She and Saira were nearly the same height when Saira wore her stiletto heels.

Saira met her gaze with a maddeningly serene expression on her face. "My plan is to make the best series possible. We have ten episodes to convince the audience that this show is worth additional seasons."

"Then why are you hell-bent on questioning every single thing. Yesterday it was wardrobe, today it's the accent. I already have the writers working overtime because of all the script changes you keep requesting."

"I am not going to make a show that embarrasses me, and my culture. I don't want to be one more Indian actress who fakes an American accent and makes fun of the traditions I hold dear to my heart." Her lips quivered and Mia's heart stopped. There was something else going on with Saira. This was about more than just the show.

Mia relaxed her posture. "I admit that there are stereotypes in the script. Had I been involved from the beginning, I would've done some things differently. But we have to make the show palatable to American audiences. This isn't the BBC or a cultural documentary. It's a dramedy, and we need to make things extreme and funny for it to work."

"I get that. What you don't understand is that the show crosses lines I'm not willing to cross."

Mia sighed. She was tired, out of words to reason with Saira and too distracted by the way her jeans hugged her legs. Not to mention that damn red bra.

"Then quit," she said wearily.

"Is that really what you want me to do?"

No! I want you to behave. If Saira really did quit the show, it would be a disaster. They couldn't replace her quickly, the filming would have to be delayed and there was a good chance the network would just scrap the show. Then Mia would be back to making low-budget, limited series that nobody watched.

Saira stepped toward her. "What's really the matter Mia? Are you having trouble working with me."

Yes. You're driving me crazy—reminding me of our time in Fiji, making me lose sleep because I spent all night thinking about you.

Meeting Saira's gaze, Mia lifted her chin. "The only problem I have working with you is that you think your way is always the right way."

Saira scoffed. "Excuse me? You're the one who's so fixated on maintaining control over our relationship that you're not even willing to consider my suggestions. Do you know how hard it was for me to get you on this show? My agent called in every favor he had just to make it happen."

Mia's heart sank as she took in Saira's's words. She had assumed that the network had chosen her based on merit. "What do you mean your agent called in favors to get me this show?" Mia's voice trembled as she spoke.

Saira moved closer to her. "I thought you knew. When

I heard Peter was leaving, I had my agent call everyone he knew at the network to get you the job."

"Why would you do that?" Even as disappointment sank in, Mia's heart perked up. Had Saira orchestrated their working together because she wanted to rekindle their relationship?

"Because I thought you'd understand my point of view. That you and I could make a good show."

Mia pressed her lips. "You thought you could manipulate me, that you could walk all over me and I'd let you."

Saira's eyes flashed, then she stepped close and lowered her voice. "When have you ever let me have my way with you? If I remember correctly, you were always the one in charge."

Mia's face went hot. She had always been the one to take charge in bed, mostly because Saira had been inexperienced and tentative. But that didn't mean Saira was passive by any means. Heat spread through her as she remembered the way Saira would brush her lips against Mia's earlobes, kiss the crook of her neck, cup her breasts and pinch her nipples with just enough pressure to make Mia growl with need. "As I recall, you knew exactly what to do to get what you wanted."

Saira's lips twitched. "I had an excellent teacher, who was quite a seductress herself."

Mia's body tensed as Saira stepped even closer to her. She smelled the same, of roses and patchouli, her lips still glossed with the faintest shade of pink. As Saira's lips parted, all rational thought left Mia's brain. All she wanted was to once again feel the heat of Saira's mouth on hers, to feel the crush of her soft breasts against her own.

It was Saira who closed the distance between them,

putting a hand on the back of Mia's head to pull their bodies closer together. As Saira's lips tugged and teased her mouth, Mia ran her hand up Saira's shirt. The feel of her soft, silky skin sent waves of heat coursing through her body. She ran her hand underneath the red top. As she'd suspected, Saira wasn't wearing a bra underneath that thing. Mia ran her thumb over Saira's hardened nipples and her own core pulsed with excitement as Saira moaned sinfully and deepened their kiss.

It was the sound of her office phone ringing that brought Mia back to her senses. No one ever used the landline, and Mia was unaccustomed to its shrill tone. *What am I doing?* Even as her brain kicked in, her hand lingered for another second on Saira's breast before she extracted her hand and disconnected her mouth.

She couldn't even look at Saira. If she did, there was no way any of her neurons would work. How could she have given in to the temptation to kiss her? As if their relationship wasn't complicated enough. Why had they even come to her office?

She answered the phone. It was Gail calling. Mia had left her cell phone in the conference room. She glanced at Saira, who was adjusting her shirt, putting her breasts back into the red top. Mia looked away before the urge to rip the damn thing overtook all rational thought.

She needn't have worried. What Gail had to say worked better than a cold shower. She hung up the phone and turned to Saira.

"Mia, we still…"

"Your husband is here. He wants to see you."

Five

As usual Rahul had the worst timing. The look on Mia's face had been clear as day. She was equal parts disgusted and furious. Whether it was with herself or with Saira, she didn't know. Saira could still feel the pressure of Mia's hands on her breasts, the touch of her lips and the heat of her skin. Mia had been so cold, Saira had wondered how she didn't feel the attraction that had been consuming Saira from the second she'd seen her in the dressing room. She had no doubts now. Part of what they had in Fiji was still alive.

Rahul had a crowd around him in the white marble lobby of the studio building. Of course he did. He was a better known star than her. He'd even acted in several North American streaming TV series. It had been his contacts that had helped her land *Life with Meera*. He wore an untucked Nehru collar printed shirt in cream and gray with straight jeans that made him look like he had legs for days. Every hair on his head was styled and sprayed perfectly to look like he'd just gotten out of bed. As soon as he saw her, he broke through his fan girls and enveloped her in a bear hug, lifting her up. She returned his hug with equal gusto. It wasn't for show. They were truly the best of friends, and despite his timing, she was glad to see him. It would be good to have someone to talk to about Mia.

"What are you doing here?" she breathed. Rahul was the extreme opposite of a homebody. He hated being at home, so whenever he had a free moment, he used his private jet subscription to be someplace else. Saira would have a hard time coming up with a corner of the world where he didn't have an Instagram post.

"I missed you, *yaar*."

"I've only been gone two days."

"Too much for me." He pressed a kiss to her mouth, making sure it was long enough for cell phone pictures to capture the moment and share live on social media. Saira smiled dreamily at him, her acting skills in full use. She took him by the hand. "We have a small break—my hotel is nearby." She made sure her words were soft enough to seem secret but loud enough to be heard.

They walked out of the studio and she hailed a pedicab. The hotel was only two blocks away but she didn't feel like walking in heels. Plus, the driver wouldn't be able to hear what they were saying over the exertion of towing them on a bicycle and the noise of the city.

As soon as they were seated, Rahul waved to the fans as if they were in a royal carriage.

"Who did they catch you with this time?"

He sighed. "Hosiang. I thought we had equal reason

SOPHIA SINGH SASSON   49

to keep it quiet, but he had a crisis of conscience and told an elder. It spiraled from there."

Saira shook her head. "When will you learn?" It was the one thing she and Rahul constantly argued about. Rahul fell in love with the frequency of a tweet, and every time he did, he got careless.

"C'mon, *yaar*, he's a monk and we've been seeing each other for months. How was I to know..."

"To know what? That he may eventually question whether he wanted to continue down a spiritual path or a hedonistic one? To think for a minute that any normal human being might go talk to a friend when faced with a major life choice, and that friend might knowingly or unknowingly betray them?"

His tanned skin paled. Rahul had been her best friend since they were four years old. They had grown up in the same apartment building in the Bandra section of Mumbai, a complex with high gates, strong security and easy access to the Bollywood studios. They were not allowed to leave the complex so they played in the hallways and at each other's homes. Saira knew before Rahul did that he was gay, just as he likely knew before her that she was. He'd been the one she'd called from Fiji, torn about Mia, panicked when their time together was ending. He'd meant well and thought he knew what was best for her, so he'd involved her parents. She had long forgiven him and hadn't brought it up in years, but seeing Mia had reopened old wounds. If only Rahul hadn't been so impetuous, she and Mia would have had a proper goodbye. Things would have ended differently. And maybe there was a small chance they would've found a way to be together all these years.

"Okay, fine. I should have known better. Thank you, once again, for saving my ass. You know my new movie opens next week. The financiers have put a lot of money into making it a blockbuster hit and we can't afford a scandal right now."

"You know what would make the movie a guaranteed hit? You coming out as being gay. Think of the free publicity."

"Yeah, that's why you've come out, *nah*? The free publicity that'll result in boycotts of the movie, social media roasting, hate mail, death threats, protests at the theaters so even those who support LGBTQ rights will be afraid to go see it."

"If this TV series is a success, then I am coming out."

He looked at her skeptically as their pedicab pulled up to the hotel. They made it to her room without being accosted, and in silence. Both had learned the hard way that hallway and elevator conversations were recorded on CCTV, which the paparazzi always managed to get hold of.

As soon as the door closed behind them, Rahul rounded on her. "You said you would come out if your last movie was a hit. As I recall, it was a blockbuster. So what happened?"

She stuck out her tongue. He looked around the small living room space of the suite, then made his way to the bedroom, plopped onto the bed and grabbed the TV remote. "My publicist says I just need to hang with you for the next couple of days. He's sending some local fans to put out posts. It'll be good for your show too."

He flipped through the TV channels. "This is a real third-rate hotel—no international sports channel. India is playing Sri Lanka in cricket."

Saira sat on the bed next to him and grabbed the remote, turning off the TV. "Your timing is really bad. Things with Mia have been tense."

He sat up. "Did you tell her about our marriage?"

"Yes. But I didn't tell her about you."

He took her hand and kissed it. "We'll figure it out. One day, we will find a way to live the way we want."

She squeezed his hand. "What did Hosiang decide?"

"He picked spirituality over hedonism. We broke up."

He put his head on her shoulder and she touched his cheek. Rahul sighed. "I can't even blame him. What can I offer him? A life of stolen kisses and hidden apartments. He has a life of enlightenment ahead of him."

"He has a life of dreaming about you ahead of him. In the beginning he will miss you and wonder whether he made the right decision. Then he'll get back into the routine of daily life and think all is fine. But every few days, something will happen to remind him of you. A scent, a song, a place. Each time that happens, it will tear his heart just a little. Bit by bit, those little tears are going to create a hole so deep in his heart that he won't even know how to fix it."

Rahul lifted his head and enveloped her in his arms. "Babe, you need to tell Mia how you feel."

"What do I tell her? That I've been pining for her for the last ten years? That all the other women I've been with paled in comparison to her? That I was hoping seeing her again would magically cure me of my obsession, but it's only made it worse?"

"That's exactly what you tell her."

"Then her next question will be, 'what do you want from me?'. What will I tell her? I don't know. If the show is a hit, maybe I'll move to LA and make a career in Hollywood. Then I'll come out to the world and hope that I can make a living here. Then she'll ask what happens if the show tanks."

"What do you plan to do if the show tanks?"

Saira sighed. If she knew the answer to that question, she would have Mia in her bed right now instead of Rahul.

"I kissed her today."

Rahul raised his brows. "I thought the plan was to focus on the show and slowly rekindle things with Mia."

"That was the plan. But..." Saira buried her face in her hands. "I didn't realize how hard it would be to..."

"To keep your hands off her? To be so close and yet not touch her?"

Rahul put his arm around her and squeezed her tight against his chest. "I know. Can I give you some advice?"

"As if I could stop you."

"The more you withhold, the harder it will get. Give in to temptation. Be with Mia, see what happens. The last time you guys were together, it was ten years ago. You were on vacation. See if what you had there can exist in the real world."

That's what she was afraid of. "What if it is real? Then what? I can't leave her again. What will I do if the show tanks?"

"Worst-case scenario. You come out and ruin your Bollywood career, and you have no working options in Mumbai. You can live off your savings for years until you figure out something else. But the more likely scenario is that you'll still get some work. There are plenty of streaming channels that'll give you a chance— it might not be the lead, and you may have to reduce the number of Hermes scarves you buy on a weekly basis, but it's not like you'll starve."

Saira shook her head. "It's not about having nice things. You know I pay for Kayra's care. She likes the place in Switzerland but that costs a bucketload. If I come out, I'll have to pay for security for my parents. They are never leaving India."

"What happened to your savings? Your last few movies did really well."

"The rupee is really weak, paying for Kayra's surgeries and rehabilitation, then Jai's MBA at Harvard, and Ma's therapies have sucked up most of what I've made."

Rahul shook his head. "Your family is taking advantage of you. Kayra can move someplace cheaper, Jai should pay you back now that he has a job, and your Ma does not need her army of astrologers, pandits, yogis, and she definitely does not need those month-long ashram visits in Rishikesh."

Rahul was right. Saira recognized her family's excesses, but it also gave her joy to be able to provide those for them. Her mother's Bollywood career had ended early, and her father hadn't really been able to hold down a job. The family had only kept their home because of Saira's acting career. Saira wasn't just risking her own life, but that of her entire family.

"It's my fault Kayra is in that center. I'm not going to make her move someplace cheaper."

Rahul shook his head. "When will you stop blaming yourself? There was no way for you to have known what would happen."

"She never wanted to do it. I put her up to it. And you

know why? Because I wanted more time for fun. I was tired of working and thought if Kayra had a career like mine, then it would take the pressure off me."

Rahul sighed. "You were a child!" He sat up suddenly. "You know, we don't have a prenup. If we divorce, you can take me for all I'm worth."

She shook her head. "I will not take money from you. I'll accept a guest room in one of your apartments when I'm homeless though." She bit her lip. "If I come out, what'll happen to you?"

He shrugged. "I'll have to find a hot model to have an affair with to drown my sorrows. I'm sure my publicist will spin it into something that makes me look like a hero or a raunchy horndog doing threesomes. I'll be fine. You've done more than enough for me. I should not be part of your calculation."

She gave him a hug. Rahul was the one person who not only understood her but actually cared for her.

"Saira, you're stressing over things you have no control over. Whether the show does well or not is not something you can control right now. But, finding out whether you and Mia can make it work is in your power. So stop sitting around playing what-if scenarios in your head. Go get your girl."

Six

Mia paced the floor of her office. *What is wrong with me?!* She had asked to speak to Saira in her office to address the accent issue. Instead, she'd ended up kissing her, and now Saira was off for a nooner with her husband and she was left to figure out how she was going to get their read through back on track. Lunch was ready, Gail had sent out a text message to everyone and the only person missing was Saira. Gail had dispatched an intern to Saira's hotel.

What bothered Mia most was that she wasn't sure whether she was more upset about Saira's behavior at the read through or her running off to her hotel room with her husband. Mia had always known that Saira's sexuality was more fluid than her own. She didn't for one second believe that her relationship with Rahul was completely platonic. They might be friends, they might even have an open marriage but Rahul was too sexy and

Saira was too hot-blooded. How could she have run off with Rahul seconds after kissing Mia with such passion?

Mia took some deep breaths and rubbed her temples. *Focus on work.* It was the only thing that made sense right now. The only part of the whole mess with Saira that she could control, or at least try to.

She shook her shoulders, then made her way to the conference room. Most people were sitting down with their lunches. Food services had set up an extravagant spread, including ten different types of sandwiches ranging from vegan to double meat, smoothies and green juices in little cups, pasta salad (vegan and regular), three different types of green salads, a quinoa salad, a couscous salad, and two meats and cheeses charcuterie boards. Mia heaped her plate. She knew how much the food cost. If she had her way, they would have leftovers for the afternoon snack and dinner.

"Loading up for dinner?"

She nearly jumped out of her skin as Saira's breath caressed her ear.

"Where were you?" Mia cringed at the nagging inflection of her voice. *This is my show. Saira works for me.*

"Sorry for not seeing the text messages. My phone was on silent."

"You're here now. Had a good time with Rahul?"

Saira's lips twitched. She leaned forward, her lips brushing Mia's as she whispered. "Are you jealous we didn't finish what we started in your office?"

Mia's face heated. *How dare she!* She cleared her throat. "Actually I wanted a second with you to discuss the issue of the accent you'll be using." At least her voice had returned to normal.

Saira straightened. "Look, I understand your and the network's concerns about accents. You want to cater to an American audience and make sure that people won't lose interest in the show because they're having a hard time understanding the main character. Also, you want them to be able to relate to me, and it's hard to do that with someone who has an accent."

Mia stared at her. *Where is this rational side coming from?* The Saira she knew in Fiji was intractably stubborn. Once, they had planned to take a hike to see a waterfall. The locals had waved them away when they'd gotten near the top of the viewing hill, saying the rains the night before had made the trek too muddy. Saira had literally dug her heels in and made them trudge forward anyway.

Saira placed a hand on her arm. Mia ignored the warmth of her touch. "How about if we go halfway. I won't talk like I normally do, but I won't go all American either. That way the character authentically has an Indian accent but it won't be so strong that the audience won't like it."

Mia sighed.

"Let's try it out with the next scene and see how you like it." Saira's tone was so reasonable that Mia found herself nodding.

They started the read through of the next scene, and Mia marveled at Saira's ability to effortlessly change her accent once again. They took a short break, then started the next scene.

"Saira, I want to you to read this scene in your normal accent," Mia said.

Saira raised her brows but didn't say anything. Mia

hated to admit it, but Saira had been right. The dialogue worked better with her precise pronunciation and slightly musical way of stringing words together. It was charming.

Gail slid a note to her that said "good call." Mia gave her a sideways look.

It was evening by the time they finished. Mia had set an early morning call for taping. The first season wouldn't be filmed in front of a live audience so they had the flexibility of being able to start early. The filming schedule was aggressive—they were taping ten episodes in sixty working days for an average of three days per episode. It was one of the hardest schedules that Mia had worked with. Mia finished the day with a pep talk to the actors and crew, promising an amazing wrap-up party when they got through the next three months. Fighting for as much time as possible was one of the many things she'd had to negotiate with the network. The brutal schedule was necessary to make sure the series could air in February, and her ability to deliver would make her career. On the other hand, if there were significant delays, no one would remember what an impossible schedule she'd had. She would simply be blamed for not being able to cut it.

Most of the actors escaped as soon as Mia was done with her instructions and wrap-up. Some lingered and socialized with each other and the crew. Mia checked in with key crew members, making sure they were ready for the next day. TV series always made it seem as though actors messing up their lines was what took so long on set but the truth was that a lot of time was spent in scene transitions, changing camera positions and a myriad of other back-end tasks. Mia had tried to minimize those as much as possible so they could transition more easily between scenes. Tomorrow would be a test of whether all her planning would work. A lot depended on Saira. If she kept requesting changes, they would fall behind, and with a schedule so tight, they had no wiggle room.

"You hate chitchat." Mia closed her eyes. How did Saira manage to sneak up to her?

"I'm not socializing. I'm making sure we're ready for tomorrow."

Saira gave her a smile. "This is the most organized set I've ever been on. I'm sure everything will go smoothly."

The compliment warmed Mia more than she wanted to admit. She didn't need Saira's approval. But she did need her cooperation. "Saira, listen, I know we've gotten off on the wrong foot with this show, but I want you to know that I am willing to listen to your suggestions. The taping schedule is just really tight, so if something will delay us, I can't do it."

Saira bit her lip.

Shit. I know what that means. Saira was going to say something that Mia wasn't going to like.

"I know the taping schedule is fast. My agent even tried to negotiate on it because it takes us double, triple, the time to tape for the same number of minutes in India."

"It takes double the time here too. That's what makes this schedule so aggressive. But we can do it because I know how talented you are, and I think we can do it in fewer takes."

Saira smiled. "Flattery will get you everywhere…"

But…

"…but getting this show right is important to me." She held out the paper script and Mia recoiled. "After the read through today, I have some additional suggestions. The script was stilted in some sections, especially if we aren't using my American accent, there are ways of saying thing in India that…"

"Saira! We're taping tomorrow. It's not fair to the other actors to change the script the night before."

Her stomach turned. Would she keep having the same argument over and over with Saira for the next three months? Mia wasn't a stranger to arguing with actors on set, but Saira wore her out. As much as she wanted to deny it, Mia couldn't ignore that there was still a physical and emotional connection between them. She hadn't forgotten Fiji and neither had Saira.

"I haven't changed anyone else's dialogue, just my own."

"Still. I have to go back to the writers, who are going to have to work well into the night. Then the script has to get approved. I need to make sure it won't require set design changes…"

"It doesn't require set design changes. You haven't even looked at my changes and you're already shutting me down. You still think of me as that naive woman you met in Fiji, but let me tell you…"

"Would you stop bringing up Fiji. What happened there was ten years ago. A lifetime. We are both different people now, and this show has nothing to do with Fiji."

Saira stepped toward her. Mia caught a whiff of Saira's perfume and her body responded immediately, her hands remembering the feel of Saira's skin, the way her nipples swelled and hardened under her touch. Her eyes dropped to Mia's lips, her own mouth remembering the kiss they shared just a few hours ago. It wouldn't take much for her to take a step and close the distance between them.

Just one step and she could claim Saira's mouth, rip that stupid red top right off her breasts and feel those hard nipples in her mouth.

Saira leaned in to whisper, and Mia couldn't help the goose bumps on her arm as her warm breath caressed her .

"This show has everything to do with you and me, and we have everything to do with Fiji."

I can't do this.

Before she could formulate words in her head, Saira took her hand and pressed something that felt like a credit card into her palm.

"We can keep arguing or do what we want to do. You know where I'm staying. Come by after you're done with work tonight. Maybe we can finish what we started in your office."

Mia squeezed her hand shut, letting the hotel key dig into her palm. She turned away so she wouldn't watch Saira walk out. One night. That's all it would take to get Saira out of her system. Then maybe she could focus on the show instead of thinking about Saira, focus on what was between her ears instead of what was happening between her legs. Would it be so bad, to give in to temptation just this once? She and Saira never had a proper goodbye. Mia never had a last time with Saira. Maybe that's why she'd never been able to get Saira out of her system. What if she did that now? What if she had one night with Saira, knowing it would be their last time together? Could it provide the closure she needed?

"Have you seen the script changes Saira's requesting?"

Mia forced herself to look at Gail. She was holding the script that Saira had had in her hand just minutes ago.

"She mentioned them to me."

Gail sighed and fanned the pages, showing Mia a whole lot of red writing. "She's virtually rewritten every single one of her dialogues. The writers' room is going to be pissed."

They weren't the only ones. Mia pocketed the hotel room key and grabbed the pages. Saira's changes would throw the timing off. The camera crew would need to re-tool; the other actors would need time to adjust to the new dialogue even if their lines weren't changed. Saira had no idea how her decision rippled through everyone around her.

"Tell her no," Mia said firmly.

"Didn't you see the email from Chris O'Toole?"

Mia sighed. "Now what?"

"Apparently, they signed a new contract with Saira this morning. I thought you knew about it. She's taking a fee cut in exchange for script approval."

Mia clenched her jaw. "I asked Chris to run the changes by me before they signed. But did our financial wiz of a network executive consider the downstream costs of these script changes? Or the potential delays to our film-ing schedule? No, he did not."

Gail put a hand on Mia's arm. "You know as well as I do that they can't see past the ends of their noses. But that's not our biggest problem. What the hell is going on between you and Saira? Are you two sleeping together?"

Mia recoiled. "What? Why would you ask me that question?"

"Because you can't stop looking at each other, and then there's the fact that she slipped you her hotel key card."

Mia's face heated. "There is nothing going on between us."

Gail put her hands on her hips. "Really?"

Mia's stomach knotted. She didn't want Gail to know about her and Saira, but she couldn't keep lying to her friend.

"Look, I told you we knew each other. The truth is that we were seeing each other for like a hot minute ten years ago when both of us were on vacation in Fiji."

"Ten years ago?" Gail said skeptically.

Mia nodded. "It was just a fling, over a long time ago." It was over. It had been for ten years. They hadn't spoken or been together. Still, one day back and all the old feelings were coursing through her body like a tornado on a collision course with her heart.

"Clearly not."

Mia changed the subject. "Let's go over the script changes. And how much Chinese, pizza, and espresso we're going to have to buy the writers so they don't go on strike." She couldn't talk about Saira. Not with her emotions so raw, and the feel of Saira's mouth still tingling on her lips.

She and Gail found a spot on the conference room table. Everyone else had cleared out. They worked through Saira's script changes. Mia had to grudgingly admit that Saira's changes weren't all bad. Many of them made the dialogue more punchy. She recalled Saira's accusation that she hadn't been taking her suggestions seriously. She was right. Mia had been too focused on making sure that she set the tone for their relationship, that she remained in control and didn't let her feelings for Saira resurface. She had failed on all counts.

Gail gathered the script after they'd made their notes. "I'll get this to the writers' room. They won't be happy that Saira did a better job than them, but there isn't much for them to do other than proofing."

Mia reminded Gail to also send the script to the other actors and crew. Once Gail had left, she took out the hotel key that Saira had given her. It would be so much easier to give in to what they were both obviously feeling. Maybe it would take Saira off her mind. Maybe it would make her forget about Fiji. Maybe it would clear her mind of all the noise that had prevented her from being in a meaningful relationship all these years.

Or it would destroy her. They still had chemistry— the kiss proved it. What if sex was even better? Would Mia spend the next ten years comparing every woman to Saira? Her last relationship had lasted four months, two months longer than the one before. She was finally moving on, finding a way to open her heart and her body to others. But a part of her was still stuck on Saira.

She picked up the key. *I know what I have to do.*

Seven

"Would you please hurry up. Mia will freak if she sees you here."

"Going, going." Rahul gave his hair one last spray and set the bottle on the counter. Saira picked it up and put it in a shopping bag. She couldn't have Mia seeing Rahul's stuff all over the place. The hotel had been fully booked, so it was harder than she'd thought to get Rahul a room, let alone a room on the same floor so the paparazzi wouldn't find out that they were staying in separate rooms. Ultimately, Rahul had decided to go visit an old "friend" in Orange County, a B-list Hollywood actor. Rahul had a one-night stand with Ned Hawkins several years ago. They'd been friends since. Ned offered up his house to both Rahul and Saira, since he was leaving town the next day. Apparently, the media had made his life miserable after an announcement from his lover's wife about their affair. He'd decided to leave town and go hide in an undisclosed location.

Rahul washed his hands and dropped the towel on the floor. As much as Saira loved him, he was a slob. He was used to an army of servants in Mumbai who picked up after him. She put his things in shopping bags and handed it to the waiting bellhop. The sound bite to the media was that they were staying with Ned Hawkins. Saira was only using the hotel room provided by the studio on the nights she had an early call.

Just as she had him out the door, Rahul turned to her. "Tell her how you feel, babe. What have you got to lose?"

My dignity. She couldn't tell Mia how she felt. Not until she knew that Mia still felt *something* for her. There was a lot that she had to make up to Mia, and still a lot of things she needed to figure out. But the first thing to know was whether she and Mia still shared a bond. Saira couldn't give up her whole life on a chance that they could be together. She had to know for sure.

She looked at her watch. It had been two hours since she'd left the studio. She fluffed her hair, reapplied lip gloss, adjusted the silk slip she had put on. When three hours had passed, she sighed, plopped on the bed and opened her laptop to look at scripts. She had two agents, one who worked the Bollywood circuit and the other in Los Angeles. Both had sent her new projects. Mumbai was offering her a high-budget film with an all-star cast and her as Mumtaz Mahal, the wife of Shah Jahan, the emperor who had built the Taj Mahal. The movie was about their love story and how it inspired the building of one of the wonders of the world. The script was emotive and powerful, and she'd be working with one of the best directors and producers in Mumbai. They were also offering 2 percent over her usual asking price because they wanted her exclusively in Agra for filming. Her agent was sure he could get her 10 percent over her usual fee for exclusive access. If she signed the project, that would put her in India for at least nine months after filming for *Life with Meera* ended.

Crossing her fingers, she looked at what her Hollywood agent had come up with. There was a cameo appearance as herself in an A-list movie, a best friend supporting role in a rom-com that had literally put her to sleep as she read the script and a meeting with an online streaming network to discuss a six-episode limited series. None of these were paying half of what she'd be getting from Mumbai.

She opened the latest balance sheets her accountant emailed her on a weekly basis. The rupee was weak against global currencies, including the Swiss franc. Kayra's rehab center was costing her nearly 40 percent more than it had the previous year. She closed her eyes. Kayra was so happy there. How could she ask her to move? Then there were invoices for her mother's ashram. Her mother had struggled after what had happened with Kayra. Since she'd started going to the ashram, she seemed happier. How could Saira take that away from her?

Her LA publicist had sent some positive articles and social media posts from her kissy scenes with Rahul today. Her own arrival in LA had gone unnoticed but, as usual, Rahul's presence elevated her own exposure. Rahul had invitations to some high-profile Hollywood parties and her publicist told her in no uncertain terms that she needed to go, and listed out the invited celebrities with whom she should try and get pictures.

Saira sighed. She was essentially starting over in Hollywood, building her presence. In India she was already well-known. Crowds greeted her wherever she went, but she'd have to build her reputation here, get the media to love and promote her. Was she ready to put in that work all over again?

Her watch told her that four hours had passed. It was getting late. Mia wasn't coming. She took a deep breath, then emailed her Mumbai agent.

Mia turned the hotel key over in her hand. She was standing outside Saira's hotel.

"Are you ready to come in?"

Mia smiled politely at the valet/doorman/bellhop who had turned from eyeing her with suspicion to regarding her with pity. He'd seen the room key in her hand and probably, correctly, surmised that she was debating whether or not to compromise herself.

What if she and Saira were still as red-hot as they'd always been? What if they weren't? She'd held the idea of Saira in her heart and head for so long that she wasn't even sure what was real versus imagined. Now was a good time to find out, wasn't it?

She looked at her watch. They had an early call in the morning. Saira needed her beauty sleep. Mia needed to be clearheaded.

According to the app on her phone, a rideshare driver was one minute away. She could be home in thirty minutes. Plenty of time to get eight hours of sleep. *Or I can sleep with Saira's naked body next to me.*

She took a deep breath, then stepped into the lobby.

When she got to the room door she paused. Should she knock or just use the key? What if Saira had changed her mind? She had passed a mirror in the hallway. Retreating her steps, she considered her appearance. She never wore much makeup, but would it have killed her to swipe some mascara on her lashes and gloss on her lips? She dug through her purse and came up with ChapStick. Something was better than nothing. She tugged down her T-shirt, then squared her shoulders.

She used the little doorbell and stood with her hands behind her back. As she waited, she crossed her arms, then moved them beside her, then in front. Why the hell couldn't she figure out what to do with the damned things. She was used to always having something in her hands: a laptop, iPad, clipboard, coffee cup. Why hadn't she thought of bringing a bottle of wine or something?

How many minutes had passed? She wasn't sure but it seemed like a lot. She rang the bell again. What if Saira wasn't there? What if she'd changed her mind? Then another thought struck her. Rahul! Was he there? What if the two of them were together? What if they were making love right now?

She turned and fled down the hall.

"Mia?"

She turned so fast that she nearly tripped and fell. Saira stood at the door. *Damn that woman.* She was wearing a cream-colored knee-length silk nightgown with no bra. The straps looked like they could barely hold the piece up. Her breasts swelled against the fabric, her hard nipples on full display. Her hair was tousled, as if she'd been asleep.

Mia closed the distance between them, grabbed Saira by the hair and kissed her hard. Saira returned the kiss with equal fervor, pulling her into the room and closing the door behind them. Mia had no control left. She squeezed Saira's breasts, enjoying the moan that escaped deep from her throat. She had Saira pinned against the hotel door. She moved her hands down Saira's waist and thighs, her own body heating and zinging with need as her hands touched Saira's soft skin. Normally Mia liked to take things slowly, enjoy the initial seduction—she got off on making her partners moan and writhe under her mouth and fingers—but tonight her body seemed to be possessed with an urgency she couldn't control.

She ran her hand between Saira's thighs. Saira bit her lip, bucked her hips in clear invitation. She wasn't wearing any panties, something Mia had expected but still found intensely arousing. Her own panties were wet with need but Mia pressed her thumb to Saira's clit, enjoying the way her body tensed and vibrated; her own body responded to the sinful moan from deep within Saira's throat. She slid one finger inside Saira, as deep as it would go, then pushed even deeper. Saira broke their kiss, bent her body, tightening against Mia's finger and burying her mouth in her neck, kissing her in that spot that drove her wild. Mia slid a second, then a third finger inside Saira, her own body pulsing, vibrating and aching with desire as Saira's moans turned into cries of ecstasy, and she clenched so tightly against Mia's fingers that for a second Mia worried they might break.

Just when Saira was close, Mia used her other hand to push the flimsy nightgown off one shoulder. Saira was more than happy to help. With her fingers still inside her, Mia sucked on Saira's nipple, its firmness and sweet taste nearly throwing Mia off the edge. She sucked hard, biting ever so slightly just as she felt Saira's orgasm shudder through her body. Saira screamed, dug her fingers into

Mia's shoulders and bit her lip as she threw her head back. It was a while before her body relaxed and Mia slipped her fingers out, her own body so raked with need that she wasn't sure how she was still standing.

Saira grabbed her shirt and tugged it up, then deftly took off her bra. Not waiting for permission, Saira mouthed one hard nipple and ran her thumb over the other. Mia put her hands on Saira's now naked waist, enjoying the feel of her hot, silky skin. She closed her eyes, letting the waves of pleasure course through her. Saira dragged her into the bedroom, pushing her onto the bed, and Mia complied with no resistance. She helped Saira take off her cargo pants and panties and spread her legs to let her put her mouth on her hot core. Saira's tongue teased her clit, in turn flicking across it and pushing hard on it. She slipped two fingers inside Mia, bending and curving them until Mia was writhing on the bed, trying desperately to hold on to control. She didn't want to give in quite yet. Mia wanted to enjoy the moment, drag it out, let her body burst into flames. But Saira was relentless. She put a third finger inside Mia, sucked hard on her clit, and just when Mia was on the edge, she withdrew her fingers, stuck her thumb inside, bending it just right. Mia's entire body pulsed, then convulsed and bucked so hard that she nearly threw Saira off-balance. Her orgasm was explosive, and Saira teased and caressed her with her mouth and fingers until Mia begged her to stop. When she was finally spent, Saira crawled on top of her and buried her face in Mia's chest. Their cores, still hot and eager, rubbed and melted together.

It was good to have Mia underneath her. Her body was warm and soft and solid all at the same time. She could hear Mia's heart thudding, and the sound was like a soothing balm on her chaotic soul. They were meant to be together. If she had any doubts about that, they had evaporated. Nothing had changed in the last ten years, they still had what they had in Fiji: love, passion and a future together. This time she was ready to do what was needed to make it happen. Mia was worth it. Saira would find a way to get work in Hollywood. She could move her entire family to America to keep them safe from public retribution. She would find Kayra a place that was cheaper and that she loved just as much. Maybe Kayra was even ready to come home. Saira would figure it out. For Mia, Saira would make it work.

Mia shifted beneath her and Saira lifted her head, her body moving instinctively so that their breasts crushed together, their hardened nipples rubbed against each other. Saira pushed her hips to rub against Mia. She was ready for round two, aching for it. Her body pulsed with need, her core slick and ready.

"Saira." Mia's voice was thick.

Saira put a hand between their legs and caressed Mia, enjoying the way her eyes closed. She was just as ready as Mia was. Saira lifted herself and rolled off Mia so she could reach the nightstand. She had all of Mia's favorite toys ready; there was no need for sleep tonight. Saira had spent the last ten years reliving Fiji, imagining this night. They would make love again and again, and in between they would talk about the future, but this time with the maturity to actually make it happen.

She had barely gotten the drawer open when Mia rolled off the bed. "Toilet or shower? If it's the latter, then I'll join you."

Mia wouldn't look at her. She walked around the bed and began collecting her clothes. Saira tensed, her heart racing, and not in the way that she wanted it to.

"What're you doing?"

Mia wouldn't answer, wouldn't look at her. She jerked into her underwear and cargo pants. Saira rolled off the bed. Mia slipped her shirt on top of her head and pocketed her bra.

No, no no no. This can't be happening. Saira placed her hands on Mia's shoulders.

"Mia, talk to me. What's going on. Why are you leaving?"

Mia still wouldn't look at her, so Saira bent her head and placed a featherlight kiss on her lips. She wrapped her arms around Mia's waist. "Babes, let's talk. Tell me what's going on. You can't just leave like this. We have the whole night ahead of us. There are so many things for us to talk about—" then, unable to resist, she wiggled her eyebrows "…—so many things still to do."

Mia reached behind her waist and unlocked Saira's arms. She took a step back and finally met her eyes. "You wanted one night. I needed to get you out of my system. Now that's it's done, we can go back to focusing on the show."

Saira sat down on the bed. She didn't trust her legs to hold her. Tears stung her eyes. "This was just a roll in the bed for you?"

Mia nodded firmly. "We never had goodbye sex. Consider this closure on our past relationship."

Closure. What a filthy, American term. As if there was a way to seal closed a gaping open wound, as if mind-blowing, life-changing passion could be zipped up and put away like a winter blanket that was no longer needed in the summer.

Mia was slipping on her shoes. Saira placed a hand on her shoulder. "Mia, you can't leave like this. We need to talk. Tonight wasn't just meaningless sex."

Mia turned to her with eyes blazing. "That's exactly what it was for me, Saira. I'm not denying that we still have chemistry. Maybe now that we have it out of our system, we can move on, focus on the show. Be professional."

Saira stepped back. "That's all you care about? The show?"

Mia nodded. "That is the only thing I care about. You and I were over ten years ago. Clearly our libidos needed one last romp. Now, let's move on and stop dwelling on the past."

With that, she walked away, leaving Saira bewildered and shattered.

Eight

Mia rubbed her eyes, hoping it would take away the dark circles and bags that betrayed the sleepless night she'd had. *Damn Saira.* Mia had hoped that once they actually gave in to their desires, it would be clear that what they had was in the past. Mia had gotten together with exes before; it was never as good as she remembered it. Mia was convinced that she'd built up a fantasy-like utopia when it came to sex with Saira and a reality check would help her move on. Except it backfired. The reality was even better than her memory.

She'd come home to her crappy apartment and spent the night reliving every moment with Saira, writhing with want and need. Her fingers and vibrator had both been useless, and now she was sleep-deprived, cranky and had the female version of blue balls.

Her watch chimed, letting her know it was time to leave. She swore, slipped on her shoes, grabbed her laptop bag and crossed her fingers that the coffee cart outside the studios was open. The damned thing opened and closed at the whim of its owner, a surfer whose schedule varied based on how good the waves were.

The way the universe was dumping on her, she wasn't surprised that the coffee cart wasn't open. She grabbed the sludge that the interns brewed in the common kitchen, then walked over to the studio where the series set had been built. She'd checked it the night before to make sure that the set design looked good. The studio was a hub of activity. The actors weren't due for another hour, but the camera crew, director and myriad other support staff had been there for a while. The director, David Rosen, was a thin, reedy man with a permanent scowl and glasses that Mia was sure were for aesthetics only. He was another source of heartburn for Mia because he was yet another control freak. But he knew how to do his job. The cameras were already positioned for the first shot, everyone knew what they needed to do and even the couch cushions were fluffed.

David strode over to her. "Script changes the night before. On this taping schedule!"

"Good morning to you too, David," Mia said evenly. "You know as well as I do that script changes happen even after the scene is filmed. What's the big deal?"

"The big deal is that it throws off the timings for my camera crew. I had to call them in an hour early to go over things. You're going to have to pay the overtime."

Great.

"Thank you for making it work, David. You know the deal the network made with Saira."

David leaned forward, his tone completely changed. "What is up with that? Is she sleeping with Chris?"

Mia stiffened. "I don't think so. She reduced her fee, and as usual, they don't always comprehend what that might mean for us on the ground level."

David nodded. "On my last show, they fired the producer halfway through filming because the actors complained about him. I had to do the directing and producing."

Mia bit the inside of her cheek. She was used to men like David. "Well, then you know exactly what a tough position I'm in. Thanks for being so great, David."

Without waiting for him to respond, she walked away. She could only take so much. Gail appeared with a dry cappuccino, and she took the cup gratefully.

"Everything ready?"

Gail nodded. "Saira's already here and sitting in makeup."

Saira, the woman who claimed that Indian Standard Time was genetic and responsible for her chronic lateness, was almost an hour early?

"She said her hair takes a while, and she wanted to make sure we started on time this morning. Got off to an auspicious start and all."

"How thoughtful," Mia said sarcastically. Saira was up to something. Was she hoping to talk to Mia? Convince her to come to her dressing room for a noon romp? Mia's traitorous body pulsed at the very thought. She took a long sip of her hot cappuccino, letting it burn her mouth.

If Saira had her way, the script for their romance was written clearly in Mia's mind. They would spend three months stealing every second they could get, quickies in the dressing room, nights filled with unbridled passion, innuendo laden looks and gestures throughout the day. Saira would talk about the future, plans to move to LA, to start a new career and live with Mia out in the open. She would even go as far as to drag Mia to look at houses she would buy for them to live together. A two-bedroom house in the hills, above the smog. They would commute to the studios together—it was worth it for the view. Then as the show wrapped, Saira would get distant. The small house she was going to rent or buy would no longer be available. The contracts she was sure were coming wouldn't materialize. There was an excellent offer from Bollywood that Saira couldn't refuse. It would just be a few months, then Saira would come back. At the wrap-up party, Saira would say goodbye to everyone but Mia, promising that she would return the next weekend on a friend's private jet. It was just a few months and then Saira's Hollywood gigs would come through.

The weekend trip wouldn't materialize. The taping schedule, jet lag, a million excuses. Weeks would turn into months, and daily video calls would become emails and text messages until Saira would finally break down and admit that she couldn't make it work. She had too many responsibilities.

The truth that Saira would never admit, even to herself, was that she was afraid to leave the security of her life in India. She liked being a beloved film star where fans swooned at her every move. Directors and producers capitulated to her demands, an army of servants made sure she didn't even have to tie her own shoelaces. Why would she trade that to become a bottom list star in Hollywood where she'd have to beg or manipulate to get what she wanted and deal with the fact that her career was on the down slope?

It could never work between them. Saira wasn't suited to be an American. She would forever blame and resent Mia for making her give up a life she loved.

Mia passed by the makeup area, eyes on her iPhone, walking with purpose. She stole a glance only to see Saira's eyes on her. She gave Saira what she hoped was a nonchalant nod. Just another actress. Today was the director's show. Mia was there to make sure it all went smoothly. Saira was David's problem today, and the thought eased the knot in Mia's stomach.

The actors took their places for the first scene. It was based in the living room of the set. Saira was wearing pajamas. A set of plaid pajamas and a T-shirt that read I Love New York would've looked drab on anyone else, but it seemed to hug Saira in all the right places, giving her that girl next door combined with sexy porn star look. Mia couldn't help but stare.

The first few scenes went smoothly. The actors adjusted to the change in Saira's lines, and Mia stood mesmerized as she watched Saira act. She had seen Saira's Bollywood movies, with subtitles on. There was no doubt that Saira was a talented actress, but it was something else to watch her live. Rarely were actors able to get a scene perfect in one take. It was even rarer for directors to accept one cut. They wanted to make sure they had editing options. But Saira was magic. It was as if the rest of the world didn't exist when she got in character. Mia watched hungrily as Saira said her lines flawlessly. As much as she hated to admit it, the dialogue changes and the accent worked much better than what she'd originally approved. Saira had been right that it made the character more authentic. No, it wasn't just that—it made the character funnier, more tragic, more likable. The audiences would eat up Saira as Meera. Mia watched the director screens that showed the various camera angles. Saira wasn't the same old American sitcom star, nor was she like the South Asian actresses of previous shows; she brought her own brand of understated dramatization. It was the way she raised an eyebrow, or twitched her mouth, the way she moved her eyes and gave that look....*that look*. Mia stood mesmerized. How could one woman be so beautiful?

Mia could scarcely believe how well things were going. By lunch time they were ahead of schedule.

Saira approached David, and they seemed to talk for quite a while. When both suddenly looked up in her direction, Mia scrambled, a little embarrassed that she was caught staring. David waved her over.

"Saira has an idea that we need to run past you."

Mia sighed.

"What is it now?"

"You seem so open to hearing my idea." Saira glared at her. Mia returned her stare with blazing eyes of her own.

"We're on a tight schedule," Mia said through clenched teeth.

"Hear her out," David interjected. Mia shot him a look. If anyone should be more stressed than she was about the taping schedule, it was him.

She folded her arms. "I'm listening."

Saira narrowed her eyes and placed her hands on her hips. "I was just saying that the next scene might work better in the kitchen than the living room."

"You want to change the location of the scene on the day we're taping it?" Mia said incredulously.

"It's the same set."

Mia looked at David. How was he not freaking out about this? It impacted him more than her. He had to move his camera crews, stage crews, and on and on.

"She's right that the scene might work better in the kitchen. Plus, she had a great idea about having the mother hold a spatula as she's talking with her hands with Meera trying to dodge the thing in addition to fighting off her mother's words."

"That's a whole change in scene, even for the Devi who's playing the mother. Plus you need to move all your cameras."

David shrugged. "There are two afternoon scenes in the kitchen so we can tape those along with this one after lunch. That will give me the lunch time to get the cameras situated."

Saira blew out a breath.

"If you two have it all figured out, then who am I to stand in the way."

She turned to leave when Saira's voice arrested her. "Can I talk to you. In private."

Saira's dressing room was the most convenient. It would take them fifteen minutes each way to walk to Mia's offices. Saira had her own trailer. Inside, the outfits of the day were hanging on a rack. A dresser, couch, and small table and chair were the only other furniture. Nothing sexy at all about the dressing room. No bed, and the couch looked uncomfortable as hell.

Mia followed behind Saira but stood by the door, one foot on the downward step. Saira took off her shoes, then began removing the pajamas that she'd been wearing for the morning scenes. Mia held up a hand. "What're you doing?"

Saira removed the pants and threw them on the couch. "I'm getting ready for the next scene. Aren't you the one that keeps reminding me what a tight schedule we're on?"

She tugged off her top and stood there in a lacy beige bra and panties that might as well not have been there. She reached behind her to take off the bra.

"Stop!" Mia hadn't mean to shout.

Saira raised a brow in that maddening way she did when she knew she'd made a point.

"I hope this is not about last night."

Once again Saira raised her brow. "I think you made it pretty clear that you didn't want more than a one-night stand."

Mia straightened. "That's right. So what do we have to talk about?"

"If you've forgotten, we are doing a show together. A show that's really important to me, and I'm tired of you rolling your eyes every time I bring up something."

"Saira, you have no idea how your little ideas create work for the rest of us. Because of your script changes, the writers were up past midnight, the camera crew and director had to be here an hour early to go over the timing changes. There are downstream repercussions that I have to worry about. Plus, there's the fact that you manipulated the network execs to get script approval into your contract ten seconds before filming was scheduled to begin. So excuse me if I don't jump for joy every time you have a bright idea."

Saira visibly flinched but Mia was not sorry for her

harsh tone. Saira deserved it. She was used to everyone capitulating to her, and it was time Mia called Saira out on her manipulations.

Saira opened, then closed her mouth. She grabbed a robe off the hook and put it on. Not that it helped. Mia couldn't not notice her hard nipples or the way the lace caressed the curve of her breast.

She took a step toward Mia. "You know what your problem is?"

Here we go again. The speech about how she's grown-up and has the experience to know better than me.

Mia lifted her chin. "I'm sure you're about to tell me."

"Your problem is that that you hate the fact that you want me. That you love me. That you want nothing more right now than to rip off my underwear and throw me down on that table."

Mia's entire body went hot. She reached behind her and grabbed the railing leading down the steps. It would take less than five seconds for her to reach the door.

"You have quite the opinion of yourself. If I remember correctly, you're the one that gave me your hotel key."

"And you came. We had an amazing time, and then you left with some mutterings about closure. If it was just about getting your rocks off, why come?"

Mia took a breath. "What do you want from me, Saira? Come out and say it. If it's not sex, then what is it?"

"I want us to talk. Not like this, but to really talk about us. There's still something between us, and it's more than just sex. I want us to sit down and hash it out, to figure out what there is, and more importantly, what there could be."

She took a step closer, and Mia felt the railing bite into her back as she leaned against it.

"Why are you so afraid to talk about it?"

"Fine, let's talk about it. What're your plans? Tell me what's changed since Fiji. Are you ready to come out? Do you want to sit down and talk about when you're going to tell your family that you're not hetero. When are you moving to LA? Do you have a lawyer drawing up divorce papers with your husband?"

Saira's pressed her lips together.

"That's what I thought. How about you invite me to have a conversation when you have the answers to those questions."

Nine

Saira sank down on the couch as Mia exited, slamming the trailer door behind her. Why hadn't she just said what she'd wanted to. *I'm ready to give it all up. But only if I can have you, Mia. I'll give up my career, my life in Mumba., I'll face my family, I'll face the world. But only if you're beside me.*

Before last night, she'd wondered whether she had romanticized what she and Mia had. First love was blinding, and Saira wanted to make sure that the happiness she envisioned with Mia was real. Just because none of her other relationships had made her feel Mia's magic didn't mean that Mia was the answer. But last night had proved that she hadn't imagined it all. Their connection was special and she wasn't ready to give up on them.

But Mia wasn't ready to forgive her. Saira had hoped that getting her into bed would melt her anger, make her see that they still had something, open her heart to exploring how they could make it work between them.

Her eyes stung as tears washed through her mascara and eyeliner. *What was I thinking?* She'd come to LA thinking she would focus on the show, make sure it was a success, and then, when she was sure she could make it work, she'd rekindle things with Mia. Instead, she hadn't been able to keep her hands off Mia. She'd jumped the gun thinking that if they fell back in love, Saira would find the strength to do what she needed. But Mia wasn't going to solve her problems.

She called Rahul and told him what had happened.

"Babe, I'm sorry. Maybe you're focusing on the wrong thing."

"What do you mean?"

"You're trying to convince Mia that there's still something between you two. But your decisions can't revolve around Mia. You came to LA to see if you can build a new life. A life where you can live in the open, be in a real relationship. That was your goal before Mia became this show's producer."

Saira sniffed.

Rahul continued. "If Mia rejects you, which she has, by the way, are you changing your plans?

She shook her head, then realized Rahul wasn't on video. "No, I still want to try and make it in LA. I'm tired of doing background checks on women I meet and making them sign nondisclosure agreements on our first date. I'm tired of being alone."

"Gee, thanks."

"You know what I mean."

He sighed. "I do."

She stood. Rahul was right. She'd lost sight of her objective. She couldn't get her life back on track until she made sure *Life with Meera* was a success. It was time for her to stop playing nice—her career depended on it.

As the actors took their places, Mia stiffened. Saira was dressed in the saree that costume had designed for her, but the underlying blouse that she'd taken issue with was different. Mia had expressly declined the request for a new blouse. Had Saira gone behind her back again?

She walked up to her and tapped her on the shoulder. Saira threw her luscious hair back. The same hair that had fallen on Mia's chest yesterday. The same hair she had woven her fingers through as Saira's mouth licked and sucked and drove her mad.

"Where did that blouse come from?"

"It's mine."

"Excuse me?"

"I told you the old blouse didn't work. You wouldn't authorize a new one, so I decided to use one of my own."

"Without checking with me? We have to consider lighting and…."

"Lighting gets adjusted after all the actors are in place. I don't understand why you're making such a big deal. I'm using one of my existing blouses. It's better stitching and fit anyway, and it looks better with the saree." She stepped back and spread her arms.

Why did she always look so good? Mia hated to admit it but the blouse was much nicer. It was a modern cut with a sweetheart neckline. Saira's waist and cleavage was on full display. The saree was wrapped perfectly to show off all her curves.

"The point is not that the blouse is bad, the point is that you can't just change wardrobe. Does this work in India? Do they let you waltz onto the set with whatever you want to wear?"

"First, they know how to dress me in Mumbai. Second, they would've stitched the new blouse. Now if there's nothing else, I believe they're ready for the shot."

What!

Saira turned away from her. No, she didn't just turn away, she dismissed her. What had happened? Just an hour ago Saira was begging for her attention, trying to talk to her, seduce her. Now it was as if Mia was an annoyance Saira didn't want to deal with.

Mia strode over to David, who was staring intently at the bank of screens in front of him. "Did you really allow Saira to waltz onto the set wearing her own clothes?"

David didn't bother looking up. "It's one piece of the costume. What's the big deal?"

Mia blew out a breath. "The big deal is that Saira is walking all over you. Yesterday she was asking for wholesale script changes, and when I wouldn't give them to her, she made a deal with the network. Today it's costume changes. We're running a show here, David. we can't let the talent…."

David held up a hand, then turned to her. "I once had to send an intern clear across town at five in the morning so my star actor could have a particular muffin from a specific bakery. Then there was the prima donna who screamed at the makeup artists because they couldn't magically make her wrinkles disappear." He looked back onto the screens. Saira was in the picture, adjusting her saree. Mia couldn't help but notice the way that blouse dipped low on her back, exposing that piece of skin that drove Saira delirious with desire when Mia kissed it. "In the grand scheme of actor issues, Saira's are not worth our time. Her script changes are actually good—she's not trying to get more airtime. And you know as well as I do that we've got an all-white writers' room, so it's good to have someone make sure we aren't doing something that will piss off a whole bunch of South Asians."

"Sunil is also part of the writing team."

"Glad to know we have the token Indian who was born and raised in SoCal and has to call his parents to translate any Hindi words we want in the script."

Mia wanted to rage at him, but the wind was suddenly out of her sails. David was right. She'd had the same concerns when she had first taken over the show. So much so that she'd gotten a sensitivity read on the script.

She dropped into a chair. Saira was getting to her. Mia's every decision since Saira had arrived had been based on an emotional reaction. She hadn't been thinking clearly. Once again Saira had swept Mia up in her vortex of chaos—and Mia had allowed herself to get swept up. She had slept with the star of her show! If word got out, Mia would be ruined. Not because set relationships didn't happen, but because she and Saira had been at odds, and any conflict between them would be perceived as personal rather than professional. Mia didn't need that for her first big show. *God, how clichéd—producer gets her first big break and she throws it all away for hot sex.* Producers were more easily replaced than stars.

"Mia!"

She looked up to see Gail standing with her hands on

her hips. "What is wrong with you? I've been texting you for the last hour. I had to run down here to find you."

Mia looked at the phone in her hand. She had it on silent for the taping, but she usually checked her messages every few minutes. On a show like this, there was always a crisis brewing somewhere, whether it was equipment malfunction, an unexpected budget spend, or a hissy fit from a writer, actor, director. It was endless.

She stood. David was getting ready to start shooting, so Gail pulled her outside the studio doors. "They want to see you on the thirty-fourth floor."

That can't be good.

"What's going on?"

"I talked to Chris's assistant but she was zipped tight."

What had Saira pulled now?

Taking a breath, she made her way to the studio offices. Apparently, they wanted her to sit in the waiting room until the network kings had a second to spare for her between meetings. She waited for over an hour, texting Gail to find out how taping was going. Apparently, it was going even better than it had in the morning. They were staying ahead of schedule.

When Chris was finally ready, Mia had reached a new level of impatience. Her email was overflowing with a million little things, and she still had to do the daily wrap and go through the checklist for tomorrow. Plus, she had to go to the bathroom, but there was no way she was going to risk missing her chance—they'd probably make her wait until yet another meeting was over.

As she walked into the room, she noticed there were a number of other people there whose faces she recognized from the portraits hanging in the lobby and hallway. Half the network executives were there. They weren't sitting on the couch drinking whiskey but were seated around the small conference room table.

Chris motioned her toward an empty chair that an assistant pulled up to the table.

"We don't have a lot of time so I'm going to just say it. We're canceling *Life with Meera.*"

Shit. Had they found out about her and Saira? She shook the thought from her head. That would be a reason to fire her, not cancel the show.

She swallowed. "Why?"

"Not enough of the streaming services have picked it up for us to be profitable."

"Filming has begun. You'll have to pay out most of the actors. We've essentially already spent over 60 percent of the budget."

"A loss we can take. We still have to consider the remaining budget, plus marketing expenses. And with Saira renegotiating her contract, more of the budget is free."

Mia felt an unexpected anger roil deep in her belly. They had taken advantage of Saira. All along she'd thought Saira had offered up a fee reduction for script approval, but now she strongly suspected that slimy Chris had talked her into it, knowing full well they'd be canceling the show.

"We've also recently acquired the rights to a tell-all for one of the European royals, so we need to free up some cash to get that made. It's going to take the slot we had for *Life with Meera.*"

Mia took a breath. She could argue, list all the reasons why the show was better than yet another royal documentary, brainstorm ways in which she could save money, even come up with marketing ideas. But one look around the table and she knew what this was about. Someone was cashing in a chit with someone else and *Life with Meera* was going to pay the price. Mia was going to pay the price, along with Saira and David and all the other actors and crew. These network weenies didn't care.

"What if I can find a way to get the streaming services interested?"

"And how would you do that?" The question came from a silver-haired man in a really nice Brioni suit.

Mia held up a finger, then pulled out her phone. With a few clicks, she pulled up Rahul Chandan's Instagram page then held up the phone. Seeing the squinting eyes, she handed the phone to Chris, who took a look and passed it around.

"Saira's husband is an international star. That one post from his Instagram account has more than a million likes. His fans posted additional photos that have hundreds of thousands. He has star power. Now imagine a few more posts like this with the hashtag *Life with Meera*. It'll create buzz."

The silver-haired man peered at the picture. "I know this guy. One of the other studios is courting him for a major movie."

Mia waited. She'd learned the hard way that in a room full of men, she needed to let them come up with the obvious plan so they thought it was their idea. Networks still worked on the GOBSAT principle. Good Old Boys Sitting Around a Table.

"Can you get him to do a cameo, do some show promos? For free?"

Sure, and while I'm at it, why don't I ask Santa Claus

*for another million dollars and two months so I can do
the show properly.*

"I'll talk to Saira."

"Report back tomorrow morning. We need to move
fast on this."

*Sure. I've been busting my ass for the last two months
working eighteen-hour days to get everything ready, but
you only have a few seconds to consider whether or not
to throw the whole thing out.*

"I doubt Rahul can make this decision without consult-
ing his lawyer, publicist and agent. You can't expect an
answer overnight. Plus, India is 10.5 hours ahead in time."

"Good, then it's early in the day there. Find a way to
make it work."

Yes your majesty.

She gave a curt nod and left before she felt the urge to
say something that could get her fired from the network,
not just the show.

Back in the studio, filming was wrapping up for the
day. They had made good progress. Mia gestured for Gail
and directed her to ask Saira to come to her office once
she was free. She debated telling David, then decided
against it. Mia wanted David focused on filming. David
was only on this show because Peter had recruited him.
Someone of his talent would get scooped up in a second. If he thought the show was going to get canceled,
he might bail, and Mia couldn't afford that. She crossed
her fingers he wouldn't hear about it from someone else.
She avoided telling Gail as well. As much as she loved her
friend, Gail could be a bit of a gossip, and Mia couldn't
risk this getting out.

By the time Mia got to her office, she was exhausted

and her to-do list had gotten longer. She got through the smaller items, then began tackling the budget reports. She and David were scheduled to meet later in the evening to go over the dailies. He was a night owl and liked to take a break after filming. It would be another late night for her, and not quite as satisfying as last night.

Mia looked at her watch. *Why isn't Saira here yet?* She texted Gail, who replied Saira had left an hour ago. Sighing, Mia texted Saira. Why was everything so difficult with her? Maybe she shouldn't talk to her about getting Rahul to endorse the show. Maybe the show getting canceled was a good thing. Saira would go back to her fabulous Bollywood life, and Mia could move on. She'd find another show, another series, maybe she'd branch out and do a movie.

When an hour went by without Saira texting her back, Mia called her. *Voice mail.*

She's ignoring me.

Mia didn't bother leaving a message. She called the hotel and asked for Saira's room. The phone rang for a good minute before a breathless Saira answered the phone.

Mia hung up without saying anything. She grabbed her purse and headed to the hotel.

Ten

Saira was more mentally exhausted than physically. She'd enjoyed her first day of filming. Her fellow actors were thoroughly professional, and David was eccentric but clearly good at his job. But she'd spent the whole day either trying to avoid Mia or find her. Despite her promise to Rahul, Saira couldn't pretend that Mia didn't exist. Or forget what had happened between them last night. When Mia asked to meet with her, Saira decided to ignore the request. She had no desire to be alone with Mia. Rahul was right—Saira had to focus on her career, on this show. Her Hollywood agent had called her before she hopped into the shower. He'd gotten her email about finding her something better, and he'd beaten the bushes, even suggested Saira read for parts, but there was nothing. Saira was not as well-known as Rahul or Priyanka Chopra. Not in America. She was still a nobody as far as Hollywood was concerned.

Rahul would help if she asked. He had contacts, and

his agent had a wider reach than her own. But she'd made a promise to herself that she wouldn't exploit their relationship. Rahul wasn't just her husband, he was her best friend, and she knew he'd do anything for her. He had been taken advantage of earlier in his life by his parents and then a childhood sweetheart, both of whom ended up wanting nothing more than money from him. He viewed every relationship with a large measure of suspicion. Saira had asked for his help in getting Mia the producer's role. She had agonized over that decision. Rahul had done it for her, but the request hadn't felt right. And what had that favor resulted in? She'd wanted Mia as the producer thinking that Mia would understand the problems with the script and work with Saira to fix them. Instead, Mia was fighting her every step of the way.

Who was she kidding? Saira had seen the producer role as a way to get close to Mia again. All that had accomplished was an hour of pure pleasure that left Saira even more wanting than she had been. When Gail asked her to go meet with Mia in her office, Saira purposely ignored the request. She didn't want to be alone with Mia, didn't want to smell her, look at her, touch her. She had enough problems; she didn't need additional reminders that she was in love with a woman who wouldn't love her back.

She sighed and picked up the room service menu. She wasn't particularly hungry but she had to eat and get to bed. The makeup artist had had to put hemorrhoid cream under her eyes today to reduce the puffiness. She hadn't slept last night, tossing and turning and going over every second with Mia in her mind, feeling her touch on Saira's skin, remembering the way she'd tasted when Saira licked and sucked her, smelling the scent of Mia on her mouth and fingers. *Damn her!*

Saira ordered a Cobb salad, decaf coffee and chocolate mousse cake. After the day she'd had, she deserved a treat. She was tempted to add wine to her order, then remembered it kept her up at night. She was getting to an age when the lack of sleep showed on her face. She needed to look fabulous for this show. Flawless and beautiful, the classic Indian beauty to win the American audience. She didn't have Priyanka's lips or Rahul's charm, but she had naturally luminous skin that was the envy of her fellow actresses.

Her hair still wet from the shower, she rubbed in an Ayurvedic hair oil, then left it to air-dry while she slept. Binita, her hairdresser at home, had done wonders for her hair in the last few years by shifting Saira from chemical products to natural oils and reducing the use of hair dryers that damaged the roots and structure. She completed her skin care routine with all natural Ayurvedic creams and settled into bed to wait for room service.

At the sound of the door knock, she looked at her watch. *Boy, they are fast.* She belted her robe firmly and padded across the suite.

She opened the door and stopped short. "Mia! What are you doing here."

"I asked to meet with you."

"I was busy. You can't come barging into my hotel. How did you even get up here?" The elevators need a key card to get to the room floors.

Mia held up a white card. "Forgot to give this back to you yesterday."

Saira snatched the card and made to close the door.

She could not have Mia in her hotel room. Not with her completely naked under the bathrobe, her body already itching for Mia's touch.

Mia held out her arm. "Please, this is not about us. It's about the show. I need your help."

This is new.

Saira waved her in. The suite had a small living area with a dining table and four chairs, a couch and TV. The bedroom was only a few steps away. When Saira did location shoots for her Bollywood movies, she got an entire apartment with multiple rooms, plus quarters for her maid. When she had FaceTimed her agent in Mumbai, he had been aghast at the "third class" place they had put her up in. But Saira knew how to pick her battles, and the hotel room was not the sword to die on.

She sat at the dining table. Best to have something solid between her and Mia.

"Please keep what I'm about to tell you between us."

Mia frowned but nodded.

"The network wants to cancel *Life with Meera*."

The words bottomed out Saira's stomach. She was counting on the show to launch her career. Her agent had pretty much told her that she needed to wait until the show released and hope it was a success if she wanted the type of offers in Hollywood that she got from Mumbai.

"What do they want?"

It didn't matter if they were network executives in LA or money laundering film producers in Mumbai, they all threatened cancellations when they were looking to get something for free.

"They want Rahul to make a cameo appearance and do

some show promotions." Mia gulped, as if embarrassed to say the next part.

"And they want him to do it for free."

Mia nodded. Saira shook her head in disgust. "The industry is the same around the world." She looked Mia squarely in the eyes. "Tell them no."

Mia jolted. "What do you mean tell them no? They'll cancel the show. Can't you ask Rahul whether he'd be willing at least?"

Saira shook her head. "I will not take advantage of Rahul. And these network people are bluffing you. They want to force you and me to give them something for free. When you refuse, they'll shrug their shoulders and move on."

Mia took a breath. "Look, things might work that way in Bollywood, but shows get canceled here all the time. I don't think they're bluffing. That's probably why they so easily gave you script approval in exchange for cutting your fee. You are the most expensive actor we have on the show."

She shook her head. "Did you read my revised contract? It says that if they cancel the show or fail to air all ten episodes for any reason, then they owe me my original fee."

Mia must have missed that. She raised a brow. "That was smart."

Saira crossed her arms. "I know what I'm doing. If you think you've got snakes here in your management, I've got snake charmers in Mumbai who are so good at manipulation that you dance to their *been*—" she mimed the flute that snake charmers used "—without even knowing it."

Mia smiled and Saira's heart caught like a string on a guitar pick. Saira loved how natural Mia was. She didn't lotion and potion her face until it shone, didn't scrub and plump her lips, tweeze and thread her brows. She had that natural beauty that was effortless. Ten years had put some lines on her face, taken away some of the fat that used to be on her cheeks and given her smile and eyes a more reserved, tentative quality. Yet she was even more breathtaking than she had been in Fiji. The way Mia's hazel eyes crinkled when she smiled shot daggers through Saira's heart. *Why? Why am I so attracted to her? There are so many beautiful women in this world. Why can't they make me feel like she does?*

"They know Rahul is in town. He's created some social media stir passionately kissing his wife in our studio lobby."

Jealous, are we?

"I told you, our marriage is not real. It's based on friendship. He knows I'm a lesbian."

"Is that what you are now? I thought you were bi, or fluid."

Saira tilted her head. "I didn't have a supportive family and culture to help me figure out what I am. Took me a little longer than you. Give me a break."

Mia bit her lip and Saira shifted in her seat. "Why can't you ask Rahul? Even if the execs are bluffing, which for the record I don't think they are, their idea is a good one. Having a cameo from Rahul and publicity might help get interest from the streaming services. That'll be good for our show."

"First of all, wouldn't a cameo change the script, costumes, lighting, and what were the other things—" she clicked her fingers "—camera timings etc. etc. Those changes take time and effort and we're already on a tight schedule."

Mia's cheeks reddened and Saira felt a jolt of heat through her. Mia's cheeks also colored like that when she was aroused.

"Look, I want to apologize to you. I haven't been fair in listening to your suggestions. I admit that you've been right about some things."

"Some things?"

"Seeing you again threw me off. I haven't been myself."

Saira leaned forward. "Seeing you threw me off too."

It wouldn't take much to lean over just a bit more and kiss her. From there it wouldn't be much to pull her into the bedroom.

"Do you know why it's important for me that we get this show right? That we don't perpetuate cultural stereotypes?" It was a rhetorical question. The only people who knew what had happened with Kayra were her family and Rahul. Mia knew about her sister's condition but not how she'd become that way.

Mia frowned. *That's right. You never thought to ask me.* Saira was tired of fighting with Mia on every little thing. It was only day one of filming. There were still twelve weeks to go. It was time Mia knew.

"Kayra was only fifteen when I asked her to do this show called *Ram ki Maya*. They had offered it to me but I wanted a break. I was tired of being responsible for paying the family bills. I thought if I got Kayra into the industry, it would ease the burden on me."

Mia reached out and placed a hand on top of hers.

"I didn't really take the time to look at the script or follow along as filming progressed. Turned out that the show was a satire on the classic Ramayana. But it went too far. When it aired, there was a public outcry that the show had desecrated a sacred text. Kayra's role was Seeta, who we call Seeta *maiya*, mother Seeta. The show questioned a really key principle about whether Seeta was still pure after being held captive by Ravana—the evil demon who kidnapped her. The show made light of this assumption, implying that Seeta had an affair with Ravana. It was in really bad humor and enraged a lot of people. The show went too far."

Saira swallowed against the lump in her throat. "The public wasn't just mad, they went fanatical. There were protests and burning of posters depicting the show, it was bad. They took their anger out on Kayra. We got her bodyguards because of all the threats against her. But they couldn't protect her from a particularly brutal crowd...." Her mouth soured as she thought about the image of Kayra after that attack. "A whole group of people descended on her, kicking and beating her with shoes and sticks. She was in such bad shape." Her voice cracked. "Took multiple surgeries and physical therapy."

Mia squeezed her hand. "Oh, Saira, I'm so sorry. Why didn't you tell me before?"

"It is not something I talk about." The truth was that she'd never wanted to tell Mia. Never wanted to see the disappointment Saira saw in her mother's eyes every time Kayra's name came up. *Kayra is not as strong as you. This wouldn't have happened to you.* There wasn't a day that went by when Saira didn't wish that she hadn't given that role to Kayra. She had ruined her sister's life. Kayra had healed from her physical injuries but never really recovered mentally. The center in Switzerland had been great for her anxiety.

"After what happened to Kayra, I don't just accept a

script. It's my name and face out there. When the public sees something they don't like, they don't blame the producer, the director, the writers or even the studio. They blame the actor. They direct their anger, and their hatred, at the person on the screen."

"Oh, Saira, I wish I'd known. I can't believe you've been dealing with this all by yourself."

How did she tell Mia that Saira was too embarrassed. Too ashamed. Mia's hand was still on top of hers and she turned her palm and laced her fingers with Mia's. "I didn't want you to know. Fiji was an escape for me. It was the first time I was myself, the first time I'd let myself forget all my responsibilities, all my guilt."

"Guilt? Why do you feel guilty?"

"That role was mine. If I hadn't given it to Kayra just so I could sleep later in the mornings and have more free time to read books, her life wouldn't have been ruined."

Mia stood and came to kneel beside Saira. "No, no Saira. You can't blame yourself for what happened to Kayra. That is not your fault. If there is anyone to blame here, frankly, it's your parents. You were a child yourself, and you needed a break. That didn't mean that your sister had to pick up the mantle…."

"I was twenty. Hardly a child. Kayra was the child, and I am her big sister."

Mia stood and enveloped her in a hug, Saira's head resting on her belly and chest. She breathed in deeply, tears streaming down her face. After it had happened, her parents had been shattered, and it had been up to Saira to figure out how to fix it all. To get Kayra the medical attention she needed and then the ongoing rehabilitation. It had all fallen to Saira to organize and pay for.

"I am so tired, Mia. I am so, so tired. Tired of acting, tired of the responsibility, of the burden of it all."

Mia held her tight. "It's a lot for anyone to take on."

"I left you in Fiji because my parents showed up, and they reminded me of the responsibilities I had. It wasn't just about having the courage to come out to my parents. I couldn't jeopardize my career. Kayra was healing physically but she was a mess mentally. The facilities in India aren't that great, so we sent her to Europe and eventually Switzerland. All that costs money. My career isn't just supporting designer handbags…."

"Oh, Saira. Why didn't you just tell me all this. Why pretend that what we had was meaningless."

"Because I know you. If I'd told you what I'm telling you now, you would've lectured me on how Kayra isn't my responsibility and somehow convinced me to prioritize myself."

"You're right. That's exactly what I would've done. No offense, but your parents are taking advantage of you. Kayra is their responsibility. They are the ones who let her take your role because they wanted another cash cow."

Saira stiffened. She'd been afraid of this. Mia didn't share her cultural values. She didn't understand that it was the children's responsibility to take care of their parents.

"See, this is why I didn't want to tell you. You don't understand. Our culture is different. We take care of family, even if it means sacrificing ourselves. Kayra is my responsibility. She is my sister. Even if I weren't responsible for her condition…"

"You are not responsible for what happened to her…."

"She is my sister, and I need to take care of her as long as I'm physically capable."

SOPHIA SINGH SASSON   105

Mia took a deep breath and Saira leaned back, pushing herself out of Mia's arms.

"I thought it would be cleaner if we just broke up. I
didn't want to spend my life wondering what could have
been. Remember I wasn't as big a star as I am now. Hollywood wasn't as much of an option. And we were young..."

"I've spent all this time being angry at you..."

Saira sighed. "I know. I thought you'd forget about me,
and I about you. But honestly, what we have together..."

Mia nodded. Saira could see it in her eyes. She still
cared about her. Still loved her. Saira felt lighter.

"I'm tired. Do you mind if I go to bed?"

Mia nodded but stood there. Saira called room service
and canceled her order. The little bit of appetite she'd had
was gone. She was exhausted.

"Can I stay with you tonight? Sleep with you? Just
sleep?"

Saira raised her brows, then nodded in relief. She
needed Mia. She offered Mia some of her pajamas and
crawled into bed in her robe. She turned to her side and
Mia spooned her, hugging her tightly.

Saira couldn't help the tears that streamed down her
face. Years of stress, shame, anxiety, frustration and lone-
liness poured out of her. Mia just held her, occasionally
sitting up to wipe her tears, sometimes with her bare
hands, other times with the sleeve of her pajama top.
They didn't talk. Saira was totally spent. Mia held on to
her, occasionally rubbing her back.

Saira fell asleep eventually and slept better than she
had in years. When she woke, she turned over in her bed
and found it empty.

Mia was gone.

Eleven

Mia hated sneaking out of Saira's room early in the morning, but she didn't want to wake her. Saira had had a rough night and she needed to rest. She had debated writing a note but hadn't known what to say. She would see Saira soon enough, and she still didn't know what to say.

All this time, Mia had assumed Saira didn't want to lose her lifestyle and idol status. The truth was so much more heartbreaking. *I wish she'd told me in Fiji.* They would've worked something out. Mia would've helped Saira figure out what to do, could have been there for her, helped and supported her. Even as she'd held Saira last night, Mia had ached for her, the pain she had endured, the constant stress she was under.

Good or bad, she had several fires to keep her mind occupied. David was mad that she'd blown off the review of dailies with him. She still had to report to Chris, and if he decided to move forward with canceling the show, she'd have to break the news to the crew. She'd have to tell Saira.

She had asked the front desk to wake Saira an hour before her reporting time. The hotel was only fifteen minutes from the studio; that should've given Saira enough time to get there. Makeup and hair would be in the studio, so all Saira had to do was shower, throw on a pair of jeans and sunglasses and grab a tea. Saira didn't eat breakfast.

When she hadn't shown up fifteen minutes past her call time, Mia began to pace. She texted, called, then dispatched an intern to her room. She should've woken Saira and said goodbye, made sure she was okay.

Thirty minutes past call time, Saira finally stormed in. Her hair was pulled back into a severe ponytail, her face devoid of makeup. She'd thrown on a T-shirt and jeans that curved around her in just the right ways. She searched the room then made a beeline for Mia.

Uh-oh. Should've left a note.

Mia held up her hands as Saira approached, her quick walk and blazing eyes clearly conveying her anger. "Sorry I left the way I did, I didn't want to..."

"Did you call Rahul and ask him to do cameo and free promo for this show?" Saira was yelling and everyone was starting to stare.

Mia grabbed her arm. "Can we talk outside?"

Saira shook her off. "No thank you, we can talk here. Did you call Rahul?"

"You didn't want to ask him, so I did. As the producer of the show."

"On my behalf."

"I made no such representations."

"C'mon Mia." She gave her a pointed look and Mia

shifted on her feet. She had called Rahul after Saira fell asleep the night before. He had been surprised to hear from her but clearly knew all about her and Saira. He'd asked Mia to stay the night to make sure Saira would be okay. When Mia had explained the situation, he had readily said yes. She'd known Saira would be upset but it had to be done.

"Rahul was happy to do it."

"Rahul isn't the one who has a problem with this—I do."

"Why? I get not wanting to ask your husband for a favor but you didn't. I did."

"He did it for me."

"As he should. You've done plenty for him."

Mia gave Saira a pointed look. She'd asked Rahul whether it bothered him that Mia was spending the night. That's when he'd told her that he was gay. Rahul also confessed that he had been the one who had inadvertently ended their relationship in Fiji. When Saira called him from Fiji, he'd been going through an identity crisis of his own. He had just been blackmailed by his first sexual partner and projected his fears onto Saira when he saw the Facebook posts of her and Mia. He had mistakenly gone to her parents, thinking he was protecting her.

After the conversation with Rahul, Mia felt even more like a shit for being angry with Saira. She had been nothing but a good daughter, sister and friend, had given up her own happiness for everyone else she cared about.

"He's my husband. That was my call to make."

All eyes were on them. This was not the time to have this discussion. "I am the show's producer and I am well within my rights to ask another star to make a cameo appearance."

Saira opened her mouth, then closed it. She turned on her heels and marched to her makeup seat. She waved her hands dismissively at the gawkers. Chris had given them two weeks to see if Rahul's social media buzz would create interest from the streaming services. The world of TV had changed since Mia had been an intern. Back then, it was all about advertisers and making sure the network affiliates would pick up the show. Now shows were sold not just to the network affiliates who aired it live, but to the streaming services, some of which got the show shortly after it aired, and others got it later. The amount they paid determined when they got the show, and the more demand there was for a show, the higher its purchase price. Rahul had already posted on Instagram announcing his cameo on #LifeWithMeera. It was approaching several hundred thousand likes just an hour after posting.

Mia sighed. She would have to set things right with Saira at the lunch break. Mia had newfound admiration for her. The woman had more responsibilities than anyone she knew. Mia felt stressed about paying her rent and the payment on her car, especially when she was between projects. She couldn't imagine what it was like for Saira, having to support her whole family, including medical expenses for her sister.

Mia made herself scarce once shooting started. Now that some of the kinks had been worked out and the actors had gotten a feel for each other, shooting was going well. During a break, David approached her. "Why didn't you tell me the network was thinking of canceling the show?" He was whispering, but Mia shot him a look and pulled him into a corner, keeping an eye for eaves-droppers. "Look, I just found out yesterday and I didn't want to panic everyone until it was a done deal. Sounds like the network is having trouble selling the show to the streaming services but I got Saira's husband to do a cameo and some promos."

"Yes, thank you for telling me about that as well. He's only available tomorrow so we have to get the script, costumes…"

Mia held up a hand. "I already talked to the writers' room. We're going to integrate him into the café scene we're already filming. Costume is going to use some-thing they already have in Rahul's size, and I'll schedule a meeting with the entire crew after we wrap up tonight so we are ready."

David crossed his arms. "You seem to have thought of everything."

"It all happened so fast. I'm sorry I didn't consult you, but you know that none of this can happen without you."

"You forget I exist sometimes."

"Of course not! You know this show was over budget. I only did it because you were the director." She gave him an appeasing smile. Stroking egos was the most hated part of her job, but one that she had become very tal-ented at.

Gail was the next one to corner her. She had heard the news from David's assistant, who had overheard him muttering to himself after *he* heard the news from an in-tern in Chris's office. Gail strongly suspected that David was sleeping with that intern, who was thankfully in her twenties but at least thirty years younger than David.

Mia sighed. She'd have to address the potential cancellation with the crew in the evening. By then, even the night cleaning crew would know that the show was on the chopping block.

During lunch, Saira walked off to her dressing room. Mia assembled a plate of food from the catering table and made her way to the trailer. She knocked several times before Saira finally opened the door. She was dressed in a long silk robe that hugged her body way too tightly. She looked at Mia with narrowed eyes, then stepped inside, letting her enter. The dressing room was a mess with clothes strewn everywhere, empty bottles of water here and there, and wilting flowers that hadn't been put in a vase. Mia made a mental note to send an assistant in to clean. Saira wasn't used to keeping herself organized.

Mia pushed some clothes off the coffee table and put the plate down. "I got you some quinoa salad and a falafel sandwich."

Saira eyed the plate. "And the mini crème brûlée is for you?"

Mia smiled. "I'd be willing to share if you let me explain."

Saira sat on the little dressing room stool, grabbed the sandwich and took a bite. As Mia suspected, she hadn't had any breakfast. "You shouldn't have gone to Rahul behind my back."

"I'm sorry. Chris gave me until this morning to confirm Rahul. You were in no shape for us to argue about this. I should've waited and woken you up early this morning, but to tell you the truth, I wanted an excuse to talk to Rahul alone." She gave her a small smile.

"You still think I'm sleeping with Rahul?"

"No!" Mia reached out and grabbed Saira's hand. She

struggled to find the right words to explain her sudden urge to talk to Rahul, knowing how intertwined he was in Saira's life. It was a ridiculous idea, but Mia couldn't help feeling that she needed to connect with him; there was a missing piece to the puzzle of Saira's life, and Rahul was it. "You've been with him for ten years, known him since you were a child," Mia said, her voice tinged with a hint of envy. "I can't help feeling a little jealous of the time he's had with you. I wanted to know what he was like. I don't know, I thought it would bring me closer to you."

Saira looked down, then leaned over and gave her a quick kiss on the forehead. "Rahul was a child star like me. Except he has a very different relationship with his parents than I do. They were very exploitative, and Rahul had to hire a lawyer when he was fifteen to get independence."

"He filed for emancipation?"

"Yes, except there is no such thing in India. Children are considered property and there are no laws protecting children from the financial exploitation of their parents. His case went nowhere."

Why didn't you file for emancipation with Rahul? Mia wisely kept her mouth shut. If there was one thing that had been clear last night, it was that Saira believed it was her responsibility to take care of her parents and sister. She didn't feel taken advantage of.

"Finally at the age of eighteen, he had to give up all of the money he made as a child, including ongoing royalties for old films, and start new." Saira took another bite of her sandwich, and Mia handed her a bottle of water to wash it down. "It didn't end there. His parents sued him for ongoing support. That went on for like ten years, and they were going to lose but then they blackmailed him."

Mia's heart lurched as it suddenly became clear. "Rahul told me he's gay. His parents used that against him, didn't they?"

Saira stared at her. "He told you?"

When Mia nodded, she raised her brows. "You must've had a really good conversation. That's not something he shares. His parents threatened to out him and ruin his career. So he pays them hush money. It's supposed to be a monthly sum but it never ends. Every few months they have an urgent cash need. You know, his mother sees a diamond necklace she must have, or his father wants to buy the new MG SUV."

"That must be awful for him."

"I try to be the one person in his life that isn't exploiting him, that isn't always asking for things. I already asked him for help getting this role, and then getting you as producer...."

You don't want to treat him the way your parents treat you. Mia almost said the words out loud but managed to restrain herself.

"I'm sorry I went behind your back. But, if it makes you feel any better, Rahul was happy to do it."

"He also hands over the checks to his parents with a smile and some dialogue about how it's important to have a parent's blessing and good wishes for a successful life."

Mia slumped into the couch, not bothering to move the saree that was underneath her. Saira stood and pulled her off the couch. "Don't sit there, you'll crush the saree. As it is, your costume people did a horrible job of pressing it."

"Pressing it?"

Saira rolled her eyes. "Ironing."

Mia stood and helped Saira redrape the saree on the couch. "Shit, this is for today?"

Saira nodded. "That's why I was late this morning. They delivered this to me and it had so many wrinkles, I had to get them to send me an iron and board."

"You ironed this?"

"You think I don't know how to iron?"

"Honestly, no. Have you ever ironed before?"

Saira smiled. "Actually no. I had to video call my assistant in India. It was like the middle of the night there. She talked me through it."

They both laughed.

"You know what, you shouldn't have to be figuring out how to iron a saree. I'll talk to costume about getting someone who knows Indian clothes."

"Thank you! I had to tie the saree myself yesterday."

"Why didn't you say something?"

Saira raised her brow. "And have you bite off my head? I've been picking my battles."

Mia sighed. "You're right. I've been so wound up about you, about us, that I haven't been really listening to you about the changes to the show."

Saira picked up the mini crème brûlée. "You can make it up to me by letting me eat this whole thing."

Mia grabbed a fork and popped a small bite in her mouth. "Not a chance. You know how I feel about sharing dessert."

Saira set down the small ramekin after gobbling the rest of the crème brûlée in three bites. "As I recall, you are perfectly willing to share your dessert, as long as I'm licking it off your body." She pulled Mia by the shirt and kissed her. Mia expected the kiss to be hard, but it was gentle, maddeningly so. Saira cupped her cheek and touched her lips to Mia's, gently kissing, tugging and tasting her. Their breasts brushed against each other, and Mia placed her hand on Saira's waist to tug her closer. She moved her hand to Saira's hips, longing to touch her through the silky robe, but Saira pulled back.

Mia's body was hot, her core wet. She needed Saira. She wanted Saira, naked and lying on that couch.

"If you're worried about the saree, I'll reiron it."

Saira smiled. "I don't want it to be like last time between us. Quick and dirty, as you Americans say." She touched Mia's cheek. "If you're ready to be with me, come spend the night. We can order room service, stay up late, wake up slowly in the morning. Tomorrow's not a workday."

It wasn't a workday for Saira—Sunday wasn't a shooting day—but Mia still had things she needed to do.

"On one condition."

Saira raised an eyebrow and Mia took a breath to try and cool her body. The idea of a night with Saira was enough to send her pulsing with need. "Wait up for me."

Twelve

Rahul showed up for his cameo appearance with his usual swagger, dressed in jeans and a deceptively bedraggled T-shirt. Apparently, he had a fan base among the crew. They were all used to dealing with stars, so were reserved in asking for selfies, but the excitement was infectious. Saira remembered a time when people just asked for autographs; now she had to look selfie perfect everywhere she went.

She sneaked a look at Mia, who was standing back. They'd spent the night together, talking, making love, then talking some more. It was different than it had been in Fiji. There was more raw honesty between them. Mia had told her all about how hard it had been for her as a female producer in a male dominated industry, how she still wished for a reconciliation with her parents, even though they still didn't accept her sexuality. She'd never seen Mia so vulnerable and it made her feel even closer to her. Mia had opened up about how hurt she'd been when her parents kicked her out of the house, how she'd missed their presence in her life all these years. Saira better understood why she was so insistent on living her life openly. Mia had given up everything she valued, her home and the love she shared with her mother, so she didn't feel the crushing vice of her secret every day. It inspired Saira, made her want the same for herself, and for Rahul. While he was smiling for his fans now, he'd been stressed all morning. The story with Hosiang was catching steam on social media. They both lived in fear that a picture, an overhead comment could ruin their lives in a hot minute. It was no way to live, and she was done with it.

Saira introduced Rahul to Mia. They hugged as if they were old friends, and Saira felt a rush of warmth and ir-ritation. "Now, now, you two better not be scheming be-hind my back." She'd meant to sound teasing, but the words came out accusatory.

Rahul kissed her on the cheek. "We are absolutely scheming. Somebody has to take care of you, and now I have a partner in crime."

"I understand you have a party to get to, so I'll see you both tomorrow." Mia raised her hand to wave goodbye but Rahul touched her shoulder.

"Why don't you come with us?"

Saira raised a brow. "Isn't it invitation only?" Her own agent had called her twice this morning to make sure she could go to this exclusive party with Rahul. She needed the exposure.

Rahul shrugged. "I'm invited. I don't think they'll mind if I bring plus two rather than plus one."

"This isn't India, Rahul. This type of thing isn't so casual here."

Rahul pulled out his phone. "I'm texting my agent now. He'll take care of it."

"Your agent is coming?" Her agent couldn't even get her a ticket let alone get himself invited.

"I told you that agent of yours is a dud. I don't understand why you don't sign with mine."

Saira sighed. "Because your agent would only take me because I'm your wife."

Rahul shrugged. "So?"

Mia turned to her. "Rahul's agent has a much bigger agency. He can probably do better for you."

Anger bubbled in her veins. She wagged a finger at both of them. "See, this is why I don't want you two scheming."

Rahul put an arm around her and kissed her head. "*Aare yaar*, we love you, and we want what's best for you."

Saira looked at Mia, who was studiously looking at her shoes. Had she said something to Rahul about loving her?

"Thank you for the party invitation, but I'm afraid I can't go. I have a lot of work to do and nothing to wear."

Rahul put both hands on her shoulders. Mia startled and Saira smiled. Rahul's friendliness took getting used to. "Work can wait, and Saira has plenty of clothes. I think you two are roughly the same size. If you don't like what she has, I'm sure your costume shop can come up with something."

Mia began shaking her head, but Rahul wasn't to be deterred. "We are not leaving without you. Go get your purse and whatever else you need. We'll stop by the hotel, pick up what you and Saira need, then go to my friend's house in the Hills to get dressed. My assistant will arrange for a hairdresser and makeup artist to meet us there."

"I really don't need all that I can do my own…" Mia's protests were completely drowned by Rahul's continued chatter. Saira smiled. It would be nice to see Mia all dressed up. She had just the dress in mind as well. It was one she hadn't yet worn and would look perfect on Mia.

When they got to the hotel, Mia seemed too overwhelmed with the clothes crammed into the small hotel closets, so Saira picked the dress.

Ned Hawkins's bungalow was a cute two-bedroom, three-bath modern house with a fantastic view of downtown LA. It had a step-down living room, open kitchen, and sliding French doors that led to a lap pool and hot tub. The living room walls were decorated with framed movie posters of Ned. Rahul had mentioned that this was Ned's "poor house," the one that he'd bought after he had to sell his mansion. Apparently, he'd never accounted for the fact that leading roles in movies decreased as age increased. To Saira, the house was perfect. Spacious enough for parties but cozy enough for a family. She and Mia could have a house like this, one bedroom for the kids, and one for them.

"How is Ned?" Saira asked. She'd heard rumors on set that he was being hounded by the media as a home-wrecker.

Rahul shook his head. "I talked to him yesterday. The poor guy thought that after George came out, they could finally be together, but it's actually harder for them to even see each other with the tabloid reporters following them everywhere. Plus, George is in a messy divorce, and his lawyer told him to keep away from Ned for now."

They only had a half hour before the hair and makeup people showed up. and Saira did not want to waste a minute of alone time. She pulled Mia into Ned's bedroom. Rahul was using the guest room.

"I feel bad for the guy but he's a little vain, isn't he?" The bedroom walls were littered with headshots of Ned through the years. Saira found a hook at the back of the door and hung up the dresses she had brought for Mia, who was furiously texting on her phone.

She grabbed the phone from Mia's hand.

"How about we focus on having fun tonight."

Mia sighed. "I have a lot of work to do."

Saira pulled Mia into her arms and kissed the spot between her neck and ear that drove Mia crazy. Sure enough, goose bumps filled her skin, and Saira ran her hands down her arms as she whispered in her ear, letting her lips brush against Mia's skin. "We won't stay long at the party, and afterwards, we'll go to my hotel and order room service for dessert. How about it?"

Mia wrapped her arms around Saira and pulled her close. Her mouth found Saira's lips, her hands slid beneath the tank top she'd thrown on after the shoot. She was wearing a bandeau bra and it didn't take long for Mia to push it over her breasts and find her nipples, rolling them between her thumbs. Saira deepened the kiss, her body eager for Mia's touch. Her own hands worked the belt on Mia's cargo pants, pushing them down along with her panties. Mia was so slick that Saira slid two fingers inside her, her own body responding to her lover's moans. Saira knew what Mia wanted. She broke the kiss and stepped back, then put the fingers she'd just had inside Mia in her mouth, tasting Mia's juices. Mia's eyes darkened.

She pulled down her jeans, chucked off her top and bra. Saira followed with her clothes. They came together at the same time, mouths hungry, breasts crushing against each other, hands exploring with fervor. Saira pushed Mia onto the bed, then grabbed her purse, pulling out Mia's favorite sex toy.

"Is that…" Mia's eyes went wide.

Saira nodded. "You left it in my hotel room in Fiji."

"I hope you've gotten good use out of it."

"It's a little hard to enjoy without you." She inserted one side of the double-headed penis inside her, then put the other side inside Mia, watching with pleasure as her head rolled back and she bit her lip. Saira moved on top of her, changing positions ever so slightly, her hand on Mia's stomach to balance herself. She tried but failed to control her own orgasm as Mia squeezed her breasts, rolled her nipples between her fingers and pressed and teased her core with her thumb.

She didn't count the times Mia orgasmed. It was hard enough to keep track of her own as years of pent-up desire and sexual frustration exploded out of her. It wasn't as if she hadn't had sex, not as if she hadn't used the toy, not as if she hadn't orgasmed with her other partners. But it was different with Mia, always had been. There was a freedom in her release, a connection with Mia that she'd tried to achieve with others and never had. It was as if there was an invisible string that connected their hearts and souls and the physical part of their relationship just allowed them to pull that string taut until they were joined together.

Afterward they lay there spent, entwined in each other's arms, kissing and touching, making up for years of missing each other's touch.

Rahul eventually knocked on the door. "I don't hear any moaning and screaming, so hoping you guys are done. The makeup and hair people have been waiting for an hour."

"Be out in a minute," Saira yelled. They both looked at each other and laughed. Saira glanced at her wristwatch and gasped. "Oh, my God, we've been in here for an hour." They'd lost track of time talking and holding each other.

They decided to take a shower separately, knowing that if they did it together, it would be another two hours before they emerged. When Saira emerged from the bathroom, Mia had already put on the dress that she'd brought for her. It was a silky, royal blue, one-shoulder dress that ended just above her knees. The hairdresser was busy getting Mia's short locks pinned so they framed her face in curls. She looked stunning. If Rahul hadn't gone through all this trouble to make the night special for them, she would've begged off, dragged Mia back into the bedroom.

Saira wore a shimmering silver dress in a twenties flapper style that ended midthigh. They were short on time so she settled for her hair in a quick updo and minimal makeup. Rahul looked stylish in designer jeans, an open collar shirt and a Balenciaga jacket. By the end, even Mia was excited about the night.

A limo took them the twenty minutes up the hills to the mansion where the party was being held. Mia stepped out in the heels that Saira had lent her and pulled down her dress. Luckily the paparazzi were not allowed past the gates. Saira and Rahul had waved to them from the window of the limo, while Mia did her best to slink as far down in her seat as possible. After being checked in by the security guard up front, they entered the foyer where they were greeted with hundreds of LED balloons floating in the ceiling, which created a mesmerizing starry night effect. Rahul's agent found them immediately. Saira turned to Mia. "Do you mind if I make the rounds with Rahul real quick? I need to get some selfies onto insta."

Mia nodded. She needed a few minutes to adjust to the party, and there were several emails that she needed to respond to. The bar was packed, so she picked up a pink cocktail that a waiter was passing on a tray and found a table on the terrace overlooking the pool. It was a cool night and most of the guests were inside, networking, socializing, gossiping. It wasn't her scene. Every now and then, she caught sight of Rahul and Saira, arm in arm, laughing, smiling, posing for photos. They were both so natural at it. Could she ever fit into Saira's world? It felt nice to dress up for a night, pretend she was going to the prom, but it wasn't something that felt natural.

When they were alone, everything seemed so easy, like they belonged together. But every time she stepped outside their cocoon, Mia was hit with the reality that Saira lived in a different world than she did. Saira was used to having hairdressers and makeup artists come to her house to get her ready for a party. Wearing designer clothes, air-kissing people, nibbling on little toasts with dribbles of sauce on them and calling it food—it wasn't something Mia could get used to. The dress she was wearing itched her skin, the pins in her hair hurt, the heels pinched her feet and she was starving. She'd taken five of the last set of cute square thingies that the waiter had passed. It took stuffing two of them in her mouth at one time to figure out it was something with crab in it. She'd drunk four screwdrivers just for the orange juice.

How would they ever make it work? Saira wouldn't be happy going to these parties alone, and Mia wasn't sure she could bring herself to do this on a daily basis. She stared as Rahul and Saira posed with the party hosts, a celebrity couple who would definitely bring some attention to their social media posts. Would Saira ever want to give up the fame and adoration? She was doing it to support her family but she also enjoyed the attention; it was clear in the way her face lit up every time someone asked to take a selfie with her.

"You in love with him or her?"

She turned to find herself staring into the brown eyes of Rahul's agent. Steve Machelan was wearing a funky plaid green suit that made him look like a dressed-up leprechaun. He gestured to the empty chair beside her, and she felt rude not nodding even though she had no desire to make small talk.

"I'm Steve by the way." He held out his hand and she took it, returning his warm smile.

"I know. I'm Mia." Despite his tragic sense of dress, Steve had a nice smile. He had a Southern California tan, well-styled sandy brown hair and perfectly white teeth.

"So, you in love with him or her?"

"I'm not in love with either of them. I'm producing her show."

"I know. *Life with Meera*. Rahul had me call in quite a number of favors to get you the gig."

She looked at him. "I didn't ask her to do that."

He quirked a brow. "Then why did she do it?"

Mia shrugged. "We were friends a long time ago. She had some issues with the show and knew I'd do a good job."

Why am I even talking to this guy. It's none of his business.

As if he'd read her mind, he leaned forward. "Rahul loves his wife. I suspect he loves her in the way one best friend loves another."

Mia stayed silent. She had no idea what Rahul's agent did or didn't know, and she was not in the habit of accidentally outing people.

"He wants me to take Saira on as a client, and I'd be happy to. She's talented and has a lot of potential. If *Life with Meera* is a hit, she'll have a lot of options. But...." He paused, as if waiting for her to fill in the blanks. Mia stared at him expectantly. She wasn't going to give him anything. He wanted to talk to her, he could keep up the conversation.

"But, I worry that their personal lives are about to implode."

Mia kept her face impassive but her pulse raced. What was Steve talking about?

He slid his phone toward her, and Mia gasped. On his screen was a photo of her and Saira from a few hours ago. They were both naked, their entire bodies on full display, Saira's hand between her legs, Mia's hand on her breast, their mouths devouring each other. The picture wasn't grainy; someone had taken it from fairly close range. Neither Mia nor Saira had paid attention to the windows in that room.

"I make it a point to have a full-time staff member who has just one task—to keep an eye on all the websites where freelance photographers—I refuse to call them journalists—put up pictures for sale. Know the sale price for these?"

Mia's stomach churned.

"It's five thousand dollars."

What?

"You're a nobody and the photographer didn't recognize Saira. He was after Ned Hawkins, hoping to get a picture of him and George. I was able to negotiate him down to two thousand."

Mia breathed a sigh of relief.

"But that doesn't mean that he, or someone else, won't be back. Two thousand for a couple hours' worth of work is good enough for most of these guys."

Mia's throat was dry. She took a gulp of the pink cocktail and coughed as the sickly-sweet liquid went down her throat.

"So tell me, Mia, was this just a one-night stand, or do I need to worry that my client's marriage is about to end?"

Mia took another sip of the horrible drink, looking away from the picture on the phone.

Steve leaned forward. "I'm only looking out for their best interest."

She very much doubted that. He was looking out for his best interest, to get ahead of any issue that would affect his ability to get top dollar for his client, and therefore himself.

"What do you want me to say or do?"

He took his phone back. "I want you to tell me whether Rahul knows you're having an affair with his wife."

She nodded. There was no harm in acknowledging that.

"Is he gay?"

She looked up in surprise.

"Oh, don't give me that wide-eyed look. They won't be the first closeted celebrity couple."

"I'm done talking with you."

She pushed her chair back but he placed his hand on top of hers. "You don't have to talk to me. But hear me out. Rahul is at the top of his career right now. So is Saira. I understand she wants to work in LA. She can do that, bright future ahead and all that. But, not if she comes out. Not right now. I'm negotiating a major contract for Rahul, a part in an upcoming superhero movie. No matter how woke we all are, he won't get the part if he comes out right now. If Rahul makes it, Saira's career will follow. They are as lovable as Harry and Megan. Don't ruin it for them."

Thirteen

Saira tried to keep an eye on Mia. Why wouldn't she come join them? She'd been sitting by herself on the lawn, nursing the same drink for the last hour. As she posed for a picture, she was glad to see Steve approach her. Maybe he would convince her to join the party. Despite how she hadn't wanted to come to this party, Saira was enjoying herself. The crowd was very different from Mumbai. People talked about art, literature, the industry. Gossip and fashion were staples in LA as well as Mumbai, but Saira found herself enjoying being a new face on the social circuit. People wanted to talk to her, get to know her. At least one director and two producers had asked for her agent's name.

As much as she hated to admit it, she liked the adoration. When she was with her family, the conversation revolved around Kayra. Even before Kayra's illness, dinner talks were filled with questions about whether she had memorized her lines, what offers had come her way, which movies were currently casting and how best to position her to get the parts. Her publicist, agent and staff were always focused on what was wrong with her—is that a pimple starting on your face? Did you eat dessert last night, because there's an extra centimeter on your waistline. It was only when she was with her fans when she felt that somebody appreciated how hard she worked. It took her hours to memorize her lines for every day of shooting. If the scene was complicated, she practiced with her assistants. She prided herself on showing up to every shoot prepared to act well enough for one take.

Mia was still sitting at the same outside table she'd seen her at almost an hour ago. Why wasn't she enjoying this? Mia loved to talk art, literature, politics, pretty much any topic you threw at her. Why was she sitting in the corner sulking like someone had given her a sour Popsicle?

Once they were done taking pictures, she turned to Rahul. "I'm going to go see if Mia is okay."

He nodded absently as he continued his conversation with a director about some superhero role they were negotiating. Maybe Rahul was right, perhaps she should take advantage of his offer and sign with Steve. It had been Rahul introducing her to Peter Denton at a party that had gotten her the part for *Life with Meera*. Her agent had just negotiated the deal, he hadn't found it for her. Steve, on the other hand, was constantly bringing offers to Rahul. It was Rahul who turned them down. Always because of a man. Hosiang was in Tibet, which was much closer to India than California. Before Hosiang there had been London-based Norris. What if Rahul hadn't turned down the offers from LA? What if he had become a Hollywood A-lister rather than a Bollywood one? He could have come out, lived his life openly.

By the time she wove through the crowd, Mia was no longer there. She approached Steve, who was still sitting at the table.

"Where did Mia go?"

He shrugged. "Saira, can we talk for a second? There's something I need to show you."

The picture stopped her cold. How could she have been so stupid? The first thing she did when she entered a room was drop the curtains. She closed her eyes, not wanting the beautiful memory of being with Mia to be tainted by the sleazy-looking picture.

"I've taken care of this picture. But you need to be more careful."

Saira nodded. There was nothing else she could say. She had been stupid and careless.

"Thank you, Steve. I'll pay you back…"

He waved her off. "It was a minor expense. Trust me, it could've been worse. Pictures like these go for tens of thousands of dollars, in the hundreds of thousands if you're an A-lister. That's why these guys spend so much time stalking all of the houses in the Hills."

She turned to Steve. "Can I ask you for some career advice?"

"Don't come out now."

"Are you telling me this as Rahul's agent?"

"I'm advising you based on twenty years of experience as an agent in LA." He put a hand on her arm. "LA is not Mumbai. You're not going to be vilified for being a lesbian. Most people will celebrate your courage in coming out. You will get some backlash from some members of the LGBTQ community for being ashamed of your identity and perpetuating the belief that you need to be straight in order to succeed in life. But that can be countered with a narrative about how you are now standing up against the heteronormative culture in India and showing your courage in coming out." Now that he had her attention, he picked up his drink, a whiskey on the rocks from the look and smell, and took a sip before continuing.

"You're at the top of your career but from here, the slope is downhill. You've got a few more big movies, maybe a couple of TV series. After that, you'll be limited to roles specifically written for you, and those are rare. If you come out now, you'll get a lot of media attention, but it won't be good for your prospects. That saying— there is no such thing as bad press—is totally wrong. Movie financiers want a sure thing. They don't want a potentially controversial figure who the public can't buy in the role that she's portraying. I can't sell you for a lead part in a male-female rom-com if you are constantly in the press as the poster child for gay rights. I can't even sell you as the girl next door if the boy is going to be interested in her."

Saira took a breath. "So much for LA being more tolerant."

"It is better than most parts of the world. You're not going to get stoned to death for being a lesbian. You can live openly and freely. But yeah, we're a lot less liberal than we claim to be. It's one of those things no one talks about. We pretend we're above the rest of the world, that we promote gay rights. If you look at the well-known actors and actresses who're out, they are front and center at parties, talk shows and award ceremonies—but not in leading roles on the big screen. Movies have to appeal to a broad audience, and that includes parts of America where being gay is considered a sin."

Saira's legs were so weak, she didn't know if she could stand on them. This whole time, she had counted on the fact that LA was a way out for her, that she could build a new life. But if she couldn't support her family, then how could she leave Mumbai? How could she make a life with Mia?

Fourteen

Could she call an Uber from a celebrity mansion? Mia stood at the doorstep debating how to get out to the front gate when Saira caught up to her. "I've been looking everywhere for you."

"I need to go home."

"Is everything okay?"

Mia looked around. There were so many people milling about, taking pictures, cell phones at the ready. "I think that pink cocktail doesn't agree with me. I feel a little sick."

Saira pressed her lips, then pulled out her phone. "I'm calling Rahul to send the driver for us."

"No, you should stay, enjoy the party. You need to network. I think I saw Steven Spielberg and Kevin Blum earlier."

Saira hesitated. It was just for a second, but enough for Mia to see the want in Saira's eyes. She squeezed her arm. "I'll take the car. Text me when the party's over."

Saira shook her head. "I'd rather spend the time with you."

The odd tone of Saira's voice rang a little alarm for Mia, but she couldn't pay attention to it with Saira looking at her like she was her entire world.

They rode in silence to the hotel. Once there, they spent the night making love, both of them hungry and eager and making up for lost years. They slept naked under the sheets, and this time when Mia held Saira, there was nothing platonic or comforting about it. It was late morning when they woke up to the hotel doorbell. Mia glanced at her wristwatch and startled at how late it was. She was used to waking up before dawn.

As Saira put on a robe to open the door, Mia checked her emails. Several from David with a bunch of tedious things she needed to take care of, one from Chris, asking her to prepare a pitch for the streaming services by tomorrow. At least the social media campaign was working. #LifeWithMeera wasn't big nationally but it was trending locally, which meant a lot in LA.

The sound of a metal trolley and the popping of a champagne bottle got Mia out of bed. She threw on the hotel robe and walked into the living room to see a room service trolley with a scrumptious-looking breakfast, a bottle of Cristal champagne and chocolate-covered strawberries laid out on the table.

"Where did all this come from?"

Saira waved to a note that the waiter had placed on the coffee table, picking up a chocolate-covered strawberry. "Rahul must have sent it. He does stuff like this all the time. Especially after he makes me pose for a million photos."

Mia wanted to say something but kept her mouth shut. Rahul was a genuinely nice person, but Saira couldn't see that he too was using her, like everyone else in her life.

Saira held out a strawberry. "I'll share."

Mia smiled and took a bite as Saira held out the strawberry, letting her mouth suck and lick Saira's fingers. She pulled Saira into a hug. "We were young in Fiji, unsettled in our lives, unsure of ourselves. We're not those people anymore. We can figure this out, Saira. We can figure out how to be together."

Saira nodded, then pulled out of her arms. "I am starving, and even the five-star hotels in India haven't quite figured out how to make pancakes, so I'm going to enjoy these while I'm here."

She sat at the table and added two pancakes to her plate from the stack. Mia picked up the card on the table and opened it. Her stomach turned. "Breakfast isn't from Rahul," she said dryly.

Saira raised her brows. "Well, are you going to tell me or keep me in suspense?"

"Steve sent this."

Saira stopped midchew, then recovered. She set down her fork. "I meant to tell you last night but we…um… got caught up with other things. I've decided to fire my agent and sign with Steve."

Mia's stomach turned even more.

"What made you change your mind?"

"I bumped into him at the party and he gave me some advice. I found it useful and realized that he knows Hollywood a lot better than my agent. He'll be better able to navigate it for me."

Mia's mouth was dry. She picked up a glass of orange

juice and nearly downed half of it. She herself had suggested that Saira sign with Steve. But that was before her conversation with him at the party. "Did he show you the pictures?"

Saira stared at her for what seemed like forever. "He showed the pictures to you too?"

Mia nodded. "With a warning to stay away from you and not ruin your career. And Rahul's too."

Saira sighed. "He said something similar to me." She reached out her arm and grabbed Mia's hand. "Look, I'm not blindly following his advice. Unlike my agent, he's got a better network of contacts to help me land roles, and he's got a whole staff that does public relations. Not all agents offer that type of full service."

"I'm not arguing that he's a good agent. What I'm wondering is why you selected him, knowing he won't support you living your life openly. He made it pretty clear that he thought you and Rahul should stay firmly in the closet."

"That doesn't mean we're going to listen to him. Rahul and I are on the same page that we're tired of living our life in secret, constantly afraid of being outed, considering each partner with suspicion. We're just trying to be smart about how we manage our careers so we don't end up like those stars who get invited to every party but don't have the money to buy a dress."

Mia pushed her plate of eggs away, her appetite gone. Those last words were not Saira's, but Steve's.

Saira moved and knelt next to her. She took both of Mia's hands in her own. "I'm going to find a way for us to be together, openly. But it's going to take time. I have to see what roles Steve can get me, develop a financial plan, talk to my family... There's a lot I have to do. I need you to be patient with me....please."

It all made perfect sense. It hadn't even been a week since that day in the costume room when she first saw Saira. So much had happened that neither of them had had time to sit back and think or reflect.

She nodded and kissed Saira lightly on the lips. But the alarm bells in her head were loudly clanging.

Weeks later, *Life with Meera* wasn't completely off the chopping block but the knives had been set down. One of the streaming giants agreed to pick it up after seeing a clip from the first day of filming. As Mia suspected, Saira's charm and talent shone through the screen. But they were still on the hook to get filming finished in six weeks, and they were currently running two days behind schedule.

Mia slung her messenger bag across her shoulder; she needed to hurry to make it to the studio. She'd spent all morning stuck in meetings, and now it was almost lunch time and she and Saira had a routine. Six weeks had gone by since she and Saira had taken up together, but they still couldn't get enough of each other. Mia didn't spend every night with Saira, especially not after her makeup artist and David had complained about the puffiness under her eyes, but they did eat lunch and dinner together when they could. Mia had cooked for Saira a couple of times, and then there was room service. Mia barely slept five hours each night but she didn't care. She had waited for ten years to be with Saira and was going to savor every second.

As soon as she entered the studio, she knew something was wrong. According to the schedule, they should be in the middle of taping but everyone looked to be on break. The actors were nowhere to be seen, the camera crew and staff were scattered about, many at the catering table, which hadn't yet been set up for lunch.

David found Mia just as she began searching for him. "We have a problem."

"Clearly. What's going on?"

"You need to rein Saira in. She requested more script changes..." Mia nodded. She had started to go over those with Saira yesterday, but it had been in Mia's bedroom and they'd gotten distracted before finishing the full review.

"The other actors are getting frustrated. They get changes the night before, they don't have enough time to relearn their lines. We were on the sixth take for the last scene when I sent everyone to their trailers to go learn the lines."

Mia sighed. She'd been afraid of this. "Saira has script approval."

"I know. But at the end of today, we're going to be three days behind. It's not just the script changes. Saira isn't coming prepared. She needs constant reminding of her lines. We've been running late for the last week and everyone is tired. Saturday was supposed to be a half day but I need to extend it to catch up."

"I'll talk to her."

David shook his head. "I've already talked to her." He leaned in conspiratorially. "I heard that she's having an affair, and that's why she's so distracted."

Mia went cold. After the pictures that Steve had bought, she and Saira had been so careful. They never entered her hotel together. Mia had even figured out an entrance through the parking lot that was less public. For their afternoon romps, Mia always knocked loudly on her door and announced that she needed to go over script changes, or went to her dressing room before Saira and left after. The window shades were always drawn and white noise turned up high.

"David, you know better than to listen to set gossip."

He shook his head. "It's not just the gossip about the affair. I think she's busy preparing for another project. I was at a dinner last night and—" he looked around to make sure no one was in listening range "—one of my fellow directors… I can't name names…he said that he was casting for a movie and Saira's name came up. But her agent said that she wasn't available to read for the part because she was busy preparing for some big Bollywood project."

Her mouth soured. She had to admit that they didn't seem to have much time to talk between Saira's filming schedule and Mia's meetings, but Saira would have told her if she signed on to some big Bollywood project. Wouldn't she? How many times had she mentioned the various roles that Steve had found for her? She had even read for a supporting actress role in a major film. Saira hadn't gotten the part.

David was looking at her expectantly. Mia sighed. "It's really none of our business what Saira is doing. But her performance on our show is something we should address, and I will."

"You do that. We need to right this ship now."

Mia made her way to Saira's dressing room. Saira greeted her like she aways did, with a kiss that made Mia forget why she'd come in the first place. She pulled away.

"We need to talk."

"Uh-oh."

"David's upset."

Saira nodded. "I know. And he's right. I've been messing up my lines, and today I forgot half my actions too. I sat down when I was supposed to be pacing and clapped by hands when I was supposed to slap my forehead."

"That's not like you."

Saira nodded. "Just been so stressed lately. I'm reading a ton of scripts, plus there's all this social stuff."

"Something's got to give. You've been going out three or four times a night. Can you skip the parties?" She kept her voice neutral. She didn't want to come across as the nagging girlfriend.

Saira sighed. "Steve thinks it's important I network in LA." She reached over and ran a finger down Mia's arm. "Then there's making sure I keep you happy." Her tone was teasing but Mia caught the stress between the words.

"We don't have to spend so much time together. I've been falling behind on my work too. I had to stay up until 3:00 a.m. last night just to get through my emails and invoice approvals."

Saira shook her head and pulled Mia into her arms. "No. That's the one thing we can't compromise on. You and I have waited so long to be together. We can't let the pressures of daily life keep us away from each other."

Mia nodded but her stomach was in a thousand knots as she looked at Saira. How had she not noticed the bags under her eyes, the paleness of her skin under the cream-colored foundation.

"Why don't I leave you to go over the lines for the afternoon taping."

"It's almost lunch. Are you sure you don't want to stay?" Saira ran a hand up her thigh and Mia's body responded immediately. She could spare some time, couldn't she? They could be quick.

She placed a hand on top of Saira's. "You need to practice your lines, and I need to go smooth things over with David."

Saira did that thing with her lips that was somewhere between a pout and a smirk, and it took every ounce of Mia's self-control to leave.

By week ten, they were six days behind on their taping schedule. David was ready to quit; one of the writers had already thrown a fit and walked off. The crew was upset because they had been working overtime, and everyone's temper was on the last string.

"No more script changes!" David screamed at her. They were in Mia's office, having just met with the editing staff. She and David had both missed an inconsistency between episode one and five.

"To be fair, David, neither one of us, or the writers caught that we had to change the episode five script."

"A problem we wouldn't have to deal with if we weren't wholesale rewriting the script as we tape."

"You were in love with the script changes. I'm the one who had a problem with it."

"For about thirty seconds, then you started sleeping with Saira and lost all control over the show."

Mia froze. *How does he know?* "That's a rude accusation."

David crossed his arms. "It's not an accusation—it's a statement of fact. You think no one notices that you two hole up in her trailer at lunch, and both of you come out looking all flushed and smelling of sex?"

Her face heated. Did everyone on set know? How could she have been so careless? Her reputation would be ruined. It was one thing to have an affair on set, it was another when their relationship was being blamed for the star's performance.

"Don't worry. The only people who know are Gail, my assistant, and me. We've done our best to quash the talk. Gail even went as far as to tell people that you're dating someone else."

Mia sank into a chair. There was no point in denying it. David pulled out the guest chair and sat opposite her. "Why are you protecting me?" It would've been so much easier for David to let the rumors take hold and have the network fire her. He'd been wanting to call Saira's agent and threaten nonperformance on the contract if she didn't improve. Mia had stopped him. Then he'd wanted to call a meeting with the network executives and change the schedule. Production delays happened on every show and film—it wasn't that unusual a request. But Mia had dug her heels in. She was still afraid the network would cancel the show.

David rolled his eyes. "Believe me, I'd like nothing more than to throw you to the wolves. But you're one of the best producers I've worked with. You're not a network ass-kisser, you care about the quality of the show and you don't try to blow smoke up my ass when something isn't working."

Mia smiled. It was actually quite a compliment coming from David.

"What do I need to do?"

He put up four fingers. "First, you need to tell Saira that she gets one last go at script changes. All of them need to be turned in in a day or two. That'll give us some time to review the changes and make sure we don't have more mistakes that require reshooting." Mia nodded. It was a reasonable request, and if she hadn't been so busy with her head between Saira's thighs, she would have insisted on that a long time ago.

"Second, you need to get us more time with the network. I need two extra weeks. We can make up the time in editing."

Mia bit her lip. "It'll be tough getting time on the actor's calendars."

"We can work around that. There are a number of solo scenes with Saira. As long as we have her, I can make the schedule work."

"The bigger issue is the budget for the crew's time."

David nodded. "That's an issue you're going to have to solve. I'll do my best to go with a skeleton crew, but you're still going to have to convince the network weenies to open their wallets."

Mia nodded. She had already calculated a week of extra budget and had a proposal ready, but that was if they had no further delays, which was wishful thinking.

"Third, you're going to give the crew the entire weekend plus Friday afternoon off."

Mia opened her mouth but David shook his head. "Don't protest. Everyone is exhausted and making stupid mistakes. They need a break. I've baked that into the time extension."

Again, Mia nodded. These were all things she'd been thinking about anyway.

"Last, you're going to break it off with Saira."

Mia froze.

"I'm not saying forever. Just until we finish filming. You are a distraction and we're at a critical point now. We can't afford to waste time. Plus, it's only a matter of time before everyone finds out. Unless she's ready to come out of the closet, it's not fair for you to keep at it."

As much as she hated to admit it, David was right.

Fifteen

Saira rubbed her temples, closing her eyes with the hope that her headache would disappear. She had too much work to do. Mia had asked for all remaining script changes by tomorrow. On top of that, Mia hadn't had lunch or dinner with her, begging off with some excuse about meetings. She was a horrible liar. There was something going on. Had she found out about the Mumtaz Mahal role? Saira had been in discussions with the movie producers; they were offering 8 percent above her regular fee. It wasn't just the money. The role was amazing. She'd get to play a tragic historical character who inspired an iconic monument of love. The movie had international blockbuster written all over it. Even Steve was encouraging her to do it.

Saira had been hoping Steve would come up with a better option for her in LA. He had done better than her last agent but also given her the same advice that she needed to wait for *Life with Meera* to come out. There was some nice buzz about the show, but because Saira was still untested with American audiences, the offers coming in were limited to supporting roles that didn't pay even a quarter of what Bollywood was offering.

She had to discuss the Mumtaz Mahal role with Mia, but every time she tried to bring it up, the thought of how Mia would react stopped her. Their entire relationship felt as though it was held together by cello tape. Any day now, one piece would get ripped off and the whole thing would collapse. Mia said she was trying to give her the time she needed to figure things out, but not a day went by when Mia didn't ask whether she'd heard from Steve, or when she planned to talk to her family. How did she make Mia understand all the pressures that were on her? On top of everything, Kayra wanted Saira to come see her. Even if she used Rahul's private jet subscription, it was twelve hours each way. They were already behind schedule on filming, a fact that was stressing Mia out. Saira couldn't ask for extra days to go visit her sister.

She grabbed her purse and shook out two paracetamol tablets, washing them down with the can of soda sitting on her bedside table.

She looked at the WhatsApp message from Kayra.

I really need to see you, di. There's something important I want to discuss with the family. I can't do it without you.

What could it be? The last time Kayra had a request, it was to permanently stay at the Swiss center. Had she found another place, or did she want to come home? She had tried calling Kayra, but all she would say over video is that she wanted to talk to Saira in person. Her mother had no idea what was going on; all she said was that Saira had to find a way to go visit Kayra.

In the meantime, she had an impossible deadline for script changes, and she still had to learn her lines for the next day. Maybe it was a good thing that Mia hadn't come over. No matter how hard Saira tried, it was difficult to focus on anything when she was with Mia. She had fallen behind on so many important tasks: reviewing her accountant's reports, reading the new scripts from both her agents, learning her lines. All Saira wanted to do was be with Mia, spend time with her, suck up every last ounce of her. But that didn't leave much time for anything else.

Her phone buzzed with a call from Rahul. He was filming in Greece. She put the phone on Speaker.

"Isn't it the middle of the night there?" she said when she answered.

"Yes, but I miss my wife. I had to talk to her."

"You do know there is no one listening on this line."

"It's the truth, *yaar*. I do miss you. What happened with Jay is really troubling me."

She sat up. "What happened with Jay?"

"You didn't hear?"

She shook her head, then realized they were on a voice call. "No. I haven't been looking at the news back home. Too busy."

He sighed. "I hope you're sitting down."

She was, but she pulled a pillow closer and hugged it tight. Jay Goshal was a prominent director, and a really nice guy. Saira had worked with him on six projects. "He was leaving his apartment complex in Bandra, just getting ready to meet his driver in the garage, when a worker—I think it was a gardener or something—approached him and threw acid in his face."

"Oh, my God! No! Is he okay?" Bile rose in the back of her throat and her stomach heaved. She clutched the pillow to her stomach and doubled over it.

"Half his face, neck and the top of his shoulder are badly burned. He's still in the ICU. For security reasons, they won't disclose what hospital he's in. Last I heard, he'll make it, but it's going to be a long road to recovery."

"Give me a second."

She rushed to the bathroom and made it just in time as the meager contents of her stomach came up her throat. She could hear Rahul calling out to her from the speaker.

She returned to the bed.

"Are you okay?"

"What the hell, Rahul? How did this happen?"

"The guy who did it was a nutjob. Apparently, his only son just told him he was gay and Jay was his idol or something. He wanted to be a director. The father snapped, got a job in the apartment complex. You know how these guys are—they blame the celebrity for their problems, thinking by hurting us, they're somehow solving their own problems."

"No, they're punishing us. They think we're the ones to blame for whatever is affecting their personal lives. I mean, if Jay isn't safe in his own home, what hope do we have?"

"India's not ready yet, Saira. It's getting there, but not yet."

"How long, Rahul? Are we going to have to wait for our children's generation to be able to live openly?"

"I don't know. Look, it's not all bad. I mean, there was *Chandigarh di Aashiqui*—that movie where Vaani Kapoor played the transgender woman…."

"Yeah, a nice movie, except that Abhishek didn't cast a trans woman to play the role. Instead, he chose Vaani, who did a nice job, but she's not trans." Saira had been approached about that role but had declined it because she'd felt that a trans woman should play the role.

"See, that's what I mean. It's changing but not fully there. Next time, they'll cast a trans woman. Look, Sonam Kapoor played a lesbian in *Ek Ladki Ko Dekha*. There's hope. Hey, imagine if you had taken that role?"

Saira wished she had. The movie was about a woman who had to come out to her traditional family in order to marry the woman she loved. It was only four years ago, but her parents had talked her out of taking the role. Kayra had finally been settled and happy and they didn't want her affected by any backlash.

"I wish I had. It would make it so much easier to come out."

"You're not still thinking of doing that, are you? Not after what happened with Jay?"

"How long are we going to wait, Rahul? It's never going to end, is it? There will always be someone dangerous out there." But even as she said the words, her stomach heaved. It was one thing to put herself at risk, but what if they came after her family? Kayra was safe in Switzerland and Mia was in America, but what about her parents?

They were both silent for a while, then Rahul spoke, "Hosiang said he's decided to leave the monastery. Being with me has made him realize that he has unresolved issues and he needs to figure them out."

"Are you getting back together with him?"

"He didn't betray me on purpose."

"It's not fair to him. He's trying to confront his truth and you're telling him to hide and lie for you."

"It's not by choice."

"Isn't it?" That's what Mia kept telling her. It was a choice. Not an easy one but it was a choice. Mia had lost her parents. It hadn't been easy for her to live openly—it wasn't as if she'd gotten the acceptance she wanted—but she hadn't taken the easy path.

As if reading her mind, Rahul sighed deeply. "If you're thinking about Mia, she had more of a choice than we do. Yes, she had to fight against her parents, but you and I both know that if it was just about standing up to our parents, we would do it. Mia doesn't get thrown out of her job for being a lesbian. She doesn't risk her livelihood, she doesn't worry every time she leaves her house that a seemingly innocent servant will throw acid in her face. I mean look at Ned—he had to stay away from his own house for months because he was being called a home wrecker."

Tears stung her eyes. "How are we ever going to be happy?"

"*Yaar,* I called you 'cause I was feeling low, and now we're both even lower."

"That's life, Rahul."

She hung up with him and closed her eyes, her stomach still heaving. How was she ever going to keep her family safe if she came out? How was she going to be with Mia? Her head hurt. She needed time to figure it all out. Was Rahul right? Was this just something she couldn't have in her lifetime and should just hope that her children could have it in the future?

Her laptop pinged with another email. It was daytime in India and people were waiting on answers. A little time. That's all she needed. Some space to catch up with everything she had to do so she could think clearly, figure out how she was going to sort out her life.

It was early morning by the time she finished with the script changes. She was tired and had to be on set in four hours. She had to get some sleep if she was going to be functional.

The next day just got worse. Saira had such a headache that she couldn't remember her lines. David sent her home. Mia was nowhere to be seen, supposedly in meetings with the network.

Saira had several emails from her Bollywood agent. She needed to make a commitment to the Mumtaz Mahal role. He'd managed to convince them to give her 8.5 percent above her normal asking fee. Nine months wasn't that long of a time to be away from Mia. *Maybe we can find a way to make it work. I can fly here once a month and Mia can come visit.* It was a nice thought, but Saira knew what filming schedules were like. Any free time she had would go toward any number of social events or endorsement deals. Mia would get busy with another project and she wouldn't be able to come. They would grow apart. Could their relationship withstand the distance? Mia understood what Saira was dealing with. She would understand, wouldn't she? If they hadn't moved on from each other in ten years, what was nine months of being apart? Steve had assured her that after *Life with Meera* came out, he'd have better offers for her.

Her accountant sent her a red envelope email. She opened it to find that an unexpected bill had come in from the ashram her mother frequented, and Kayra's facility bill was again higher than normal. He was asking permission to break one of her fixed deposits to cover the payments. Saira rubbed her temples. The fixed deposits were her savings, and she lost money if she broke the deposit before the due date. She looked at the invoice from the ashram but the numbers swam before her eyes. She slammed the laptop lid shut. There weren't enough hours in the day.

A WhatsApp message pinged on her phone. It was Kayra asking whether they could talk. Normally Saira tried to talk to her sister a few times a week, but calls with Kayra took at least an hour and she still had to memorize her lines for tomorrow. She couldn't have another bad day on set. A second later another text came in, this one from Mia, saying she was on her way to the hotel. Saira rubbed her temples. For the first time since she'd come to LA, she was not looking forward to seeing Mia. With Mia there, Saira wouldn't be able to focus on her lines, plus she couldn't keep putting off telling her about the Mumtaz role.

She washed her face and changed her clothes. Mia keyed into the hotel room. Saira knew something was wrong the moment she walked in. It was in the way her smile didn't reach her eyes, in the stiff way she walked and sat down on the couch with her legs crossed. She was wearing a black business suit. Mia hated business suits. She only wore them when she had to. Things must be really bad with the network.

"I'm sorry I didn't get my lines right today. I stayed

up all night working on the script changes and didn't get enough sleep."

"So it's my fault?"

"I never said that." Saira went and sat beside Mia. She put a hand on her knee. "What is going on?"

"We need two more weeks to finish the show. The network isn't happy about it, but thankfully it's too late to pull the plug. They *are* going to torture me by giving me a ridiculously small budget in which there is no way I can have all the staff I need to finish filming. I'm going to have to fire Gail."

Saira squeezed her hand. She knew how much Mia valued Gail's friendship. "I am so sorry. But filming was scheduled to end anyway, right, so it's not like you're really firing Gail."

Mia squeezed the bridge of her nose. "Actually, she was supposed to be my assistant through the end of production. But the only way I can make the budget work is to let her go now. Which means more work for me, by the way."

"I am sorry." She didn't know what else to say. Mia seemed miserable, but Saira didn't have a way to make her feel better.

Mia opened her mouth, then closed it.

"You blame me, don't you? This wouldn't have happened if I hadn't screwed up my lines all those times."

Mia shook her head. "This happens on all shows. There are always production delays, the bosses are never happy, and at this point, I'm usually questioning my career choice."

"Then what is it?"

"A few people know about us on the show."

Saira's throat closed. "Who? How?" she choked out.

"It's just David, his assistant and Gail."

Saira's pulse raced. "Gail is a huge gossip. By now the whole crew probably knows."

Once again Mia shook her head. "We can trust David and Gail."

That was easy for Mia to say. She hadn't been betrayed over and over again, nor did she have to worry about what would happen if someone did leak their relationship.

She stood and paced the length of the small living room. "We can't meet in my trailer anymore. And you can't come to the hotel."

Mia was silent. Saira paced some more. How much did Gail and David know? Had they taken any pictures? She turned to Mia. "We should take a break. Just for a little while. Until filming is over."

"That's exactly what David asked me to do."

Saira stopped. "Okay, then we're in agreement."

Mia stood. "Actually, I told him no. I promised that we wouldn't get together while on set, but that our relationship is not up for negotiation." She gave Saira a hard look. "Glad to know where I stand with you."

Saira stepped back, her chest and throat so tight that she wasn't sure if she was even getting enough air. "That's not fair. I can't have our relationship go public now. We've talked about this. You know how much I have at stake."

Mia placed her hands on her hips and Saira stiffened. She knew this posture. "We've talked a lot about what you have at stake, but have you considered that I'm affected too? David has already implied that our relationship is affecting the show, that I've been too soft with you, that I've been distracted. This is a big show for me.

I mess this up and I'm going to be stuck doing projects no one else wants. I don't want our relationship getting out any more than you do. But, unlike you, I'm not willing to throw away our relationship every time there's a bump in the road."

She still doesn't understand. They'd been having the same argument since Fiji. Mia saw everything as black and white; either Saira was willing to come out or she wasn't, either she was willing to give up her life in Mumbai or she wasn't; either she loved Mia or she didn't. How many times did she need to ask Mia for more time? Mia knew the position she was in, the stress she was under. Why couldn't she be more understanding?

Saira rubbed her temples. "That's not fair. I didn't say we should break up, I just think that a break might not be a bad idea—to protect us both."

As soon as the words were out of her mouth, Saira knew it was the wrong thing to say. The look on Mia's face sent daggers through her heart.

"Have you ever taken a break from being a daughter or sister?" Mia grabbed her purse and wrenched the door open. "You don't take breaks from the people you love."

Sixteen

The fact that things improved on set only made it harder for Mia. Saira had sent her an apology text and begged her to come back to the hotel room so they could talk. Mia suggested that they take the night to think on it. Saira had appeared on set looking fresh and bright. She'd delivered her lines flawlessly, and David had beamed. Had he been right? Was their relationship affecting Saira's performance? Maybe they had been spending too much time together. She had to admit that having the evening to herself yesterday gave her the time she needed to rework the budget that Chris had requested. She'd figured out a way to pay for two more weeks of the crew's time.

Maybe a break wasn't such a bad idea. Things had been so intense for the last two and a half months, neither of them had any breathing room.

"Can I talk to you?"

How did Saira always manage to sneak up on her? Mia

had just finished pouring herself a cup of coffee from the catering table.

They found a quiet corner in the studio. The crew was setting up for the next shot and Saira could get called any second.

"Look, I'm sorry about yesterday. I was stressed about messing up my lines, and I had just been thinking about how there is so much to do and so little time and...."

"And spending less time with me felt like a good way to make space in your day."

"Yes... I mean no. Wait.... just give me a second."

She put a hand through her hair and Mia instinctively reached out to stop her. "Don't ruin your do."

Saira leaned forward. "I love you. I've loved you since the day we met."

David called for the actors. Saira sighed. "Please try and understand where I'm coming from."

Mia stood rooted as Saira walked away. Saira loved her. They'd said it to each other in Fiji, but that was different. Mia had spent a sleepless night wondering whether Saira was tired of her. Whether Mia had misconstrued really amazing sex for love. Whether she was once again in a one-sided relationship and destined to be left alone.

The day couldn't end soon enough for her. She kept herself busy in her office, afraid that if she were in the studio with Saira, she wouldn't be able to resist pulling her into a dark corner or her dressing room. She'd promised David that she would not be distracted during working hours and would leave Saira alone to focus on her lines. He hadn't been happy that Mia wouldn't break it off, but she reminded him of the countless relationships that happened on set, including one that he notoriously had with a previous actress. After being pinned in his glass house, he resisted the urge to throw any more stones at her. But that didn't mean he wouldn't go low and spread rumors if he felt she wasn't keeping up her side of the bargain.

Gail stuck her head in just as Mia was getting ready to leave. "Can I talk to you for a second?"

Mia nodded guiltily. She had yet to break the news to Gail that she wouldn't have a job. She was trying to find a way to keep her, but it wasn't looking good. Mia had put out feelers for other positions. It would be easier to break the news if she had options to give Gail.

Gail sat in the guest chair across from Mia. She clasped her hands. "You can't fire me."

"Excuse me?" It took a second for Mia to process what Gail had said.

"I know you're working the budget, and there's no way you're going to make it work unless you get rid of some people. Naturally I'd be at the top of the list."

While it was true, it still irritated Mia that Gail had come to that conclusion. "Why would you make that assumption?"

She folded her arms. "Am I wrong?"

Mia couldn't lie to her. She shook her head. "I'm not done with the budget yet. I'm trying to find options. That's why I haven't mentioned it to you."

Gail leaned forward. "You're a horrible liar, Mia, always have been. You've been avoiding me the last two days, and you've stopped cc'ing me on the budget emails to Chris. I see the writing on the wall, but I'm here to ask you not to do it."

Mia sighed. "I'm sorry, Gail. I will do my best to try and find you something good."

"Oh, I'll find another job in a minute. My old show has been begging me to come back. I'm not worried about me, I'm worried about you."

"Excuse me?"

"Saira. I've been worried about you since you started seeing her."

"That's not fair." Mia and Gail were close but she'd been limited in how much she shared. She didn't need Gail to tell her all that was wrong about her relationship with Saira—her inner critic did a pretty good job of that.

"I've worked with you before. When the show is filming, you are hyperfocused. On this show, you've been distracted. You haven't been yourself."

"It's the biggest show I've done. There's a lot to do... it has nothing to do with Saira."

Gail pinned her with a hard look. "Tell me something, Mia—are you happy living your life in the closet?"

"What're you talking about?" Mia said wearily.

"You talk about how important it is to live openly, and here you are, sneaking around with a married woman. Tell me, are you enjoying hiding out in hotel rooms? Getting good at looking away when someone catches you staring at her? Having your friends lie for you?"

"Gail... I'm grateful you covered for me and Saira. Our relationship is complicated, I don't deny it. She needs some time to sort things out. She's got a lot of responsibilities. As soon as she finds a good project in LA, she'll come out and our relationship can be more open."

"I hope you're right but are you sure you can trust her? I hear she's signing some big period film for Bollywood."

"What? When did you hear this?"

"There has been chitchat about it for weeks now. Didn't Saira tell you?"

Gail had to be mistaken. There were always rumors and gossip about movie contracts.

"I'm sorry about the budget, Gail…"

Gail stood and gave her a hug. "Take care of yourself. Try and remember why you have your principles."

Mia put her forehead on her desk once Gail left. Her friend's comments had poured salt on the gaping wound that was her relationship with Saira. Hiding, sneaking away was wearing on both of them, but Saira had asked her for time and understanding and Mia had agreed to be patient. But, was Gail right about the effect it was having on Mia's job? Had she been so focused on protecting Saira that she'd jeopardized her show and career? David had accused her of the same thing, of losing control over the star of her show and letting it run over schedule and over budget. She took a breath. If the show got a second season, she would resign as producer. It wasn't fair to the crew if she couldn't handle Saira. She could get another job as producer, but she couldn't replace Saira as the love of her life.

The last month of shooting went smoothly. After Saira's declaration of love, they'd made up, but Mia saw less and less of Saira as their working days got longer and Mia got busier with editing. As much as she hated to admit it, Saira was better at remembering her lines when Mia didn't spend the night at her hotel.

The wrap party to celebrate the end of filming arrived way too soon. Saira was scheduled to leave the next day to see her sister in Geneva. Saira had promised to return to LA in a few days. Though filming had wrapped up, there was always something that came up in the editing process, and sometimes they needed actors to come back in to redub lines in the sound studio.

Mia had a bad feeling about Saira leaving. She couldn't explain what it was, but there was a gnawing ache deep in her belly about saying goodbye to Saira. They were spending the night together, and Saira kept saying it was only a few days that she'd be gone but there was no real reason for Saira to be in LA. She didn't have another project lined up, and Mia was going to be very busy getting the show ready to air.

Mia made it to the hotel before Saira, who had texted to say that she was meeting with Steve and would be late. Mia hoped that Steve had come up with something good for Saira. They'd discussed the offers he'd brought her to date, and Mia hadn't been impressed. As much as she wanted Saira to pick up a project in LA as soon as possible, she knew the offers he'd brought Saira were not right for her.

The smell of flowers greeted her as she opened the hotel room door. A beautiful bouquet of pink and white peonies sat on the dining room table. Mia set down her messenger bag. The envelope with the card was open. Was it wrong to see who the bouquet was from?

Mia picked up the envelope. Saira was a star; plenty of people knew peonies were her favorite. Plus, any number of agents, studio execs, directors, producers, even costars sent flowers to each other, especially on wrap day. But something about the flowers called to her.

She opened the envelope, read the note, then placed it back on the table.

Congrats to the new Mumtaz Mahal. See you in Mumbai soon.

It was from her Bollywood agent. This was the movie David and Gail had told her about. She had asked around about it. There was a big project being financed out of Dubai, a period piece about the wife of the guy who built the Taj Mahal for her. The role was huge, but there was no way Saira would take it. The shooting schedule would be months in India. Saira hadn't even mentioned it to her. They had talked about all the other offers that Saira had received. Mia assumed Saira hadn't brought it up because she wasn't considering it. *She lied to me.* Was she even going to Geneva or was she headed to Mumbai?

Mia sat on the couch and buried her face in her hands. She had written this script from the beginning. Saira was never going to stay. Mia didn't doubt that she wanted to, that Saira loved her. But it took more than love and wanting to do what Saira needed to do, and Mia knew her well enough to know that she wasn't ready. Saira was used to being the heroine—of her family, of her country. She liked taking care of her family, being the provider. She enjoyed being the darling of a country. It was a lot to give up to come live with Mia in a crappy one-bedroom condo.

Saira had asked if Mia would be willing to give up her own life to come be with her. The truth was that Mia didn't have the courage either. Sure, she made excuses: she didn't speak Hindi, or any of the Indian languages; she had no job prospects in India. There wasn't exactly a demand for American TV producers with mediocre titles behind their name. The real issue was that she wasn't ready to go live in hiding, pretending to be Saira's friend or whatever, watching her lover go to parties with her husband and carry on with a fake marriage. This whole time, Mia had assumed she was on the moral high ground, wanting them to live openly. But wasn't she asking Saira for a sacrifice when she wasn't willing to do the same? When Gail had asked her whether she was willing to live in secret, Mia had recoiled. She wanted Saira to give up her whole life and come out, but if Saira seriously asked her to do the same, Mia couldn't.

Saira breezed in late at night. "So sorry I couldn't break away earlier. Steve and I had a lot to talk about, so we went and had dinner and drinks."

"Good meeting?"

Saira nodded. "He's in discussions to get me a small walk-on role in a really cool espionage thriller movie."

Mia let her go on telling her about the project. Her stomach was in knots, her mouth completely dry. "You got flowers."

Saira hadn't noticed. "Oh...who are they from?"

"Your Mumbai agent. Congratulating you on that role you just took."

Saira froze. "Listen, I was going to talk to you about that."

Mia narrowed her eyes. "When were you going to tell me? After you got to Mumbai, when you wouldn't have to face me?"

"After I got back from Geneva. I'm meeting with the film financiers there. The deal isn't final."

"I thought you were going to Geneva to sort out whatever is going on with Kayra."

"I am. Look, I haven't signed the final papers and the

movie financiers want to meet with me. I think they're going to offer me more money. The financiers are from Dubai, and since I was going to be in Geneva, my agent got them to meet me there."

Mia didn't trust herself to speak.

As if reading her mind, Saira took Mia's hands in her own. "I am going to Switzerland to see Kayra. That was always the plan. This meeting only happened yesterday. This role, Mia, it's huge. It has international appeal. Even Steve thinks I should take the role because it'll help me land better in LA. I am only considering this project because it helps me ultimately get to LA."

She was looking at Mia so earnestly it cut through her heart. Saira really believed she was doing the right thing. "How long is the project?"

"Nine to ten months. But that doesn't mean I'll be gone the entire time. I'll come here, and maybe you can visit me."

"Visit you on set? Where you'll introduce me to everyone as what? Your ex-producer? Your friend? Your former lover? Or your secret girlfriend?"

Saira let go of Mia's hands. "I haven't figured it all out yet."

"Why didn't you tell me you were considering this movie?"

Saira looked away and Mia had her answer.

Mia swallowed against her tight throat. "You and I both know what's going to happen. You're going to go back to India and resume your life as a beloved and happily married star. You'll leave me waiting here for years before finally admitting that you can't give up your life there."

Saira was shaking her head as she spoke. "That's not fair Mia. You haven't even given me a chance. I can't topple my whole life in a day. I have to start with my family, prepare for what's coming. It's about their safety too. You know what happened to Kayra. I can't risk something like that happening to them." Her eyes were wet and Mia's chest burned. Saira would keep getting sucked into her responsibilities. Until she admitted to herself that she couldn't do it all, she would keep sacrificing her happiness, and Mia's.

Mia sank down on the couch and buried her face in her hands, unable to look at Saira. *I'm tired of waiting for you.*

Saira clicked on her phone and turned it toward Mia. She recoiled. "What is that?"

"That's a picture from a news story about a director I worked with in India. He's openly gay. Some guy threw acid in his face because he thinks Jay is responsible for his son being gay. That's a picture of him in the hospital. He's looking at months of plastic surgery and even then he's never going to look right. This happened just a few days ago."

"That's horrible." Mia sat on the couch and grabbed Saira's hand. "I'm so sorry that happened to your friend."

Saira squeezed her hand. "I know there's a certain risk involved in being a public figure. You get threats and stalkers no matter what. But you have to understand that India is where America was fifty years ago with gay rights—most of them still think the way your parents do. They think that when celebrities come out, they are corrupting their children, Westernizing them. Things are changing, but slowly. It was only 2018 when our Supreme court struck down the penal code that made homosexuality illegal. Until then, police threw people in jail and beat them for no other reason than a neighbor or family member's complaint."

"We've had this conversation so many times, Saira. I understand the risks in India are different than they are here. I thought you were ready to leave, to start a life here with me."

Saira sighed. "I am. I just need more time. We've waited ten years, what's a few more? It's just until my career takes off. Then I can move my family, and we can live together openly."

"That was your plan ten years ago."

It was her fault. Mia knew this was where it was headed from the very beginning, but she'd let herself get sucked into a fantasy.

She cupped Saira's face. "I know you love me. I don't doubt it for a second. But you can't have it all. You can't have your fame, your lucrative movie contracts, keep your sister in that expensive facility, take care of your parents and live your life openly with me. You want things to be perfect for everyone, but that's just not possible. You have to decide, Saira. What are you willing to sacrifice for your happiness? For us?"

Tears streamed down Saira's face. Her own eyes were wet. She'd known they were headed toward this. Had avoided it, tried to tell herself there was a way they could work it out. It was too much to ask of Saira. She wasn't ready yet. Maybe she'd get there, but Mia couldn't spend her life waiting, hoping, living in the shadows.

"Can't you wait, just for a little while?"

The plea in Saira's voice shook her resolve. She could

wait for Saira, couldn't she? What was a few years for the love of her life? It's not as if she'd had luck finding a life partner in the last ten years. Except she hadn't been looking for a life partner. Now Mia was ready for permanence. If anything, the time spent with Saira talking about the future, a home, children, date nights—it had helped Mia realized she was ready for all that. She wanted to come home to someone each night, have that special person she could take to the insufferable parties; she wanted to plan a future, including children.

"It's not fair to you or to me to put our lives on hold, waiting, hoping that things will change."

Mia pulled Saira into a hug, closing her eyes and breathing in her scent. Saira kissed the corner of her neck, then her check, and her mouth found Mia's. They kissed with all the pent-up passion of the past ten years, and the future they each knew they wouldn't have. They held each other for a long time, their bodies melded together. Mia finally broke free before she lost the last of her crumbling nerve. "At least we get to say goodbye this time."

She picked up her messenger bag and walked out of Saira's hotel room, and her life.

Seventeen

Saira waited in the family lounge of the Clinique Lake Geneva. The glass wall overlooked snowcapped mountains and a landscaped garden that could've inspired a Monet. She sat on a lemon-yellow sofa that was hard on the back but too stylish not to like anyway. Mia would've hated this place. It was pretentiously beautiful and uncomfortably luxurious. Saira had spent the entire plane trip alternatively crying and arguing with herself. Finally after eight hours, she'd realized that she couldn't give Mia what she wanted. Saira couldn't choose between her own happiness and that of her family. She'd thought about begging Mia to give her more time. Mia was right, it wasn't fair to her.

Kayra came breezing in and gave her a warm hug, which Saira returned. Like last time, Kayra looked happy and healthy and Saira instantly relaxed. Whatever Kayra wanted to talk about, it wasn't bad news.

"Saira, I want you to meet someone." It was only then that Saira noticed a tall man, athletic, with sandy brown hair. He was wearing a stylish khaki jacket, jeans and a black T-shirt.

"This is Paul."

Saira stuck out her hand and Paul leaned in and hugged her. "It is so nice to meet you. Kayra talks about you all the time." He had a European accent that Saira couldn't quite place.

"Well, I must admit that she has kept me totally in the dark about you."

Kayra grinned and pulled Saira back down to the couch. Paul pulled up a chair across from them. "I wanted to tell you in person, after you met Paul. We're in love. Paul wants me to marry him."

Saira looked at Paul, who smiled back at her. He leaned forward. "I'm in love with your sister, and it's important to both of us that you approve."

"This all sounds wonderful, but how about you start from the beginning. How did you two meet? How did you fall in love? I want to hear it all." Paul and Kayra were only too happy to tell her the whole story. Paul was the son of a Swiss banker. He had come to Clinique Lake Geneva six months ago for a one-month stay. He didn't elaborate on why, just that he was stressed and needed to figure some things out. They fell in love. Initially Paul extended his stay but then his father refused to pay for it, so he'd been visiting every weekend.

"How does your family feel about Kayra?" Saira asked carefully. She was happy for her sister but Paul had yet to mention what he did for a living.

"They think she's been good for me. They've been on

me to finish my degree and I've been making really good progress since Kayra's been helping me."

Saira smiled at Kayra. Her sister had managed to do her schooling online and even finish an international bachelor's degree. Saira herself hadn't studied further than the Indian equivalent of high school. It was hard enough to get tutoring on set and find time to study to pass her exams; there had been no time for college, especially once she'd had to start paying for Kayra's medical care. Saira had hoped that eventually Kayra would find a job and become independent.

"So what're your plans after you get married?"

Kayra leaned forward. "That's what we want to talk to you about. Paul needs a year to complete his studies but we don't want to wait to get married. I want him to live here with me."

Saira was sure she'd misheard. "Why would he live here? Don't you have a home of your own?"

He nodded. "I live with my parents, but they're not willing to support us until I finish my degree."

Saira shifted in her seat. She didn't want to rain on Kayra's happiness.

"*Di*, please, Paul makes me so happy. It's only a matter of a year, two tops. Plus, if we're living together, you're just paying a little more for him."

"Kayra, you know I'd do anything for you but... I am not sure I can afford to keep *you* here, let alone Paul too. This place is really expensive, and they just raised their rates."

The look on Kayra's face pierced her heart. Saira grabbed her sister's hand. "I can't afford to pay for you to stay here, but we can work something else out. Maybe you can get an apartment. I'll pay for everything until Paul gets on his feet."

"You want me to leave here?" Kayra's eyes got big. "*Di*, I can't. I feel safe here, I can't go somewhere else."

Saira sighed. She'd had this conversation with Kayra many times. "You have to at some point, Kayra. You can't live here forever. It's a hotel, not a home." She looked at Paul with some hope. "You two will want to start a real life together, in your own home."

Paul nodded at first. "Of course, but we just need a few years, to figure it out, you know. This place, it's so peaceful, so healthful, I can focus on my studies."

It didn't escape her notice that they started with a year, then two years, and now it was a few years. She rubbed her temples. She could barely afford to pay Kayra's way with the new rates at the facility. There was no way she could pay for Paul too. "Kayra, I'm getting on in age, I have maybe a few more years of being able to earn what I do now. I can't keep paying for you here." She looked at Paul. "I want to help you guys, I really do, but you're going to have to ask your parents for support if you want to live here."

Kayra stood. "So what, you're abandoning me? After everything I've been through because of you."

Saira's mouth soured. "Because of me? If I recall correctly, you wanted to do that movie. You were always jealous that I was the star. You begged me to get you a role."

Kayra's eyes blazed. "And you gave me the one role you didn't want."

"I gave you the only role they'd take you for. Do you think I didn't try? You think Ma didn't try? She sent your photo for every role that came my way. She hounded my agent. I didn't deliberately give you that show. It was bad luck you ended up with that show."

"Luck!" Kayra scoffed. "What luck I have, spending half my life in hospitals and treatment facilities while you get to enjoy the luxuries of being a big star."

Maybe it was the view of the snowcapped mountains, or the appearance of a waitress with three tall glasses of lemonade served in cut glass crystal. Everything that Mia and Rahul had been saying came crashing down. "Luxuries? I've had luxuries? I work eighteen hours a day, nonstop. If I'm lucky, I get Sunday off, and in that time, I think about more ways in which I can make enough money to support the family. Here you are living in the lap of luxury, going to the spa every day, taking nature walks, all charged to my account with no consideration as to what it takes to pay for all this."

"I didn't ask to be here, what happened to me…"

"Was not my fault."

"You're saying it was mine?"

Saira shook her head. "It was bad luck, fate, call it what you want. It was my duty as your sister to get you the best medical care possible, which I did. But now you're asking me not only to pay for you to live in this palace, but also support your fiancé?"

"You know I'm still getting therapy."

Saira tapped on her phone and pulled up the latest report from the center. "Your psychiatrist discharged you two years ago. The therapist you see is a wellness specialist. He's not a medical doctor. There is nothing you're getting here that you can't get at home." Then it hit her. She held up a finger and pulled up the invoice her accountant had sent her when he asked to break one of her fixed deposits to pay for the latest bill from the facility. He'd said the bill was much higher than usual. "Has Paul been living here with you? Have you been putting his expenses on my account?"

Kayra lifted her chin. "It's not that much….and we had no choice….I couldn't just see him on the weekends…"

"Do you have any idea how much this place costs? Do you know how much I've been stressing about money. How I'm making decisions based solely on how much money I'll earn? I just broke up with the love of my life because…."

"*Di*, I don't want to hear anything. I love Paul and you'll have to find a way to support us."

How had she never noticed how petulant Kayra was? How spoiled her sister had become? Saira had been so focused on protecting her, shielding her, giving her everything she wanted to make up for what she'd had to go through that she'd never noticed how entitled her sister was. Rahul had been telling her for years that Kayra was like an only child who was given everything she ever asked for.

Saira stood. "I am leaving, Kayra. You can finish out the month here, after that I'll let you know what arrangements I've made. I'm not paying for you to stay here anymore."

Kayra stared at her wide-eyed. "Ma is going to want to talk to you."

So Kayra had already discussed this with her parents. Of course she had. How had Saira missed it? Her parents and Kayra were always on the same page. Against her.

"I'm headed to Mumbai now." It was time for her to have a serious talk with her parents.

* * *

She breathed out when she stepped onto the tarmac at Mumbai airport. It was hot, sticky, and the air smelled of salt, fish and jet fuel.

Her regular car and driver were there to pick her up. She was greeted at her apartment complex by a crowd of fans. Someone had posted her arrival at the airport on social media and despite the early morning hour, a crowd had gathered. She told the driver to stop right before the building gates. She lowered her window and grasped the hands that came forward, blowing kisses at the gathered crowd. A little girl was hoisted on shoulders until she made her way to the car and handed Saira a bouquet of flowers.

Saira asked the girl her name, accepted a kiss on her cheek and took a picture with her. These were the moments she loved.

As she entered the building, the security guards lined up to greet her. There was a new person there she didn't know. He'd been hired a few days ago, and when he stepped forward to introduce himself, she thought about Jay and the acid in his face. Like her, he would've felt perfectly safe walking into his own home, wouldn't think twice about a new face. All that would change if she came out. She would have to live in a bubble, unable to interact with her fans, fearful of anyone she didn't know. Her life would be very different.

Her parents were waiting for her when she arrived. Their two-level, five-bedroom condo smelled as it always did, like sandalwood incense from the morning prayers. The living room was marble white floors, glass coffee and accent tables, and comfortable black leather couches. Her parents greeted her with warm hugs. Her favorite cutting chai, a strongly brewed cup with ginger and cardamom, appeared as soon as she sat down on the couch. She took a sip. "I've missed chai. Americans have no idea how to make a good cup of tea."

Her mother smiled. Parvati Sethi had been a beautiful and talented actress. She claimed her career had been derailed by the arrival of Saira first, then Kayra. Saira never knew what her father really did for a living. He had some family money, which he'd lost early in life, then was involved in several failed businesses. For a while he'd managed her mother's career and then Saira's, until she realized that he couldn't resist starting more businesses than he could manage. As soon as she turned eighteen, Rahul had made her hire a proper accountant. It hadn't been easy to take the power away from her father, but she'd had to do it—at the time, the family was close to losing their home. She took a deep breath as she sipped her chai. If eighteen-year-old Saira had the courage to tell her father he couldn't manage her money anymore, then she could do this now.

"You look tired dear, why don't you go rest for a little while." Her father patted her hand.

"Tell me what you want to have for lunch. I'll have the cook make it," Parvati added.

Saira was exhausted. She hadn't slept on the plane from Geneva. Her head hurt and nothing sounded better than some sleep and the cook's rajma chawal. Their cook had been with them since Saira was a child and old Lata *didi*'s red beans and rice were her comfort food.

She looked at her watch and shook her head. Due to the fog in Mumbai, the plane had had to delay departure from Geneva. She had a meeting with the movie producers in a couple of hours. The meeting with the financiers in Geneva had gone really well. They'd agreed to 13 percent above her usual fee. The casting wasn't even complete, and *Mumtaz*, as the movie had been named, was already creating buzz.

"I wish I had time to rest but I have a meeting in two hours."

"You sound so tired, *jaan.*" Her mother put an arm around her. "Is everything okay?"

Saira smiled and leaned into her mother, taking some comfort in the way she squeezed her tight.

"I have to talk to you about a few things." She took another fortifying sip of the tea, letting the hot liquid strengthen her.

"Is this about Kayra?" her father asked. "Sweetheart, I know how much pressure you're under trying to launch your Hollywood career, but God willing, your show will be great and then you'll be earning in dollars."

Saira pressed her lips. "Dad, don't you think it's a bit much to have to pay for Kayra's fiancé, who is perfectly healthy, to stay in that really expensive place?"

"Don't think that way. You're supporting your sister. You know how hard it's been for her to be in a relationship. Paul is a nice guy."

"How would you know?"

"He came to the ashram last month to ask us if he could ask Kayra to marry him. So wonderfully old-fashioned."

The extra charges from the ashram.

"And you paid for him to stay at the ashram."

Her mother frowned. "So what, he was our guest."

"Ma, I had to break one of my fixed deposits to pay last month's ashram and clinic bills. Do you understand what that means? The money coming in couldn't cover the expenses, I had to dip into my savings. I'm getting old now, the leading roles are going to stop coming. We'll have to live off our savings, and then what? How long can that last?"

Her mother pulled her arm away, clearly upset. How could she not understand? Her mother had gone through the very same thing; when she'd tried going back to acting after taking a break, she'd been told she was too old for leading roles.

"Maybe after the next role it's time for you to start thinking about having children. The next generation."

She can't be serious?

"You want me to have children so I can work them the way I've worked all my life?" She must be misunderstanding her mother.

"What's so bad about the life you had?"

Saira stared at her mother. Rahul and Mia's voices were playing in her head. All her life, she'd vilified Rahul's parents and been grateful for her own family, assumed that they were letting her take care of them because they had no other choice.

"My entire childhood was spent on a set. I can't even remember what's real and what was a scene in a movie. I didn't go to school, play with friends or do anything other than work. I wouldn't wish that life on my children."

Her mother looked away. "If you were that unhappy, why didn't you tell us?"

"What choice did I have? We needed the money and

you made it very clear that we'd lose our home if it weren't for the money I was bringing in."

Her parents were silent and Saira downed the rest of the tea. "But there's an even bigger reason why Rahul and I will never have children."

She had their attention now. Saira took a deep breath. This is what she'd come to do, and she had put it off long enough. "I don't love him, not in the way a wife should love her husband. In fact, I never have and never will love a man. I've been a lesbian all my life."

She met her parents' gazes, expecting shock and anger, but they just stared passively back at her.

"Is this about that girl in Fiji?"

She nodded."

Her parents looked at each other and her mother sighed. "When you were a teenager, you were only obsessed with the female actresses. Girls your age had posters of Salman Khan on their walls, but you had Madhuri Dixit. Then there was Fiji. At first, I thought you were just experimenting, but you were so depressed when we brought you back, it was clear what had happened there."

Saira could scarcely believe what she was hearing. Her parents had known all along. After Fiji, they made it seem as though it had been a one-time thing, that she'd lost her way, that she was experimenting. Saira had spent years agonizing over the decision to tell them that Fiji wasn't just her experimenting, cried buckets of tears over the guilt of how she'd treated Mia. It had all been for nothing. Her parents had known!

"If you knew, why did you push me to marry Rahul?"

"Saira, you're a grown woman now. I thought you understood when I explained it to you back then. You can't live your life like that. You heard what happened to Jay? Forget Jay, you've lived through what happened to Kayra, and that was because she misrepresented a religious figure. It would be one thing if you were a nobody. Maybe you could live your life quietly. But people look up to you. The public will blame you for every young girl that tells her parents she's a lesbian, and they'll take their anger out on you."

It was Saira's turn to look away from her mother. She couldn't argue with anything Parvati said. They were the same concerns and fears she had.

"I can't keep living a lie. I want to come out with the truth, go live in America where I can live openly."

Her mother shot her father a look. "Let me talk to my daughter alone."

Narayan didn't argue; he was more than happy to escape to the upstairs terrace.

Her mother turned to her after he'd left. "Saira, do you think I've spent my life in love with your father?"

It wasn't really a question Saira had thought about. Her parents weren't always lovey-dovey but they seemed to get along.

"Your father has been like my best friend. The same way Rahul is yours. Do you think I don't know about him? I've known both of you since you were children. Do you think any Indian mother would allow her *jawan* daughter to be alone in her bedroom for hours with a boy?"

Saira's eyes widened. "Then why did you want us to marry?"

"Because you are good friends, you understand each other and will keep each other happy. Marriage is not about love and romance. Sex and passion fade, especially when your arthritis kicks in—" she gave Saira a small smile. "—but what endures is when you have an understanding with your partner. When you are willing to share in their successes and their failures. That's what a lifelong marriage is. I knew Rahul would take care of you, treat you well, give you comfort. What can you hope to have with a woman? You will be shunned from India. All those fans that give you flowers and balloons when you walk through the door will throw rotten tomatoes and eggs at you. You want to leave your home and go live in America? Then what? You think you'll live happily ever after as a nobody?"

"I can be an actress in LA. The woman from Fiji, Mia, she's the love of my life. I can be with her there."

"What about us? You think that public, those people that are sitting outside our building right now will leave us alone? Kayra hasn't come to Mumbai because just the sight of the crowds stresses her. How do you think she'll handle the media attention?"

Saira looked away. Her mother grabbed her hand, pulling Saira's attention back to her.

"There was a time when I thought that I could have everything in my life. But I've learned that life is all about compromises. No matter what people say, women really can't have it all. We are mothers, daughter, sisters, and because we are stronger than the fathers, sons and brothers in our lives, we are the ones who make the sacrifices, who hold the family together."

Saira's stomach turned. Wasn't that exactly what Mia had said to her? That she had to choose—between her family's happiness and her own.

Parvati grasped her hands. "We need you to hold this family together. You don't want to pay for Paul, fine. You want us to reduce our expenses, fine. Whatever you say. But don't give up your life on the hope that you'll find happiness with that Mia woman. How long have you known her? Is she willing to give up her life for you?"

Saira bit her lip. Her mother squeezed her hands. "What if it doesn't work out with her? You'll have destroyed your life, and all of our lives—for nothing."

Saira closed her eyes, letting the tears flow down her cheeks. She knew what she had to do.

Eighteen

"Earth to Mia!"

Mia looked at David, who was frowning at her. "I've asked you the same question three times and you are off in space."

"I'm sorry, David. Just a lot on my mind right now."

They were in the screening room reviewing the first episode. The network wanted to release it as soon as possible, even before the other episodes were ready, to garner more interest in the show.

"I know what's on your mind. It's that announcement that Saira's going to star in the Mumtaz movie. She's not coming back and giving you your happily ever after, is she?"

Mia sucked in a breath. "No, she is not." David had become a friend in the last few weeks. Turned out that he was a romantic and a fair share of heartbreaks had inspired his empathy.

He put a hand on her shoulder. "It's for the best. Trust

me, actresses are a pain in the ass to deal with. They are so full of themselves, always wanting the spotlight."

That's what I used to think too. "I knew she was going to sign that movie. That's why I broke up with her."

"Still hurts to see it in print. I will say I notice a few more wrinkles on her forehead. I predict she won't age well."

Mia smiled and punched David playfully in the arm. "I appreciate what you're trying to do but it's not necessary."

"She's coming to the release party next month."

Mia sucked in a breath. That, she hadn't heard. "I can handle it." It had been two months since she'd last seen Saira. The last message she'd received from her had been a text—*I love you*—a few hours after Mia had left the hotel room, probably before she left for Geneva. That's it. Nothing since then. No "I've reached Mumbai safely." Or "I miss you." Mia hadn't really expected it, but that didn't stop her from wanting it. She had avoided Saira's social media, but her days had been filled with images of Saira. Even now, her face was paused on the big screen, frozen in a half smile, half smirk. Mia closed her eyes. They had another month of editing before she could take a break. Except, how was she going to get Saira out of her heart and soul?

"You need to get out, meet people."

"I've lost count of how many women Gail has swiped right for me."

"Meet anyone?"

"About five someones." They had all been intelligent, beautiful women. The type of women who were ready to settle down and were perfect matches for Mia. She'd had five great dates, and none of them came close to making her heart beat the way Saira's image on screen did.

"You have to move on."

"Easier said than done."

"So you're going to spend the rest of your life pining for her?"

"Pretty much."

"If the show gets a season two, she'll be back here for several months."

"And will be another producer's problem."

David raised his brows.

"It would be too tempting to fall into her bed again. I can't do that to myself and to her. I won't produce another season."

"So I've been nice to you for no reason?"

Mia smiled. "Total loss for you."

"You wouldn't take up with her, even if you're single?"

Mia shook her head. "It's not the way I want to live my life, sneaking around, pretending... I'm trying to respect that Saira isn't in the same place in her life. But I'm not going to torture myself with stolen moments." She turned away from David. It was so much easier to say than to do. She'd spent every night away from Saira longing for her, crying for her, barely holding on to the last vestiges of control she had left to keep from texting or calling her. She pulled out her phone. "Do you mind if we take a break?"

David shrugged. "I could use a coffee." As he left, she opened up her Facebook account. Her birthday was two days ago. Her mother had sent the usual message wishing her a happy birthday and asking if she was "normal" yet. It was the only communication she ever received from her parents. The same message every year on her birthday. Mia never responded. She hadn't talked to her parents since she graduated from high school. They hadn't even come to her graduation, just signed the final school forms before she turned eighteen. She had lectured Saira about courage, but there was one thing she hadn't gotten the nerve to do, and it was about time she did.

Mom, I am normal. I always have been and always will be. It's time you accepted it. If you can't, please don't contact me again.

A part of her had been waiting for her parents to come around. She'd never said goodbye to them. It was time to do that. She hit Send on the message.

A text message popped up from Jessica, the woman she had gone out with two nights ago, one of the dating app matches from Gail's online swiping spree. Jessica was a lawyer, had nothing to do with the entertainment industry and was classically beautiful.

Saira's face was still on screen.

She texted Jessica, inviting her to dinner. It was time to move on.

"You're wearing that to the premiere party?"

Saira twirled in front of the mirror. "What's wrong with it?"

Rahul clicked his tongue. "A little risky, isn't it? Too much on the nose?"

"Are you sure you want to come with me?" she asked.

"I wouldn't miss it for the world. Don't worry, my publicity machine is ready."

Saira took a deep breath. "Are we ready to do this?"

Rahul rolled his shoulders. "We will never be ready. But, it's time."

"I will miss your money. This hotel suite is far better than where the network puts me up." The hotel room was indeed splendid. A top floor suite, it had two bedrooms, a spacious living and dining room and closets that fit all the clothes she'd brought, as well as Rahul's.

Rahul laughed. "You know you get a settlement, whether you want it or not. It's in our prenup."

She shook her head. "I'm not taking it." She applied a last coat of lipstick, checked her makeup one last time in the mirror, then turned to him. "I don't want to be one more person who takes from you, Rahul. I'm fine, really I am. I got a great deal on Mumtaz. They're paying me 1 percent above my usual fee."

"I thought they were giving you a lot more."

"They were, but I negotiated alternative terms."

Rahul offered her his arm. "Shall we?"

The party was being held in the rooftop ballroom of their hotel. Networks didn't always throw lavish premiere parties, but this one was doubling as a PR event. Selected press outlets had invitations. When Rahul and Saira stepped out of the elevators, they were directed to walk down the red carpet so the media could snap pictures.

Saira's eyes searched for Mia but she was nowhere to be found. *What if she doesn't come?* She took a breath as they made their way to the gathered media. It didn't matter whether Mia was here or not. Saira wasn't doing this for Mia. She was doing it for herself.

"Saira, love the dress. Can you tell us what you're wearing?"

Saira smiled. She'd had the dress custom designed. It was a strapless gown that fell to the floor with a front middle slit. It was a beautiful silk in rainbow colors.

"I'm wearing this dress to show my pride, and announce that Rahul and I are getting a divorce."

There were murmurs in the crowd, some in surprise, most in confusion.

"Why are you getting a divorce?" someone shouted.

Rahul put an arm around her. "We're getting a divorce because she's found the woman of her dreams, and I've found the man of mine."

There was a momentary pause before the gathered journalists all began hurling questions at once. Rahul and Saira spent thirty minutes explaining it all before an assistant finally moved them off the carpet. They were immediately accosted by actors and crew who wanted their own scoop of the announcement. It took a while before Saira was able to break free of the crowd and find some quiet on an outside terrace. The night was still warm. She took a deep breath, feeling amazingly free.

"Never a dull moment with you." Saira turned to find Mia, looking gorgeous. She was wearing a strappy emerald green dress that wrapped around her in a way that caught Saira's breath. Mia hated dressing up. Had she done it for Saira's benefit? *I hope she did it for me.*

Saira smiled. "I told you to give me some time and I'd figure it out."

Mia was still standing several steps away, looking wary. "What made you do this now?"

Saira wasn't going to wait for Mia to come running into her arms. She stepped toward her. "I finally realized what you and Rahul were telling me all along—my family has been taking advantage of me. All my life, my parents have made decisions based on what was best for them. I decided it's time for me to choose my happiness over theirs."

Mia stood there, maddeningly still. Saira took small

steps toward her. She looked like a deer caught in the headlights, ready to flee any second.

"I know you, Saira. You won't be happy abandoning your family."

She was only a few steps away from Mia, close enough to see the tears in her eyes. "You know me so well. I'm still going to take care of them. Just not in the style they've become accustomed to. I'm giving them the money I'm getting from Mumtaz, plus the apartment we own in Mumbai. They can live a comfortable life with that money if they spend it well. If they don't, then they have to figure out a way to earn some of their own. That includes Kayra. She's an educated woman, who is perfectly healthy and capable. I'm done being their ATM. If there are security concerns, I'll have to figure out a way to pay for that, but I have some ideas."

"What about your career? What about that big movie you just signed?"

Saira could hear the fear in Mia's voice. She couldn't believe it was really happening. Saira could barely believe it herself. She and Rahul had spent the last month planning their announcement. Both of them had lost at least five kilos because they were too anxious to eat. Now that it was done, Saira finally felt like a weight had been lifted off her shoulders, a lifetime of weight. It almost felt surreal, like a dream that she might wake up from.

"Mumtaz might be the last film I do, but I made a deal with them that they'd support my announcement. Turns out the main financier has a son who's trans. He's all about bringing social change."

Saira was close enough to see the tears on Mia's cheeks. She reached out, cupped Mia's face and wiped the tears with her thumbs.

"You shouldn't have done this for me," Mia said softly.

"I didn't do it for you. I did it for me. I knew my family had been been taking advantage of me, but I truly believed that they wanted my happiness. That's why theirs mattered so much to me. But when it came to it, what they wanted was for me to sacrifice my needs and wants for theirs. I am done living my life for them, and in hiding. I don't want to be without you."

She touched her forehead to Mia's. "I love you. I've loved you for more than ten years. If you'll have me, I want us to be together. I want a life with you. I want you to marry me."

Mia closed her eyes, and for a second, Saira thought her knees would give out waiting for Mia to answer. Then Mia lifted her chin, found her mouth and kissed her hard. When she finally pulled away, her eyes were shining. "I love you so much. Do you know how hard I tried to get over you? For more than ten years?"

Saira nodded. "I know exactly how hard. That's why I don't want to live another second without you. So will you stop torturing me? Will you or won't you marry me?"

Mia smiled. "Yes Saira Sethi, I will marry you." She wrapped her arms around Saira's waist. "I will marry you, have your babies, I'll even produce your show if I must. I'll do whatever it takes to make you happy for the rest of my life."

This time when they kissed, it was with the sweetness of their past and the future to come.

* * * * *

COMING SOON!

We really hope you enjoyed reading this book. If you're looking for more romance be sure to head to the shops when new books are available on

Thursday 9th November

To see which titles are coming soon, please visit

millsandboon.co.uk/nextmonth

MILLS & BOON

OUT NOW!

Available at
millsandboon.co.uk

MILLS & BOON

OUT NOW!

3
BOOKS
IN ONE

A
Christmas
DARE

AVRIL
TREMAYNE

ZARA
COX

CARA
LOCKWOOD

Available at
millsandboon.co.uk

MILLS & BOON

OUT NOW!

Available at
millsandboon.co.uk

MILLS & BOON

OUT NOW!

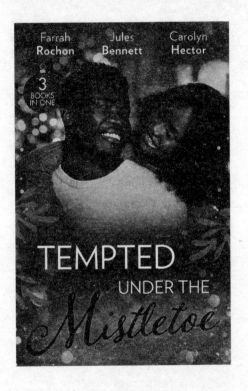

Farrah Rochon Jules Bennett Carolyn Hector

3 BOOKS IN ONE

TEMPTED
UNDER THE
Mistletoe

Available at
millsandboon.co.uk

MILLS & BOON

LET'S TALK

Romance

For exclusive extracts, competitions and special offers, find us online:

- **f** MillsandBoon
- **🐦** @MillsandBoon
- **📷** @MillsandBoonUK
- **♪** @MillsandBoonUK

Get in touch on 01413 063 232

For all the latest titles coming soon, visit
millsandboon.co.uk/nextmonth

MILLS & BOON

THE HEART OF ROMANCE

A ROMANCE FOR EVERY READER

MODERN
Prepare to be swept off your feet by sophisticated, sexy and seductive heroes, in some of the world's most glamourous and romantic locations, where power and passion collide.

HISTORICAL
Escape with historical heroes from time gone by. Whether your passion is for wicked Regency Rakes, muscled Vikings or rugged Highlanders, awaken the romance of the past.

MEDICAL
Set your pulse racing with dedicated, delectable doctors in the high-pressure world of medicine, where emotions run high and passion, comfort and love are the best medicine.

True Love
Celebrate true love with tender stories of heartfelt romance, from the rush of falling in love to the joy a new baby can bring, and a focus on the emotional heart of a relationship.

Desire
Indulge in secrets and scandal, intense drama and sizzling hot action with heroes who have it all: wealth, status, good looks…everything but the right woman.

HEROES
The excitement of a gripping thriller, with intense romance at its heart. Resourceful, true-to-life women and strong, fearless men face danger and desire - a killer combination!

To see which titles are coming soon, please visit

millsandboon.co.uk/nextmonth

MILLS & BOON
A ROMANCE FOR EVERY READER

- **FREE** delivery direct to your door
- **EXCLUSIVE** offers every month
- **SAVE** up to 30% on pre-paid subscriptions

SUBSCRIBE AND SAVE

millsandboon.co.uk/Subscribe

GET YOUR ROMANCE FIX!

Get the latest romance news,
exclusive author interviews, story
extracts and much more!

blog.millsandboon.co.uk